MW01490674

THE
SECRET
KEPT

HERBERT C. ROBINSON

PAGE PUBLISHING, INC.
New York, NY

First originally published by Page Publishing, Inc. 2015

ISBN 978-1-68139-437-4 (pbk)
ISBN 978-1-68139-438-1 (digital)

Printed in the United States of America

PROLOGUE

As he stepped into the boardroom after his father, Jonathan looked on in amazement while the sea of CEOs and executives shuddered in fear as Jack Tobias walked slowly to the head of the table to be seated. It wasn't just an ordinary table; it was a broad triangular piece made from the finest walnut burl in the world. Jack Tobias wanted the table shaped that way so everyone who sat at it could face him while he sat at the tip of the triangle. It also represented the fact that as a triangle expands from the tip, everything expanded from the man sitting there, and that man would always be a Tobias.

Jonathan knew that, one day, he would be at the head of that table, glaring out into the eyes of fear as his father did this morning—the eyes of men and women who had a right to be afraid for what they saw was no ordinary man. He was the CEO and controlling shareholder of Tobias Industries, and he held the power to shatter careers and ruin lives with a flick of the wrist.

Tobias Industries was a textile conglomerate and America's number-1 producer and distributor of cotton, and today, it was just business as usual—the takeover of another company that couldn't compete in an industry that seemed to be tailor-made just for the Tobiases.

"We call this meeting into order!" yelled Millicent Daniels, the chairperson of the board. "This meeting is to finalize the merge of UniMed Chemicals and Tobias Incorporated. All against, say nay!"

The room was silent. No one would dare disagree with the direction of Jackson Tobias III, even if he were taking them off a cliff.

"Well then, all in favor please raise a left hand," she stated.

Jack's head rotated slowly around the table; he was a very suspicious man, and with oral agreements, some people wouldn't say anything at all and just go along with everyone else in the room. He instituted a hands-up rule so he could see that everyone was on the same page whether they liked it or not. Every left hand at the table reached for the ceiling.

"If that concludes business this morning, this meeting is adjourned," Millicent said as she got up from the table. As the executives began to rise and exit the boardroom, Jonathan remained seated along with his father.

Once the room was empty, Jonathan stood and walked over to a row of windows that seemed to never end and looked out over the New York skyline. From there, it felt as if he owned the entire world. High off another one of his father's conquests, he turned to him and asked, "Dad, why is it so easy?"

Jackson looked over to his eldest son and said very coolly, "Simple self-preservation. Either be acquired or be run into the ground through competition."

"You mean noncompetition, right?" Jonathan asked with a smug grin.

"Precisely," added the equally arrogant father.

Jackson knew something that the future heir would soon come to know—the reason why he was so successful as his father and other Tobiases were before him. He also figured that there would be no better time than the present, so he gestured for Jonathan to take a seat.

"Is everything all right?" his son asked.

"Everything is fine, but what I'm about to tell you requires your full attention," Jackson replied. The eager son was all ears.

Jackson gazed deeply into his son's eyes as he prepared to tell him the reasons why life was so easy and prosperous; the secret behind the most lucrative contracts in the country, including the government. He wanted to explain all of this to Jonathan, and he would, but he knew he'd have to journey back more than 150 years.

BOOK ONE

CHAPTER 1

It would all begin in the year 1859 in what felt like the coldest winter in years. Jonathan would know since he'd been sent here for his education six years ago. He hated Philadelphia for its cobblestone streets and large smoke-spewing factories. It astounded him that after a half decade, he still couldn't get used to the industrialization of the North.

He detested it all—immigrant merchants from everywhere peddling anything to anyone willing to buy, the stenches rising from every corner and alley, not to mention the rats he seemed to encounter at every pile of rotting garbage he passed while high stepping through the city's filthy streets.

"Damned Yankees!" he said to himself. Why couldn't he stay in the South with his father and the rest of his family?

He could remember his father saying, "Son, slaving won't last forever." Deep inside, he knew his father was right for sending him here for his degree in business law. Jonas Tobias knew that the country was moving in the direction of the North, especially with all the grumblings about slave abolishment coming from Washington, DC. He also knew that in order for his brood to survive these changes, a Tobias would have to learn amongst the Northerners.

Jonathan's family owned Azalea, one of the largest slave plantations in the South. His father had amassed a great wealth off the blood and backs of Negro slaves. Jonathan didn't want to see that fortune disappear, so when asked, he agreed with his father and went to Philadelphia. But at times like now, he regretted that decision.

Watching each breath cloud up in front of his face, Jonathan steadied himself while navigating through the patches of slush and ice separating him from his destination. He took his eyes away from the ground to glance around at the barren streets and realized that he was the only man foolish enough to be outside on this night.

"This had better be worth it," he muttered to himself while walking past a mountain of week-old shoveled snow.

With every step, he began to think of Azalea, longing to be home and away from this frigid weather. He missed the warm days when he watched for hours as the slaves tended to their bountiful cotton fields. He missed waiting in the kitchen for Olina to slip him her spicy salt pork and dumplings while she prepared dinner for his family and the hands. He chuckled to himself remembering how he would sneak the food out of the back of the house because Jonas disapproved of the children taking food from her when no one was around.

A gust of wind swiftly brought him back to reality, a harsh reminder of his surroundings. *It would all be over soon*, he thought to himself as he clenched his fists while searching for a bit of warmth inside of his pockets. After his trip to Illinois, he would be back in Alabama where he belonged.

He didn't want to make the trip to Springfield, especially in this weather. Traveling four states to the northwest in the winter was suicidal, but it was at the insistence of Thomas Woodburn that they bear the journey.

Thomas had been Jonathan's only friend in the North and the only person here who he could stand to be around for more than an hour. They had been very close since meeting in law school at the University of Pennsylvania when Thomas first arrived from England. He would be the only person to know that Jonathan was from the South and of slave money—all of which mattered for the Northerners because they outlawed slavery even though they looked down on Negroes as well. The moralist Northerners were just as bigoted as the rest of the whites. Jonathan surmised that because they had no tobacco and cotton themselves to harvest, the jealous Yankee wanted to ruin slavery for everyone else.

Over the years, he had gotten involved with advocacy groups aimed at championing the rights of enslaved Negroes. There were many groups that came and went, and he joined just about all of them to stay socially correct. Thomas thought it was quite amusing to see the son of the largest slave owner in the South pushing for laws to end his father's trade.

Jonathan saw it as an opportunity to blend in and make contact with the people who would become vital to his family's future plans. Most of the time, it drove him mad to be around so many snobbish men and women. Jonathan was also a bit conceited, but even the South's most elite were no match for these blue bellies.

After finally arriving at Woodburn's colonial townhouse, Jonathan yanked the door chime and impatiently waited on the stoop. Chauncey, Thomas's manservant, let Jonathan in and took his hat and coat before returning to the kitchen. Chesterfield sofas and a large mahogany coffee table adorned with gold and silver ornaments stood between Jonathan and the warmth radiating from the far end of the living room. He squeezed past the furniture, being careful not to knock anything over, to get closer to the fireplace. Once there, he extended his partially numb hands toward the crackling flames.

"Jonathan Tobias! My good friend, you've finally made it," Thomas said as he sauntered down the steps to greet him.

"Yeah, I'm here, but I nearly froze to death on my way over," Jonathan replied as he gave his friend a once-over. The complete opposite of himself, Thomas was a short and portly man with a balding pate and stained teeth that were the results of indulging in too much tobacco and cognac.

Jonathan, on the other hand, was tall and built powerfully with a head full of curly black hair that surrounded his rugged, but handsome, face. His pitch-black eyes, directly inherited from his father, seemed to become more menacing whenever he furrowed his bushy eyebrows. The slaves at Azalea called them "evil eyes" and often whispered that if they stared at you for too long, expect a lashing from the whip. Of the many traits he received from Jonas, he loved that one the most.

"Well, if you almost froze traveling eleven blocks, how will you possibly make it three days in Illinois?" Thomas asked with a toothy grin.

"Lots of long drawers and a healthy supply of your favorite cognac," Jonathan quipped, thus resulting in a hearty laugh out of both the men.

Thomas gestured for Jonathan to follow him into the dining room then motioned for him to sit down. He called for the butler to bring them two glasses and a bottle of scotch.

"Chauncey, how long before we eat?" Thomas asked. Being the more experienced drinker, he didn't want to consume too much alcohol before the meal.

"A little under an hour, sir," the elderly man replied.

"Very well then, Jon, let's have a taste," Thomas said as he filled the two glasses with brown liquor.

After the first sip, Jonathan looked across the table and asked, "Is this trek necessary? Three days of cold, mountains, and possibly encountering Indians."

Thomas took another swallow before answering, "Jon, I know you believe that getting back to Alabama is more important than going to Illinois, but you must trust me. This trip will give you more reason than ever to get home to your family."

Jonathan looked puzzled as Thomas continued to speak. He hadn't been given much detail about the trip, so he only focused on the dangers, the cold, mountains, and possibly encountering Indians.

"My dear friend, the winds of change are blowing again in the sea of politics in this nation. The division of the North and South has reached its boiling point. The Democrats want a separate slave nation, and the Republicans want to end slavery altogether. Personally, it makes no difference to me what happens in this country. I'll be headed back to England in the near future." He paused to take another swig.

"We've known each other for a long time now," he stated as Jonathan nodded his head in agreement. "And through the years, I have gotten to learn quite a bit about you. I know how you love your family and how desperately you want to get back to them. More than anything, I know how much you hate it here." Jonathan agreed with another nod. Thomas went on, "One thing I do know is certain is that if there is a civil war, the North will prevail. Tell me, Jon, where would that leave the mighty Tobiases?"

Jonathan glowered across the table at the obvious truth coming out of Thomas's mouth. He didn't like what he was hearing, but he had to accept it. "Thomas, I agree that we would be in a terrible position, but why do you think I'm here?" He paused to let Thomas think it over. "My father sent me here in preparation for the future. He knew that my time spent here would earn alliances with whatever government that rises out of the North," Jonathan answered with unmistakable pride in his father's wisdom.

"Precisely!" Thomas shouted. And in an even tone, he added, "You came here for an Ivy League education and also to gain the contacts who will guide this nation's future. Well, friend, that's the reason for our journey to Springfield. We are going to side with the next president of this country." As Thomas finished, Chauncey entered to announce that dinner was ready to be served.

"The next president?" Jonathan asked, clearly taken aback. "How can you make such a guarantee in these uncertain times? There are numerous parties and candidates among them. What makes your man the shoe-in?" Jonathan demanded. He was bothered by Thomas's assuredness but also enticed by the idea of meeting the next man in the White House. But with the aroma of roasted lamb and Chauncey's other delights wafting from the table, Jonathan knew he wouldn't get his answer tonight. It was time to eat.

CHAPTER 2

The following morning, Jonathan had awakened to the sound of leafless branches being blown against his bedroom window. The wind outside was fierce, and he dreaded going out today. But this was the day he and Thomas were to set off on their trip.

His trunks had been packed two days ago, so he didn't have to hurry to get prepared. He lay in bed and pondered the events to come. He had so many questions for Thomas, but mainly, he thought of how proud his father would be of him once he returned home. For a long time, he suspected that Jonas had thought more of his brother and was envious of the time Claude got to spend at home while he was stuck here in Philadelphia. As he stared at the ceiling, Jonathan began to reminisce of when he and Claude were younger, how they vied for their father's attention. There were many episodes, but nothing compared to the time three of Azalea's slaves murdered a field boss and escaped into the wilderness.

While feeding horses in the stables, a field boss had been surprised by a slave driver named Jasper, and before he could react, the large Zulu rammed a pitchfork into his stomach. Wallace Stump, one of the elder bosses on the plantation, hardly managed a belch before he fell lifelessly to the ground. Jasper dropped the makeshift weapon and ran off toward the swamps.

Two other slaves saw what happened and decided to go along with him. As the bells signaling for help rang, they knew there would be no turning back. The looks on their faces were as uncertain as their futures—because they had no idea where they were headed. The land owned by the Tobiases stretched as far as the eye could see. They decided to split apart. Their only strategy was to run away from the sound of the bells. Jasper went on alone while Ben and Moses stayed together. They all knew the consequences if caught, so they were ready to kill and prepared to die.

When the bloodhounds were released, Claude and Jonathan instinctively went with separate squads of trackers. Both boys had hoped that he would be the one fortunate to capture the fleeing vassals and show their father that his lessons never fell on deaf ears. Jonathan knew it wouldn't be a difficult task finding them; the nigger dogs, as they called them, were trained to sniff out the scent of any slave that ran away. The dogs were barking and howling as if it were mating season. They were on the trail of something.

The butterflies in Jonathan's stomach began to flutter as he sensed a confrontation was near. He wasn't alone; there were ten angry white men armed with rifles alongside of him. Some rode horseback while the rest were on foot, but they all had one common goal while heading into the dense forest—capturing the slaves before sundown. Without the sunlight, the slaves could blend in with the darkness, making them impossible to find.

That's just what Ben and Moses had in mind, but in the distance, they could faintly hear the dogs barking.

"What we's gon do? They done sicked the dogs on us," Ben frantically said to Moses.

"I reckon we move fasta. No time for worry'n now. So git goin'," Moses told him. The men were visibly tired from running in circles and hearing the barking only led to more panic.

"Let's hide, Mowsuss, up in those trees," the words came quivering out of Ben's mouth as he trembled with fear.

Moses saw something moving between the trees. "Go on, Ben, up dat tree right there," Moses whispered.

"Whatchu see, Mowsuss?" Ben asked.

"I said up dat tree," Moses said in a stern tone.

Ben immediately began to scramble up the tree as Moses backed away into a nearby bush and knelt on one knee. At the exact second his knee touched the ground, a bloodhound appeared in sight. Moses held his breath. Without barking, the dog paced back and forth until its master came into view.

When the lone tracker reached the dog, he petted the hound on the back of its neck. Instantly, the dog began to sniff the ground around the area. Ben watched in horror while clinging onto a branch as the hound sniffed and writhed in the very spot he and Moses were just standing in. Moses silently watched as the hound started to bark and make its way to the oak Ben had climbed. The tracker walked over to the tree and looked up.

"You got somethin' boy?" he said while stroking the dog's mane. The dog barked. "I see it too," the tracker whispered to the dog as he brought his rifle into a firing position and aimed it in Ben's direction. "Nigger, get down here! Outta that tree now, nigger!" he shouted at Ben.

The hound began to bark and growl, becoming as aggressive as its master. Ben's eyes began to water, and the lump in his throat grew larger by the second as he saw his bid for freedom come to an end while looking down at the tracker and his rifle.

Slowly, Ben climbed down the tree hoping the tracker and his dog wouldn't be there once he reached the ground. "Don't shoot me, suh, please!" he wailed. "I didn't hurt nobody!"

Moses watched as the tracker yanked Ben down form the tree by his britches. He stood over Ben and yelled, "I should kill you now, nigger, for whatchaw done ta poor Wallace!" The rifle's barrel was no more than five inches from Ben's face.

"No, not me, suh! I wouldn't never hurt no white man!" Ben shrieked while putting his palms in front of his face as if that would stop the bullet.

The tracker whistled for the dog, which immediately came to his side. "Look what we got us," he told the dog. "Now get some help. Go, boy!" He slapped his thigh, and the hound ran off barking into the wilderness.

The tracker began to kick Ben in the ribs. "Turn over, nigger!" he yelled as Ben winced and whimpered in pain.

"Please don't kill me. I'ma be good," Ben cried out while slowly turning over onto his stomach.

The tracker grabbed both of Ben's hands and bent over to tie them together. He never knew what hit him when Moses struck him on the side of the head from behind. Ben didn't know either as Claude Tobias came crashing down on top of him. Moses grabbed the rifle from the unconscious man and kicked at Ben.

"Go on, hurry and tie that white bastard up," Moses said as Ben slowly got himself together.

Off in the distance, Jonathan struggled to get through a patch of waist-high weeds. The humidity-mixed scents of poison ivy and eucalyptus made it very difficult for him to breathe. The lines of sweat running down his face were evidence the slaves picked the hottest day of the year to attempt an escape.

He constantly swiped at the air because his sweat made the perfect drink for a swarm of gnats buzzing around his head. What the gnats didn't get ran across his lips, leaving a foul, salty taste in his mouth, making him wish that the others were more successful because he desperately wanted to get back to the plantation.

After managing to get past the weeds and into the woods, Jonathan took a minute to lean against one of the many weeping willows that littered the area. He was trying to seek protection from the scathing sun, but the effects of the shade soon wore off because the humid air was sticky and kept him very uncomfortable.

Alone and a bit afraid, his stomach began to bubble uncontrollably. While looking for a place to hide, Jonathan came across a thick expanse of bushes. He figured it would be the perfect place to relieve himself—because with three runaways on the loose, he didn't want to get caught with his pants down.

Once he found a secluded spot, he pulled down his pants and got into a squatting position and waited. After about two minutes of nothing, he realized it was not his bowels bothering him but panicky nerves making him feel this way. Standing up to put his pants back on, he heard the sound of voices, and the returning urge to shit instantly filled his body. But he knew he'd have to investigate.

He picked his rifle up from the ground and headed in the direction of the noise, hoping to God the voices belonged to the trackers he got separated from. Unfortunately for him that wasn't the case, because after trudging through another thicket of shrubs, Jonathan couldn't believe what he saw—Claude lying unconscious at the feet of two runaway slaves. And to make things worse, one of them had his brother's rifle.

As Jonathan's body trembled with anxiety over the idea of having to save his brother's life, he noticed the two men seemed to be quibbling over something. So if there was a time to do anything it was now. He crouched down and crawled to the edge of the bushes trying to get as close as possible without being seen. He got so close, in fact, that he could actually hear what the bickering was about.

"Mowsuss, let's leave dis cracka where he is and go," Ben said while nervously pacing in circles. Having been captured once already, he clearly wanted to put more distance between him and the other trackers.

"No, we leave him alive, and he gonna tell the others we's tagetha," Moses shot back at Ben.

"Mowsuss, there's no time fa killin'. He sent that hound for more help. We's got to go now!" Ben said, emphatically trying to get his point across.

"Time, dat we got. This won't take a bit," Moses said while raising the rifle by its barrel. "No noise neither," he added with a sly grin as he hoisted the rifle way above his head in order to crush Claude's skull with its stock.

Kneeling on one knee, Jonathan began to steel himself as his body replaced his anxiety with anger. He dared not breathe as he aimed his rifle with deft precision. He squeezed the trigger and sprang to his feet.

"CLAAUUDE!" he screamed as he ran to the area where the men were standing.

"Oh Lawd, oh Jesus!" Ben wailed as Jonathan came charging through the cloud of smoke left over from the lone shot he fired.

"Lay down, nigger, or I'm going to shoot you!" Jonathan yelled at Ben, who did as he was told. "Claude?" he called out to his brother. "Don't you move, nigger!" he told Ben while surveying the area. His heart thumped rapidly as the adrenaline coursed through his veins. He saw Moses sprawled on the ground at the base of a tree with Claude's rifle at his side; the gaping hole in his neck was all the proof Jonathan needed to know that he was dead.

"J-J-Jon . . . Jon," Claude faintly called to his brother. The shot from Jonathan's rifle had startled him awake, but he lay still during the commotion.

"Claude, dear Jesus," Jonathan said as he hurried over to his brother. He sat Claude up against a tree while never taking his eyes away from Ben. "Claude, are you all right?" he asked.

"I'm fine. Just untie me, 'at's all," Claude told him.

Jonathan untied his brother and tied Ben's hands behind him with the same rope. Claude got up from the tree rubbing his head where Moses had struck him. Slowly, he made his way over to Ben; once there, he kicked him in his side. Ben cried out in pain as Jonathan shot a concerned look in his direction.

"Damn niggers were goin' ta kill me," Claude said with an indifferent look on his face as he walked to where Moses lay dead and retrieved his rifle.

Jonathan looked over at his brother and caught a glimpse of Moses. He had never killed a man before, and even though slaves weren't considered men, the severity of his actions began to weigh down on him. The melancholy moment passed quickly when he focused his attention back on Claude who was alive and well. Jonathan realized at that moment that he would've killed anyone, black or white, to save his brother's life. He embraced Claude. As the brothers held on to each other tight, the hound returned with a group of trackers, and they were both surprised to see their father with them.

Jonas Tobias led the pack of men with his rifle clutched in his large hands. When he saw his sons, he rushed over to them and pulled them in close for a tight bear hug. "Boys, y'all all right? We heard the shot, but we were too far away," he said as he squeezed them with all the love in his heart.

"We're fine, Paw," Claude said when his father let them go. Jonas stepped back and asked what happened.

Before Jonathan could utter a word, Claude chimed in, "I killed 'em, Paw. One shot, and I surprised the other coon over there," he said while pointing at Ben, who had a crowd of trackers standing around him ready to pounce any moment.

Jonas would have none of that here; both Moses and Ben would be brought back to the plantation to be put on display to show the rest of the slaves what happens when they try to escape. Ben would be whipped and burned alive to deter any hint of a revolt—which had always been a slave owner's biggest fear because slaves outnumbered whites on any plantation. Jonas knew that the only way to stay in control was to keep the smell of death in the air. The heinous treatment Ben would receive was necessary since a white man was killed, but mainly because Jasper had gotten away.

Meanwhile, Jonathan couldn't believe what he was hearing, Claude lying to his father in order to take all the credit for the capture.

Bastard, Jonathan thought to himself. *I could have let those niggers kill him.* He started to speak on his behalf but decided not to. After losing Jasper's trail, this was a proud moment for Jonas, and Jonathan didn't want to ruin it in scandal.

With no other reason to endure the humidity any longer than necessary, Jonas ordered the men to carry Moses and lead Ben back to the plantation. But before they set off for home, Jonas embraced Claude one more time. A mixture of emotions stewed inside of Jonathan as he watched the bond between his father and brother strengthen, knowing that from this day on, things would never be the same between Claude and him again.

The knock on his door had startled Jonathan from his memory, and he found himself back in his bedroom. He sat up in bed, and after thinking about Claude once more and his incessant potential for treachery, Jonathan realized that he had more important reasons than the outcome of Thomas's trip to get back to Azalea.

CHAPTER 3

Jonathan's servant knocked on the bedroom door to tell him that his bathwater had been heated. He refused the bath, fearing pneumonia because he was soon going out in the frigid weather. He told Gerald to prepare tea instead.

He crawled out of bed and went over to the washstand to shave his face and give his sideburns a trim, sneezing when a cloud of talcum entered his nostrils as he powdered his cheeks and neck. After wiping his hands, Jonathan stepped into his garment room where his clothes were neatly laid out for him.

Fully dressed, he headed down the stairs and wasn't surprised to find Thomas Woodburn sitting comfortably in the living room.

"Ah, good morning, Jon. Glad to see you amongst the living," Thomas said in a jovial tone. After six years, Jonathan had gotten used to Thomas's sarcasm and quick wit.

"I was about to have some tea and biscuits. Why don't you join me," Jonathan told Thomas, who was always ready to feed his face.

Gerald served the men steaming cups of tea and placed a tray of biscuits with various flavored jams between them. Once the servant left, Thomas pulled out a silver flask and began to pour liquor into his teacup.

"Thomas, Jesus, man, the day hasn't even started," Jonathan said.

"Tobias, please, this is for Old Man Winter out there," Thomas quipped in his defense. "I'd pour some of this in yours if I were you," he added while shaking the flask in front of Jonathan's face. He gave Thomas a dismissive look and finished his biscuit.

"Are you packed yet?" Thomas asked, never liking to be inconvenienced with wasted time.

"I've been packed for two days now. I've known you long enough to count on you being here at the crack of dawn damn near and ready to go," Jonathan told him.

"That's good, Jon, because Chauncey is outside with the carriage. I'll have him load your trunks immediately," Thomas said while heading to the door to instruct Chauncey to load Jonathan's things.

When Thomas opened the door, the wind howled as a chill rushed into the house. Feeling the uncomfortable air, Jonathan became reluctant about going out there. "Why are we leaving so early, Thom? We've got all day to set out. At least let the sun shine," Jonathan said as he rubbed his hands together.

"Oh, Jonathan, that's enough!" Thomas said. "We are leaving now and that's the end of it. You would think that someone in your position would be eager to get on with it. I don't want to hear any more about the weather!"

Jonathan wasn't used to anyone taking that kind of tone with him, but he knew his friend was right. Thomas was offering the opportunity of a lifetime, and to continuously gripe about the weather was a bit disrespectful. He called for Gerald to bring his coat, hat, and gloves. "I'm ready to go," he told Thomas after putting on all his items.

"Not quite," Thomas said while patting the breast pocket of his overcoat.

"Right again, friend," Jonathan snorted with a look of embarrassment on his face. Thomas reached inside his overcoat and pulled out his flask. He took a swig and passed it to Jonathan.

"Aahhh," Jonathan said after taking a generous swallow for himself, "now I'm ready." A warm sensation began to fill his entire body.

Gerald opened the door for them, and they all ventured out into the steel-gray morning. The missing chirps of the birds that flew south for the winter were replaced by the drumming sound of the impatient carriage horses beating their hooves against the road. And coupled with the whistling through the trees, it created an eerie tune to their ears.

Jonathan's eyes watered as the wind blew directly into his rose-colored face. Clenching his scarf tighter around his neck and tipping his head forward so the brim of his hat could deflect the gusts, Jonathan was the first to attempt to cross the ice-covered lawn.

Frozen grass crunched beneath his boots as he charged vigorously toward the carriage while Chauncey stoically braved the cold, shivering at attention while waiting for them with the doors wide open. Jonathan stepped inside and plopped himself on one of the cushioned benches facing the front of the carriage. Thomas climbed in, taking the bench opposite of him, and wasted no time lighting his pipe. Gerald shut the doors behind him and joined Chauncey up front.

"We're on our way," Thomas said as the carriage began to roll.

The sun finally began to peek out from behind the clouds when Chauncey guided the horses through the gates of the Philadelphia Railroad Depot. The carriage rolled slowly as they trotted past the various stations lining the frozen dirt road that snaked throughout the entire rail yard.

The stations were just warehouses thrown together to accommodate the boom in the country's newly discovered travel industry. The quality of the buildings varied, depending on the success or failures of the companies that owned them. The same rule applied to their locomotives.

Also along the road were rows of merchants selling food and goods to a countless number of men and women who wanted to take advantage of their last chance to gain provisions for their trips. Jonathan was surprised to see so many people out on this blustery morning, and now he could understand why Thomas wanted to leave so early.

The carriage came to a stop in front of the Pennsylvania Railroad station, and they exited to be amid a crowd of people scurrying about as if the entire city of Philadelphia was going to explode at any moment. After jostling their way to the entrance, Thomas, pipe in his mouth, turned to Chauncey and waved him off to see their trunks packed into one of the storage cars.

Inside the crowd was no different than the one they left on the street, everyone pushing and shoving their way toward the three giant locomotives docked side by side at the rear of the station.

"Which one are we taking?" Jonathan asked Thomas, who was struggling to get past two women dallying along in broad hoopskirts.

"Unfortunately, the Ohio Robin is the last one of the three," he yelled back to Jonathan, who kept pace right behind him. The only benefit of squeezing through the women came when the sweet scent of their perfumes gave his nose a break from the steam and wood-burnt fumes that filtered through the air.

The locomotives were majestic. They looked like three kings with their red-painted wheels, copper tubing, and polished brass trimmings. Plumes of white smoke puffed out of the large balloon smokestacks that crowned the front of their engines. Scalding steam hissed from the pressure valves running alongside of the length of the boilers, giving the illusion that the locomotives were breathing.

Even though the trains were stationary, the water had to stay preheated in order to enable them to move on command. So crews of firemen, or "ash cats" as they were called, were always on standby to feed planks of wood into the engine's firebox. Directly attached to the engine was the tender, a large wagon with the name Ohio Robin painted in gold on its sides, fully stocked with firewood to fuel the train to its destination.

When Jonathan finally caught up with Thomas, he was sitting on a bench next to one of the passenger cars linked behind the Ohio Robin. Tapping the remaining ashes from his pipe, he moved over so Jonathan could take a seat next to him. Exhausted, he sat down and let out a long, exaggerated sigh feeling like a salmon that just swam upstream to spawn its eggs; Jonathan was grateful for the opportunity to rest his legs.

"It's a madhouse in here," Jonathan said while eyeing two young boys running along the platform in awe of the trains, while their black nanny skipped behind to keep them from getting into any trouble. "Would you look at that, Thomas, niggers have just too much freedom here," he said with a scowl on his face.

"I guess *you* would rather chase after those boys," Thomas replied.

"It's not that, Thom. For six long years, I watched blue-bel-lied Northerners hand niggers rights my granddaddy fought against England for. Goddamned Yanks let these niggers practically raise their children. Niggers were brought here to this country for one purpose only, slaving."

Thomas slipped his pipe into his pocket and gave Jonathan an incredulous look. He couldn't understand his friend's reluctance to accept the changing times. "You bloody well better get use to it, chap, because soon they will all be free," Thomas said matter-of-factly.

"I'll never get used to it. Niggers shouldn't have any freedoms beyond breathin'," Jonathan shot back.

Thomas started to speak but caught a glimpse of Chauncey approaching them with two satchels hanging over his shoulders. He turned back to Jonathan and said, "It's time to go. We'll finish this on the train." Then he heaved himself up from the bench.

They walked along the platform until they reached a conductor taking tickets and directing traffic.

"Three to Springfield, Illinois," Thomas said while handing his papers over to the elderly man, who, after looking them over and checking their validity, ripped them in half.

Handing three halves back to Thomas, he said, "Keep these with you at all times. Without them, you'll be forced from the train. Your car is the second behind the engine."

Walking toward their car, Jonathan passed a crowd of women in shawls and bonnets boarding the "Women Only" car located directly behind theirs. He turned and looked the length of the platform, past the boxcars, and saw a group of black passengers boarding a car labeled "Negroes Only" at the rear of the train. Smiling to himself, Jonathan found solace in the fact that at least the railroad industry still considered Negroes third-class citizens.

The din of the station quieted when they entered the Pullman sleeper car. Passengers calmly moving about the car trying to find their seats were quite the contrast from the helter-skelter view Jonathan saw when he glanced out of one of the windows. They fol-lowed Chauncey, who led them to their row of booths.

Each booth had two pew-like benches that faced each other with overhead stows to put your things into. Pullman sleepers boasted first-class quality with its plush floral carpeting, stained polished teak walls, and ceilings with small brass lamps affixed to them spaced throughout the length of the car. The booths also had black velvet curtains for privacy, and the two facing benches collapsed together to form a small bed.

Chauncey took their coats with him to his booth while the men got settled. Normally, servants rode in a separate car, but Thomas wanted him close by to wait on his every beck and call.

After getting himself acquainted with the bells and whistles in his booth, Jonathan peeked into the one next to his and found Thomas loading tobacco into his pipe for another smoke.

"Settled in, Jon?" he asked while tapping his pipe against the wall to make room for more tobacco.

"Everything is fine, and you even made sure that my booth was the closest to the heater. You really thought everything through," he said while sitting down on the bench across from his friend.

Thomas looked up from his project and smiled at Jonathan. "You have been a great friend to me since I came to this country. My family didn't even consider that I might be a loner when I arrived here. I guess they were in such a rush to be free of me that the thought hadn't crossed their minds. This wasn't the most welcome place for an Englishman when I got here. The War of 1812 was almost a generation ago, but many men had lost loved ones during that period, and somehow, the unfortunate ones found it easy to blame me. I was a wee lad when our countries were at war, but that doesn't seem to matter because any opportunity they get to step over and shun me, it's taken."

Jonathan looked solemnly at his friend, feeling guilty about how Thomas had been treated; he wanted to interrupt but decided to let Thomas continue.

"Look at me, Jon. I'm not dashing like you. I'm squat and bald. I rely on my fortune and sense of humor to get by. You didn't have to befriend me. The people here thought you were one of them. You looked past the money and the jokes and saw who I really am. You trusted me with a secret that could have exposed you and made you a social outcast. I'm grateful for the trust and loyalty you saw in me when others hadn't—including my family who dispatched me to this god-awful country. That's how your purpose became my concern. I'm sure you've wondered what stake I had in all of this."

Jonathan raised his eyebrows and shook his head slowly, trying to mask the fact that he had been curious at times. Though he would never tell Thomas, he also felt alone dealing with the Northerners and having to keep his background a secret.

With a long sigh, Thomas continued, "Well, Jon, there isn't any. I just want to help out a true friend." Thomas extended his open hand out to Jonathan, who in turn clasped his large hands around it and held tightly. It was an intense moment that would only be interrupted by the sudden jerk form the train's brakes dislodging and the deafening whistle signaling that the Ohio Robin was leaving the station.

Jonathan watched from the window in his booth as people either stopped in their tracks or scurried out of the way as the behemoth locomotive rolled slowly through the bay doors to exit the station. Outside, the sun gave way to the clouds, and the sky turned bright gray as if it were going to snow. Jonathan could not have imagined making this trip by carriage; it would have been foolish to try something like that.

The whistle blew again but louder and longer as the train left the rail yard and began to pick up speed, passing people on the streets that stopped to gaze at the new form of transportation as it chugged by at speeds never before imagined.

Sights that were familiar to Jonathan after six years had only become a blur as the train moved west toward the edge of the city. Finally, he was leaving Philadelphia, its blue bellies, and all of the things he hated about the North, and getting one step closer to Azalea.

After a few hours of watching the scenery change from frosted pines to frozen meadows and then back again, the swaying of the train had lulled Jonathan to sleep. He slouched so far down in his seat that his face landed flush against the window where the cold, penetrating through the glass, woke him up immediately. Straightening himself out, he got up and peeked into Thomas's booth. Not finding him there, he noticed that the entire car was almost empty. Puzzled, he looked into Chauncey's booth and found him polishing a silver cup set.

"Chauncey, where is Thomas? As a matter of fact, where is everyone else?"

Chauncey turned his head slowly toward the rear of the car and, in the most condescending Old English tone he could find, said, "The women's car, sir," as if Jonathan should have already known, and returned back to his chore.

Jonathan leaned back out of the booth and made his way to the car's rear door; yanking it open, he ignored the temperature while stepping across the short empty space between the cars and pushed through the door.

A wave of heat rushed to greet him when he stepped into the crowded car that stank of liquor and cigar smoke that had remained stagnant in the uncirculated air. Men, who thought that this was a better way to spend their time than looking out at the frozen countryside, clogged the aisle leaning over women's shoulders, spewing liquor-laced words into their ears. Some of the women enjoyed their company while others felt as if their space had been invaded by the drunk and garrulous men.

Now perspiring, Jonathan squeezed down the aisle past the chatter, making his way toward the boisterous laughter emanating from the rear of the car. Reaching the point where he couldn't push any further, Jonathan used his height to look over the crowd and saw the one and only Thomas Woodburn at the center of attention.

Sitting between two smiling women, Thomas took a quick sip from his trusted flask and wiped the sweat from his forehead in one motion, all the while telling the crowd tales from his sordid childhood back in England.

They hung on to every word he said, especially the story about him literally falling in love with the sheep on his father's manor. They laughed at all his stories, all of which Jonathan had heard before. To him, they weren't amusing anymore but quite sad; and hearing them again, he could see why Thomas's family would send a grown man away to a foreign country in the first place. He was an embarrassment.

Even still, he could see that Thomas was enjoying himself and showed no trace of the man pouring his heart out to him earlier in the afternoon. Disgusted, Jonathan went back to his car, leaving Thomas alone with his audience.

Jonathan had just finished removing his boots when he heard footsteps and loud chitchat from the men returning form the women's car. Everyone seemed to be in a good mood since having spent some time with the opposite sex.

"Jon, my dear friend," Thomas slurred while sticking his fat head through the curtains. "Come on, Jon, have a drink with your old chap."

Thomas slid inside of the booth cradling a full bottle of scotch under his arm and holding two silver cups in his hands. He passed one of them to Jonathan, who, upon seeing his reflection, snickered at the thought of Chauncey laboring to get them their mirror finish. After pouring the scotch into the cups, Thomas raised his for a toast, but Jonathan didn't budge; he just stared emptily into Thomas's bloodshot eyes.

"Come on, get with it," he said to Jon, who quickly obliged once he caught a whiff of Thomas's wicked-smelling breath.

By now, the sun had set, and the light from the lamps made their shadows loom high against the walls behind them. "So, Thom, tell me how you stumbled upon this mysterious figure we are going to meet," Jonathan managed to ask after the fire in his throat burned out. Thomas raised his hand and told Jonathan to hold on while he gathered his thoughts.

Besides the constant coughs and chugs from the engine's smokestack, no other sound could be heard inside of the cabin. Thomas swayed erratically with the movement of the train, leaning so far it looked as if he would fall out of the booth and into the aisle. But as with all drunks, just when he would likely keel over, he straightened himself up and began to speak. "Very well, Jon, where would you like for me to begin," he said while striking a match to his pipe.

"Anywhere you want," Jonathan said flatly, wanting him to get on with it.

"Do you remember the True Republican Abolitionist's dinner party last November?" Thomas asked.

"Yeah, the one held at the widow Martha Stapleton's mansion," Jonathan replied while nodding his head.

"That's right, the one you made some poor excuse so you wouldn't have to attend. Thankfully, we all don't think like you because you missed one bloody good time. You should have seen the cleavage bursting with ample white breasts or the wine that was generously poured as soon as your glass left your lips. Stuffed Cornish hen so tender that the meat practically melted in yo—"

"Come on, Thom, get serious." Jonathan wanted Thomas to spare him the frivolous details.

Thomas began again, "It was the gala of the year, so all of the bigwigs from the Republican Party were there. After we ate, Martha Stapleton read off a list of the year's most charitable and active members. Your name received a hearty applause, I might add."

Jonathan squirmed from hearing the news of him being one of the antislavery's best supporters. It pained him to be involved in any of their functions at all, let alone be honored at a party where they insisted on patting themselves on the back. His patience was wearing thin, so he told Thomas to continue.

"Where was I? Oh, that's right, the honors. After the honors were read, the entire party toasted to a future of free states at any cost. I happened to be seated at the same table as Secretary of Congress Graham Westhead, his wife Mabelle, Supreme Court Justice William Mabrey, and his lovely daughter Marilynne."

"We drank sherry and hobnobbed over boysenberry tarts when Mr. Westhead suggested that I stay behind after the reception ended. Even Justice Mabrey added that it would be a wise decision for me to do so. I spent the rest of the evening trying my damnedest to get Marilynne to fancy me a waltz, but for some odd reason, she wasn't even interested in looking at me," Thomas said, baffled by her unconcern for him.

"When the reception was over, I followed Justice Mabrey to a private dining chamber at the other end of the mansion. Graham Westhead was already there, and he introduced me to the others: Senator Salmon Chase of Ohio, Jay Cooke—a financier from New York, and Robert D. Watson, a cotton speculator from the Treasury Department.

"Everyone was rather stone-faced during the introductions, but the mood changed altogether after Westhead passed around cigars and snifters of brandy. They began by talking about the party, and a couple of them joked about the women there they would like to ravish. Justice Mabrey sat next to me, so I had to keep my thoughts about Marilynne to myself.

"Anyhow, the subject quickly turned to politics, and Robert D. Watson was the first to speak. He went on vehemently about why the Republicans must act fast, projecting that if slavery were allowed to continue for ten more years, the South will have their economical independence. The power would shift from the Union to the Southern states. He even eluded that if the Mayflower would have landed in South Carolina instead of Plymouth Rock, this wouldn't even be an issue."

"Sons of bitches, I knew it!" Jonathan said excitedly, confirming what he had always suspected: the Yankees coveted the South's fertile lands.

"What is it, Jon?" Thomas asked curiously.

"It's nothing. Go ahead," Jonathan replied, smiling to himself at what he seemed to know all along.

Thomas took a long drag on his pipe and continued, "When Watson finished, Salmon Chase, a rather fiery gent, bid a toast to what was, in his words, 'correcting a godforsaken mistake.'"

"What was the mistake? Slavery?" Jonathan asked.

"It's funny you asked because it's the same thing I did after we toasted. At that point, I drew stares from everyone in the room. But none were as piercing as the senator's. In the iciest tone he could muster, he told me that the mistake wasn't the allowance of slavery, it was the Union not benefiting from it. Then Westhead added that the most lucrative trade in the country shouldn't belong solely to a bunch of hillbillies and farmers when the Union was obviously the brain trust of the nation."

Jonathan listened intently as Thomas described his encounter with the greedy cabal, who felt as though a Southerner's blood wasn't blue enough to reap the profits of slavery. His hatred toward them grew with every word that came out of Thomas's mouth.

"After making their views clear to me, I finally got to hear why I was asked to join the meeting. This was Jay Cooke's cue to fill me in on how they were going to bring their plans to fruition. He slowly walked around the table and stood behind each man as he eloquently laid out their roles for me.

"They are actually going to vault their own man into the White House during the next presidential election. It's a detailed scheme with every contingency thought of, from Templeton Marshal to ensure the ballot, all the way down to Chief Justice Mabrey ruling against any challenge of the vote in the supreme court. Jon, I believe they can do it," Thomas said, clearly convinced.

"All right, Thom, I believe it too. But you still haven't told me what they wanted with you." Jonathan wanted to get to the center of the story and find out what he had to gain in all of this.

"Patience, Jon, I'm getting to that now," he said, still feeling the effects of the liquor. He went on, "Graham Westhead, who I figure to be the man in control, told me that there is only one variable that the success or failure of this elaborate plan hinged upon. Anonymity. Afraid that any connection between them and their candidate could ruin everything, they felt it was important to include an outsider with no governmental ties whatsoever, someone wealthy enough to financially back their candidate, and who's been involved in all of the right Republican and abolitionist circles in order to stem any suspicious conspiracy theories.

"Somehow, they felt as though I fit the criteria. There is no doubt my being an Englishman swayed their decision, ensuring that I couldn't be a mole spying for the South. When he asked me to join their plight to bring the South to its knees, I immediately thought of you. I asked him what exactly did he need from me, and he told me he wanted five million dollars to finance their candidate's campaign."

"Five million?" Jonathan asked excitedly. He and Thomas were more than wealthy, but five million dollars was a lot to ask by someone Thomas had just met. "Bold fella, huh? What did you tell him?"

"Obviously, I agreed. Then Westhead informed me that Jay Cooke would instruct me on how to handle the financial dealings at a later time. He also added that after this meeting, I would never see or hear from the gentlemen at the table or anyone associated with them again."

"If you weren't going to have any contact with them, how in the hell were they going to reward you for your involvement and five million dollars?" Jonathan asked as he stood to let the blood in his legs circulate.

"I mentioned that to Westhead, who laughed when he reminded me that I just agreed to finance the next president's campaign—and once he was in office, the president would reward anyway I wished. Satisfied that we were all in agreement on our plan and its benefits, everyone left me alone with Jay Cooke to make arrangements on how my money would be spent on the candidate. Afterwards, each of us slipped out of the mansion and disappeared discreetly into the night."

Thomas dug inside of his vest pocket and pulled out a square envelope with a broken wax seal. "A month ago, I received this by telegram," he said while handing it to Jonathan, who opened it to find two cards elegantly scripted in golden ink inviting Woodburn and a guest to a private Republican nomination party in Springfield, Illinois.

Staring at the invitations, Jonathan became so transfixed by what he held in his hands that he didn't even hear Thomas say that he was retiring to his booth to get some sleep. As he read the words aloud, an unsettling feeling crept into his stomach as the weight of everything that Thomas had just revealed came crashing down around him.

The two beautifully crafted invitations were the evidence of Westhead's plot in motion, and meant the beginning of the end for the privileged and powerful lifestyle that slavery had afforded him. After looking up and finding himself alone, Jonathan blew out the lamp and sat quietly in the darkness thinking about the impending peril of Azalea and what, if anything, he could do about it.

CHAPTER 4

The Ohio Robin sliced through the rain as it rolled into Springfield early the next morning. Leaving trails of black smoke in its wake, the train nearly ran out of firewood as it raced nonstop through four states to make for a shorter ride.

It had not been a shorter ride for Jonathan, who sat up half the night pondering the news Thomas had given him, and spent the other half unsuccessfully trying to get some sleep on the tiny makeshift bed inside of his booth. Now he sat impatiently waiting for the train to make its way to the station so he could get to their hotel and lay down in a bed made for a man his size.

Restless, he got up to look in on Thomas, who slept as peacefully as a newborn baby nestled in its bassinet. Green with envy, he kicked the bed and felt a hint of satisfaction when Thomas sprang up at attention.

"What in bloody hell are you doing?" Thomas asked after wiping his eyes and seeing Jonathan standing over him.

"I came to tell you that we're here already," he answered with a sly grin.

"Damn it, Jon, you damn well know that's what Chauncey's paid to do," Thomas said while putting on his glasses. "You look awful. Did you get any rest?" He noticed the bags under Jonathan's eyes.

"None at all, especially after what you told me. And only a pygmy could've slept on that thing," Jonathan said while looking in the direction of Thomas's bed.

"Oh, to hell with you. It's not my fault that you are the son of a goddamned giant. So you lost a night of sleep. Don't worry, Jon, with the things we are going to accomplish here, you can look forward to a lifetime of pleasant dreams. Now let me get dressed so we can flee this machine," Thomas said while struggling to pull his suspenders over his chubby shoulders. "Chauncey!"

When they got off the train, they were approached by a rain-soaked gentleman holding a sign with Woodburn's name on it.

"Thomas Woodburn?" the man hesitantly asked, but when he realized that Thomas fit the description he had been given, he stepped closer and introduced himself. "Mr. Woodburn, my name is Gavin Meade, and I'm here to proudly welcome you to our city and escort you and your guests to the Widmark, our finest hotel," he said while tipping his hat and flinging water on Thomas at the same time. "Oh, sorry about that," he added while trying to wipe the splatter of water from Thomas's large forehead.

"That's fine," Thomas said, waving him away, irritated. "And our things?"

"Well, I already put them onto the carriage. That's how I got all wet," Meade answered, showing all of his teeth.

"You lead the way," Thomas said as they turned to follow him out of the station. "Make sure all of our luggage is there when we get to the carriage, and that it's ours. This man's not too bright," he whispered to Chauncey out of Meade's earshot.

Satisfied all their luggage was present, Chauncey climbed onto the carriage and rode up front with Meade. Since their bench was uncovered, he tried his best to share his umbrella while the younger man struggled to maneuver the horses through the puddled streets of Springfield. However, the umbrella proved useless because the wind blew the rain in on them from all directions and drenched every article of clothing he had on.

"Do we have far to go?" Chauncey asked angrily, spoiled by his ride in the Pullman sleeper car. He was embittered that now he had to ride up front and get all wet with the driver.

Inside, Thomas smoked his pipe while Jonathan silently looked out of the window as the carriage rolled slowly through town. The torrential rain emptied the streets, giving Springfield the same deserted look of the small towns he remembered from back home. And except for the snow that the rain didn't wash away, it could have been easily mistaken for Birmingham, Alabama.

By no way did it remind him of Philadelphia or the other "power" cities that were situated throughout the North, but he knew this place was crawling with the same type of people who believed he and his kind were social and political afterthoughts. And between yawns, he wished that he could torch the entire town, sending the blue bellies to hell and their evil reform conspiracies right along with them.

The carriage came to a halt in front of a gigantic Victorian structure that dwarfed the rest of the buildings along Jefferson Avenue, the largest street in Springfield. Jonathan pushed open the door to be greeted by a wide burgundy canopy covering a bright red carpet that stretched from the curb to the front doors of the Widmark Hotel. Gavin Meade and Chauncey unloaded the carriage while Jonathan and Thomas had gotten acquainted with the comforts of the lobby where they completely forgot about the present downpour that caused the streets of Springfield to run brown with mud.

Opulence radiated throughout the entire lobby from the mahogany-covered walls and the paintings that adorned them, all the way down to the large marble fountain that rested in the center of the hotel's atrium. Walking toward the front desk, Thomas noticed a school of carp swimming around inside of the fountain.

"I'm impressed," Thomas said while nodding his head approvingly. His remark paid a high compliment to the Widmark Hotel, coming from a man who had dined with the most royal families in England. Jonathan was so tired that he could care less about the Widmark's ambiance. And after more than twenty-two hours on the train, he was just happy to have his feet on stationary ground.

Meade and Chauncey caught up with them right after they received their room keys. "Mr. Woodburn, if you don't mind, I would like to walk with you to your room," Meade said while making his best attempt to straighten his damp clothing.

"I have no problem with that," Thomas said as they fell in step behind the bellhops who led them up a grand staircase that split apart at the first landing, separating the Widmark's east and west wings.

When they reached their rooms, Meade stepped in front of Jonathan and dropped a few silver coins into the bellhop's hand after he put Jonathan's things into his suite. He did the same for the other bellhop when he finished with Thomas's suite, which was located directly across the hallway. As Jonathan turned to close his door, he caught a glimpse of Meade following Thomas inside of his suite.

"There seems to be a grave misunderstanding here," Meade said as soon as he closed the door. Gone was the buffoonish act he put on at the train station. Thomas's mouth began to sag open, fearing that his role in Westhead's plan had been sniffed out.

"There is?" he asked quizzically.

"Yes, there is. When I gathered your things from the train, I couldn't help noticing that you didn't plan on staying around after the party this evening," Meade said after wiping his face and hands off with a towel Thomas had given him.

"Well, I didn't think my being here would have been necessary," Thomas said, nervously reaching for his tobacco pouch.

"You have to understand, Mr. Woodburn, your position as the campaign financier involves more than your money. It requires your presence throughout the entire campaign trail. Your insight may or may not determine the outcome of this election," Meade said as Thomas made his best effort to conceal the fact that he already knew the election's outcome.

"So you want me to stay and help with the campaign?" Thomas asked as his face slowly began to regain its color.

"Yes, the Republican Party thanks you for your support and generosity. I have been appointed as your assistant to accommodate your every need during your stay here," Meade said while Thomas sat on the sofa filling his pipe with tobacco.

"I have an early request. I would like to have dinner, privately, with our candidate the evening after the nomination party," Thomas said.

"That's not a problem. We are all at your disposal. I suppose you want him here in your suite," Meade said while jotting the request down in his notebook. "Is there anything else I can do for you?" he asked before turning to leave.

Feeling a bit confident, Thomas stroked his chin slowly as he mulled over one more request. "As a matter of fact, there is, but you needn't take any notes for it," he added with a devilish grin.

Later that evening, the sound of footsteps had awakened Jonathan from a deep, comatose sleep. He crawled out of bed patting himself all over, and discovering he still had on all of his clothing, he lethargically sought out the person in his suite.

"Chauncey, how'd you get in here?" he asked after finding the butler moving about completing a host of chores from unpacking Jonathan's things to preparing a hot bath for him.

"Master Woodburn had the concierge let me in when you wouldn't open the door. That was hours ago when lunch was served," Chauncey said while handing him a steaming mug of coffee.

"Where is Thomas?" Jonathan asked between sips.

"He is rather occupied at the moment," Chauncey said, giving him the look from last evening, "but he insisted on you being ready for tonight's event."

Jonathan placed his mug on the coffee table and headed in the direction of the bathroom where a tub of hot water waited for him.

Well rested from his sleep and relaxed from his bath, Jonathan emerged from his suite dressed in the black tuxedo that Chauncey left neatly laid out on his bed for him. He entered Woodburn's suite and encountered two scantily clad women who looked well worn from the drinking and lascivious behavior that went on while he slept the day away.

"Say hello to Jon," Thomas said to the women, who replied with languid waves as they sat cuddled up with each other on the sofa sharing a bowl of grapes. Jonathan knew too well what they were, having been around Thomas long enough to know he would never miss an opportunity to add another escapade to a life of wild stories.

Jonathan sat quietly across from the half-naked prostitutes while Thomas frantically walked about trying to locate something that was missing. "Looking for these?" Jonathan said, holding the invitations in his hands.

"What would I do without you?" Thomas said as he snatched the invitations and wiped the beads of perspiration from his forehead.

Jonathan wondered just the opposite, knowing that by being apart of the conspiracy, Thomas was the key to his entire future. But even after having almost a whole day of knowing, he still hadn't thought of a way to cash in on the information he had been given.

After promising to have dinner sent to the suite for the women, Thomas joined Jonathan in the hallway, and they made their way toward the lobby.

"What was that?" Jonathan asked, mentioning the women in the suite.

"Perks, Tobias. Perks, that's all," Thomas said dismissively. "As it seems, I've been delegated a role here since I'm the campaign financier. Meade informed me earlier that I must stay on throughout the entire campaign trail and help get the nominee elected. We both know that's a joke because the outcome is already set in stone, so those lovelies are just compensation for my time."

Having been taught by his father that the tool in his pants is only to be used for true love, Jonathan could never imagine himself lying with a harlot. He shrugged Thomas off as they stepped onto the first landing of the staircase where he could see the entire lobby filling up with staunch Republican Party members making their way to the Widmark's grand ballroom.

The sight of them began to make him sick, knowing that the country would soon be dominated by their ideology. Hearing the music and laughter that poured out into the lobby, Jonathan prepared himself for what waited on the other side of the doorway.

Inside, the ballroom was packed with men suited in tuxedos that mirrored his and women dressed in satin ball gowns trimmed with lace that were garishly draped in their finest jewelry in hopes of standing out the most. The sights and sounds were dizzying, so Jonathan tried his best to ignore it all as he and Thomas followed an usher to their table.

From there, he watched as the Republican Party's elite fraternized with one another while waiting to see their presidential nominee for the first time. Noticing a few groups of men gathered together laughing and sharing in small toasts, Jonathan began to imagine that they were organizing ways to divvy up his land once the takeover of the South was complete.

He turned to Thomas who, until then, had only focused on a plate of food in front of him. "Look at them all, just waiting to pick over our land like a flock of greedy vultures," he said in contempt of the crowd. "There has to be a stop put to all of this."

"Jon, you're being foolish," Thomas said as he turned to look at him. "By even thinking that, you are going against every reason your father had for sending you here. The men I described to you last night are gods. Nothing will stop them from getting what they want."

Thomas took a sip of wine and continued, "The South has already been lost. This here is just a matter of making if official."

"What do you suppose I do, sit here and enjoy myself knowing what I know?" Jonathan asked sardonically.

"I'm not saying that at all. Instead of harping on what you can't control, think about your family and what's important to them." Thomas took another drink before adding, "Then concentrate on salvaging what can be saved."

The crowd began to clear the floor as the music being played by the band changed from a slow waltz into a vigorous drumroll.

"Ladies and gentlemen!" the master of ceremonies yelled as he stood on the dais that had been placed at the center of the ballroom floor. The retired opera singer waited patiently until every guest had been seated and he had everyone's full attention, then he spoke.

"We are all gathered here in this ballroom tonight for one reason! Not for the fine food that the Widmark has prepared or the harmonizing music that has been elegantly played for us either! Change is what led us here tonight! We are here because we are fed up with the savagery that runs rampant in the South! Fed up with the greed that motivates their behavior . . ." His resonant voice boomed over the ballroom as he held the captivated audience hostage with his speech.

Jonathan, in particular, paid close attention to every word the orator had said. Words like *disrespect, savagery,* and *greed* had stuck out to him the most, not because they were being used to describe everything he believed in, but because they represented the motivation behind Westhead's conspiracy.

He looked around and wondered how many people in the audience actually knew what drove this campaign besides Thomas and himself. He shook his head as he figured that probably none of them did. *Fools,* he thought to himself, *being led like lambs to slaughter, all because of one man's greed.* A man who didn't even have the decency to be in attendance, but then he remembered something his father had once told him, that the deadliest snakes always operated in the shadows.

He turned his attention back to the emcee that appeared to be winding down his speech. "It is time to restore order! Time to take back our country! It is time," he let a long pause hang in the air, "to meet the bearer of change! Please give a round of applause for our next president! Ladies and gentlemen, I give you Abraham Lincoln!"

The applause was deafening even without Jonathan's contribution, and it went on until the tall bearded man rightfully took the emcee's place upon the dais. To call him tall would have been an understatement; standing six feet five when the average height was five feet seven, he towered over anyone who stood next to him— especially his wife, Mary Todd, the short and plump, dark-eyed woman at his side.

Jonathan seethed at the sight of the olive-skinned nominee humbly accepting the praise from the audience. After studying law at the University of Penn, he had known all about the legend of Abraham Lincoln, a self-educated farmer from the hills of Kentucky who earned a law degree in his spare time between chopping wood and harvesting potatoes. He had been elected to Illinois state legislature and parlayed that into a career in politics with a seat in the house of representatives.

The rumor mills had also spun stories about him, notably that he married a domineering prude who held check over their household and forced him to call her "Mother." The most severe rumor of all questioned his sexuality, and behind his back, his detractors called him "the big flower."

Now he stood in front of the Republican Party's most respected dignitaries and members as the "chosen one," the only man brave enough to make the cataclysmic decisions that will forever change the face of the nation.

To Jonathan, Lincoln was just the final piece of Westhead's puzzle, following a course that has already been laid out for him. He saw no power or bravery when he looked at the dais, just a puppet whose only reward would be the title of President of the United States for doing another man's biddings.

"President of the United States of America," he silently mouthed to himself. It was a title that many men would kill for—and die for as well. Jonathan didn't know what the future held for Lincoln beyond him being elected president, but he knew the president would be instrumental to him when the time came to save Azalea. Jonathan's palms began to sweat as the thought of his plantation's future crossed his mind for the hundredth time.

Lincoln opened his address with his famous declaration, "A house divided against itself cannot stand. I believe the government cannot endure, permanently half slave and half free."

He was a notoriously short speaker, and Jonathan knew that he wouldn't be on the dais too much longer. When he finished, Lincoln was mobbed by the entire audience who were trying to make last-ditch efforts to offer the future president anything they could to make him remember them once he was in office.

Thomas noticed that Jonathan had become visibly agitated as the rambunctious crowd surrounded the newly designated candidate. Placing a steady hand on Jonathan's shaky fist, he leaned in close and said calmly, "Relax, Jon, have a drink," as he passed his flask to his friend. "We'll have him all to ourselves tomorrow and then we'll set everything straight."

Alone in his suite after the party, Jonathan sat quietly in front of the fireplace as myriad thoughts raced around his head. The past two days were starting to take their toll on him; he could hardly eat, and now even sleep was evading him. It seemed as though the only solace he could find came from Thomas's silver flask.

Gazing intently at the crackling flames, he envisioned the entire South going up in smoke, everyone dead and everything destroyed. Suddenly, Thomas's words began to echo over and over inside of his head. "The South has already been lost, salvage what can be saved, the South has already been lost, salvage what can be saved, salvage what can be saved . . ."

Quickly, Jonathan turned away form the fire, ultimately realizing what he needed to do.

The next evening, Jonathan relaxed on the sofa in Thomas's suite as he waited for their guest to arrive. Long gone were the whores, and the suite was as pristine as the day they checked in. No matter how calm he tried to remain, he still couldn't escape the fact that the fate of his family would be decided tonight. He hadn't even discussed his idea with Thomas, who had been preoccupied with making sure that everything would be to Lincoln's liking.

After making arrangements with Thomas to repay the five million dollars that all of this was costing, Jonathan knew that he could not return to Azalea empty-handed. He hoped to bring something to his father that would justify the six years he'd been away. If not, he would look like a fool, and there was no way he would ever give Claude that kind of satisfaction.

The knock at the door caused everyone in the suite to pause momentarily and check around to make sure that everything was in place. After Chauncey opened the door, Lincoln slowly walked in holding his twelve-inch top hat, which he was increasingly becoming famous for, at his side.

Thomas was the first to greet him. "Abraham, it's a pleasure to finally meet you," he said after a firm handshake.

"Call me Abe. And you are?" he said after scanning the room and noticing Jonathan.

"Jon Tobias," he said while reluctantly shaking Lincoln's hand.

"I thought we would be alone here," Lincoln said after turning back to Thomas.

"We are alone, Abe. Jon here is privy to everything we are going to discuss. Let's all sit down at the table and have a drink," Thomas said, trying to ease the tension.

Chauncey filled everyone's glass with scotch and then excused himself from the suite, leaving them to sit quietly and wait for the first person to speak.

"Thomas, I wanted to thank you personally for your generous donation to my campaign. Meade mentioned to me that he informed you about staying on. I promise to keep your duties as effortless as possible," Lincoln said before having a drink.

"It's good to see that you have been practicing your prom-ise-making skills. You'll be doing a lot of that during the campaign trail, making promises, that is. And once you're in office, you'll spend the rest of your term breaking them," Thomas said, seizing the first opportunity to lighten the mood. The two of them laughed while Jonathan could only manage a smirk as he unsuccessfully tried to conceal his aversion toward Lincoln.

"Is there something wrong?" Lincoln asked Jonathan, who had been staring daggers at him since the moment they sat down.

"As a matter of fact, there is," Jonathan said, wasting no time drawing battle lines between them.

"Well, I don't have all night!" Lincoln shot back at him.

"Gentlemen, gentlemen, please!" Thomas cut in. "Abe, there's something you don't understand. I didn't put up the money for your campaign. He did."

Lincoln took another drink from his glass. "That's fine with me. We are all Republican here, right?"

Thomas held up his hand as if to slow him down. "Well, that's another thing. He isn't a Republican either."

Lincoln sat back in his chair and began to shift his eyes between the two of them. "What the hell is going on, Woodburn? What is this? I was told that you were on board," he said sharply.

"Abe, I am on board, but I had to make the financial situation clear to you before we went any further," Thomas said in his defense.

"Nothing is clear to me now. It hasn't been since you both started talking," he said to Thomas before turning his attention to Jonathan. "What are you doing here? You're not a Republican, but you paid five million dollars to finance my campaign. What do you want from me?"

Jonathan could hold on to his emotions no longer. "I want protection!" he erupted.

"Protection! From who? For what?" Lincoln asked, even more confused.

"You, that's who! And the rest of your cocksuckin' partners who are schemin' to take what's ours!" Jonathan answered in a tone that made Lincoln flinch. He could never control his Southern accent once he lost his temper, and now he spoke as if he was among his family.

"You're spies!" Lincoln said as he quickly stood up from the table.

Thomas followed and went over to him. "Abe, listen to me," he said, looking up to the taller man. "You know very well that Graham Westhead wouldn't pair you with a spy."

"But this is clearly a Southerner," Lincoln said, pointing a long index finger in Jonathan's direction.

"Yes, he is, but he's the one that put up five million dollars to get you into the White House. He's not against your cause because he needs your help. He's just having a difficult time asking for it," Thomas said, trying to placate the growing hostility between his guests.

Tired of Thomas speaking for him, Jonathan slammed a heavy fist against the table, rattling the silverware in the process and drawing everyone's attention to him. "Abraham, please come and sit down," Jonathan said very coolly, knowing that if he didn't calm himself, a golden opportunity was about to slip away. "Please," he said again, "just hear me out."

Lincoln mulled the request over and retook his seat. Jonathan refilled their glasses and began to speak.

"We are all men in here, and none of us want to be told what to do. But I want you to imagine something. Imagine that, one day, you had to unwillingly give up everything you worked all of your life for and everything that you believed in. You have no say whatsoever—you just have to do it because the law says so. Then, suddenly, you find out that the law only says so not because it's morally right but because the powers that be are manipulating the law to serve their own greedy agendas. How would you feel about that?" he asked passionately.

"You don't have to answer," Jonathan said when he saw that Lincoln was about to respond. "Because, being a man, I already know how you'd feel. The way I feel right now." He looked Lincoln straight in the eyes.

Feeling the need to engage him, Lincoln asked, "Why would you support the Republican Party if you know what we're after?"

Jonathan let out a light chuckle. "Abe, we're not all idiots below the Mason-Dixon Line. The Federal Union is powerful, and even the strongest resistance will eventually meet with defeat," he said submissively.

"So you pay for my campaign, and now you expect a favor in return. Is that how this is supposed to go?" Lincoln asked sneeringly as he stroked his bushy beard.

After regaining his composure, Jonathan had Lincoln right where he wanted him, feeling sympathetic and in control. He figured that if the rumors about his wife were true, given the opportunity, Lincoln would jump at the chance to wield his forthcoming executive powers. And Jonathan would see to it they served his purpose.

"So tell me, what can I do for you?" Lincoln asked before having another drink.

"It's simple. I want Azalea to remain untouched. Our land, our slaves, and our crops are to be left alone," Jonathan said as the wide-eyed man stared back at him. "I know you plan to end slavery once you take your seat, but I want my family's plantation to go on unchanged."

"Is he serious?" Lincoln asked Thomas, who was just as shocked by Jonathan's demands as he was. When Thomas didn't answer, he turned back to Jonathan. "How do you suppose something like that can happen?" Lincoln asked the brazen young man sitting across from him—who wanted something so preposterous he couldn't believe he was entertaining the thought of giving it to him. He admired Jonathan's passion and willingness to stand up for his family, so he continued to ponder the idea of granting his request.

It was true that once he made it to the White House, there would be no one who could stop him from doing what he wanted to do, not even Westhead. And after all, it was Jonathan's money that put him in such a lofty position.

Jonathan tried his best to remain calm, but the anticipation was killing him. He hoped that he had gotten through to Lincoln, but the expression on his face told him nothing.

"Tell me, what does your plantation produce?" Lincoln asked after another silent moment.

"Cotton. We have the second largest plantation in the South, but the largest production rate overall," Jonathan answered with pride.

"King Cotton," Lincoln said, calling the crop by its nickname, which stood for the dominance it held over any other exportable product in the world. Knowing that at any moment, every living human being could be wearing or using cotton, Lincoln made his decision. "I'm going to help you. I don't know how, but you can rest assured that your plantation will be spared," he said firmly.

"Wonderful!" Thomas added excitedly and raised his glass for a toast. "To great men being able to agree and to the continuous success of our endeavors."

As he hoisted his glass, Jonathan felt an incredible sense of relief as the burden of Azalea's future seemed to rise from his shoulders.

"Let's eat. I'm starved," Thomas said when the last man finished his drink.

"I have to decline," Lincoln said as he started to get up. "Since my nomination, my schedule has been filled with pressing engagements. Will you gentlemen forgive me?"

Not wanting to spend any more time with him than necessary, Jonathan said that he understood and walked with Lincoln to the door. As they firmly shook hands, Jonathan began to wonder why

Lincoln quickly agreed to help after learning that Azalea was the country's largest producer of cotton.

Lincoln looked Jonathan in the eye and reassured Jonathan again that he would be hearing from him soon after he won the election. They bid farewell and Lincoln departed, leaving Jonathan alone with Thomas and a table full of food.

"I told you so. Didn't I say that everything will be okay?" Thomas managed to say through a mouthful of chicken. "We should celebrate. I swear, Jon. I thought your attitude was going to cost you everything. Somehow, you were able to convince him—"

"Convince? What are you talking about?" he cut in, unfazed by Thomas's celebratory mood.

"I'm speaking about the way you got him to understand Azalea's importance to you," Thomas said, trying to rationalize with him.

"Thomas, don't you get it? This entire conspiracy is about one thing. Greed. And what he understood was how wealthy he could become by owning the only cotton plantation left in the country," Jonathan said, cursing himself for believing that he could strike a fair deal with the likes of Abraham Lincoln and his cohorts.

"No matter what you think, he agreed to spare Azalea," Thomas said, trying to shed light on the situation. "You'll be able to return home with the good news your father is hoping for."

"But for how long?" Jonathan replied, wanting Thomas to be right, but Lincoln's curiosity compounded his worst fears. "What do I do when he shows up at the gates to make a claim on our land?"

Thomas put down his fork and turned to Jonathan. "I don't understand you. Just a few hours ago, you had nothing. You were in the same predicament as the rest of the South with no hope for the future. And for a fraction of what would have been lost, you purchased immortality. Now you stand here telling me that you still feel threatened because he inquired about Azalea? Talk about looking a gift horse in the mouth," he said while rolling his eyes in disgust.

Jonathan couldn't blame him for feeling the way that he did, but he would not be influenced by his naïvety either. Thomas had been more than a brother to him, but with his family safely tucked away across the Atlantic Ocean, he could never experience Jonathan's anxiety from the threat of losing everything that mattered to him the most.

"Thomas, I'm not ungrateful or unsatisfied. Believe me, I can't wait to return to Azalea, especially with news that will help my father rest easy," Jonathan said as he returned to his seat, "but I have to be careful. There is no honor amongst thieves, and as it stands, I just made a deal with the man that's going to become the biggest thief in American history."

Thomas removed his eyeglasses and squeezed the bridge of his nose between his forefinger and thumb. He let out a long sigh before speaking, "Okay, you've made your point. But remember, I'm going to be here, and you can believe I'll keep a watchful eye on him during the course of the campaign." He placed a firm grip on Jonathan's forearm. The gesture had given Jonathan a small sense of security, knowing that even though he was headed back to Alabama, he was leaving someone behind that he could trust and who would also look out for his best interests.

With his business in Springfield concluded, Thomas knew that early tomorrow morning, Jonathan would be headed back to Azalea, so he excused himself from the table and returned holding a small wooden box in his hand. It was polished to a shine, and when he placed it on the table, Jonathan could see that his name was neatly inscribed on the lid.

"Thomas, this isn't necessary now," Jonathan said while shaking his head, embarrassed.

"I know it isn't. That's why I want your word that you won't open it until the moment you arrive at Azalea," Thomas said while lighting his pipe.

"You have more than my word. I'm forever indebted to you. You should be going back with me just so you could see the beautiful place you helped to save. I love you, Thom," he said with all of the sincerity in his heart. Jonathan had waited for the opportunity to go back home to Azalea for six long years, and now that it had finally come, it was bittersweet because he had to leave Thomas behind.

CHAPTER 5

Founded by Jebadiah Tobias in 1790, Azalea had been named after a colorful flower that grew abundantly in the state of Alabama by his wife Charla, who fell in love with the name as well as its seductive beauty the moment she first laid eyes on one. He purchased the vast land with the small fortune he had earned by smuggling arms to the Patriots during the Revolutionary War and selling slaves in the years that followed. When he grew tired of watching others become rich in the slave trade, he moved his family, along with thirty slaves, south with the intention of joining the country's burgeoning cotton industry.

The gamble paid off. Almost overnight, the world's need for cotton grew exponentially. Praised for its softness and strength, the fabric it produced became the staple of every home in North America as well as across the Atlantic in European countries too.

With the world evolving into a more sophisticated society, cotton's potential to be dyed in a variety of colors appealed to women—who used the cloth to fashion dresses, bonnets, and kerchiefs that until then only a few bland colors had been made available from other woolen materials. Barring a few bumps and bruises, Jeb Tobias was able to successfully meet the world's growing demands.

Unfortunately, success almost always comes at a price. In order to raise cotton correctly, the subtropical combination of heat, wetness, and humidity was required. But that same mixture also spawned fatal diseases like malaria, cholera, dysentery, and yellow fever. Yellow fever or yellow jack, as it was called, claimed the lives of three of his four young children. And the pain of watching them die slowly drove Charla to the brink of insanity, leaving Jeb to raise his youngest son, Jonas, all on his own.

Growing up at his father's side, Jonas quickly developed a strong business acumen as Azalea's prosperity solidly continued to increase, year after consummate year. An astute student, Jonas learned the value of punctuality and control while watching his father rule over Azalea with a cold heart and an even colder iron fist.

Over the years, Jebadiah monitored his son's development with pride as Jonas grew into a powerful man who would be respected and feared by his slaves and peers alike. And when death came to visit in late 1835, Jeb went peacefully, knowing that Azalea would forever remain firmly grasped in a Tobias's hands.

Now, as with every late winter or early spring at Azalea, the continuous sounds could be heard of hoes scraping the unturned dirt and old cotton stalks being broken and pulled to make room for the seeds that would grow into stalks that would be harvested by the slaves for its valuable white fluff that blossomed in the fall. White gold, as it was called by the speculators and prospectors who came from as far as Germany to bargain for it, had been the lifeline of the South's newfound prosperity. And Azalea had thousands upon thousands of square acres of fertile soil to produce America's most prized cash crop.

Slaves were summoned to the fields by daybreak after a meager breakfast of cold bacon and corn cake, and forced to spend entire days performing the meticulous and monotonous task of tilling and furrowing every available inch of that soil until well after the sun went down. There were no breaks, unless the field boss gave permission to drink water from the trough—and that only came when a slave was close to dying from heat exhaustion. Time was always of the essence because the sooner the seeds could be planted, the sooner the cotton could be harvested and sold.

By midafternoon, the sun had shone brightly, and the slaves milled around the plantation completing a host of chores ranging from wiping down the white wooden fence that lined the road leading up to the main house, to cleaning up the animal's stalls and feeding them too. Those tasks were mainly relegated to the small children and the cripples because every able-bodied slave was required to do the more serious work out in the cotton fields.

Today would have been as mundane as any other except for the unfamiliar carriage kicking up dust as it headed toward the main house. Inside, Jonathan could barely contain his excitement because, for him, this day had taken forever to come. After finally making it home, he promised himself that it would be an eternity before he would ever leave Azalea again.

As the carriage rounded the huge pond located directly in front of his home, Jonathan picked up the box that Tomas had given him during his last night in Illinois. He kept his word as promised and waited until his carriage came to a complete stop before taking a look at his gift.

"Classic Woodburn," he said to himself and smiled when he read the inscription on the gold and jewel-encrusted pocket watch that his most trusted and loyal friend had given him.

"Master Tobias, Forever Cotton's King and Lord of the Lash."

The words were significant to Jonathan because, obviously, Thomas had the watch inscribed long before they made the trip to Springfield, which meant that Thomas always believed in him and knew that Azalea would be safe, and that made Jonathan thank his lucky stars that someone as honorable as Thomas Woodburn stayed behind to make sure everything went as planned.

After a few minutes of reminiscing, he stuffed the watch into his pocket, not wanting to think about conspiracies, shady deals, or anything of that nature. Jonathan only wanted to focus on today and his surprise return home.

Stepping out of the carriage, he immediately began to take in his surroundings, marveling at how things had changed but more so at how things stayed the same. The tiny slave children still played in front of the house under Gam Ma's watch, who he swore was one of his granddaddy's original slaves. Flocks of geese still floated in the pond where he and Claude used to fish with their father as children.

Everything was just as he remembered it. During his time in Philadelphia, his thoughts of home helped get through the years, but now that he was actually here, those memories began to seem less vivid—especially when a light breeze blew by, bringing with it the smell of blackberry pies that were somewhere cooling off on a windowsill.

"Oh my Lawd, Jonny, is datchu?" he heard once Gam Ma spotted him.

"Yes, ma'am," he said boyishly as she hobbled over to him. Even though he had been raised to look down on the slaves, Gam Ma had been a surrogate mother to him as well as one to Jonas when he was a child. So he knew to treat her with the utmost respect.

"Jesus done brought you home. Praise Gawd. You was gone so long them children there ain't even been born yet," she said while looking in the direction of a dozen or so children playing hopscotch and tag in front of the house. "Well, don't be wastin' no time chattin' with me. Go on in dere boy and see your pa. Das watcha waitin' for anyhow." The wily old woman nudged Jonathan toward the house.

In the antebellum South, the hallmark of a plantation's success had always been measured by the grandeur of its mansion, and the Tobiases had no qualms about flaunting their wealth. Painted glossy white, the squared coliseum-type structure stood four stories high and boasted second- and third-floor colonnaded porches that wrapped around the entire house, giving them the option of watching the sun rise or set and everything in between. Colossal Doric columns supported the porches, making Azalea's centerpiece appear as though it once belonged to ancient Greek royalty.

Magnolia and dogwood trees draped with spanish moss not only added to Azalea's palatial beauty but provided shade for anyone who wanted to bask in the aromatic fragrances of the floral gardens that surrounded their home.

Jeb Tobias had a saying, "No one respects wealth that goes unseen." And beneath the blazing sun, the mansion glistened like a gigantic pearl that could be spotted from miles away. Their home was the main reason why over the last thirty years, Azalea had been the envy of the South's "vulgar rich" who tried their best to emulate the Tobias's unattainable power and wealth.

Jebadiah had the gargantuan home built in hopes that one day Jonas would have the family that yellow fever had stolen from him. But unfortunately, tragedy had struck again. While giving birth to Jonathan, Cecilia Tobias hemorrhaged to death, making Jonas Tobias the South's most eligible bachelor and leaving Jebadiah with an empty house to fill.

As he made his way to the front door, Jonathan caught a glimpse of the ramp that ran alongside of the steps making the mansion wheelchair accessible. He paid it no mind, figuring that it probably belonged to one of the retired field bosses that his grandfather had invited to move in with them after his mother died. As soon as he reached for the door, it swung open, and a strong hand pulled him inside.

"Awe shucks, look at you, boy! Jon, I'm sure glad to see you. You're almost as tall as me," the man said as he squeezed Jonathan and mussed his hair. It was Gus McMiller, the senior field boss and Jonas's most trusted friend.

"I was as tall as you before I left," Jonathan said, happy to see a familiar face.

"Cleevon! Cleevon!" Gus yelled.

"Yassuh?" the servant said as he entered the living room.

"Go on and fetch Jonas and ring the bell so the boys can come on in. Jon is home!" Gus barked as he clapped his hands together in jubilation. "Your father told me you were away doin' some great work for the family," he said after Cleevon disappeared.

"Nah, it was nothing Gus," Jonathan humbly said, not wanting to discuss anything until he spoke with his father first.

"What in hell is taking that damn nigger so long with your father? Wait here, I'll be right back," Gus said after a few silent moments.

Left alone, Jonathan began to feel like a stranger, so he quietly crept from room to room reacquainting himself with his own home. With each step bringing him a memory from his childhood, Jonathan decided to walk through the entire mansion. But upon hearing the bell ring, he hurried back to the living room where he met with a lovely but unfamiliar woman.

"Are you the reason that bell is ringing?" she asked while sitting crossed-legged on one of the rococo sofas lining the walls of the living room, upset that her daily walk through the gardens had been cut short by the signal for all whites to return to the mansion.

Stunned by her beauty, Jonathan could only manage a nod. "Who are you?" she asked, knowing that he must be important for the Tobiases to end a day's work early over him.

"I'm Jon Tobias, and who are you?" he said while trying not to appear awestruck by the Southern belle sitting in front of him. He'd seen many attractive women in his lifetime, but none were as striking as her.

"Debra Carlysle. I would curtsy, but I don't feel like getting up," she said while flirtatiously rolling her eyes.

Her name had sounded familiar. He wondered if she was related to the Carlysles of Henderson County, another prominent plantation family. And what was she doing here interrogating him?

"Here he is! I told y'all so!" Gus yelled as he ushered in a group of field bosses who were all happy to see Jonathan. They mobbed him with hugs and pats on his back, all while separating him from Debra Carlysle. He felt helpless, like a piece of wood drifting farther out to sea as the gap widened between them when more people poured into the room.

"Goddammit, the prodigal son has returned home!" someone yelled from the other side of the room.

The voice sounded raspy, probably from years of drinking whiskey, but Jonathan knew exactly whom it belonged to. "Claude!" he yelled while trying to squeeze through the crowd to find his brother. Even though he felt the way he did about him, Claude was still his blood, and he missed him.

"Jonny, let me look at you," Claude said after a tight embrace.

"I'm all here. I see that you added a little weight," Jonathan said after giving his brother a once-over.

"You mean this?" Claude said while rubbing his big belly. "This is just good old lovin'. Come here. I want you to meet somebody," he added with a huge smile.

"Jonny, this is Debra Carlysle, soon to be Debra Tobias," Claude said after he led Jonathan to his fiancée.

"Nice to meet you, Debra," Jonathan said as he shook her soft hand.

"Isn't she somethin'," Claude said, beaming with pride.

Totally deflated, Jonathan meagerly nodded his head. Infected with jealousy, he could barely look at the two of them without thinking of a million reasons why Claude didn't deserve her, number 1 being that he wanted her for himself.

Looking around the room, Jonathan assumed the festive mood was probably more about the half day off than his unexpected return home. He clearly could see that Gus was happy to see him. Even Claude seemed overjoyed, but given their history, that could be a façade.

"Claude, where is Daddy at?" Jonathan asked, growing a bit impatient.

"I'm right behind you, son," Jonas bellowed, causing Jonathan to turn around and experience a severe case of heartache.

As Cleevon pushed the wheelchair toward him, Jonathan's spirit sunk to an all-time low. A morose hush blanketed the room as Jonathan fought back the tears while kneeling to embrace what he believed was a shell of his powerful father. He knew things would change and people would age, but no way in hell did Jonathan expect to see this.

He sounded like his father. He even looked a bit like Jonas except that his hair, once thick and black as coal, had become withered and gray. The skin on his face looked leathery and sagged a bit on the left side, giving him a permanent half frown. His entire left side was paralyzed from the neck down, making it impossible to return his youngest son's tender embrace.

"Oh, Dad, what happened?" Jonathan struggled to ask through quivering lips.

"Son, not here. Not now," Jonas said coolly when Jonathan broke down, losing the battle with his tears. "I'm all right, Jon. Get a hold of yourself," he calmly told his son, not wanting to be pitied in front of an audience.

Reading Jonas's mind, Gus began to clear the living room so the Tobiases could have some time alone.

"I had a stroke," Jonas said after Jonathan had a drink and had gotten himself together.

"A stroke? How?" Jonathan asked, confused because for as long as he could remember, his father was an image of good health.

"I'll tell you how," Claude said with a scowl on his face. "That goddamned bitch Olina had been puttin' hemlock in Daddy's food for years. And when his body couldn't handle the poison any longer, he had a stroke."

"I was riding my horse when it happened. I hurt my back. Now I'll be ridin' for the rest of my life," Jonas said as he tapped the wheelchair for emphasis.

"Olina? Why would she do that to you? We treated her decent," Jonathan said, still horrified at the sight of his father.

"You been round them Yankees too long," Claude said. "No matter how good we treated her, she still was a nigger. They're untrustworthy and only loyal to the whip. We took our eye off of her, and look what she done to Daddy." He pounded his fist into his palm.

"Dad, you sent me a telegram once a month while I was away. Why didn't you tell me?" Jonathan implored.

Jonas placed his hand on Jonathan's knee and looked him in the eyes and said, "Look at you, Jon. Your strong concern for me is why I sent you away in the first place. I refused to let it be the reason for you returning prematurely. Just as I refuse to sit here and have you pitying me like some goddamned cripple. Don't worry about me. This is a great day, and we should treat it as such. My boy has finally come home, and I want to hear all about it."

It had taken Jonathan a few days to fill Claude and Jonas in on the past week's events. The three of them would meet after supper in the library for privacy where they sat at a table with a bottle of whiskey between them.

Under candlelight and surrounded by walls of first-edition books, Jonas and Claude learned of the Republican Party's plot to steal the election and raid the South in one well-calculated sweep. At times, Jonathan felt like he was telling ghost stories to small children as their faces would cringe at his revelations of a Republican nation and Negro slaves being set free.

"I don't like it," Claude said when Jonathan finished recounting his arrangement with Abraham Lincoln. "The idea of helping to destroy the South just to spare our skin don't sound too invitin' to me." During the past few days, Jonathan learned that since the accident, Claude had assumed the majority of Jonas's control of the plantation, thus giving him an opinion that had to be listened to. "I mean, what about Debra and the Carlysles? What happens to them? She's going to be my wife, and her family is our concern too."

Jonathan didn't need to be reminded of that, seeing Claude being led around the plantation by his nose was already more than he could stomach. "You'd rather suffer the fate of everyone else?" Jonathan asked, knowing firsthand the consequences the South was facing.

"We don't need to do this, Dad. This is the South. We are powerful enough to rally together and defend ourselves," Claude said before turning to Jonathan. "You said we're the only ones who know the truth right now. If we could get the word out and warn everyone about what those Yankees are up to—"

"Warn who, Claude?" Jonas said, interrupting him. "No one would listen. Slaving and the cotton boom have made us all arrogant. We believe the world needs us. We believe the world will protect us from the Yankees because they love our cotton. We're wrong, Claude. You'd be better off telling them the sky was falling. No, this information was gathered by us, and that's just who it's going to serve," Jonas said while shaking his head.

By the way he rolled his eyes and hissed loudly, Jonathan could clearly see that Claude didn't like to be overridden. "Dad's right. If word gets out that we were trying to awaken the South, you could rest assured that Azalea would become the first casualty of war. So not a word of this to anyone," Jonathan said. "Not even to Debra," he added for spite.

"Damn you, Jon! Don't think you can come here with your fancy lawya's degree and some cow-shit story about sly politicians and freed niggers and think you can boss me around," Claude said as his face took on a crimson tone. "I have been runnin' Azalea for three years, and I'll tell who I please!"

In a swift motion that startled Jonathan, Jonas backhanded Claude across the face. "Don't you dare speak that way in my presence again! You forget that you've been running Azalea by using my name. So until I'm dead and buried, the final word will always come from me."

Claude rubbed his cheek and sulked quietly while Jonas told him that he would do as told and not utter a word to a soul. Jonathan looked on, astonished at his father's display of superiority. And from that evening on, even though he was crippled by a stroke, Jonas Tobias would always appear to him as the strong and able-bodied man who had raised him from birth. Needless to say, Claude never sat on his father's right side again.

During the months that ensued, Jonathan divided his time at Azalea between learning the inner and outer workings of the plantation and monitoring Abraham Lincoln's progress along the campaign trail. He and Woodburn had remained in constant contact, and despite the details of his encounters with alcohol and seedy women, Thomas had nothing to report except that Lincoln's progress was steadily increasing and things were going along okay. No news was good news to Jonathan, and while waiting for the impending election, he discovered a way to tighten his family's grip on the cotton industry.

It happened when Jonas urged Claude to allow Jonathan to accompany him on a trip to the Cotton Exchange in New Orleans, Louisiana. There, every year at harvest, plantation owners from the South and brokers for the cotton mills of the North would meet at a large warehouse in the French Quarter to haggle over the price of the year's crop.

The plantation owners would bring a sample of their cotton to be plucked, pulled, and tested by inspectors who would then give the cotton its final grade. The inspectors, or classers, as they were called, used sharp eyes and sensitive hands to test the texture, fiber, length, and look for discolorations and impurities, which were all determining factors in whether a plantation had a profitable year or not. White or "pure" cotton with long, soft fibers would receive the highest grade while cotton that was yellow tinted and loaded with impurities such as leaves or seeds would fetch the lowest and be relegated to the bottom of the auctioning block once the bidding started.

The exchange system had never been an issue with the Tobiases because they sent grade A–quality samples to New Orleans every year. Their crop received the highest bids on the auctioning block by brokers from the craftiest financial institutions in the country, who would then sell the crop to the cotton mills in the North and England at a premium. There, the cotton would be spun into fabric and distributed at a huge markup to retailers around the globe.

Cotton was the most lucrative trade in the nation, the only thing that could make sworn enemies conduct business every year at the Cotton Exchange in complete harmony like long-lost brothers. Through phony handshakes and fake smiles, they managed to ink deals that made both sides richer, all the while hating to breathe the same air as one another. It was quite a childish sight, but it proved that even though their morals had kept the North and South apart, their lust for money would always bring them together.

Having lived on both sides of the Mason-Dixon Line, Jonathan knew firsthand of the rival faction's dependency on each other; mainly the South's need to sell its cotton to the Northerners, and the Northerner's need for the South to continuously produce cotton so they could sell their goods to the rest of the world. It reminded him of a failed marriage where the spouses didn't love each other but stayed together because neither could survive on their own.

Even though the South produced 100 percent of the nation's raw cotton, there were no mills there, and almost all their cotton products were imported from either England or the Northern states. To Jonathan, this had always been a ludicrous practice, and he figured that if Azalea built its own mill, they could manufacture their own fabric and become independently wealthy by selling their product to the retailers themselves.

"Son, that's a mighty fine idea," Jonas said as he nodded his head approvingly. "Where did you come up with that?" They were back in the library, which had now become the official place to discuss Azalea's future.

"It was something I noticed when we were in New Orleans. Looking at all of those brokers made me realize that we could cut out two or three middlemen if we produced our own fabric," Jonathan said while Claude looked on, perplexed because he didn't hear of the idea until now.

Fearing that Jonathan would replace him as acting head of the plantation if Jonas agreed with his idea, Claude spoke up. "Who are we going to have working in a mill? You can't possibly think of putting them slaves in there. Niggers are too damn stupid to work all of those gadgets," he said in an ornery tone.

"You know somethin', Claude? Your lack of vision truly amazes me. You've been to New Orleans ten times before, and you couldn't see an opportunity like this starin' you in the face," Jonas said, disgusted by Claude's haste to attack the solid idea Jonathan had presented. "Instead of havin' your nose up Debra's ass, you should try to find a way to help Azalea too."

As Claude tried to speak in his defense, Jonas raised his right hand and yelled, "I don't want to hear another word outta you." Then looking in Jonathan's direction, he added, "Son, take me to Cleevon. I've had enough of this fool for one evening."

Upon entering his bedroom after leaving his father with Cleevon, Jonathan wasn't surprised to find Claude there waiting for him. To a stranger, standing over six feet tall in the dimly lit room with his fist clenched, Claude would have looked intimidating. But with his long golden hair and soft facial features, he only reminded Jonathan of the portraits he had seen of his mother.

Claude hated the fact that he resembled her, and he sported a heavy beard so whenever he looked in the mirror, he wouldn't be reminded of it. And since he wasn't blessed with Jonas's rugged looks, Claude spent his entire life bullying and intimidating his peers, trying to prove, more so to himself, that he was a genuine Tobias.

"You son of a bitch! I know what you're tryin' to do!" Claude yelled as he moved in closer. "But I ain't gonna just sit back and let it happen!" Only inches away now, his breath reeked of alcohol, and Jonathan could see the dots of perspiration on his face.

"What are you talking about?" Jonathan asked, sticking his arm out so Claude couldn't come any closer.

"You know damn well what I'm talkin' about. You constantly making me look like a fool in front of Daddy. You tryin' to replace me as head of this place!" Claude yelled as his temper started to get the best of him.

Sensing that his brother had come for a physical confrontation, Jonathan kept his cool and took a seat on the bed. "You're being paranoid. I don't want your position. I'm not looking to impress Dad because I don't need any credit. Didn't I prove that to you when we were younger?" Jonathan said smugly.

"Oh, is that what this is all about?" Claude yelled. "You're still mad at me for tellin' Daddy that I killed that nigger. Is that why you didn't tell me about your plans for the mill? You don't trust me?"

"You're goddamned right I don't trust you! Can you blame me?" Jonathan yelled back as the emotions he held in check for more than fifteen years were about to explode. "You are the lyin', treacherous bastard who betrayed me, and now that you feel threatened, you have the nerve to be in here accusing me of trying to take something from you. I oughtta kick your fat ass," he yelled as he leapt up from the bed. Unable to control his contempt, Jonathan unloaded on his brother with a barrage of punches when their bodies crashed together in the center of the room.

Realizing that his younger brother was getting the best of him, Claude grabbed a hold of Jonathan's wrists, and they grappled for what seemed like an eternity. "You bastard! I'll kill you!" Claude said after Jonathan flung him into a dresser, smashing it into pieces.

"Hey! Hey!" Gus McMiller yelled as he burst into the room to find Claude in a headlock gasping for air and sweating profusely. "What in hell is goin' on in here?" He rushed in-between the feuding brothers.

"Outta my way, Gus! This boy needs a lesson!" Claude yelled as he struggled to get past the older man.

With a firm grip, Gus held onto Claude. "Settle down! You're tired and drunk. Now do you want to wake your father?" he said, looking at both of them.

Because neither of them wanted to face Jonas's wrath for fighting one another, the brothers began to relax and straighten themselves out. "I don't want to see this kinda shit again, or I will tell your father," Gus said to them. "I mean it," he added, looking specifically at Claude.

"Yeah, whatever Gus," Claude said while staring daggers at Jonathan. "He just better stay the hell outta my goddamned way," he added before storming out of the room and slamming the door behind him.

"What was that about?" Gus asked, staying behind to help straighten out the mess that was made of Jonathan's room.

"It's nothing. Just sibling rivalry, that's all," Jonathan said after picking up the jagged pieces of wood that used to be his dresser.

"Okay, nothin'," Gus said in disbelief. "Your father won't tolerate no family feudin'. So whatever it was, it better be over," he added sternly.

"It is, trust me," Jonathan said dishonestly, knowing that his fight with Claude was only the beginning.

After consulting with a handpicked selection of architects and engineers, the Tobiases immediately began construction. It was an enormous risk, but also a calculated one. Nonetheless, with Jonas's blessing and almost no help from his brother, Jonathan assumed the arduous task of overseeing the project completed—which meant spending entire days enduring the sweltering heat—while making sure the foreman and crews lived up to the reputation of their expenses.

The mill was to be erected on a huge parcel of land next to the warehouses where Azalea's bales of cotton were stored. It was an ideal location because of its proximity to the stream that ran through Azalea that they always used to ferry goods to and from the plantation. More importantly, its short distance from the mansion also allowed Jonathan the opportunity to periodically visit his father throughout the day with progress reports.

Following another brief meeting that ended with Jonas berating his brother, Jonathan had himself a tall glass of lemonade prior to heading back out to the construction site. It was an unusually humid day, and he needed something to cool him off before walking through the dense woods that separated the mansion from the warehouses.

Upon stepping out of the house and taking notice of the overcast sky, Jonathan decided to put a move on it. The woods were a deadly place to be caught in the violent thunderstorms that frequently occurred during this time of the year.

Walking along the gravel-strewn pathway that provided the fastest route through the forest, Jonathan suddenly heard the footsteps of someone creeping up behind him. Fearing that it was Claude looking to go another round, he immediately became upset—because with the pressures of overseeing the construction of the mill and the coming presidential election, Jonathan was in no mood for another silly confrontation. He slowed his pace to let his brother come into striking range before quickly turning around to attack with a tightly cocked fist.

"Oh, it's you," Jonathan said to Debra as he exhaled and slowly brought his arms to his sides. "What are you doing out here?" he asked the startled woman, amazed that even in the state of fear, she still looked beautiful.

"I see you walk through here every day, and I wanted to ask you a question," she said while her face regained its color.

"You want to ask me something?" he asked, clearly taken aback.

"Yeah, is there a law against that?" she shot back, standing there with her arms folded.

So far, this had been the longest conversation they had since the day he returned home. He decided to engage her. "Go ahead, ask."

"Why does your brother hate you?" she asked, looking at him with her piercing blue eyes.

"What?" was all Jonathan could manage to say, completely thrown off by her bluntness.

"Claude, he hates you. And I want to know why," she said.

"I don't know. Have you asked him?" he said, wondering what the motive was behind her concern.

"I did, but he wouldn't say. And he usually tells me everything," she said with a sly smile that told him she wasn't lying.

They had been in each other's company before, but it had always been in the presence of Claude or others, and Jonathan could only steal quick glances of her flawless beauty. But out here, alone, he could admire her without worrying about anyone becoming aware of his desire.

"See something you like?" she said flirtatiously when she saw that Jonathan was taking notice of the way her curvy body moved with each graceful step she took.

"What I see is a bunch of trouble if Claude knew you were out here talking to me," he said while trying to pretend he wasn't the slightest bit turned on.

They were walking slowly along the path when he stopped abruptly and turned to her, "Look, Debra, I'm busy here. Now what is it that you want?" he said rigidly, but before she could answer, thunder roared and the sky began to pour huge drops of rain onto them. Concerned that lightning would be following, he grabbed a hold of her petite wrist, and they raced back toward the mansion.

By the time they reached the edge of the woods, they were both tired and thoroughly drenched, so they ducked into a small utility shed for shelter. Fully stocked, the shed only provided enough space for one person. So they squeezed into each other's arms and hoped that the violent storm would pass quickly. But Debra was extremely exhausted, and when she gently rested her head on his shoulder, her warm, panting breath titillated the sensitive skin around Jonathan's neck, making him wish the storm would last forever.

Now he truly envied Claude—especially when the thunder crackled loudly, and she clutched his body tightly for protection. And in a desperate attempt to comfort her, Jonathan ran his fingers through her hair and told her that everything would be okay. But the rain beat heavily on the tin roof making him impossible to hear, and when she looked up to ask him what did he say, Jonathan found the temptation of Debra's succulent lips impossible to resist.

Closing his eyes and leaning in gently, Jonathan began to passionately kiss his brother's fiancée. He took a chance, and she responded by sensually coiling her tongue around his, setting off tiny explosions of bliss inside of his head. They held each other so close they could feel the other's heart palpitate as a rush of carnal electricity flowed wildly through their veins.

"No," she breathed to Jonathan, who was completely entangled in the heat of the moment and had hiked up her dress to rub his hands gently over her delicate thighs. Wriggling free when they came too close to her nether region, Debra smacked him with an open hand across the face. "I said no!" she stated while emphatically wiping her lips with the back of her hand. "I am to be your brother's wife. We can't do this!" she added before pushing on the door to head back outside.

Even though he was utterly disappointed, Jonathan was still concerned for her safety. "Debra, wait! Don't go out there! What about the storm?" he frantically asked while reaching out to grab her, but she had already made it to the other side.

Standing there, framed by the heavy rain falling around her, Debra looked at him with forlorn eyes. "I'm sorry, Jon, but I'd rather take my chances with the thunder and lightning than ruining my engagement in that shed with you," she said before running off toward the mansion, leaving Jonathan alone to sulk over the blown opportunity to finally get even with his brother.

The next six months began with an air of precariousness as Abraham Lincoln barely eked out the presidency by garnering 40 percent of the ballot in a very tight four-way election. During that time span, Jonathan witnessed firsthand the determining factors that would send the nation barreling toward the brink of a civil war, while completing Azalea's own fully operational cotton mill.

As promised, immediately after his inauguration, Lincoln started his term by levying huge fines and taxes on the Southern states that legally allowed slavery to continue. The penalties he imposed for not adhering to his new antislavery laws were so burdensome to the plantation owners that within three months, seven states seceded from the Federal Union.

Proslavery advocates labeled him a lunatic. They said because of his strange hold on the cotton industry, Lincoln would run the United States directly into the ground. After all, cotton exportation was the lifeblood of the nation's economy. Even the North's older Republican fundamentalists, who often favored money over morality, agreed that he was out of control and began to whisper about finding someone else to take his seat.

It didn't matter; fully supported by the powers that put him into the White House, Lincoln continued to use whatever legislative authority he had available to lead the South's constituents further down a path toward an eventual conflict. He would get his wish, approximately two and a half months after the first seven states seceded. Four more joined them to form the Confederacy.

Playing directly into the plans of Westhead's conspiracy, the Confederacy or the Confederate States of America, as they were officially known, began to operate independently of the Federal Union as their own separate entity. They created their own currency, designated Richmond, Virginia, as their capital, and even chose Jefferson Davis, a former secretary of war and current Mississippi state senator as their president. It was a bold move by the Southern states, but also a costly one because their decision to secede legitimized any reason Lincoln had for launching a military campaign against them.

Meanwhile, as the tension in the nation thickened and the entire South scrambled to prepare for the Union's inevitable invasion, business went on at Azalea as usual. Naturally, when the rumors were first heard of the country's impending conflict, every able-bodied white man across the South took up arms and donned the gray uniforms of the Confederacy. But the men at Azalea, who were all born and raised there, knew their devotion belonged to the Tobiases. They decided to stay at home and endure the crisis whether Jonathan's arrangement with Lincoln turned out to be legitimate or not. To Jonas, it was a courageous display of loyalty, and he rewarded them all by increasing the already generous wages they earned at the plantation.

With all the predictions of Lincoln and the conspiracy gradually unfolding before his eyes, Jonas decided to make Jonathan the official head of the plantation. After thinking long and hard about the promotion, which would have otherwise been bequeathed to Claude upon his death, Jonas concluded that in the year since his return, Jonathan demonstrated the uncanny ability to lead Azalea all on his own.

"There is somethin' I have to say to you," Jonas said as Jonathan pushed him slowly along in his wheelchair. It was midafternoon in early April, and not a single cloud appeared in the cerulean sky. They spent most of the morning together at the fields, watching the slaves work diligently to get the soil prepared for the upcoming cotton season. Lately, Jonathan had been spending a lot of time with his father, mainly to take his mind off the fact that he hadn't heard from Lincoln or Woodburn in the last two months, and the fate of the nation was quickly coming to a head.

"About what, Dad?" Jonathan asked after he activated the brake and walked around to the front of the chair to face Jonas. They were alone, over by the serpentine stream that ran past the warehouses and the cotton mill.

"Son, I'm talkin' about Azalea. I want you to have total control and give the final words when necessary," Jonas said as the steely look in his eyes displayed the unwavering confidence he had in his son.

"What about Claude?" Jonathan asked, already foreseeing the devastating effect the decision would have on his brother. "I decided before I returned that I didn't want to take anything away from him," he added before picking up a few stones to throw into the water.

Jonas chuckled, a rare sight for Jonathan. "Claude wouldn't have anything to take if it wasn't for these," he said looking down at the blanket covering his atrophic legs. "That fool doesn't care about this place, its history, or its future. All he cares about is whippin' on slaves and beddin' their womenfolk when they're not in the fields. And now that he is engaged, he can't separate the forest from the trees. Do you see that?" he asked, pointing at the enormous cotton mill made of stone and brick looming high in the sky in front of them. "Boy, that's leadership. That's direction. Claude's got none of that. You are exactly what this plantation needs."

"I don't know if I'm ready for that kind of responsibility," Jonathan said apprehensively, tossing another stone into the stream.

Jonas would hear none of it. "You've been ready since the day you killed that nigger to save your brother's life."

Ready to fling another stone when he heard what his father had said, Jonathan dropped the rock and quickly turned to him. "What?"

"Yeah," Jonas said, nodding his head affirmatively, "I know the truth. I've known since the day it happened."

Jonathan couldn't believe his ears, but "You knew? How?" was the only thing he managed to say.

"After we found you and your brother, Gus handed your rifles to me. I smelled the barrels and realized that yours had been the only one that was fired. So I questioned Ben before we killed him, and he told me what really happened out in those woods."

Completely intrigued, Jonathan wanted to hear more, but Jonas paused to savor the jasmine scent of a breeze that blew in from the east. "Boy, it sure feels good to be outside. I never went out much before you came back," he said while slowly tilting his head toward the sky.

Jonathan was infuriated, but watching his father inhale the rousing spring air, he decided to let him relish the moment. Quickly, the moment passed.

"Damn it! You're telling me I spent the entire time in the North believing that I failed you, wondering if you sent me there because you thought I wasn't fit to handle the rigors of slavery." Jonathan sighed heavily as his eyes began to well with tears. "Hating myself for not telling what really happened when I had the chance. Hating Claude for what he did to me," he said as a single tear rolled down his cheek.

"I don't want you hating him," Jonas said. "I know Claude is a goddamned pompous idiot, but he is your brother and my son. And there ain't no room for hate in this family."

"Did you tell that shit to him," Jonathan shot back angrily.

"I know you're upset, but choose your tone carefully when talkin' to me, boy," Jonas said rigidly. "Claude was a mama's boy before you were born. Always clinging to your mother, never giving her any room to breathe. When she died, he blamed you for it. I guess he still does."

Jonathan was still confused. "Is that supposed to be some excuse for what he did? Is that supposed to make it right? She was my mother too. And she was your wife. Do you blame me for her death?" he asked, suddenly feeling like the black sheep of the family.

"Now hold on a minute Jon," Jonas said, wishing that he could somehow embrace him. "Cecilia was a beautiful woman, and I loved her dearly, but what happened to her was nobody's fault. I told your brother that many times, but it's not my job to make him believe it. This isn't about Claude or his feelings right now. This is about what I'm asking of you," Jonas said, trying to steer the conversation back into the right direction.

"Son, that day in the woods, you knew your brother told an unforgivable lie, but you knew that speaking up about it would have embarrassed me in front of my men. You chose to put my honor before your own personal recognition. The selflessness and maturity you displayed in your youth still amazes me.

"Now I don't know how much longer I have left to live," Jonas said solemnly, "but I do have to make sure that my father's plantation will be left in capable hands, deserving hands. Yours," he added vehemently before blankly staring off into space.

Jonathan had gotten the message; his father would not take no for an answer. Even though being anointed as head of Azalea had always been the achievement he dreamt of, he didn't expect it so soon and under such perilous circumstances.

"I'm honored that you have that kind of faith in me, but the war could break out any day now, and I haven't received any word from Lincoln telling me exactly what needs to be done to save this place," Jonathan said, gazing directly into Jonas's glassy eyes, trying not to focus on the horrific features the stroke had given him.

Looking down at him, Jonathan realized that no matter how powerful or wealthy his father was, being fed, clothed, and changed like a baby had to be difficult to live with. And after taking a few seconds to gauge the many disappointments life had relentlessly thrown Jonas's way, Jonathan knew there was no way he could let his father down.

"I'll do it," Jonathan said confidently. "But first we must wait until I hear form Lincoln before anyone gets to know. Especially

Claude," he added after he released the brake and aimed the wheel-chair in the direction of their home.

Barely out of the woods, Jonathan spotted Gus McMiller on horseback, racing swiftly up the road to meet them. "Jonas! Jonny! Hurry!" Gus yelled as he pulled the reins to bring the muscular beast to a halt. Instantly, anxiety began to slowly permeate through their veins as they watched the usually coolheaded field boss leap from the horse and frantically run over to them. This could not be good.

"It's happening! It started two days ago!" Gus struggled to say as his chest heaved from being out of breath.

"What's happening, Gus? Calm down and get yourself together," Jonas said, never before seeing his old friend act like this.

"Sumter! The Yankees attacked Fort Sumter! They bom-barded it with cannon fire!" he said, referring to the federal for-tress that stood on a man-made shoal located in the middle of the Charleston Harbor. The Confederacy seized it when the state of South Carolina seceded, making it the official line of demarcation dividing the rival factions. Up until now, a standoff had ensued there between the Confederate soldiers holding the fort and the Federal Union's navy.

"What does that mean?" Jonas asked to anyone that was willing to answer.

"It means we are at war," Jonathan said, struggling to get the painful words out of his mouth.

"That's right," Gus chimed in and added, "Jefferson Davis has called for every available white man to take up arms. That's why I'm here. Claude told me to rally our men together and order them to assist the Confederacy!"

Jonathan could not believe the timing; a civil war had started between the North and South, and he had no word on Azalea's pro-tection. "The bastard!" he said aloud as his heart began to beat faster. "How could he start a war and leave us to hang dry like this!" he added irately, cursing the man who he thought he had an honest deal with. As his temperature steadily rose, Jonathan started to sweat profusely.

"Jon, are you alright?" Jonas asked. "Look at him, Gus, he's sweatin' bullets!" he added with much concern.

"You do look a little flushed," Gus said as he took a step closer to look at him.

"I'm fine!" Jonathan told him. "Let's get back to the house before Claude does something stupid," he added before stepping behind the wheelchair to push his father home.

Jonathan had only made it a few steps before he started to feel dizzy and see multicolored spots in front of him. "Oh God!" he breathed as his eyes blinked sporadically.

"What is it?" Jonas asked, craning his neck, trying to see what was going on behind him.

"I . . . I don't know," he struggled to say as his mouth dried up making it difficult to speak. "I can't feel my . . . I can't feel," Jonathan barely whispered, slumping lifelessly over the back of the wheelchair's seat, "feel my legs."

"Oh no, no, no," Jonas whimpered as Jonathan fell face-first onto the ground, knowing there was nothing he could do to stop him. "Come on, boy, get up. Don't do this to me now. Get up, Jon," he whined as his hand shook violently while reaching down, desperately trying to wake his son. "Gus!" he yelled before the field boss could ride off leaving the two of them stranded.

When Gus turned around, he saw a sight he thought he would never live to see. Jonas Tobias, a man who never shed a tear in his adult life, crying uncontrollably as Jonathan lay deathly still at his feet.

CHAPTER 6

As the sun slowly descended beyond the horizon, and its fading light cast an auburn hue across the sky, a large horse-drawn carriage, bringing an unexpected visitor, turned up the road that led to Azalea. It had only been four days since the start of the Civil War, and the people of the plantation were visibly distressed over the past days' staggering events—especially at the mansion, where the mood was so sullen that no one seemed to care when the young man exited the carriage and asked politely to speak to whoever was in charge.

"Master Tobias? Is you awake, suh?" Cleevon asked after knocking on the bedroom door and peeking his head inside. The majority of the room was dark except for the diminishing rays that crept in through the windows, allowing him to see the shadowy figure lying face-up in bed. Cleevon asked again, "Masta Tobias, is you awake? There is someone here to see you."

The man slightly waved his hand, letting the servant know that he was understood.

"Alright, suh, take your time," Cleevon whispered timidly. "He's in the study whenever you're ready," he added before slowly backing out of the room.

Jonathan didn't budge. He lay still in his bed, staring at the ceiling, wondering who could have possibly come to see him. He hadn't left his room since his physician diagnosed him with heat exhaustion two days ago. "Get plenty of rest and drink lots of fluids," he could hear old Dr. Sampson say repeatedly in his head. It had been an incredible scare, losing control of his faculties and collapsing the way he did. So Jonathan completely followed the doctor's orders. But unfortunately, drowning himself with fluids kept him constantly filling his bedpan, thus limiting the amount of time he had for sleep.

Now tired and hungry, he crawled out of bed and slowly tried to get himself together. After struggling to get dressed, he emerged from his bedroom unshaven and sporting only a bathrobe and a pair of bedroom slippers. Hardly any one had seen him since his accident, so Jonathan took a deep breath and a moment to muster his strength before gingerly descending the winding staircase, one marble step at a time. When he let go of the banister after reaching the first floor, he wasn't surprised to find his father there waiting.

"Boy, it looks like you could use one of these," Jonas said, referring to his wheelchair as he tried to put a smile on his partially paralyzed face. He almost died when Jonathan collapsed, and only Dr. Sampson's reassurances that his son would be okay could console him. Jonas Tobias had lost too much of what he valued in life, and the possibility of losing the only thing that was still golden to him was something he could not live to bear. "How are you feeling?" he asked, extending his quaking arm out to his son.

Jonathan knelt on one knee and embraced him, squeezing tightly to convey the powerful feelings that resided in his heart for his father. "I'm fine, just a little hungry from not eating, that's all," he said when he got back to his feet.

"Cleevon, you see to it that my boy gets whatever he wants to eat, and bring it to the study," Jonas said to the servant who waited on his every beck and call. "Can you push me?" he asked after Cleevon took Jonathan's order of fried pork and rice and then went scurrying off toward the kitchen.

"Is my brother around?" Jonathan asked after pushing Jonas past the living room and catching a glimpse of Claude's men sitting around aimlessly with their heads hung low as if someone really close to them had just died.

"He's gone," Jonas said as the chair rolled quietly along the mansion's main hallway.

"Gone where?" Jonathan asked quizzically.

"He's joined the Confederate Army," Jonas answered indifferently. "I told him if he wanted to die fighting another man's fight that he must go it alone and that he could not take another man here with him. I really don't feel like speaking about him right now," he added painfully, knowing that the fiery encounter with Claude two days ago could have very well been his last.

"Who's in there?" Jonathan asked after bringing the wheelchair to a halt in front of the polished french doors that separated them from the study.

Jonas gave him a confused look. "All I know is that he asked for you personally. We're about to find out," he said as Jonathan separated the double doors, and they both made their way inside.

"Gavin Meade! It's good to see you!" Jonathan said, surprised to see a familiar face. "It's been more than a year. How are you?" he asked while firmly shaking Meade's hand. Jonathan could barely contain his excitement, knowing that Lincoln's top emissary could only be here to bring them encouraging news.

"I'm all right. What about yourself?" Meade asked, pointing at the bulging knot over Jonathan's right eye.

"I'm fine. That's nothing, just had an unfortunate spill a few days ago, that's all," he said dismissively. "This is my father, Jonas Tobias," he added before urging Meade to retake his seat.

"Are you hungry? Can we get you anything?" Jonas asked, extending the Tobias's legendary Southern hospitality to him.

"No, no, I'm okay. This is all that I need," Meade said, looking down at the mint julep he'd been sipping on when they entered the room.

After taking another sip of the drink made from bourbon whiskey, sugar, and crushed mint leaves, Meade got right down to business. "I know you're wondering what took me so long. Believe me, I set out long before the fighting commenced, but the borders between the North and South are quite difficult to cross. I have to be careful travelling through the South without a valid reason," he explained. "Right now, I'm posing as a merchant for Eye-are-land," he added in his best impression of an Irish accent. The three of them laughed.

"It's okay, Gavin. All that matters is the fact that you're here now," Jonathan said while gently patting him on the shoulder. Immediately, Meade reached into his jacket pocket and pulled out a folded piece of paper and handed it to Jonathan.

"What is this?" Jonas asked after Jonathan looked at it and passed it over to him.

"This is the Magen David, a gift from President Lincoln," Meade said as he pulled another folded sheet from his pocket bearing the same likeness.

"It's the star of Israel and the symbol of the Promised Land," Jonathan chimed in, flaunting his Ivy League education. "But what does this have to do with us?"

Meade took another sip of his mint julep and then he put the piece of paper on the table and placed his finger directly in the center of the six-pointed star. "What you have here is incredible. Your plantation is by far one of the most beautiful places that I've ever been. But this," he said, jabbing at the star with his index finger, "will make Azalea sacred."

Jonathan and his father looked at each other with raised eyebrows and then slowly turned back to Meade. "How?" Jonathan said, asking the question for both of them.

Meade was enjoying this, piquing the two powerful men's interest by giving them small bits of information at a time. "May I have another?" he asked, wiggling his empty glass for emphasis. Jonas called on Cleevon, who quickly returned with Jonathan's food and another tall glass of the syrupy drink. "These are good. Maybe if the Union would have known about the South's mint julep, we might have thought twice about going to war," he said wryly. Jonathan and his father didn't respond.

Noticing that the Tobiases weren't interested in his dry sense of humor, Gavin Meade quickly got back to the point. "This star is to be used for your protection. It will keep any Union infantry division from crossing Azalea's borders."

"The idea of Union troops not setting foot on our land sounds great, but how will the Magen David achieve this?" Jonathan asked.

"It's quite simple. Under strict and secret orders from the president, no officers serving in the state of Alabama shall lead their men past the shining star's perimeter," Meade said before having another drink. "You must paint this star precisely eight feet high on every fifth tree along your border."

"Why every fifth tree? What if someone misses the sign? Why not paint it on all of the trees?" Jonas asked anxiously.

"Too many stars might draw unwanted attention. Besides, there will hardly be any troop movement in this part of the state. But if by some chance a division finds itself anywhere near Azalea, the officers will alert their scouts to exactly what they should be out there looking for. We don't want to have any accidental battles in the middle of your cotton fields, do we?" Meade said confidently. "Don't worry, Mr. Tobias, this has been well thought out. Trust me. No, trust the president, Azalea will be safe."

Jonathan, who had taken a moment to devour his pork and rice, listened intently and was satisfied with everything Gavin Meade had to say. "When can we get started?" he asked, feeling relieved that Azalea will finally be protected from the conspiracy he helped to create. Now, without any remonstration from Claude, Jonathan would affirm his position as head of the plantation.

"Everything has been made official on our end. All that's left is for the stars to be painted on the trees," Meade said casually. "You'll need these," he added before reaching into the satchel he brought with him and pulling out a stack of stencils with a larger version of the Magen David etched in each one of them.

Jonathan was impressed. Looking at the stencils, he realized that Lincoln and Woodburn had taken every necessary precaution to ensure Azalea's safety. They were also evidence that Thomas had done his job of making sure Abraham Lincoln stayed true to his word.

"Woodburn, how is he?" Jonathan asked, inquiring about his best friend. The mention of Thomas Woodburn immediately caused Meade's face to light up, an effect his name had on most of the people he came in contact with.

"Thomas is great. He really burned up that campaign trail. There was never a dull moment when he was around. He left a lasting impression on all of us," Meade said while flashing his pearly white teeth.

"Left? What do you mean left? He's not in Washington? Where did he go?" Jonathan asked while furrowing his brow at Meade.

"Thomas went back to England. He left a month ago. Claimed he couldn't deal with the violence of war and decided to go home," Meade told him.

"That's like old Thom, afraid of his own shadow," Jonathan said reflectively. He was smiling, trying to mask the discomfort the news of Woodburn's departure was causing him.

"If there's any consolation, he said he would return once the war was over," Meade mentioned, noticing Jonathan's uneasiness. "Well, I delivered the message that I was sent to bring," he said as he started to get up from his seat.

Meade walked over and shook Jonas's hand. "Mr. Tobias, everything will be fine," he said before turning to Jonathan. "Oh, I almost forgot. The president said it would be very helpful if you could send any information you might come across from time to time that would be of any importance to the Union. As it stands, it is in your best interest that we win this war as well," he added with a hint of arrogance while cutting eyes over at the pile of stencils lying on the table.

Jonathan knew that it was true. The North had to win the war, but the gesture of spying for them instantly turned his stomach. And even though Meade's subtle threat had infuriated him, Jonathan smiled. "Tell the president that whatever he needs, to just ask it of me," he said ingratiatingly.

"I will tell him indeed. And I know he'll be pleased to hear of your willingness to help," Meade said before stepping out into the hallway.

"Smug son of a bitch!" Jonathan said when he returned to the study after personally seeing Gavin Meade to his carriage. He slammed the doors shut and took a seat across from his father.

"What's eating at you, Jon? We are finally out of the woods," Jonas said as he picked up one of the stencils to marvel at.

"I'll tell you what's bothering me," Jonathan said, also grabbing one to examine along with his father. "I want to be finished. I want to wipe my hands of this goddamned conspiracy. I helped him get into office, and he's repaying us with these. Goddammit, Dad! That should be it. I didn't expect to be coaxed into spying for them."

"Unfortunately, son, that's how it goes when you're involved in shady dealings. As long as we're in a position to help, and he can hold Azalea's protection over our heads, there will be no such thing as finality," Jonas said without taking his eyes away from his stencil. "I would do the same in his position."

Jonathan put down the stencil and looked at his father incredulously. "You would do the same? How could you agree with Lincoln's underhanded tactics? Have you forgotten that the Yankees are attacking the South as we speak?"

Finally taking his attention away from the object in his hand, Jonas turned to his son. "Even though you have been blessed with your mother's honesty, intelligence, and integrity, there is still a whole lot you need to learn about this business," he said coolly before raising his index finger. "Number one being that it is never personal, because if it were, you and the rest of my men would be alongside of Claude, fighting for the Confederacy. So you need to separate yourself from what's going on in the rest of the country and concentrate on this plantation.

"Jon, don't get me wrong, son. I do give a damn about what's going on around us, but Tobias blood, not Confederate, runs through our veins. The sooner you realize that, the better off you will be."

"Dad, I do understand," Jonathan said in his defense. "I don't want to help them any more than we already have, especially spying. Protecting ourselves is one thing, but the idea of betraying other Southerners doesn't sit well with me."

Jonas groaned loudly. "Jon, if you are going to run this plantation as I know you can, you'd better get a firm grip on your conscience. Slaving is a ruthless industry, and you're going to be faced with choices that will seem downright sickening, but in order to maintain your control over the niggers, you'll be forced to make them. You don't have to like it, but no matter what, you have to accept it," he said as his glare bore deep into Jonathan's soul.

"The same goes for your arrangement. You're going to have to bite down and accept Lincoln's terms until this war ends. Passing on information is a small price to pay for what we're receiving in return. The only thing we can do is pray for a speedy conflict, because the sooner the war ends and Lincoln has what he wants, the sooner we will be left alone."

Jonathan sat back in his chair and processed everything his father had told him. And as always, Jonas was right. There was no way Azalea would be thoroughly protected unless Lincoln won the war. And in order for him to do so, the Tobiases had to completely sell out and assist the Union wholeheartedly.

"Alright, Dad, you've made your point," Jonathan said and gathered up the stencils and neatly placed them in the satchel Gavin Meade left with them. "I have to let go of my inner conflict with the Yankees and focus on the well-being of my family and the plantation." Jonathan slung the satchel over his shoulder and walked around to the back of his father's wheelchair.

As he pushed his father toward the door, Jonathan ordered Cleevon to go ring the bell and assemble the men in the living room. Upon hearing his son's unusual command, Jonas remained silent and smiled to himself, knowing exactly what Jonathan was planning to do.

When they reached the living room, it was jam-packed with field bosses and hands that were waiting patiently to hear what Jonathan had to say. They were all hardened men, young and old, who spent the same amount of time in Azalea's sunny fields as the slaves they oversaw. And as Jonathan scanned the room, he could feel their eyes on him, observing, looking for any clues of apprehension or weakness from the man that was going to lead them into the future.

"Men, friends, brothers," Jonathan said confidently as he tried to make eye contact with everyone in the room. "I assembled you all here tonight for two reasons. Number one because I wanted you to hear it first, from me, that I am replacing my father as head of this plantation. That means nothing will change except that Gus will report to me instead of my father with issues concerning Azalea. Before I go any further, if there is any man here who has a problem with what I've just said, this is the time to speak." No one uttered a word.

"As you all know, a war has broken out between the North and the South. A fight that everyone in the country believes is over slavery and morality, but I know for a fact that it isn't. Soon a large portion of the men in the South will die, their wives will be made widows, and their children will grow up fatherless," Jonathan said, pausing long enough to let them envision the horrific picture he painted inside of their heads, "and it's all going to happen because the Yankees covet the slavery industry.

"That brings me to reason number two. You are also here tonight because I want to assure you that none of us here will suffer the fate of those who live beyond the boundaries of this plantation. Azalea will go on unaffected by the events taking place in the rest of the country," he said before digging into the satchel and pulling out a stencil and holding it up for all of them to see. "With this symbol, I guarantee that Azalea will see its most prosperous and profitable days since my grandfather planted his first cotton seeds here seventy years ago. Now go home and sleep well knowing that your wives and children will live through this crisis with absolutely nothing to fear!"

Jonathan stood back and watched as his employees, faces flushed with relief, filed out of the living room and headed off into the night knowing their futures had just been promised brighter days.

"That was amazing, son!" Jonas said when only he and Gus were left inside of the room. "I've known these men all of their lives, and I can tell that they are behind you, Jon. It's hard to believe that just a few days ago, I thought I'd lost you, and Azalea's future looked dire. Now you've given us all hope," he added while nodding his head.

Although Jonathan was elated by his father's vote of confidence, he knew there was more work to do. "Gus, first thing in the morning, I need ten men to go with me along the perimeter to paint these symbols on the trees."

Jonathan's position at Azalea did not require him to oversee any work done on the plantation, but a task as important as making sure the Magen David was properly positioned demanded his full attention. There was absolutely no room for error.

Later that night, Jonathan stood alone on the porch outside of his bedroom, staring off into the murky, starless sky. His mind wandered, thinking of Thomas, his best friend, safely tucked away across the Atlantic in a peaceful place, probably with a tumbler full of liquor in a room full of women, laughing it up without the tiniest care in the world. Then he thought of Claude, off shrouded by the same darkness, waiting for the bloodiest war America would ever see. He sighed heavily at the irony of the two people who impacted his life the most, although at opposite ends of the spectrum, abruptly disappearing without telling him good-bye.

It had taken almost a week for Jonathan and his crew to paint the images of the Magen David along Azalea's border. And in the months that followed, the plantation became an oasis buried deep inside of the chaos and bloodshed that began to mire the South. Meade's foresight was accurate. No Union troops had come within miles of Azalea, and the Tobiases operated peacefully as if the Civil War never existed.

During that time, Jonathan became a hero amongst his men. After sparing their wives and children the heartache that the other families of the South were facing, they vowed to give their lives for him. Their devotion showed in their work as their efficiency and attention to detail had the Tobiases looking forward to reaping their best harvest in years.

As the annual harvest swiftly approached, Jonathan found himself spending the majority of his time over at the cotton mill. It had to be a success, and Jonathan would guarantee it by hiring Charles Shepard, the most skilled loom operator and foreman out of Lowell, Massachusetts—the birthplace of America's fabric-producing industry.

He wanted to watch personally as the instructor he hired showed a large group of slaves and a dozen field bosses the tiny intricacies of the gears and pulleys that were scattered throughout the factory. Sometimes they would spend up to twelve hours a day practicing inside of the hot and muggy building. So when the time came for the first bale of cotton to be sent through the combing machines, the slaves would possess the same skill and knowledge as their counterparts operating the mills in the North.

With Jonathan's assumption of his duties, Jonas was left with an abundance of free time on his hands. He didn't complain about his lack of responsibilities because for years he wished for a break from Azalea's unrelenting demands. Even when Claude assumed control of the plantation after his accident, he still had to go over most of his son's decisions with a fine-tooth comb.

So on a sun-filled September afternoon, Jonas had no qualms about sitting on the front porch to sip lemonade and take in the garden's gentle, scented breezes.

"My oh my, we have a visitor," he said to no one in particular. He was remarking about the trail of dust sprouting up from the road far on the other side of the pond. By the time Cleevon could squint his eyes, the man was already close enough for Jonas to recognize.

"Masta Jonas, I thought we wouldn't be seein' no souljahs round these parts!" Cleevon said, focusing only on the man's military uniform.

"My God!" Jonas said, astonished. "That's no soldier. That there is my son!" he added as Claude rode up to the front of the steps and brought his horse to halt.

"Daddy!" Claude yelled as he climbed off the horse and raced up the steps to greet him. He was fully dressed in his Confederate regimentals with a long single-edged saber fastened to his left side.

"Claude, come here, boy!" Jonas said, reaching out to make sure it was really him. For months, he had hidden the fact that he worried about Claude's safety almost every moment of each passing day. "Let me look at you! I'm so glad you're home, and you're all here. Usually, men would return from that kind of hellish madness with a peg leg or missing an arm or two!" he added, relieved that his son wasn't a part of the war's horror stories that someone would return from town with at least once a week.

"Yeah, Dad, I'm back for good," Claude said after downing a whole glass of lemonade and excusing Cleevon for privacy. "I was a fool for leaving. I'm sorry, Dad," he added remorsefully.

"It's okay, son, I understand," Jonas said softly, trying to console his son whose face was buried deep in the palms of his hands.

"It's not okay. I was wrong. I've been wrong most of my life. And being alone out there on those battlefields made me see the error in my ways," he said, struggling to fight back his tears. "I should have never left. Jonny was sick, and I shoulda been here by his side."

"Jon's all right. You're here now, so stop beatin' yourself up, Claude," Jonas said, gently rubbing Claude's shoulder.

"I can't help it, Dad," he said in a tone so low that it barely equaled a whisper. "I never seen anything like that out there. White men scattered around like uncooked chicken parts. Arms and legs everywhere. Dead, all of them, never goin' back home to their families again," Claude said, luridly relaying the images that shook him to the core. "Seeing those men made me realize that I had to make peace with you and my brother."

That night, after a hot bath and a shave, Claude went to the library to meet with Jonathan and his father. He entered the dimly lit room and found them sitting at a table full of his favorite cooked foods and a bottle of whiskey between them.

"Dad," he said and acknowledged Jonas with a quick nod before walking over to Jonathan standing directly in front of him.

Since they weren't on good terms when they last saw each other, Jonathan felt a little uncomfortable with Claude towering over him. He quickly rose to his feet, and now only a tiny pocket of tense air stood between them. Jonathan had no idea what his brother was about to do and was surprised when Claude reached out and embraced him.

"Jesus, Jon, I'm sorry," Claude blurted out as the tears began to run steadily out of his eyes. "I've been a terrible brother. I've been blamin' you for Mama when I knew it wasn't your fault, and I want to tell you right now that I'm sorry!"

Jonathan was totally taken aback. His father did not prepare him for this. "Come on, Claude, you don't have to do this," he said pleadingly while looking his brother in the eyes.

"No, Jon, let me do this," Claude said, pushing him away. "Dad, I lied. It wasn't me who killed that runaway. It was Jon. They were going to kill me, and he stopped them. He saved my life, and I repaid him by saying that it was me," Claude told his father shamefully.

"It's okay, son, I understand" was all Jonas could say after waiting sixteen years for Claude to finally tell the truth, amazed that some strange epiphany Claude had on the battlefield could make his arrogant son return home to wipe his slate clean.

Whatever it was, it didn't matter because Claude's decision to clear his conscience completely restored every ounce of faith Jonas once had in him. Now the proud father sat quietly and watched as his two boys reconciled with each other.

Since he grew up without any siblings, it had always been Jonas's dream to see his sons working hand in hand, running the plantation. A dream that he realized could possibly come true as Jonathan explained to Claude, in full detail, everything that was happening at Azalea, from Magen David to the potential of the cotton mill's success.

"Jon, you really did it. You saved us," Claude said, sincerely impressed by his brother's ability to stave off an entire military's invasion. "No one would believe it if we showed them," he added before scarfing down another slice of blackberry pie. After spending four months on a daily diet of hardtack, a quarter-inch thick, three-inch square biscuit made from unleavened flour, Claude was not embarrassed to make a pig of himself at the table.

"I don't know if we're totally safe yet," Jonathan said humbly. "Who knows how much longer this goddamned war is gonna last. Until it ends, we have to consider ourselves partly at risk," he added, speaking on the odd chance of a Union battalion stumbling upon Azalea and destroying the entire population.

"Which is why we have to work along the Yankees and give them any kind of advantage they need to help them win the war," Jonas mentioned casually, cautiously waiting to see Claude's reaction to what he just said.

Claude slowly brought his attention from his food and looked at the both of them suspiciously. "Did you just say that you're spying?" he asked reticently, not sure if Jonas's words had registered properly in his ears.

"That's not what I said, but it is what I'm implying," Jonas replied bluntly, subliminally telling his son that there was nothing left on that subject to be said.

Claude clearly got the message and decided to leave it well enough alone. He turned to Jonathan. "I'm here. However you want to use me, just call on me," he said demurely before extending his long arm across the table in an attempt to shake his brother's hand.

"Oh, believe me, I will. There is a lot for us to accomplish," Jonathan replied, smiling and firmly clutching Claude's hand; relieved that after sixteen years of quarrelling, he and his brother could finally operate on the same page.

Claude wiped his mouth and smiled at them both devilishly. "I hate to leave you two like this, but y'all are gonna have to excuse me because for five long months, Debra has been at home patiently waiting for me," Claude said as he rose from the table. "Dad, Jon, I'll see y'all in the morning."

"What got into him?" Jonathan asked after Claude left them alone in the room.

"I don't know, son, but it's said that war brings out the absolute worst in men. I guess the experience your brother had out there forced out his best," Jonas said smiling, not only happy that Claude made it through the war safely, but that he also returned home a completely changed man.

After another three-minute bout of unfulfilling sex, Debra lay naked next to Claude with her head resting snugly against his broad shoulder. Most evenings when they finished having sex, he would go directly to sleep; but tonight, he said there was something important he wanted to tell her.

"Debra," he said softly while lying face-up and gently gliding his fingers along the nape of her neck, "I love you. And I want you to know that you're the only person here that I can trust."

"I know, dear," she whispered in his ear and used her soft hand to rub imaginary circles across his chest. "Now tell me what it is before I drift off to sleep," she added languidly as the bottle of wine they shared earlier began to weigh heavily on her eyelids.

"It's going to be mine, all of it. And I'm gonna make you the richest woman in the South," he told her proudly, speaking as if he discovered some long-lost treasure.

"What's going to be yours? Claude, what are you talking about?"

"Azalea. Not long from now, I'm going to be the only one left in control," he answered with a sinister giggle.

Wide awake now, Debra quickly opened her eyes. "What about your father and Jonathan? What are you planning to do with them?" she suspiciously asked after wiggling out from under the covers and sitting upright in bed.

Claude calmly placed his hands behind his head while looking up at her and smiling ostentatiously. "Darlin', you don't need to worry about them, because immediately after the harvest, their fates are going to be permanently sealed. Soon as those slaves are ready to run the cotton mill, the plantation will be mine for the taking. Jon and my daddy don't even realize it yet, but since they decided to become two treasonous bastards, they hand-delivered Azalea over to me."

Aroused by Claude's deception, Debra slid back under the covers and sidled up close to him until there wasn't any room between them. "Hmm, Debra Carlysle, the richest woman in the South," she said, trying on the new title. "I like the sound of that. Tell me more," she breathily added as she began to sensuously kiss Claude's lips and gently fondle his tiny erection.

In the following weeks that led up to the harvest, the Tobias brothers worked together in perfect harmony. Whenever Jonathan called on him, Claude was there, playing his part well and never giving anyone a chance to catch on to his deceit.

"Claude's been a blessing since he returned. Spending all my time in that broiling cotton mill was going to be the sheer death of me," Jonathan said to Jonas while Cleevon served them hominy grits, hot buttered corn muffins, sizzling bacon, and bright yellow soft-scrambled eggs. This had become their morning ritual, breakfast together, since the responsibility of running the plantation left Jonathan with absolutely no other time to spend with his father.

"I'm thankful that he's back too, son. Maybe now you can give that damn mill a break. You've been coddling it like a mother with a newborn baby," Jonas said with a half-crooked smile.

"In a little while, Dad, I will. I promise," Jonathan said while crunching on a crispy piece of bacon. "The harvest ends in just two days, and I want to make sure that every boss and every slave in that mill will be ready. Don't you know that one quarter of our finished cloth product will be worth twice as much as our entire raw crop alone? We're going to make eight times the amount of money we've made in past years," he added, excited about Azalea's expected capital gains.

"All right now, Jon. You remember what happened the last time you overworked yourself," Jonas said with an overly concerned look while cautiously pulling on his son's reins.

Jonathan remembered, and just the thought of that day made him drink an entire pitcher of water. "Don't worry, I'll be home early. Claude's coming over to the mill this afternoon to relieve me. I gotta saddle up," Jonathan said as he got up and left his father alone at the breakfast table.

The morning sun had shined brightly, causing the drops of dew to sparkle like diamonds on the garden's neatly sheared blades of grass. Ever since the day he took over, Jonathan relished his morning walks to the stables because the crisp air coupled with the flowers' sweet fragrances were an invigorating start to what always turned out to be a taxing and laborious day.

And like clockwork, Jonathan sighed when he got a few steps beyond the garden because the sight of Azalea's enormous horse stable meant that his workday was about to begin.

Having been taught as a boy by his father to have a special bond with his stallion, Jonathan picked up a bucket of feed and a large wooden brush when he entered the stable and proceeded to Whisper's stall. He was all alone inside of the dusky building, but since the bosses had to have the slaves out in the fields picking cotton before dawn, he knew it was normal for the stable to be empty at this time of the morning.

"Mornin', Whisper, it's time for work," Jonathan jovially said as he eased the gate open to the horse's stall and walked in slowly before running his hand gently along the stallion's muscular side. The horse jerked and snorted at Jonathan as if to display its happiness to see him. "I brought you a treat," he said as he slung the bag of oats around Whisper's neck so the horse could eat.

"Ahh, that's a good fella. Eat up," Jonathan said softly while brushing the kinks out of the horse's mane. "We got a big day ahead of us, so eat up, fella. That's a good—"

"Do you always talk to animals?"

It was Debra standing on the other side of the wooden gate, her big blue eyes watching him stammer as he struggled to find something to say. This was the first time she had said a word to him since their ordeal a year ago inside of the toolshed. In an essence, breaking the unspoken pact they made to never have any contact with one another again.

"What are you doing here?" he asked her aloofly, sorely reminded of the many awkward moments they shared following their passionate kiss, especially at family gatherings when he had to sit directly across the table from her and pretend she didn't exist, still wanting to steal a glance at her but fearing his desire would be picked up by everyone in the room.

Debra didn't answer him, and after a silent moment passed, Jonathan grew concerned when the usually spirited woman stood there looking confused as her eyes welled up with tears.

"Debra, what's the matter? Tell me what's wrong!" he said as he slid out of the stall and quickly took her into his arms. Still she remained silent, but this time, she timorously shook her head. It was too early in the morning for this, and even though holding her close felt like the right thing to do, Jonathan was becoming irritated with her unwillingness to respond.

"If you're not going to answer me, what the hell are you out here for!" he yelled while pushing her away, although still holding on to her shoulders the way a parent would chasten a disobedient child.

"I don't know how to tell you!" she shot back at him, surprised that Jonathan could take that kind of tone with her.

"Tell me what?" he asked.

"That your brother's trying to kill you!" she told him before twisting out of his grip and turning to walk away.

In the second it took to process what she had just said, Jonathan saw a horrifying image of himself dead pass before his eyes. He felt sick at the thought and stood there doubled over until he realized that Debra was getting away.

"Debra, wait!" he yelled before finally catching up to her and grabbing a hold of her wrist. "What do you mean he's trying to kill me?"

She led him into a shadowy corner that had been recently cleaned and stocked full of freshly cut hay. They sat on two unopened bales so if anyone returned early to the stable, their heads would be low enough that neither of them would be seen. Debra leaned in close to him.

"Claude wants to take over the plantation. And he's going to give you and your father over to the Confederacy," she said after regaining her composure and wiping away her tears.

Jonathan did not want to believe what he was hearing. "But things have been okay since Claude's been back. I've seen it!" he said, faintly hoping what he was telling her could be true.

"No, it's all been a ruse," she calmly told him. "Claude has been telling me everything he's planning to do since the night he returned. He's waiting until the harvest is over and the slaves are ready to operate your mill, then he's going to have you arrested for treason."

"Treason!" Jonathan said excitedly. "Goddammit! The bastard wants us hanged? Why would he wait until now to do this? Everything is starting to come together for this plantation. Why now?" he added as he pounded his open hand with his fist.

Debra felt so sorry for him. "Jon, Claude hasn't waited. His first attempt was unsuccessful," she murmured before looking the other way.

"What?" he said after slowly lifting up his head. "Debra, what are you talking about?"

"He's tried to kill you before!"

Jonathan shook his head in disbelief. "Debra, that's impossible. I would know it if someone tried to kill me. You're wrong about that," he said, now beginning to wonder if anything she had told him was the truth.

"You don't believe me, do you?" she asked, noticing the skeptical way he looked at her. Jonathan said nothing. Realizing that he needed to see something more convincing, Debra reached down into her sundress and pulled out the tiny leather pouch that was tucked inside of her brassiere.

"What is this?" he asked as she passed him the drawstring bag containing a gray powdery substance.

Debra hesitated, knowing what she was about to say was going to devastate him. "It's hemlock, and Claude's been putting it in your food since the day you returned. Small amounts. He expected you to die sooner or later. So happens, Jonas was there to get you help. It wasn't heat exhaustion," she said, passing on the terrible secrets that Claude had been sharing with her over the past weeks. Debra swore that she could see the color gradually drain from Jonathan's face.

Jonathan sighed heavily after finding out that his brush with death was premeditated. "Why?" he asked. "I devoted my entire life for this family. Himself included."

Again, Jonathan looked at the tiny bag of hemlock that he held in his hand. He was amazed that his brother could be so heartless that he would use the same poison on him that Olina had used on their father.

Instantly after that thought, Jonathan began to shake his head violently. It could not be true. Claude couldn't possibly be that calloused.

"Please, Debra, please tell me Claude had nothing to do with my father's poisoning," he said to her pleadingly.

She cast a gaze on him with dolorous eyes. "I'm so sorry, Jon," she said while slowly nodding her head.

"No, no, not my daddy," he muttered before bursting into tears. "How could he do that to my daddy?" Jonathan added as he envisioned his father transform from the able-bodied figure that he left behind seven years ago into the wheelchair-bound paraplegic he was today.

Debra sat quietly and watched him sob uncontrollably before realizing that there was something he could do. And with the grace of a Siamese cat, she lithely eased next to him and began to whisper into his ear. "I'm here, Jon, please take me. Save me, Jon, the way you've saved Azalea. Please save me from him."

Jonathan felt her gentle touch on him. His entire body heated up when she used her soft hands to wipe his tears away. When she began to kiss him, Jonathan wanted to tell her to stop, but he found the words impossible to say.

"Oh, Jon, take me now," she begged of him as she used her weight to pull him off the bale until they were both lying side by side in a bed of hay.

In an unbridled display of passion, Jonathan responded by kissing Debra feverishly. He gently touched and groped her while undoing the ribbons of her dress, only stopping to gaze at the curves of her naked body. He'd never before seen a woman that was flawless from the crown of her head all the way down to the soles of her feet. He had waited his entire life for this moment.

After Jonathan shed his clothes, Debra took him inside of her, and their bodies became a vision of entangled ecstasy, spending the rest of the morning physically displaying their love for each other until neither of them had anything left to give.

"Oh my," Debra exhaled as she rolled off him, still managing to stay nestled in his arms. They were both spent, and she couldn't believe that even after a few minutes had passed, fresh beads of sweat were still forming on her face. "What did you do to me?" she asked as her body twitched sporadically, each spasm becoming more pronounced than the last.

Jonathan said nothing. He just held her close while despondently staring at the rafters. He wanted to relish what had just taken place between them, but he couldn't take his mind away from Claude. Something had to be done.

"I think you should get back before he realizes that you've been away," he said while reaching for his things.

Immediately, Debra began to get dressed, running her hands through her hair to remove a few loose strands of hay. "When will I see you again?" she asked as she leaned in to kiss him.

"Soon, Debra. You will soon, believe me," he said with a piercing look before she turned to walk away, leaving as mysteriously as she came.

"Dad, he has to die! There is no way around it!" Jonathan said angrily.

After he and Debra parted ways, Jonathan spent the next hours alone in one of the garden's gazebo's watching the house, waiting for Claude to leave. Jonathan wanted to avoid his brother at all cost, knowing that his temper would cause him to give his knowledge of the plot away.

When he spotted Claude leaving for the mill, Jonathan buried the urge to confront him and quickly ran into the house to look for his father. And when he found him, Jonathan wasted no time in wheeling Jonas to the library.

"Is there anybody in cahoots with him?" Jonas calmly asked, continuously looking himself over as if he just discovered that he was paralyzed for the first time today. The news that Claude was responsible for poisoning him was reopening those painful wounds all over again.

"No, Dad, he's going at this all by himself," Jonathan said as he paced back and forth, full of raging energy.

"How in the hell does he expect to get anyone to follow him after he double crosses us?" Jonas asked curiously.

Jonathan stood across the table from his father. "Claude figured that once he informed on us, he would be rewarded with Azalea for his loyalty to the South. Then he would use his favor with the Confederate military to keep everyone else in line. Either side with him or get strung up along with us."

Jonathan continued, "What we have here is a crafty bastard who won't let nothing stand in his way of gaining control. He doesn't care about love or loyalty. Hell, he made sure Olina was dead before you could recover because he knew that you would get to the truth. And if he didn't yak everything to Debra, the day after tomorrow, we would have fucking nooses around our necks hanging from the gallows. I know you love him, but there can be no more chances. Dad, what are you going to do?"

"Jonathan, enough!" Jonas yelled as his fist came crashing down on the table, knowing that everything Jonathan had just said was true, realizing that the dream of his sons working together to further the Tobias's legacy was just that, a dream. Jonas's face began to turn hard as stone. He looked up at his youngest son with an ice-cold glare. "Go get me Gus McMiller."

After Jonathan left him alone, Jonas looked down at his legs again. He picked up the bottle of whiskey and began to think long and hard about his life before the wheelchair. Angrily, he tossed the bottle, smashing it against the wall. "Damn you, Claude!" he yelled as a single tear streamed down his face.

To a stranger, nights in the South could be interpreted as frightening, especially when the cloud cover prevented the moon from illuminating the sky, and the birds get replaced by fruit bats that wait patiently for the darkness to fall before they fly. Strange noises from animals and insects that wouldn't make a peep during the day created an eerie symphony that could be heard all around.

But for Claude Tobias, those nocturnal elements were perfect company. As a child, he always stayed up late, well after everyone else went to sleep, to roam the hallways of the mansion pretending he was the king of some faraway castle. It was the only time of the day he could talk out loud to himself and let his imagination run astray. So when Jonas requested that he go on an errand that would require him to be out past midnight, Claude was eager to oblige.

Returning from Dr. Sampson's with medications for his father, Claude couldn't help laughing at the irony, and when he thought of what was going to happen to Jonas in a couple of days, he decided to throw the medication away. "Dad's not gonna need these where he's goin,' he muttered before tossing the bottles of elixir and bags of herbal teas into the dense brush and weeds lining both sides of the road he travelled on. He would tell his father that the doctor never answered, hoping that Jonas spent his last days on earth in excruciating pain.

As his horse trotted along the murky road, Claude began to think about the future. Finally, he would have what he believed was rightfully his since birth. When he was acting head of Azalea, he hated having to run every decision he made by his father for inspection; he would have the final say and never be second-guessed again. Claude became so transfixed by his thoughts of the power he would soon have and how he intended to wield it that he didn't notice Gus McMiller and five of his men standing in the middle of the road waiting for him.

"Claude! Claude, get over here!" Gus said in an excited whisper.

As Claude got closer, he could see that they were all armed with rifles. "What's goin' on, Gus?" he curiously asked after he climbed off his horse.

"We got runaways! Four of 'em. The dawgs tracked 'em this way. Tie up your horse and come on!" Gus said as he turned to lead them through a thicket of weeds, away from the road and into the dense forest. After tying his horse to a tree, Claude grabbed his rifle and followed them.

Gus and his men held their rifles tightly and crept through a cacophony of shrill cricket chirps and owls cooing as they searched for the group of runaways that ran off into the night. Claude, who always had a thirst for blood, was eager to catch them so he could be the one to dish the torturous punishment they would receive for trying to escape.

"I wish we could hurry up and catch them niggers," Claude said as he swatted a mosquito that was sucking blood from his neck. "I would love to skin one of them sumbitches alive. How about you, Gus?"

"Sssshhhh!" Gus responded, giving Claude a stern look before pressing his index finger against his lips.

They were approaching an expanse of bushes where Gus suspected the slaves could be hiding. For years, he had been regarded as a master tracker and marksman, and as far as anyone could remember, only one slave had successfully escaped from Azalea. In situations like these, when Gus had a hunch, the seasoned boss was usually right.

Claude fumed. *Old bastard. Shushing me. In a few days, he's gonna beg me to keep him alive,* he thought to himself.

They were all crouched a few feet away from the bush, which until now had been rendered indistinguishable by the night. From a distance, it appeared as a void that was darker than everything else around it, that's how Gus knew it was there. They moved in closer.

With a few hand signals, Gus ordered three of his men to go around the bush one way while he, Claude, and a third man would go the opposite way and meet up on the other side, trapping whoever was hiding there in between.

"Claude, you go on ahead and lead. I'll be right behind ya," Gus whispered as they began to make their way around the bush.

Claude crept lightly, trying his best not to step on any twigs and alert the slaves that he was coming. His rifle was firmly gripped in both hands, ready to shoot the first slave that he saw. Tonight, no one would escape alive.

"Gus, there ain't nobody here!" Claude said when they met with the others and realized they had come up empty.

"Yes, there is. You!" Gus replied as he swung the butt of his rifle, striking Claude on the side of his head.

Since he was standing behind Claude when he struck him, Gus couldn't see that Claude's rifle was still clutched in his hands and was shocked when he shot the man standing in front of him.

"Get him, he's getting' away!" Claude heard Gus yell after he shot one of his men and then turned to run away. His heart pounded against his chest as he raced through the pitch-black woods—bumping into trees, stumbling over rocks, and losing his rifle in the process.

Claude could barely breathe, but he wouldn't stop running until he was absolutely sure that no one was behind him. Exhausted, he leaned against a tree and sucked in as much air as he possibly could. He began to feel dizzy as the warm blood from his wound oozed down the side of his face.

Alone with no weapon and four men scouring the area looking to kill him, Claude began to panic. His mind raced to find the reason why Gus would try to ambush him, ultimately realizing that his father and brother must have found him out.

"Debra," he blurted out, figuring that she was the only person who knew what he was planning and could have given them the information to trigger tonight's events.

Pressing his hand against the wound on his head, Claude surmised that this was all a trap—Jonas sending him to Dr. Sampson at this time of night and Gus waiting on the road to tell him that some slaves had escaped.

"Shit! How was I so stupid?" he asked himself after realizing that he never heard any dogs barking at all, a sign that no slaves had escaped to begin with.

Before he could get too down on himself, Claude realized something that his father and Jonathan hadn't anticipated, the company of Confederate soldiers he saw entering these same woods earlier in the night. If he could just find their camp, he would inform them of what was going on at Azalea and return home with an army as he had already planned. Then there would be hell to pay—for everyone.

Claude began to mentally retrace his steps from earlier, trying to calculate the distance between the spot where he saw the company enter the forest and where he was now. From there he began to walk towards an area where they might be set up for the night. He moved gingerly, trying his best not to make a sound because he knew that Gus McMiller wouldn't give up until he found him.

After spending almost an hour wandering around the wilderness, Claude finally caught a break when he smelled the familiar stink of military rations and saw campfires burning in the distance beyond a cluster of trees. He exhaled with relief as he neared the campsite, coming so close that he could see a few soldiers guarding the perimeter. He smiled widely and thanked sweet Jesus.

Hurrying in their direction, Claude's confidence increased with every step he took until Gus appeared from behind a tree and startled him.

"Don't you make a goddamned sound," Gus said as he leveled the barrel of his rifle between Claude's eyes.

Instantly, two of Gus's men came out of nowhere and took Claude from behind. This time, they firmly grabbed a hold of his arms to ensure that he would not get away.

Claude was deflated, and in the minute it took to turn him away from the camp and lead him deeper into the forest, his body lost every ounce of strength. Physically, he had resigned to his fate; but mentally, he would not go down without a fight.

"Gus, this is between them and me! This ain't got nothing to do with none of y'all!" Claude cried to anyone that would listen. "I swear, Gus, I was gonna leave you outta this!"

"That's a bunch of hog shit, Claude, and you know it. What you were tryin' to pull would have affected all of us. You were gonna turn us into your slaves, you lyin' bastard!" Gus said as his men dragged Claude to the secluded spot they had prepared for him, far away from any unsuspecting ears if he ever decided to scream. Once there, they forced him back against a tree and tied him to it.

"Wait, Gus! You don't have to do this! Let me live, and I can make you a very rich and powerful man!" he said excitedly in a last-ditch effort to gain clemency.

Gus shook his head. To him, Claude was the embodiment of absolute treachery, and the sight of him was disgusting. "You just don't get it, do ya? What you did to Jonas is unforgivable. My loyalty to your father is not for sale," he said while stepping back away from Claude.

Almost as if on cue, Gus's men stepped forward with a large pail of turpentine, soaking Claude from head to toe with the volatile fluid. Its pungent vapors ate away at his nostrils and burned the tears from his eyes.

Many times before, Claude had been the one holding the pail, dousing a slave with turpentine while he or she was helplessly tied to a tree. He knew exactly what was coming next.

"Wait, Gus, please! Not like this!" he yelled while using all of the strength he could muster in an attempt to wriggle himself free. "Just shoot me, Gus. Please! I'm begging you to just shoot me," he added between wails.

"Hey! Don't you dare cry now, boy! You asked for this. If it was up to me, I'd shoot you between the eyes and move on, but your daddy wanted it this way. He said you should burn like a no-good nigger," Gus told him while striking a match against a piece of flint.

Claude flinched when the match finally lit, and he could feel his heart sink to the pit of his stomach as Gus approached him with the flickering flame. Without a word, Gus tossed the burning match in his direction, igniting the turpentine, and a loud whoosh could be heard as Claude burst into a large ball of fire.

The entire area lit up, and the light from the flames cast an eerie glow on their faces as they watched in awe as Claude burned alive. A few of them covered their ears because, later in life, they didn't want their dreams to be haunted by his ghastly screams.

Unfazed by childish folktales, Gus stood only a few feet away from Claude, watching and listening to it all, only calling for the buckets of water after the smell of burning hair and flesh became too difficult for him to stand. And when the men put out the flames, all that was left of Claude was a pile of smoldering ash and bits of charred human remains.

Gus walked over to the gory mess and shook his head solemnly before spitting a mouthful of tobacco juice on it to signify that Claude's run of deceit had finally come to an end.

Early the next morning, Jonathan made sure that he was the first person to arrive at the cotton mill. He wanted to get one last look at the pristine facility before the slaves and bosses showed up and the operation got underway. The heels of his boots scraped against the wooden floor as he walked through the cavernous building, gently running his hands along the gigantic spinning machines. He was in awe of the brand-new equipment in the way the children revel in their most sought-after gifts after unwrapping them on Christmas day.

After completing his tour of the building, Jonathan was greeted by a wave of slaves, who poured inside and headed directly to their stations. To Jonathan, everyone looked pretty nervous, but he knew that if he had a mirror, he would find the same tense look on his face. Today was one of the most important days of his life.

When Charles Shepard finally arrived, Jonathan could see the tension gradually erode away. Everyone relaxed as the portly New

Englander with boyish features made his rounds throughout the building assuring them all that everything would go smoothly. He was an ardent taskmaster with a reputation for putting his workers at ease before rigorously ratcheting up the workload throughout the rest of the day.

"Did you get much sleep last night, Mr. Tobias? It clearly doesn't look that way," Shepard said, making small talk as they walked together through the factory, retracing the steps that Jonathan had taken earlier when the building was empty.

"Couldn't keep my mind away from this place. I guess the anticipation was getting the best of me," Jonathan told him, not wanting to let on that Gus's gruesome details of Claude's death was the real reason he'd stayed up half the night.

When they reached the loading bay at the rear of the factory, Shepard abruptly stopped and turned to him, then like an usher, he extended his chubby arm out and turned back around, stepping aside so Jonathan could see the scene taking place behind him. Azalea's largest slaves were unloading and opening four-hundred-pound bales of cotton that had been delivered form the warehouses. Heaps of white cotton were scattered all over the place, being spread out with rakes in preparation to be sent through the combing machines. The sight reminded Jonathan of the many winters he spent in Philadelphia when the children played in mountains of freshly fallen snow.

"You see, there's nothing to worry about," Shepard said confidently. "I'm not an expert on sleep, but milling is my life. I have run mills the size of small cities. This place is no different. You go get some rest, and I guarantee that by sundown, this mess you see will be turned into the finest fabric the South has ever seen."

Even though Jonathan found solace in Shepard's confidence, wild horses wouldn't be able to drag him away from the cotton mill today. "I'm sorry, Charles, but I have too much time invested in this place to go home and rest now. I have to stay and see this all the way through," he said emphatically.

"Suit yourself," Shepard said before walking off toward a group of slaves who were loading the raked cotton into large rolling bins.

He snapped his fingers at them, urging them to pick up the pace as he headed over to the mill's main operating switch. And with the pull of a lever, the coal-fed steam engines roared to life.

The clamor was deafening. Between the whir of three thousand spindles spinning and twisting cotton yarn at lightning speeds, and the clanking of the gears and pulleys of two hundred looming machines, Jonathan could barely hear himself think. To compound matters, invisible hairs from cotton lint floated throughout the building making the already sticky air difficult to breathe.

For the next seven hours, Jonathan endured the factory's hellish conditions as he tried to follow each step of the milling process until the first roll of fabric was complete. Drenched with sweat, he waited with the patience of a father expecting the delivery of his firstborn child.

"Mr. Tobias!" Shepard called out when he found Jonathan down by the loading bay stealing a few breaths of fresh air. "Follow me, there's something I want you to see."

He led Jonathan to the largest room of the factory where the gigantic looming machines were located. The floor vibrated as the powerful machine's belt-driven harnesses rose and fell in precise rotation, opening alternating vertical rows of wrapped thread on heddles that separated like jaws. And as they did, a horizontal row of weft filler shot across them on shuttles. The process repeated itself rhythmically as the loom magically weaved threads of cotton into delicate sheets of cloth.

"It's beautiful," Jonathan said while holding a piece of cloth in his hands. After rubbing the soft fabric against his cheek, Jonathan scrunched it into a ball and pulled it apart as far as he could to test the cloth's strength and durability.

"Oh, it's very strong, and it has been mercerized to increase its color absorbability and improve its luster. Right now, you're holding a piece of cloth that boasts the country's finest quality, guaranteed to fetch the highest dollar," Shepard said smilingly, proud of his latest creation.

"How much can we produce?" Jonathan asked without taking his eyes away for the fabric, amazed that something so valuable could grow from the planting and cultivating of a tiny cotton seed.

An expert mathematician, Charles Shepard looked around the room and quickly replied, "Being careful to mind wear and tear, I can only run these machines for fifteen hours a day. Six days a week, we can produce over 3,500 yards. That's 180,000 yards a year. However, given the political climate of the nation, that's nowhere near enough to feed the demand. Soon you'll have to build more mills."

Shepard's estimation totally delighted Jonathan, and his face broke out into an uncontrollable smile, knowing that his contributions to Azalea were going to pay off for years to come. He neatly folded the piece of fabric that Shepard had given him and left the mill with its noise, heat, and polluted air to head back to the mansion and share the success with his father.

"Look at it, Dad. It's more valuable than gold. Touch it," Jonathan excitedly said as he tried to pass the piece of cloth over to his father.

Reeking of alcohol, Jonas was unconcerned. He was clearly depressed, and Jonathan surmised that he was trying to deal with Claude's death. It didn't help that they were alone in the library where the three of them met regularly. Jonas refilled his glass with more whiskey.

"Dad, you have to let him go. He was no good," Jonathan said pleadingly.

"You don't tell me when to let go, boy! Goddammit, I know he wasn't shit, but he was mine. My son!" Jonas shot back, poking his chest out for emphasis. "I have a good reason to grieve!"

"But, Dad, look at this," Jonathan said while waving the fabric back and forth. "We have to move on."

"Move on? You're so obsessed with Azalea's future that you're forgetting about ours," Jonas said as Jonathan looked on in confusion. "Tobiases have been successful since my daddy first came here, but no generation had yet to escape tragedy. My brothers and sister, your mother, and now Claude. At times, I wonder if this family is cursed," he added before taking a large swig of his drink.

"You can't count Claude as a tragedy. What happened to him was a result of the choices he made," Jonathan said.

"Son, that's the point I'm trying to make. Whether he made the choice or not, he's still dead. Now what if something happens to you?

Everything, all of this," he said while snatching the cloth from the table, "will have been for nothing."

"What are you talking about?" Jonathan asked.

"I'm talkin' about children!" Jonas yelled. "If you died right now, who would be left?"

Taken aback, Jonathan finally understood what his father was trying to say. He poured himself a drink.

Noticing the dumbfounded look on his son's face, Jonas continued. "You've gone great lengths to establish the Tobias name and further our legacy. But, son, in order to have a legacy, there's got to be someone to pass it on to. What's going to happen between you and Debra?" he abruptly asked to his son's surprise.

"What do you mean?" Jonathan asked curiously.

"I know there's something between you two, or she wouldn't have told you about your brother's plan. Say what you want. I already spoke with her earlier today," Jonas informed him dismissively.

"You spoke to her? What did she say?" Jonathan asked, unable to control the tone of desperation in his voice.

"She came clean. She's in love with you. Said it's been since the day the two of you met. I'm old-fashioned, and under any other circumstances, I wouldn't approve, but we owe her a great deal of gratitude."

"I know," Jonathan said distantly while staring off into space, thinking of where Jonas and he would be right now if Debra hadn't warned him. Suddenly, he felt the urge to find her and profess his feelings to her. "Where is she now?"

"I sent her home."

"Why?" Jonathan asked.

"I told her to speak with her father and try to convince him and his wife to stay here with us until this whole war thing blows over," Jonas replied.

Jonathan wasn't sure he heard his father correctly. He looked at Jonas's glass and wondered if he had too much to drink. "You gave her permission to speak about us to her family? Are you sure about that?"

Jonas slowly shook his head. "For someone to be so smart, how can you be so naïve? Don't think for one moment that her family's safety never crossed her mind when she told you about Claude. Debra's no fool. She knows her family won't stand a chance unless they come here with us. She also knew that Azalea would have gotten rolled up with the rest of the South if she sat back and let Claude take control," Jonas smiled wickedly. "You have to hand it to her, the lady's a survivor. Definitely someone I'd want havin' my grandchildren."

"I don't know," Jonathan said, reluctant to agree that allowing Debra to invite her family to Azalea was the right idea. "What if her father tries to use our arrangement with Lincoln against us the way Claude did? What's to stop him?"

Jonas took another swig of whiskey. "I've known Preston Carlysle for about forty years now. Our parents were cordial, and we've been on good terms too. The man's got a lot of pride. So much, in fact, that he would never accept an offer of protection from another man, but on the other hand, he would never turn us over and jeopardize his daughter's only chance of surviving this war."

"Still, Dad, after what we just went through with Claude, it feels like we're putting ourselves back in the same position to be crossed again. I just think it would be best if no one else knew about us," Jonathan said before igniting his taste buds on fire with a generous sip of his drink.

Jonas leaned forward, and while looking his son in the eyes, he couldn't help being overcome with pride at the man Jonathan had turned out to be. Strong, wise, and incredibly loyal, Jonas saw his father in his son.

"Jon, that woman loves you, but believe me, she would have resented you for not offering her family refuge. The offer I made to her was for the best. She'll be back," Jonas said, nodding his head reassuringly. He reached over and picked up the piece of cloth that he ignored earlier, and after running the light fabric between his fingers, Jonas looked up and said, "You've done well for us, Jon. Goddammit, you've done well."

For two weeks, the moments slowly crept by while Jonathan impatiently waited for Debra's return. To occupy his days, he stalked the corridors of the mill and watched as the rolls of newly weaved fabric began to multiply. But at Jonas's request, Jonathan always made sure he came home early so they could eat supper together as a family and then retreat to the porch to watch the sun go down.

From there, Jonathan spent his nights lying awake in bed wondering when he would again be able to hold Debra in his arms. He knew she was destined to become his wife, bear his children, and share in his fortunes eternally. Secretly, he pined over her every day.

From the looks of it, today would end no differently than the others. After a fulfilling meal, Jonathan shared a pitcher of mint julep with his father and watched the sun lose its daily tug-of-war with the night. But as daylight gave way to the twilight, Debra's carriage rolled up to the front of the mansion, bringing Jonathan a pleasant and unexpected surprise.

Before the wheels of the carriage had a chance to stop, Jonathan had already run to the door to greet her, happily walking in stride with the slowing vehicle until it came to a grinding halt. And when the driver climbed down from in front and opened the door, Jonathan was both surprised and relieved that Debra had returned with only her mother in tow. The driver helped the ladies exit the carriage one by one. Debra was first. Apart from the vexed look on her face, she was still as beautiful as the first time he laid eyes on her.

"Jon, this is my dear, sweet mother, Petunia," Debra said sardonically as she quickly walked past him, trying to put as much distance between her and her mother as she possibly could. She grabbed the front of her skirt in a bunch and ascended the steps, only stopping on the porch to kiss Jonas gently on the cheek before disappearing into the mansion.

"Ma'am." Utterly confused, that was all Jonathan said while dipping his head politely as Petunia Carlysle extended her chubby hand for him to kiss.

"Just call me Petty. That's what everyone else calls me," Petunia said as Jonathan obliged her.

Petunia Carlysle was a robust woman whose beauty-queen features were beginning to diminish with age, and she tried to hide that fact with garish clothing and accessories. Her lilac-colored dress had been made from the finest silks and linens that money could buy. The matching silk bonnet she wore covered her thick strawberry-blonde hair but exposed her graying temples. She accentuated her ensemble with jewelry that only the wife of a successful slave baron could afford. This woman was the embodiment of Southern arrogance.

Looking at her, Jonathan could clearly see where Debra had inherited her striking eyes. Blue as the Caribbean Sea, he knew that with all of her fine clothing, sparkling jewelry, and dainty posturing, her eyes were what garnered Petunia Carlysle the most attention. But this evening, they betrayed her, for they displayed the fears of a woman who was possibly about to lose everything she had ever known. Jonathan would do his best to put her at ease, but he would have to find Debra first.

After scanning her empty bedroom, Jonathan finally found Debra in his room staring through one of the windows. He approached slowly. By now, the sun had set, and as he got closer, he could see her reflection on the darkened glass. She was crying. Gently, he touched her shoulder.

"Debra, what's wrong?" he asked her softly.

She turned to him. Her cheeks were streaked with tears. "He said no. He told me he wouldn't come here," she said before burying her head into his chest. She was speaking of her father, and of course, just as Jonas had predicted, he refused their invitation. "Oh, Jon, I begged him. I pleaded with him, but he constantly pushed me aside. Instead, he sent me back here with that bitch. Why would he stare death in the face instead of swallowing his pride?" she asked between heavy sobs.

"Debra, I'm sorry, but I can't tell you what's going on in your father's head," he answered honestly.

Instantly, she looked up at him, and though she was crying, Jonathan could see the fire in her eyes. "Yes, you can! Don't you dare lie! You all are the same!" she yelled, pounding her tiny fists against his chest. "You're a man. You're all prideful bastards, and you all think alike," she ranted as her swings grew more and more violent.

He grabbed her flailing arms and pulled her closer to him. She struggled to get loose from his grip, causing Jonathan to become angry. "Woman, get a hold of yourself! Don't be angry at me, and don't compare me to anyone else. I'm not like anyone you've ever known. A prideful bastard wouldn't have invited your family to stay here. Look around here. It's evident that family comes first. We need to be starting our own," he said forcefully.

Embroiled in a stew of emotion, Debra looked up at him wantonly, and Jonathan returned the same lascivious gaze. He kissed her, passionately, pressing his lips hard against hers while dipping his warm tongue deep into her mouth. As she rotated her tongue around his, he felt the tense muscles in her body slacken as he guided her to the bed.

Now in the confines of his bedroom and no need to rush, Jonathan carefully undid the buttons of Debra's blouse, exposing her cream-colored torso and comely breast. Slowly, they helped each other out of their clothing until they were both completely naked.

He continued to kiss her, gently tracing the curves of her body with his fingertips, their journey beginning at the edge of her navel and ending at the nape of her neck. She groaned in ecstasy. He was just getting started.

Deliberately, Jonathan pulled away from her mouth while cradling her soft mounds and brought his wet lips and tongue to her swollen nipples. As he gently squeezed and groped her breasts, Jonathan could feel Debra's heartbeat while sucking and slurping on her tits like a newborn child.

In an erotic frenzy, she ran her fingers through his hair and squirmed feverishly beneath him. Her entire body was catching on fire.

"Oh please, Jon, take me," she hissed after her hands reached down between them and gripped his rock-hard penis. "I can't wait. I want you inside of me now," she begged while spreading open her legs and pulling him closer.

Slowly, he eased his massive rod inside of her. Wet, but not too wet, tight and warm, Debra engulfed every inch of Jonathan's erection. He squeezed his eyes shut with satisfaction as the thought of being one with the woman he loved titillated every nerve in his body from the tips of his toes to the neurons in his brain.

His strokes were slow and methodic, wanting to savor every second of sexual bliss, and the bed rocked back and forth choreographically with every wave of their lovemaking motion. The candles burned slowly, and he pushed harder, becoming more aroused while watching Debra wince in delight as he plunged to depths that no other man had ever been to before.

"Oooohhh, Jon," she panted while gripping his muscular back, her fingernails digging into his skin. As his pulsating hardness clashed with her softness, Jonathan ignored the pain and watched as his quickened strokes produced tiny ripples in her breast.

His muscles started to tense, and the uncontrollable urge to come began to grow deep from within as each thrust brought him closer to his climax. In perfect harmony, Debra's breathing became more intense, and her legs quivered and became spastic as she prepared to come in unison along with him.

Suddenly, without warning, Jonathan let out a muted groan as he ejaculated, planting a budding seed inside of his lover. Totally drained, he collapsed beside her, and they effortlessly fell asleep tightly embraced in each other's arms. Tonight marked the beginning of the rest of their lives.

CHAPTER 7

With increased sentiment fueling both the North and the South, the Civil War raged on. But progress at Azalea continued unaffectedly as though it existed inside of another realm. At a time when it seemed like things couldn't get any worse for the country, things couldn't be any better for the Tobiases.

The summer had met its end in 1862, and the plantation was poised for a fruitful harvest after another successful growing season, and unlike anywhere else in the South where the obligations of war left many plantations weakened with only the wives of the owners remaining in control. The inherited responsibilities proved a daunting task for these women whose only occupations up until then were hosting soirees and flaunting their wealth. Needless to say, upon their return home, their husbands considered themselves lucky if their plantations had amassed only 50 percent of their potential growth.

There would be no such worries for the Tobiases, who were making a fortune off the need for loomed cotton. After President Lincoln imposed an embargo barring the purchase of slave-picked cotton, the once almighty mills of the North were no longer consistent, causing the demand for the material to grow out of control. The drought created complete pandemonium in the industry, and even though some of the craftier plantations managed to smuggle their cotton up North, it still wasn't enough to quell the increased demand; thus, leaving Azalea in the enviable position to make another killing.

As Jonathan stepped out onto his balcony this morning, making a killing was the only thought on his mind. Lately, this had become his awakening ritual, looking out over the vast cotton fields the way a king would survey his domain.

The sun had barely risen, and already the sparrows' chirpy spirituals had filled the crisp Alabamian air. Consequently, upon hearing the sedative music, Jonathan smiled to himself because even in his wildest dreams, he never envisioned that life would be so perfect. After a lifetime of betrayal and hardship, Jonathan felt he had finally been given everything he desired and deserved; safety, prosperity, and—turning his gaze to the sleeping figure in his bed—most importantly, love. Only a glutton would ask for more. But as Jonathan returned his attention back to Azalea's ever-extended cotton fields, there was one thing that he wished for: more mills.

Jonathan cursed himself while watching his always efficient slaves trudge up and down rows and rows of stalks, filling their burlap sacks with fluffy bolls of cotton. If only he had foreseen the true damage the war was doing to the industry, he would be selling ten times the amount of material he was selling today.

He sighed at the thought, knowing that any plans to add more mills would have to wait until the war came to an end. Most of the manpower in the South was dedicated to the Confederacy's cause. Besides, he didn't want to expose the plantation to any unnecessary eyes.

In the past year, there had only been one visitor to Azalea, and Jonathan wanted to keep it that way. It had been on a sunny afternoon in the spring when Preston Carlysle made an appearance to give Debra away on their wedding day. He hadn't returned since, much to the delight of Petunia Carlysle, who had been finding herself waking up in Charles Shepard's bed as of late.

"Absence makes the heart grow fonder—of someone else," he whispered to himself.

The passing thought of his mother-in-law's indiscretion led him back into the bedroom where Debra slept peacefully. Sunlight poured into the room, bouncing off her white nightgown, giving her the appearance of a celestial being. She was his angel. Jonathan sat down on the bed beside her and began to gently stroke the hair around her face. Slowly, she began to awaken. Her eyelids fluttered as she adjusted to the light.

"Mmmmhh," she purred. "Good morning."

"It's always a good morning when I look at you," he responded with a smile. "Did you sleep well?"

"As well as the baby would allow. It's been kicking all night," she said while rubbing her hand over her stomach.

Jonathan joined in, lightly massaging the gestating belly. "He wants out, that's all."

"He? What do you mean he?" she asked playfully. "Everyone knows that I'm baking a little girl in this oven."

"You must be having twins because I'm counting on a boy to come out of that oven."

"Jon, hush! You sound just like your daddy," she said, alluding to the fact that Jonas had been talking about a grandson since the moment they discovered she was pregnant. "We just better pray for a healthy baby with ten fingers and ten toes. Besides, it ain't like this child is gonna be our last."

Jonathan smiled and planted a wet kiss on her lips.

"Oh, Jon, do you have to go?" she asked morosely while grabbing onto his arm. "It's going to be any day now, and I want you here with me."

Jonathan looked at her then sighed heavily when his eyes cut over to the telegram sitting face-up on the nightstand. The unique symbol on its letterhead stood out in bloodred ink distinctively—the Magen David. When the letter from Gavin Meade arrived a few nights earlier, summoning him to Washington, DC, at once, it didn't surprise Jonathan at all because he somehow knew this day would come.

"Debra, I want to stay, but you know how important it is for me to answer this call," he said, frustrated that the letter never mentioned what his visit would be pertaining to. "This could be about anything—a warning, an opportunity, who knows. I can't afford to guess. Any miscalculations on my part would be disastrous for this child," he added while returning his hand to her stomach.

"I'm afraid to do this by myself," she said cautiously.

Jonathan knew exactly what Debra was referring to, the tragic happenstances that befell the Tobias women before her. As her pregnancy came closer to term, the so-called curse had been on his mind, but he refused to make his feelings known to anyone. He took a deep breath before pointing his gaze directly into her eyes.

"There's nothing to be afraid of. Everything is gonna be just fine. You have everything here that you need, and everyone here is going to do their best to help you get through this. Hopefully, I'll be back before the baby comes." He squeezed her hand affectionately. "I have to go."

"I know," she said softly with an understanding nod. He leaned over and kissed her forehead. "I love you. Hurry back!" she called out as he left her alone in the room.

As Jonathan made his way to the awaiting carriage, he hastily descended the staircase as if it would shave valuable minutes off his travel time and allow him to return home sooner. He was angry about having to leave his wife at a time when she needed him the most, and he had intentions on making his feelings known once he arrived in the nation's capital.

"On your way?" Jonas asked when Jonathan stepped out onto the front porch.

"There you are. I just went to your room to say good-bye," Jonathan said before trailing off into a deep thought. He remembered the last time he left Azalea to go north; he didn't return for six long years. Now looking at his father, he was reminded of the drastic changes that awaited him upon his return. Jonathan wasn't sure if he could handle any more unfortunate surprises.

"What is it, son?" Jonas asked with concern, snapping Jonathan out of his stupor.

"It's Debra. She's upset that I'm leaving. She's worried something could go wrong with the baby. I have to admit, I'm worried too," Jonathan said pensively.

"You're thinking of your mother, ain't ya," Jonas said, reading Jonathan's mind. "You both can't be that way, thinking negative.

Don't you know that if you go through life always expecting the worst, you'll never be able to leave the past's tragedies behind. Let them go," he ordered.

"Dad, you don't believe that. As much as Grandpa wanted you to have a big family, why didn't you? There were enough available women around. You were afraid that what happened to my mother would happen again," Jonathan said ingeniously.

Jonas shook his head slowly. "Son, you've got it all wrong. The only reason I didn't try for more children was because your mother was the only woman for me."

Jonathan's eyes closed, and his head hung low as his father's sincere words descended upon him. "Debra's the only woman for me," he uttered.

"I know she is," Jonas said, laying a heavy but comforting hand on Jonathan's shoulder. "That's why it's important that you tend to this business in Washington."

Jonathan knew that his father was right. He stood up to go. "Look after her," he said while locking eyes with his father.

"Like she was my own child," Jonas replied before Jonathan climbed into the carriage and headed off on his journey.

Following a two-day train ride out of Montgomery, Alabama, Jonathan had arrived in Washington, DC, on a dreary afternoon. From the fresh mud and huge puddles on the ground, it looked as though he had just missed a downpour, but the dark sky signaled that there was still more rain on the way.

Fortunately for Jonathan, Gavin Meade had been at the station to greet him, and he didn't have to worry about getting drenched. After exchanging a few pleasantries while Meade's driver loaded Jonathan's belongings into the carriage, they hopped inside of the vehicle and were on their way.

As they rode through the streets of Washington, Jonathan remarked to himself at how, despite the weather, so many people were out and about today. And since this was the nation's capital, he noticed that everyone scurried around with their noses tilted upward with an air of self-appointed importance. The sight of it all instantly reminded Jonathan of everything about the North he spent the last two years trying to forget. Having only been here less than thirty minutes, he already wanted to turn around and go back home.

"What the hell is this all about?" Jonathan asked, turning his ire toward Meade. "You really picked the wrong time to bring me here" he added, his eyes becoming more menacing with each word.

Jonathan's tone caught Meade off guard, causing him to blanch. "I didn't do anything but send you the letter," he replied cowardly. "I don't have a clue what this is about. I just do what I'm told," he added, clearly laying the blame on the man in charge.

Sensing Meade's fear, Jonathan eased up, and they rode the rest of the way in complete silence. When the carriage finally stopped, Jonathan stepped out to discover that he wasn't on the grounds of the White House but, instead, on a block that had been jam-packed with brownstone houses and red brick buildings.

He followed Meade into a three-story brownstone located directly across the street from a large theatre. They were greeted by a servant who took their coats and led them into a small but cushy waiting room. Once there, Meade disappeared behind a mahogany door, and Jonathan was left alone with the Gothic paintings that adorned the silk-covered walls.

After a few minutes, Meade returned. "The President will see you," he announced formally, leading Jonathan from the waiting room into an identically decorated den. The only difference between the two rooms had been the large mahogany desk that Abraham Lincoln was standing behind.

"Mr. President," Jonathan said piously.

"Abe!" Lincoln blurted out as he came from around the desk to shake Jonathan's outstretched hand. "My friends call me Mr. President, but my good friends refer to me as Abe. Jon, you're one of my good friends," he added jovially, laying it on thick to set the tone of the meeting.

"Gavin, that will be all," Lincoln said to his lackey, who instantly made himself scarce. "Have a seat," he said, gesturing Jonathan to a pair of facing sofas.

"Gavin tells me that I might have called on you at an inappropriate time. Please accept my apologies," Lincoln said after passing Jonathan a glass of scotch once they were seated.

"No apologies necessary. I'm a little uptight because my wife's having a baby," Jonathan said, waving Lincoln off dismissively.

"Congratulations are in order," the president said while raising his glass.

Jonathan raised his glass with him and then let the velvety liquor warm the back of his throat. He began to relax. "Abe, tell me, what exactly do I owe the honor of this invitation?"

Strangely, almost immediately after the words left Jonathan's lips, the president's blithe demeanor had become crestfallen. It was as if a stench of hopelessness and gloom had suddenly pervaded the air in the room. Lincoln took a moment to answer.

A moment was all that Jonathan needed to read the features on the president's face and see the expensive price he was paying for leading an entire nation to war. He looked old, almost nothing like the man he met in Springfield two years ago, seeming to have aged ten years as the bags on his gaunt face cried out for one peaceful night of sleep. Even his trademark beard was now stained with gray hairs.

Finally, Lincoln spoke up. "We're going to lose," he said, barely audible.

"What did you say?"

"The war! We're going to lose the damned thing!" Lincoln growled.

"How's that possible?" Jonathan asked curiously, remembering that Woodburn and his father had assured him that the Union's victory over the Confederacy was all but guaranteed.

"It's my fault. It's the embargoes. I did it to strangle the Confederacy's economy. I thought it would be a strategic move, but it's turning out to be a gross error of judgment on my behalf," Lincoln said while shaking his head dejectedly.

"I don't understand. From what I can see, the embargoes are working," Jonathan said, noting that the ban on free trade with the North had crippled the Confederacy's ability to fund the war. Lincoln even had a naval fleet patrolling the Atlantic Ocean to stop the flow of slave goods heading to Europe.

"I know it's working, but it's a goddamn Pandora's box! We choked our own supply. Winter's approaching, and I can't properly clothe our troops. Jon, this could destroy us!" Lincoln said before letting out a long exaggerated sigh.

Us? Jonathan thought to himself, now realizing why he had been summoned here so urgently. They needed his help, and sensing a change of the guard, Jonathan took a generous sip of his drink, sat back, and let Lincoln continue.

"Somehow, if we were to match wits, there may be a way to get through this," Lincoln said candidly.

"What do you propose?"

Jonathan's question was like music to the president's ears. "I need you to put a halt on the production at your mill and sell the Union all of your raw cotton," he deadpanned.

Jonathan grimaced. It wasn't confusion that distorted his face but the thought of his immense profits going up in flames if he reverted back to selling raw cotton. He began to shake his head, but before he could say no, Lincoln threw up a hand.

"Wait, Jon, I'm impressed with your foray into the production of textiles, and I know that over the last year, you've been capitalizing a great deal from your cotton mill. I don't want to take that away from you. I'm willing to pay you dollar for dollar for every pound of your raw cotton as if it were loomed. I can guarantee you won't lose a single cent."

"I have to say that's a very generous offer, but why me?" Jonathan asked suspiciously.

"Because even if the Confederate ships don't sink the vessels bringing us cotton from India, it will still take too long for the cotton to get here. The only way to save valuable time is to purchase it domestically," Lincoln replied.

"But I know of many Union sympathizers in the South. Wouldn't it be cheaper to purchase the cotton from them?" Jonathan suggested.

"Cheaper, yes—but safer, who knows? I'm past the point of cost cutting. I have to win this war. Sure, I know of the Unionists in the South, and I'm pretty sure they would be willing to sell me their cotton, but I can't trust them. I can only—"

"Of course, you can only trust someone with just as much to gain by the Union winning the war as yourself. And who would have the most to gain or lose but me," Jonathan said, cutting in and finishing Lincoln's sentence for him.

Again, the president exhaled. "As dubious as it sounds, that's the reason why you are here," he said genuinely.

"It's dangerous," Jonathan said aloud as he mulled over the idea. "This goes way beyond spying. If it got out that we were supplying the Union, Azalea would surely be burned to the ground. Even you wouldn't be able to stop it."

"Of course it's dangerous. The danger factors directly into the inflated price of your cotton," Lincoln said.

There was a knock on the door followed by the servant peeking his head inside of the den. "Excuse me, sir, dinner's ready to be served. Shall I set up in the dining room or would you like to eat in here?"

"The dining room will suffice," Lincoln said, and the man disappeared quietly. "Good, we can eat and then head on over to Ford's for the show."

"Show?" Jonathan asked, slightly bewildered.

"Yes, the opera. The only time I stay here is when I intend to see the shows at Ford's," Lincoln replied with an injection of newfound spirit. "Forgive me for not mentioning my itinerary when you first arrived."

"But we're not finished with this," Jonathan said.

"We can put if off until tomorrow," Lincoln said dismissively.

"Abe, I beg your pardon, but I didn't come this far to be entertained. I want to be heading home by tomorrow," Jonathan shot back, surprised at Lincoln's sudden lack of concern for the matter at hand.

What the president wasn't letting on was that despite everything that was going on in his chaotic world, the Italian operas and plays at Ford's Theatre were the only thing that soothed him and afforded him a peaceful night of sleep. He never missed an engagement, and tonight would be no exception.

"Let me make a suggestion," Lincoln said, throwing up an index finger. "After we eat, you return here and work out any kinks that may exist in my offer. We'll discuss them first thing in the morning. Hopefully, we can reach an accord before lunch. If so, I promise you you'll be on your way back to Azalea by the evening. Agreed?"

"Agreed," Jonathan said while nodding his head.

"Then lets eat before the food gets cold," Lincoln said before leading the way to the dining room.

After enjoying a succulent meal of lamb and potatoes, Jonathan found himself all alone in Lincoln's den. He poured himself a glass of scotch and immediately began pondering Lincoln's proposal, figuring that the sooner they could come to an agreement, the sooner he would find himself back at home.

Sitting behind the president's desk and staring at a blank piece of paper, Jonathan realized that the amount of money he was being offered would not be enough. There was too much to lose if he was found out, and he wouldn't be gaining much if things went along without a hitch. He was going to make the same amount of money if he hadn't been called here. It might have taken longer, but Azalea wouldn't have been put in harm's way. And now that he was bringing a child into this world, the value of what he was risking grossly multiplied.

Ironically, with the thought of his child, the gears in Jonathan's head suddenly started to turn. His mind was made up. If the president truly desired his cotton, Azalea would have to be properly compensated.

Jonathan finished his drink and began to write fervidly on the blank sheet of paper, smiling devilishly to himself, knowing that Lincoln was about to pay dearly for the risks that his plantation was about to take.

"You can't possibly be serious?" Lincoln asked as he read over Jonathan's proposition with wide eyes. They were back in the den, returning there immediately after breakfast. "This is extortion!" he added cynically.

"I say it's a fair deal," Jonathan said, steadfastly holding his ground. "In monetary terms, the deal is the same as the offer you made yesterday."

"I see that! It's what you want after the war that disturbs me," Lincoln blurted. "This is a monopoly!" he added while tapping the paper with the back of his free hand.

The president was holding a draft written by Jonathan promising that any purchase of cotton or its by-products by the US government will come exclusively by way of the Tobias corporate entity.

"I wouldn't call it a monopoly because we don't have the crop cornered," Jonathan said in his defense, "which means we can't set any price higher than the going rate of the competition."

Lincoln winced with confusion. "If you're not going to profit more than your competition, why do you want this?" he asked while waving the paper as if it were a flag.

"Abe, do you have to ask? For all that I'm doing for you, I feel as though I should be rewarded with the sole right to government contracts. You told me that we're good friends, and I trust that you would reward me as such, but I want to be ensured that I'll continue to be rewarded long after you complete your term," Jonathan said pointedly.

Lincoln understood, bitterly accepting the fact that he couldn't be the president of the United States forever. He knew that once his term was up, all the promises he made while in office would quickly be forgotten. "Exactly how long after my term do you expect to be rewarded with these contracts?"

"Indefinitely," Jonathan shot back, staring the president right in the eye.

"Goddammit, that could mean forever!" Lincoln bellowed.

Jonathan expected that reaction. "Abe, that's exactly what it means. It's the same amount of time Azalea would be lost for if your plan fails. There's too much at stake, and only the terms on that piece of paper will make it worth it." He paused to let his words seep in. "We can go on back and forth like this all morning. Nothing's going to change. So we can either agree on this now and both get what we want—you winning this war and forever changing the face of this nation, and me supplying the government with my cotton. Otherwise, I'm going back to Alabama and our futures will just have to be left up to fate," he added coolly, painting the president into a corner.

Without a word, Lincoln stood and walked over to the window. He pulled back one of the curtains, and a sliver of sunlight beamed into the room. For a few moments, he remained silent while staring out onto the busy street. And after regaining his composure and choosing his words carefully, he began to speak.

"Passion. It's such a sweet-sounding word. But as sweet as it sounds, by no way should the word be considered weak. It's almighty in that it can easily separate a winner from a loser. Those who posses it prevail, while those that don't fall bleakly to the wayside." He turned from the window to face Jonathan.

"Jon, never in my life have I met a man as passionate as you. Standing firm behind your convictions, you refuse to be led astray. You would make a fine general. I admire that, your passion. My passion?" A question unto himself. "My passion would have me accept defeat this morning rather than accept it as the outcome of this war. I'll concede to your terms."

Jonathan looked on as Lincoln walked back to the desk and scooped up the now powerful piece of paper. "I'll have Gavin take this to my secretary general, who will transform this into an official document. When he returns, we'll read it over together, and I'll sign it before you and my attorney general as witnesses. Thus rendering your contract into government record, and you'll have your reward."

While the bested man spoke, Jonathan fought hard to stifle the smile that came with the rush of elation and self-satisfaction that he was feeling. He had just delivered a coup that would serve his family for generations to come. But as delighted as he was, Jonathan knew that there was no time to celebrate because he was now faced with the arduous task of supplying the Union with enough cotton to enable them to win the war.

After ironing out the details of their covert exchange, Jonathan found himself arriving at Azalea three days later on a hot and sticky night.

Returning home sooner than expected, Jonathan felt an eerie calm upon entering the mansion. The entire place was dark and quiet, totally opposite of its usual signs of life. The sun had long since retreated, so it was normal for him not to see any slaves or hands, but Cleevon, who always had been a visible fixture in the mansion, was nowhere to be found. The hairs on the back of Jonathan's neck stood up as he sensed that something here was wrong.

"Dad! Daaaaddd!" Jonathan called out as tiny beads of sweat began to form on his face. When no one answered, he panicked. Trepidation encompassed every inch of his body after checking his father's room and finding it empty. Jonathan began to believe that what he feared the most about leaving was occurring again. He raced toward the stairs in an attempt to check on his wife.

"Debra!" he yelled as he bounded up the steps, only to be met at the top by Petunia, standing there with her hands resting on her wide hips.

"Sssshhhh! Jonathan Tobias, what on earth are you doing at this time of night howling like a mad wolf?" she whispered angrily.

"Petty, where is everybody? Where's my father?" he asked, showing no concern for her demeanor as he wiped the sweat from his brow.

"Boy, your daddy's fine," she replied dismissively. "That old coot is out there in the garden under the gazebo. Him and Gus have been drinking up a storm and making so much noise that I had to chase them outta here before they woke up the baby. Now you come in here right after them with a bunch of racket—"

"Did you say baby?" Jonathan asked, interrupting her prattle.

"Yes, I said baby. That's what your daddy has been celebrating for the past two days . . ." Petunia's voice trailed off as Jonathan glided past her and quickly made his way to his bedroom where, after easing the door open, he found Debra sitting up in bed cradling their newborn child.

"Did I wake you?" he asked sheepishly.

"Mmm hmm," she replied with a slight nod.

"Did I wake the baby?"

Again, the nod.

Jonathan spent a few seconds nervously standing by the door. He was transfixed by the sight of them. He couldn't move; somehow, the reality of him being a father began to quickly set in, turning his feet into stone. He'd never been around a newborn baby before, let alone one of his own.

"Jon. Jon," Debra softly called out to him after noticing his apprehension. "Come on over here. The baby's not going to bite you," she added with an innocent smile.

Jonathan inched his way over to the bed and sat down beside her, never taking his eyes away from the infant nestled peacefully in her arms.

"Sweet Jesus, you had the baby," he said gently, trying not to startle the child, who stared up at him innocently. "When?"

"The baby came as soon as you left," she responded with a triumphant smile.

"Look at him. He looks just like me," he said elatedly. "It is a he, isn't it?" he asked, hoping she would say yes.

"Yes, Jonathan Tobias, this here is your son," she answered with pride in the fact that she was able to give her husband exactly what he wanted. An heir.

As he looked his little boy over, Jonathan marveled at all of the Tobias traits that had been passed on to him. His tiny head was covered with thick curls of jet-black hair. The boy's long limbs ensured Jonathan that he would grow to be as tall as him and his grandfather. And when the baby's tiny fingers squeezed his thumb, Jonathan felt the grip of a hand that would wield the power of many men in the future.

"He has your eyes," he told Debra, remarking on the boy's sapphire orbs.

"But he has your stare. The Tobias look of determination. Jon, what are you going to name him?"

Jonathan let out a giggle, embarrassed that the notion never crossed his mind. He was so enraptured with his newborn son that he didn't realize that his child was still nameless.

After Debra carefully placed the baby into Jonathan's arms, he began to think long and hard for a name to give his son. A name appropriate enough to christen the child for the life he was about to embark upon. A name as strong and as powerful as the blood flowing through the boy's veins.

"Jackson," Jonathan stated resonantly. "Jackson Jonathan Tobias is what our son will be named."

"Congratulations are well deserved, son," Jonas said the next day as he beamed a perpetual smile. They were in the library, and Jonathan had just finished recounting the details of his meeting in Washington and Azalea's lucrative contract with the government that he was able to force the president to sign. "I told you, son, a long time ago that the tide would one day turn in your favor," he added, reminding Jonathan of his seemingly infinite wisdom.

"You did, Dad. And did it ever turn," Jonathan said before disappearing into a thought.

"What's got you, Jon?" Jonas asked.

"You," Jonathan replied. "You've been a rock for me throughout my entire life. I only hope that I can be at least half the father you are to me for my own son's sake."

"Nonsense," Jonas said while shaking his head. "Look around here. You've done more for that boy in the six days he's been on this earth than many men could accomplish in a hundred lifetimes. Jackson will be fine."

As Jonas finished speaking, a thunderous roar filled the air. Oddly, the noise repeated itself again and again, causing Jonathan to get up and look out of the window. He expected to see rain, but the sun was still shining, and not a single cloud could be seen in the clear blue sky.

Slowly, as if he were somehow possessed, Jonathan backed away from the window, realizing that the bright skies and thunderous roaring could mean only one thing.

"What is it, Jon?" Jonas asked.

"Cannon fire!"

Jonathan quickly rolled his father out of the mansion and ordered Cleevon to ring the bells along the way.

The clamor was deafening, the combination of clanging bells and mortar shells flying high over his head, but Jonathan ignored the ringing in his ears and raced back into the mansion to retrieve his wife and son.

"What is that?" Debra yelled over Jackson's frightened screams the moment Jonathan burst into their room.

"Never mind that now! Let's go!" he said while guiding her to the door. Amazingly, over the noise now mixed with Jackson's wails, Jonathan had somehow heard the reverberating boom of the shells landing on their targets. He rushed out onto the balcony and saw that the shells weren't landing on Azalea. They were landing on the town of Henderson, about three miles away. He went back into the bedroom and told Debra to wait.

Once Jonathan got a hold of Cleevon, the bells ceased to ring. Then after sifting through the crowd that gathered in front on the mansion, he informed his father that Azalea wasn't being attacked, and they both breathed a collective sigh of relief.

Realizing that the plantation wasn't in any danger, Jonathan ordered Gus to disperse the crowd and get the slaves back out to the fields. They would only have to contend with the noise, but otherwise, Azalea would be okay. Jonathan wished he could say the same for Debra.

"Well, what is it?" Debra asked impatiently as Jonathan closed the balcony doors and shut all of the bedroom windows to cushion their ears from the outside noise.

He took a deep breath to steel himself and told Debra to put the baby down. She obliged by gently placing Jackson inside of his bassinet. She turned to him with a worried look in her eyes. "Jon, please tell me what's going on out there."

"The Yankees are bombing Henderson."

"Oh no!" she said with shock before her hands covered her agape mouth. "My father's there!"

"I know," Jonathan said. "There's nothing that we can do to save him."

"Yes there is. Someone can ride into town and bring him back," she shot back naïvely.

"Debra, be serious. No one in their right mind is going to ride into that hell storm and risk getting killed!"

"Damn it, then I'll go myself!" she screeched at Jonathan as she made an attempt to get past him.

"Where do you think you're going?" Jonathan managed to say as they wrestled in front of the door, struggling back and forth until he used his brute strength to overpower her and force her onto the bed. "What the hell is the matter with you? Do you actually think I would let you go out there to get yourself killed and have my son grow up without a mother the way I did?"

"But my father—," she tried to say but was cut off.

"There ain't no buts," Jonathan said furiously. "Your father knew the consequences when he chose to stay. If he wanted you dead, he would've kept you with him instead of sending you back here!" he yelled. His voice was so loud and emphatic that it startled Jackson, causing the baby to cry.

Defeated and frustrated with Jonathan, Debra took Jackson out of his bassinet and stormed out of the room.

Later that night, long after the bombing stopped and Debra and Jackson had cried themselves to sleep, Jonathan stood on the balcony and watched as the fires burning in Henderson lit up the darkened sky. Looking in the direction of the once sprawling town, he couldn't help shaking his head in pity at the aftermath of the death and destruction that had rained down on it earlier in the day.

"What have I done," he muttered to himself knowing that the blood of the town's unsuspecting citizen's were partially on his hands.

He knew all along about the attack on the riverfront town because it was the only way the Union could secretly retrieve their supply of cotton from Azalea.

The president had explained it all to him before he left Washington. The waterway flowing through Henderson emptied into the Tennessee River, which the Union navy now had control of, and ran north into Kentucky, a state above the secession line.

Once the cotton reached the Bluegrass State, it would be off-loaded and transported by railroad to Lowell, Massachusetts. There, the cotton would be spun and mass-produced into everything the military needed—from socks, sheets, blankets, and long underwear to coats and uniforms.

The only problem would be Union steamships docking in Henderson, which sometimes doubled as a Confederate hub. But as Jonathan gazed at the billowing flames, he knew it was a problem that existed no more.

Still, Jonathan was surprised at the swiftness and merciless nature of the attack, the relentless shelling of a civilian town until it disappeared from the face of the map. He truly underestimated Lincoln's desire to win the war.

The thought of the president's desire caused Jonathan's culpability to nag at him because he knew that intertwined with it was the unrelenting desire of his own, a desire so strong that he signed off on the death of his own people—Southerners just like him. A decision Jonathan was so ashamed of, he conveniently forgot to mention to his father that the attack on Henderson was a part of the plan.

Stepping back into the bedroom, Jonathan realized that even his wife's heartache resulted form a machination put together with help of his own hands. He began to wonder what kind of monster he had become.

Jonathan sighed heavily before he crawled into bed, hoping to put the demons of guilt to rest as he closed his eyes and tried to fall asleep.

Three weeks later, after Preston Carlysle's remains were put to rest, Azalea's harvest was completed. Union steamships docked on the banks of what was once known as the town of Henderson.

Cloaked by the darkness of night, Gus McMiller supervised as his men and Union sailors worked together to load the ironclad vessels with tons of cotton. Once the last bale had been strapped into place, the ships would leave the port as discreetly as they came. The

clandestine exchange took place once every week until the plantation's warehouses were empty.

Subsequent to receiving Azalea's cotton that winter, the Union
sent their troops into battle outfitted in military dress made from
cotton born out of the very institution of slavery that they were dying
in droves to end. The Civil War had become an irony in and of itself.

CHAPTER 8

The intonation was sonorous, and Jonathan detested every bit of it. He craned his neck around the crowded auditorium and saw that everyone, even his wife, was enjoying the libretto.

Perched high in a private box at Ford's Theatre, he and Debra were guests of President Lincoln and the First Lady. They were viewing an operatic version of *Othello*, which, for Jonathan, had finally reached its climax. He began to thank his lucky stars that the play would soon be over.

It was late January in 1865, and Abraham Lincoln had recently been inaugurated for a second term after winning the presidential election with a landslide victory over George B. McClellan the previous year. By now, following the events that had taken place since Jonathan's last visit to the nation's capital, it clearly was no longer a question of which side would win the war, but rather a matter of when.

The embargoes that earlier almost cost Lincoln the war were finally taking drastic tolls on the South. And with the inducement of two hundred thousand freed slaves into the Union army, the Confederate military found itself overwhelmed.

None of this, in Abraham Lincoln's opinion, would have been possible without the influx of Azalea's cotton. The president considered his good fortune a cause for celebration and invited Jonathan and Debra to stay with him and Mary Todd at the White House for a week.

Initially, Jonathan had been reluctant to attend, but he accepted the invitation after realizing that the change of scenery would be good for Debra, who, after almost a year and a half after the death of her father, still seemed to be ensnared in the toils of her grief.

Amazingly, the operatic plays and lavish dinner parties at the White House were just what her spirits needed, and Debra began to feel like the debutante she used to be. Although he had to pay the high price of rubbing elbows with Washington's denizens, after seeing his wife enjoying herself, Jonathan knew the trip was worth the fee. Fortunately for him, they were leaving for Azalea in the morning.

After returning to the White House following the show, Debra went off with Mary Todd to view her expensive and extensive collection of handmade silk gowns while Jonathan joined the president in his private study for drinks.

Stepping into the chandelier-lit room, Jonathan noticed that the study was more of a lounge with its stained-oak wainscoted walls, oversized fireplace, and clusters of large leather high-back chairs. What classified it as a study were the volumes of books neatly shelved on the bookcases lining the walls of the cavernous room.

Only the wall above the crackling fireplace remained bookless, and it was adorned with the stuffed and mounted heads of exotic wild beasts from around the world. The entire room oozed grandeur, but so did every other square inch of the palatial executive mansion.

"They've been behaving like long-lost cousins," Jonathan said after Lincoln handed him a snifter of cognac. He was speaking of his wife and Mary Todd Lincoln, surprised that Debra had taken a liking to the First Lady, who had a long-standing reputation for being a prude.

"Mary's originally from the South, so there's probably a lot of mutual things they understand," Lincoln said before raising his glass. "To women able to get along," he toasted in jest.

"I'll drink to that," Jonathan replied as he brought the glass to his lips. He swashed the liquor around in his mouth, savoring its distinct flavors before swallowing the smooth drink.

A moment of silence had passed between them as they sat across from each other, and Jonathan used it to study the president from head to toe. When he finished, he didn't know whether it was the cognac invading his senses or the week they had just spent together because he was beginning to regard Abraham Lincoln as a genuine friend.

Granted, Lincoln was a Northerner and their ideas and opinions differed greatly, but he stayed true to his word and kept Azalea safe from the Union armies that were systematically destroying the plantations of the South.

"Abe, I want to thank you for the hospitality you've shown me this week," Jonathan said, breaking the silence.

"No, no, Jon. It is I who should be thanking you," Lincoln replied graciously. "You and your cotton are greatly responsible for the Union's optimistic position in the war. Besides, during your last visit, it was you who truly opened my eyes."

"I did?" Jonathan asked, his voice flecked with confusion.

"Oh yes, Jon. You sure did," Lincoln said while casually crossing his long legs before continuing. "I'm sure you know by now that once this war is over, everyone involved in this conspiracy of ours will live on like kings. Well, everyone but me, of course. The only compensation I received for my role was the opportunity to become president of the United States. I should have asked for more, but I blame my contentedness with only being the president on the naïve politician in me. Purely a mistake I won't make again," he added slyly.

"Jon, I don't come from anything resembling money, but you can look around and see that living like this can spoil the most humble of men. After you brought it to my attention that one day this all had to end, I sat back and wondered what would life after the presidency be like for me. It became evident that once my term is up, I'll be forfeiting all of this power and prestige."

"Abe, what are you saying?" Jonathan asked curiously, steadily growing uneasy with the direction the president was taking.

"I'm saying that just being remembered for freeing slaves in historical documents won't be enough for me. After serving as president of this great nation, I believe that I deserve a more tangible reward. There's something I want you to see. Jon, do you read the Bible?"

Without waiting for a response, the president picked up the large oxblood-colored Bible that rested on the table beside the flagon of cognac. Puzzled, Jonathan looked on as Abraham Lincoln leafed through the book until he found the appropriate page.

"Ahh, here it is. Genesis, chapter 12, verse 7. Jon, I want you to read this," Lincoln said while carefully handing over the book to him.

As Lincoln sipped on his drink, only the fireplace could be heard while Jonathan silently read the verse. "And the Lord appeared unto Abraham and said, 'Unto thy seed I will give this land.'"

After he finished reading the scripture, Jonathan looked up and asked, "What is this supposed to mean?"

"It means exactly what it says. I am to receive a sacred land— and only Azalea qualifies as such these days," Lincoln said in a tone that was no longer smug. His words were now delivered cold and calculatedly.

"I must admit, back in Springfield, I thought it was ridiculous when your only request was that your plantation remain untouched during the war. But since then, Azalea has continued to flourish while other plantations either struggled or were destroyed. The decision to construct a cotton mill displayed your business savvy, and the indefinite contract with the government was a pure stroke of genius and will deliver fortunes for your family well into the next millennium. Even I couldn't see that far into the future. All the while, I took you for another dumb farming Southerner, but quite frankly Jon, you've succeeded in making me look like a fool."

Gradually, Jonathan's cheeks turned bright red. It had nothing to do with the president's flattery. Instead, he was fighting the impulse to tear Lincoln limb from limb as white-hot fury surged through his veins. He tried to speak up but Lincoln threw up a hand.

"No, Jon, you had your chance to speak the last time you were here!" he snapped viciously. "I came to you humbly asking for your help, but instead, you used my desperation as an opportunity to take full advantage of me. I was forced to concede to your ultimatum, but tonight, I'm sitting in the catbird seat!"

"It must have felt good to put that contract over on me, knowing that I was in no position to refuse you. Ironically, because of your cotton, any day now, the Union will win the war, and the future that once looked bleak to you then is back in my control. And since I can have Azalea ripped from the face of the earth at any time, it seems as though your future is under my control too.

"You've witnessed Henderson firsthand, so you already know what I can do. My only question for you tonight is how much are the lives of your family and that golden goose of yours worth to you?"

Jonathan seethed at the casual mentioning of his family and plantation being destroyed. He searched Lincoln's face in an effort to find the gracious host that he and Debra had been with throughout the past week, only to come to the conclusion that that person never existed.

When Jonathan didn't answer, Lincoln continued. "Half, Jon. I want half of every cent you'll ever earn from Azalea. But if you don't remove that scowl from your face, I'll take it all."

Jonathan's stony expression wouldn't budge. Lincoln ignored Jonathan's cold glare and went on.

"I'm going to give you exactly ninety days to name me as full partner on your company's charter, granting me 50 percent control. Also, you're going to hand over my share of the company in stock certificates, which I'll have the liberty to liquidate as I please. It's not that I don't trust you, Jon, but I would like to have my money where I can see it. I have a funny feeling those certificates are going to become very valuable one day. Don't you agree?" he asked with a sinister grin before suddenly rising to his feet.

"Is that it?" Jonathan managed to ask through clenched teeth.

Lincoln casually yawned as if he hadn't a care in the world. "I think I've made myself clear. It's been a long day. It's about time for me to get some sleep," he said before turning to leave, and then after taking a few steps, he turned back around and added, "And Jon, do see to it that you handle my request in a timely manner. If I don't have what I want by the first of May, I guarantee you'll rue the day you ever doubted me. I would hate to have to remind my stalwart generals that during their cleansing of the South, they left one stone unturned."

After delivering his final threat, Lincoln headed off to his quarters, leaving Jonathan alone with the mounted game in the room. Eerily, he felt their eyes on him as he pondered the implications of the president's demands and wondered what about it—if anything—he could do.

He walked over to the fireplace and began to study each of the conquered beasts very carefully, thinking of how he was lured here to Washington this week and trapped in the study tonight to suffer their same fate. The only difference was that instead of using a rifle, Lincoln utilized threats and intimidation to claim his prize. Jonathan felt a hand on his shoulder. Startled, he quickly turned around to discover that it was only his wife.

"Jon, are you all right?" she asked her husband with a concerned look in her eyes.

He gently kissed Debra on the lips and reassured her that everything was fine. The last thing he wanted to do was put a damper on the wonderful time she was having, so he used every ounce of strength in his body to force a smile.

"It's getting late, and we have to leave first thing in the morning, so could you please say good night to the animals and come to bed," she said while ever so slightly tugging on his arm and looking up at him lustfully.

Slowly, Jonathan extended his arm and gestured for her to take the lead. But before they could exit the study, Jonathan stole one last glance at the wall above the fireplace. And silently, as he followed Debra to their bedroom, Jonathan vowed to himself that he would never end up that way.

After feigning good spirits for Debra's sake during their entire journey home, Jonathan needed a release. So upon returning to Azalea, he sought out his father's wise ears. And later that night, long after everyone in the mansion had gone to sleep, they sat in the library where Jonas listened intently to the details of Jonathan's encounter with President Lincoln.

Jonas, who had developed an affinity for flavored tobacco, calmly puffed plumes of sweet-smelling smoke into the air while dissecting every telling word, never once interrupting Jonathan's frantic speech. He casually nibbled on the stem of his briar before asking the only question that seemed important.

"So you knew all along about that attack on Henderson?" he asked while shaking his head in disgust.

"Yes, I did," Jonathan answered sullenly, ashamed that he had deceived his father, who clearly made his displeasure known by showing more concern about his prior knowledge of the Union's artillery siege on Henderson than Abraham Lincoln's demands. "It was the only way they could've received our cotton without anyone becoming the wiser," he tried to explain.

"Dammit, I know why it had to be done. I'm mad because you kept it from me! That day, you paraded around here like you didn't know what was going on. I expected that kind of behavior outta Claude, not from you!" he snapped. "I love this place too, but I'd rather see Azalea go up in flames before I have you around here deceivin' me!"

The words cut deep, but Jonathan understood. "I'm sorry, Dad," he said contritely as his eyes met the table. "It'll never happen again."

Slowly, Jonas pulled the pipe out of his mouth. "You're damned right it won't happen again. I'm gonna make sure that all of this cavortin' around with the enemy comes to an end," he vehemently told his son as he contorted his already gnarled face.

Every day following his return home, it became more evident that the Civil War was nearing its end, so Jonathan set out to purchase all the plantations surrounding Azalea. He offered a king's ransom for land that had been utterly wrecked by the necessary savageness of war. Without the employment of their newly freed slaves, many owners considered their mammoth-sized parcels of land too burden-some to control. And when Jonathan approached them with satchels full of money, the plantations were quickly sold.

Oddly enough, Jonathan seemed to notice that no one grew suspicious of his motives or showed the slightest bit of concern. But he dismissed the thought, figuring they were all too preoccupied with the opportunity he had given them to head West and join the country's fervid rush for gold.

Once the last acre was purchased, the Tobiases would lease the land at a piddling rate to their new tenants—Azalea's field bosses and their families, who would, in turn, sublease it to struggling farmers and ex-slaves for a lion's share of the harvest. As simple as the idea had seemed to be, it was ingenious in that it served two crucial purposes. The sharecropped land would create the illusion that it accounted for the majority of the Tobias's cotton production, but more importantly, the newly purchased land became the barrier that would further insulate Azalea and its illegal activities from the outside world.

The scheme to hide Azalea had been in place for more than a year, and Jonathan was surprised, after he informed his father of his last meeting with the president, that Jonas had told him to proceed with the plan. Wholeheartedly, Jonathan followed his father's instructions, vigorously acquiring property until it seemed like they owned an entire county. He even had Charles Shepard cordon off land along the banks of Henderson for the addition of new processing plants and cotton mills.

The empire he created was now poised for everlasting success. But as Jonathan worked hard to see his ideas to fruition, there were days when he thought his efforts were futile, knowing that one day in the near future, he would be forced to give Abraham Lincoln half. And almost certainly, those days were followed by sleepless nights where he lay awake in bed wondering how long after the first of May would it be before Lincoln came to the take the rest.

Meanwhile, deep in the swamps of northern Alabama that bordered along the state lines of Georgia and Tennessee, a meeting was about to take place that would have a lasting effect on the nation.

Either by raft over murky waters or by horseback through a labyrinth of secret pathways cut through the overgrowth of cattail and peat, a small group of men descended upon a large cabin located far from the reaches of civilization.

As the moonlight sparsely peeked through the trees, one by one, each man entered the lushly furnished cabin. Once inside, they took their designated seats, and following the rules of their fraternity, no one uttered a single word until the last member of the group had arrived. They called themselves the Knights of the Golden Circle, and over the last decade, they secretly held their meetings here since their inception in Natchez, Mississippi.

Nicknamed the Jewel of the Mississippi, Natchez was a small port town on the southwestern tip of the state with breathtaking views overlooking the Mississippi River. Speckled with luxurious mansions on verdant tracts of land, it was home to the most prized pieces of real estate in the southern half of the country.

Every year in the antebellum South, the slave industry's elite would escape to their "summer homes" in Natchez for one- or two-month getaways. Where the rich went to see and be seen, it became the South's answer to the blue-blooded Gold Coast in Long Island, New York.

During the summer months, Natchez played host to a string of cocktail parties, formal galas, and masquerades. It was the only place that allowed spoiled wives to show off their expensive jewelry and elaborate silk brocaded gowns while their husbands bragged and boasted over bourbon about the production of their slaves.

For years, Natchez reigned as the slave baron's paradise until sentiment toward abolishing slavery grew from a tiny whisper into a shrill yammer in the Northern states. But it was only after scathing books demonizing slavery were published by the likes of Harriet Beecher Stowe and Hinton R. Helper that Republican politicians were struck with a sympathetic chord, and slavery's most prominent beneficiaries were forced to unite and form the KGC.

Secretly, they lobbied and threw abundant sums of money at the North's seediest politicians in hopes of placating the issue of abolishment away. To no avail, these all-powerful and influential men met regularly to devise ways to thwart the inevitable clash that had been brewing between the Northern and Southern states.

When their efforts failed, they agreed to secede from the Federal Union and pledged a great deal of their fortunes to back the Confederacy throughout the Civil War. Now, almost five years after making that decision, they were on the verge of failing again. With millions of dollars lost and the Union ravaging the South, tonight, the Knights of the Golden Circle were hell-bent on getting revenge.

It wasn't until the moment Gus McMiller wheeled Jonas Tobias into the cabin did the meeting begin.

"Men, I don't think that I need to remind y'all of the reason we're here," Jonas said to everyone after Gus helped him into his seat.

"No, we know why we're all here. After all the time and money that went into this mess, the Confederacy's gonna lose the war," bellowed Hardee Gaines, the most outspoken member of the group. His gargantuan plantation in Durham, North Carolina, produced the most tobacco in the nation. He had been nicknamed Satan, but no one knew whether it was because of his arched eyebrows and pointed goatee or the sadistic manner in which he treated his slaves.

"Dammit, I knew all along that we should have taken our slaves and invaded Mexico when it was ripe for the taking. Now the Confederacy's not even strong enough to do that. We're gonna be left with nothing!" Gaines added before slapping his thigh in frustration.

"Oh, Hardee, please! Enough about the Mexico business. Land down there ain't worth a hog's shit anyway. Stop complaining. We tried our best. It didn't work out the way we planned. We need to be thankful that we still got our land—"

"Speak for your goddamned self, Jarvis!" William T. Sibley, the great grandson of Georgia's first cotton-grower had cut in. "And I speak for most of us here tonight. If you took a moment to stick your optimistic nose in the wind, you would smell that our plantations are burning as we speak," a fact that ignited an uproar among the men the room.

Toward the end of the war, Ulysses S. Grant, the command-ing general of the entire Union Army, issued an edict to his troops to set fire to any plantation they see. Many of the men here in the cabin tonight had been victimized by the order, and they all despised Jarvis Bedford, whose prosperous sugar and tobacco plantations were located along the Florida panhandle, which had gone virtually untouched by the war.

Like an orchestral conductor, Jonas allowed the noise to con-tinue, permitting the men to deservedly vent their frustrations before banging his cane against the floor to silence the entire room.

"All right! All right! We all lost something important to us because of this damned war. A house can be rebuilt and land recultivated, but ain't nothing gonna bring me back my oldest boy." Instantly, everyone's head dipped in a gesture to offer their condolences. Jonas continued, "I didn't ask y'all here tonight to bicker about our losses. We have to handle them on our own. I asked y'all here to suggest we deal with the one who saddled us with our grief. I asked y'all here to suggest we send them Yankee bastards a message that the South will surely rise again!" Jonas said passionately.

"Well, what do you recommend?" Gaines asked.

Momentarily, Jonas cast a wicked one-eyed gaze upon the semi-circle of men as an eerie quiet enveloped the room. "At the start of the war, the Union came up with a plan to surround the South by placing troops along the Atlantic coast, around the Gulf of Mexico and up the Mississippi. It was designed to isolate the South and choke off the supply lines to the Confederacy. It worked. They called it the Anaconda Plan, but now I say we cut off the head of that snake. Raise your left hand if you agree with me."

Out of everyone in the South, these men were the most affected by the war. Financially hurt and angry, they knew exactly what Jonas had meant, and without hesitation, one by one, each man raised their left hand toward the ceiling.

After the last man signaled his approval, Gus immediately helped Jonas into his wheelchair and pushed him to another section of the cabin where a shadowy figure had been patiently waiting in one of the rear rooms.

"Mistah Tobias, I must say it is an honor to finally meet you, suh," the younger man said, totally in awe of Jonas's presence. He extended his arm, and Jonas's meaty palm swallowed his hand.

"Likewise, I've heard a lot about your many efforts out in the field. It's quite a pity they weren't met with much success. Maybe all of this could have been avoided had you succeeded," Jonas said, remarking on the man's failed attempts to kidnap President Lincoln over the past year.

"Suh, if you don't mind me sayin' so, that son of a bitch is more slippery than oil dipped in grease," the man said in his defense.

"I know he's guarded heavily at all times, but I just happen to know of a place that he likes to frequent," Jonas said before handing over a sheet of paper that had been folded in half.

After briefly skimming over the carefully laid instructions, he curiously looked at Jonas and pointed to a group of jumbled letters at the bottom of the page. "What's this?"

"It's old Latin," Jonas replied, "and before you make your exit, it must be announced loud and clear for everyone there to hear. It's more significant than the actual deed. Memorize these words as if it were your own name. Do you hear me, boy?"

"Yes, suh!" the man quickly replied, respectfully adhering to the imperative tone in Jonas's voice. "Mistah Tobias, you can count on me not to disappoint you."

"I sure as hell hope that's true," Jonas said with a tinge of worry. "The entire reputation of the South now rests with you."

"I'll do my best."

"I don't want assurances! And I don't want your best! I just want the goddamned thing done, ya hear?" The man nodded that he understood.

Jonas gave him a once-over. No older than thirty and thinly built, the man used a thick handlebar mustache to hide his boyish good looks. But it was his eyes, the steely deadness of them; although the young man was in total awe of Jonas's legendary presence, not once did his eyes display an iota of fear. Jonas was convinced he was up to the task.

"Your payment will be here waiting for you once your job is completed. Now go on, boy, and do the South some good!" Jonas said to the man, who tucked the instructions inside of his boot before slipping out of the back door of the cabin and quietly disappearing into the night.

Immediately after the man left him alone, Jonas struck a match and lit his briar. He began to suck desperately on its sweet-flavored fumes. He was anxious, an emotion he never before felt in his entire life. Now he was depending on pipe tobacco to free him from the stressful thoughts of sharing a fate far worse than his confederates in the other room.

Throughout his life, Jonas Tobias held a firm grip on his destiny and was never known as a man to be steeped in religious beliefs. But tonight, out in the middle of nowhere, he dug deep down into the depths of his soul and prayed to an almighty God for John Wilkes Booth to succeed.

After four years of intense fighting, almost six hundred thousand deaths between the Union and the Confederacy, and an uncountable number of injuries, the Civil War culminated in a small town in central Virginia the following spring.

Marching for six straight days on near-empty stomachs, General Robert E. Lee's Army of Northern Virginia found itself cut off from their supply trains, which had been captured by the Union forces at Appomattox station. Hungry and exhausted, many of his fifteen thousand soldiers stumbled out of the walking columns along the way to Appomattox and were never seen again.

Unfortunately, the soldiers who completed the journey saw the full extent of the Union forces waiting for them. Lee and his troops were surrounded by Union General Ulysses S. Grant and an abyss of eighty thousand troops. Greatly outnumbered by the heavily armed Union cavalry and infantrymen, Lee knew it would be suicidal to engage in battle. And with no energy to fight or run, the Confederacy's commanding general realized that the end had finally come.

Faced with an agonizing decision, he sent a man on horseback to the opposing force armed with only a message and a white flag.

Lee, who once remarked that he would rather die a thousand deaths than surrender, knew that if he didn't, thousands of his men would needlessly die.

On Palm Sunday, April 9, 1865, wearing his best dressed uniform, Lee waited to meet General Grant at a neutral site in a home not far from where his troops and the Union soldiers were positioned. Accessorized with a red silk sash, a jeweled sword given to him by some woman in England, red stitched boots and a pair of long gray gloves known as gauntlets, he planned to discuss the terms of his surrender but wanted to look his very best if he was to be taken prisoner.

But once General Grant arrived, Lee's freedom never came into question as negotiations between the esteemed adversaries quickly got underway. Humbly, Lee asked for a few simple things such as food for his men and permission for them to keep their horses and firearms.

Grant only agreed to feed them and allow them to have their horses, but the defeated men would have to hand over their weapons. In no position to argue, Lee meekly agreed to the terms and firmly shook hands with Grant before mounting his horse and riding back to his men to personally give them the news.

Three days later, what was left of Lee's army relinquished their weapons and received their paroles, which allowed them all to return back to their homes. The war for the Confederacy was officially lost.

As a result of the Union's victory, celebrations abounded in the northern half of the United States. Parties were planned. Parade routes in Washington, DC, were designated and scheduled to enable the Union to put its victorious armies on display. After overcoming four long years of fighting and shedding blood, there wasn't a soul in the nation's capital that didn't exhale an exhausted sigh of relief.

On Good Friday, April 14, 1865, the temperature steadily dropped as darkness blanketed the evening sky. It was only two days after Robert E. Lee's army surrendered, and the presidential carriage raced through the streets of the nation's capital carrying President Lincoln, the First Lady, and their two invited guest to view a showing of the comedic play "Our American Cousin" that was being performed at Ford's Theatre.

After last-minute cancellations by General Grant and the secretary of war, Edward M. Stanton, the president, hard-pressed to find a guest to accompany him and the First Lady, detoured from their route to pick up Major Henry Rathbone and his fiancée. Now they were running late.

The play had been well underway when they finally arrived at the theatre. On stage, Ms. Kay Hart and E. A. Emmerson were delivering their lines when they caught sight of the president and his party entering the auditorium. The actors immediately began to applaud the chief executive, and almost on cue, the orchestra began to play "Hail to the Chief" as Lincoln and his entourage followed an armed escort to his private box.

Once there, the president uncharacteristically walked over to the rail and graciously bowed for the entire crowd to see. The entire place erupted into a thunderous applause that went on for minutes until Lincoln motioned for everyone to sit down, and the play continued.

Meanwhile, as Lincoln settled into his rocking chair, John Wilkes Booth dismounted his horse in an alley behind the theatre. After securing his horse and checking to make sure his one-shot derringer was cocked and loaded, he placed the gun inside of his pocket and entered the theatre through one of its rear doors.

Inside, Booth had no problem navigating the bowels of the large theatre. And being a seasoned actor known throughout thespian circles, he was greeted with smiles and pleasantries from the actors and stagehands he passed that were patiently waiting for their cues. Ever the actor, he returned their gestures as he crossed the theatre below the stage and emerged on the other side and made his way to the lobby.

Upon entering the lobby, Booth glanced up at the clock and saw that it was nearing 10:30. It was time. The play was in its third act. He took a deep breath and walked toward the stairs that led to the president's box.

With each step that he took up the darkened staircase, Booth fought off the tiny bits of apprehension that he couldn't wash away with whiskey earlier in the evening. But he tossed his misgivings aside remembering the many times that he had gotten so close only to have Lincoln slip through his fingers, realizing that an opportunity like this won't ever come along again. He also thought of the influential men counting on him to complete this mission. Both knew he'd come too far to turn back now. He unsheathed the large bowie knife strapped to his side.

As he held his breath, Booth could actually hear his heart beat while standing behind the door at the top of the stairs that opened into the anteroom of the president's box. He rushed inside after gathering the nerve, in hopes of taking Lincoln's armed escort by surprise. But to Booth's astonishment, the anteroom was empty. Lincoln's guard was gone. Booth returned to his side and drew his derringer.

Inside the president's box, all eyes were glued to the stage as Harry Hawk stood alone delivering a monologue laced with comedic lines. A slight chill in the theatre caused Mary Todd Lincoln to snuggle closely to her husband who sat comfortably with his back to the door, oblivious to the man on the other side.

On stage, Harry Hawk finished his soliloquy, and the entire audience burst into a roaring laughter that filled every corner of the auditorium. This was the moment Booth had been waiting for. He eased open the door to the box and slid inside, finding himself three feet from the back of Abraham Lincoln's head. With the pistol in hand, he extended his arm and squeezed the trigger.

The explosion tore through the laughter as the .44-caliber slug bore deep into the president's brain. Mary Todd Lincoln was the first to scream.

"They've killed him! Oh God, they've killed my husband!" she wailed in absolute horror as her husband lay slumped against the wall.

The shot turned Major Rathbone's head, who, through a thin cloud of smoke, saw Booth standing behind the fallen president. He sprang to his feet and charged at the assassin.

Bowie knife in hand, Booth swung violently at Rathbone's chest when the unarmed man lunged at him. Instinctively, Rathbone threw up an arm, and the blade sliced deep into his skin. Spatters of blood squirted from the wound. The entire audience looked on, stunned in shock and awe at the fracas taking place almost two stories above them.

Booth rushed to the rail and screamed out, "Sic semper tyrannis!"—which, in Latin, meant "Thus always to tyrants." He added, "The South is avenged!" before leaping over the railing to the stage apron twelve feet below. He landed awkwardly on his left knee with bits of the American flag that was draped around the president's box caught in his left boot's spur. The snag on the way down broke his left tibia just above the ankle. The pain was excruciating, but the adrenaline surging through his body quickly got him to his feet.

Booth heard the cries "Stop that man!" and "Don't let him get away!" as he ran across the stage past Harry Hawk, who stood frozen stiff with fear. Backstage, the orchestra leader was returning to the pit when he encountered Booth, who hit him so hard the old man spun around before hitting the ground. No one else impeded Booth and his bowie knife as he hurried to the back alley to retrieve his horse.

It had been less than two minutes since the shot was fired when Booth mounted his horse and charged through the streets of Washington, DC, before crossing the Navy Yard Bridge over the Potomac River into Maryland and disappearing into the night. Despite a nationwide manhunt, he was never seen or heard from again.

Meanwhile, back at Ford's Theatre, a crowd of onlookers and good Samaritans gathered around Abraham Lincoln's body. The president lay still as two physicians that were on hand at the theatre did all that they could to bring life back into the nation's leader. Their efforts were futile; there wasn't much that could be done inside of the crowded theatre, and one of the physicians requested that the president be moved.

An infantry commander who had arrived on the scene ordered four of his men to pick up Abraham Lincoln's long body. Then he drew his sword to clear the crowd standing around in a hushed bewilderment as he led his men through the theatre and over to one of the brownstones directly across the street.

After the president was placed on a bed, Dr. Charles Leale, a young surgeon, dug his fingers inside of the wound in hopes of recovering the bullet lodged behind Lincoln's bulging right eye. The doctor was unsuccessful, and even though the president's vital signs gave off faint readings, his life could not be saved. The deathwatch began.

Throughout the night, a procession of Washington's most respected leaders and politically connected citizens from Vice President Andrew Johnson to Gavin Meade filed in and out of the house to say their final good-bye to Abraham Lincoln and pay respects to Mary Todd Lincoln, who braved the horrific night at her husband's side.

The vigil went on until Abraham Lincoln breathed his final breath at exactly 7:22 in the morning. At the age of fifty-six, the sixteenth president of the United States of America departed from the world, leaving behind a wife, two sons, and the legacy of defeating the Confederacy to end slavery, while taking the sinister designs he had for Azalea with him to the grave.

CHAPTER 9

"Come home" were the only words on the telegram that the messenger had delivered, but Jonathan knew exactly what it meant. He gathered his things together and headed for the carriage waiting to take him back to Azalea. After he settled in for the long ride from Tobias Incorporated's headquarters in Montgomery, Alabama, Jonathan began to reflect on the past ten years that seemed to fly by in a staggering blur.

The Reconstruction began immediately after Abraham Lincoln's death, bringing visionaries to the South from all over the world—all of them wanting a hand in the rebuilding and reshaping of the Southern states' future, as well as their hands on the seemingly unlimited funds that the government had appropriated to see Lincoln's dream of freed slaves reintegrated and functioning equally in a society that held them captive for over two centuries come true.

It was a noble idea, the Reconstruction, but the Civil War left the South in utter chaos. In most areas, anything that wasn't burned to the ground had been bombarded back to the Stone Age and destroyed. And although some had been spared the physical damage of their unfortunate neighbors, everyone was left to deal with life after slavery, which proved to be more devastating than engulfing flames or descending artillery shells.

Loss of slave labor made cotton production less profitable, and whites, who, before the war, swore they would never pick a single boll of cotton were now out in the fields going back on their words. Barely scraping by, most of them were content with just being able to put food on the table and make payments to the government on the fines and back taxes they owed. Without their slaves, they struggled to hold it all together, and they watched helplessly as their once palatial plantations became grossly unkempt and dilapidated. The South never returned to its pre-war affluence again.

The ex-slaves didn't fare much better. With no place to go, many of them wandered the South enduring lynches and other aggressions from disgruntled whites while surviving on meals supplied by a newly formed government agency called the Freedmen's Bureau. Most returned to work for pitying wages at the plantations from which they were freed, content to live under conditions barely above the ones they lived by before the war. Freedom for them had become nothing more than a technical word.

The remarriage between the ex-slaves and their employers proved trying for both sides involved. But it was the cotton-field owners who felt the blunt changes the Civil War brought on the most. After the war, the once regal crop seemed to lose its luster. With wages, no matter how small, being paid to employees who once worked for free, cotton became expensive to grow. And since the mills of the North elected to share the growing transportation expenses with the plantation owners, cotton's profits suffered another damaging blow.

Miraculously, life for Southern growers began to improve when industrialization and the railroad's tentacles spread deeper into the South and efforts were made to establish new enterprises in fields such as textiles, lumbering, and steel. While others in the South prospered from the new innovative ventures, the cotton growers were too stubborn to conform. Instead of evolving, they planted more seeds with hope that "king cotton" would one day retake its throne. It didn't, and since the excess cotton and its decreased demand caused a glut in the market, the industry essentially starved on its own food.

But while arrogance and ignorance caused every cotton grower in the South to starve, the stomachs at Azalea steadily grew.

Immediately after the war, Jonathan took to the road to join in on the Reconstruction, fighting tooth and nail against the carpetbaggers who descended upon the South like a flock of vultures on a mission to pick the remaining meat from a dead animal's bones.

Using his contract with the government to his advantage, Jonathan sold three quarters of his cotton to the Freedmen's Bureau, enabling them to donate clothing and other cotton goods to the legions of displaced ex-slaves. The rest of his inventory was used to garner linen contracts with the many hospitals and hotels that were sprouting up in and around the rebuilding cities of the South.

Although Azalea's cotton quickly sold, Jonathan wasn't anywhere near done. Refusing to rest on his laurels, he devised ways to increase Azalea's already substantial profits while other plantations in the South struggled just to break even.

Every year following the harvest, the ginning of Azalea's cotton left the plantation with billions of leftover cotton seeds—seeds that, in the past, were sold to oil mills to be compressed into cottonseed oil. But in the years following the war, Jonathan had an oil mill constructed in hopes of producing the high-quality oil on his own. It was only during this process that it was discovered that attached to the seeds were tiny cotton fibers, called linter, that escaped the ginning machine. Initially considered worthless, linter was discarded with the rest of the mill's waste, and it wasn't until a routine inspection of the plant did Jonathan recognize the potential for the hairs to be sold.

While leaving the oil mill, Jonathan noticed a row of waste bins full of linter being pushed to the facility's dumping site. Drawn to the material's fluffiness, Jonathan reached into one of the bins and took out a handful. And after squeezing the linter into a tight ball, he was impressed with its softness and ability to retake its shape. He ordered all of the bins to be put away for storage.

Jonathan wasted no time in finding suitable buyers, travelling to the major furniture manufacturers of the North with samples of linter and returning to Azalea with lucrative contracts promising the delivery of bulk quantities of it to their factories to be used as padding for mattresses, chairs, pillows, and sofas.

Realizing that Azalea's profits would increase by developing as many by-products of cotton that could be found, Jonathan hired the most knowledgeable scientist of the era to prod and stretch the cottonseed to its limits; an innovative idea that paid dividends when they discovered that oil could still be extracted from the seed after removing its hull. Hull combined with the seed meal left over from the oil extraction created a premium quality animal feed that Jonathan packaged and sold to the United States cavalry. He was turning garbage into gold.

In time, his crack team of scientists and engineers discovered that with chemical treatment, cottonseed oil became a major component in the manufacture of paints, cosmetics, detergents, and soaps. The breakthroughs prompted Jonathan to broker deals with railroad and freight companies to deliver his goods to farms and factories around the nation. It wasn't long before Tobias Incorporated became a force to be reckoned with in other enterprises, as well as the one that had dominated the cotton industry for so many years.

As the Tobias empire consistently grew into one of the most sought-after businesses in America, Jonathan understood that the well-being of his company would be better served if he set up headquarters far away from Azalea's cotton fields. Rightfully so, he didn't want to risk anyone accidentally stumbling onto his most valuable asset and the secret behind Tobias Incorporated's success: slaves.

In 1870, Jonathan purchased a four-story limestone building in Montgomery, Alabama's business district and, as a testament to his success, appointed it with furniture and fixtures made from the finest materials in the world. He christened it the Tobias Cotton Emporium, making the entire third floor his office while using the fourth as an apartment for the nights when he couldn't make it back to Azalea. The first and second floors were occupied by the staff of executives and agents that Jonathan meticulously hired to represent the growing facets of Tobias Incorporated.

Jonathan's employees spread out like weeds, aggressively marketing Azalea's commodities to an array of businesses around the entire country. And with the advent of telegraphic lines linking Europe through Morse code with the United States, in five short years, the Tobias Cotton Emporium became the nerve center that helped turn Tobias Incorporated into a multinational conglomerate that Jonathan autonomously controlled.

As Jonathan's carriage rolled past the iron gates of Azalea, his body began to slightly tremble when a foreboding tragic notion entered his brain. It was an intuition he'd been steadily fighting off for the past year while preparing for this day. Jonathan prayed that he wasn't too late when he exited the carriage and was greeted by an overcast sky and his two teary-eyed sons.

"Jack, Tommy, where's your mother?" he asked after giving them both a tight embrace.

"She's inside with Grandpa," Tommy replied between sniffles.

"He's not doing too good," Jackson said as he locked eyes with his father.

"I know, son," Jonathan said while throwing his arms around their broad shoulders as they somberly walked into the house.

Inside, Jonathan could feel the dourness lingering in the air as only a few candles burned inside of the chandeliers, leaving the mansion a dimly lit residence of gloom. Gus McMiller and a small group of field bosses were huddling quietly in the living room after paying respects to their old friend and one-time leader. Jonathan gave them a stoic nod while making his way toward his father's room, steeling himself for what awaited on the other side of Jonas's door.

Slowly, he eased open the door to find Debra and his young daughter, Lucy, sitting wistfully at his father's bedside. In contrast to the rest of the mansion, every candle and lamp burned brightly in the room in an attempt to keep Jonas awake and attentive during his last days on earth. Jonathan and his sons entered the room.

"Daddy!" the five-year-old yelled when she saw her father. Excitedly, Lucy ran over to Jonathan and jumped into his awaiting arms. With a forced smile, he held her high above his head. "Pa Pa's sick!" she said ingenuously, and at that precise moment, Jonas began to cough and shiver spasmodically, prompting Jonathan to put her down and send all the children out of the room.

Debra, pregnant with their fourth child, got up from the rocker that was placed next to Jonas's bed. "You need to be here alone," she said before leaning over and stamping a kiss on her father-in-law's forehead. She squeezed Jonathan's hand and gave him a supportive kiss before leaving the two of them alone.

When Debra closed the door, Jonas's labored breathing enveloped the room. Jonathan inched closer to the bed. He looked down on his father, who, for the last twelve months, had been bedridden with lung disease, and the sight instantly brought tears to his eyes.

Even though he was covered from the chest down, Jonathan could see that the gaunt figure lying beneath the blankets matched perfectly with the protruding cheekbones on Jonas's sunken face. Jonas's flesh was so taut it looked as though at any moment, the sharp cheekbones would burst through his skin. His fate was sealed. The cancer was eating him alive. He let out another series of violent coughs.

Jonathan sat down and wiped the remaining strands of hair that Jonas had left away from his face. "Dad, I'm right here beside you," he said softly, and after a brief flutter of the lid, Jonas opened up his one good eye.

"Don't be sheddin' no damn tears over me, boy," Jonas struggled to say before coughing up a glob of blood and phlegm.

"Yessir," Jonathan rigidly replied in an effort to echo his father's unflinching bravery.

"I've lived a long and good life, Jon. I can't go on sufferin' like this. Besides, your mother has been waitin' on me to join her for forty-seven years. And I've been waitin' just as long to see my sweet Cecilia again."

Jonathan slowly shook his head. He couldn't believe what he was hearing, and he couldn't believe that this was the end. Jonathan struggled to fight back a wave of tears. "Dad . . . I . . . I can't imagine my life without you."

Painfully, Jonas tried to heave a sigh; instead, he produced another agonizing hem. "It's too late to worry yourself over me. You have your own family to look after now, especially them two boys," Jonas said, remarking about Jonathan's inseparable ten- and twelve-year-olds. "You've become for them what I once was for you and Claude. Only you've done much better with them. I won't even speak on the work you've done for this plantation except to say that because of you, I can die a fulfilled man," he added as he began to shudder violently as his eyes gushed forth with tears.

"Dad!" Jonathan sobbed while reaching out for his father, who responded by firmly gripping Jonathan's arm. As Jonas struggled to hold on, Jonathan could see the beads of perspiration on his father's face gradually morph into intense drips of sweat. "Daddy, wait!"

Jonas's right arm quivered while using all of his might to pull Jonathan closer to him. "I've held on for far too long," he struggled to say, choking in an attempt to gasp for air. His eyes blinked sporadically before locking onto Jonathan's face for one last father-to-son stare. "Son . . . it's time for me to let go." Slowly, Jonas exhaled his final breath then his body went limp. He was gone.

"Dad . . . Dad," Jonathan said as he began to shake his father frantically, only to grow more and more distraught when Jonas failed to respond. "Dad, wake up, please!" he added while crying and shaking Jonas wildly, causing his lifeless body to flail like a rag doll in Jonathan's arms.

Upon hearing the commotion, Gus stormed into the room and placed a firm grip on Jonathan's shoulder. "Jonny, come on son, look at what you are doing. Your daddy's gone now, let 'im go," he said in a soothing tone.

"He's dead, Gus."

"I know, Jon. I know," Gus replied with moistened eyes. "It was time. He don't have to suffer no more. Let me take care of him now," he added while easing Jonas out of Jonathan's arms. He gently placed Jonas back on the bed and pulled the blanket up around his neck as though he was tucking his old friend in for a good night's sleep as he had done for Jonas so many times before.

He turned to Jonathan, who sat on the edge of the bed with his face buried in his palms. Again, Gus laid a comforting hand on Jonathan's shoulder. "Jonny, I want you to stand up and look me in the face," he said sternly, and Jonathan rose to his feet and looked Gus square in the eyes. "That's better. Now listen. Jonas was one hell of a man, and he lived one hell of a life. And he wouldn't want anybody cryin' or upholdin' some kind of sadness over him. He would want us all to move on. And that's what I'm asking you to do."

Jonathan furrowed his brow in confusion, and Gus continued. "I'm not telling you to forget about him, and the good Lord above knows we couldn't if we tried. He left a little piece of himself with all of us. But the biggest chunk of all, his strength, courage, leadership, and wisdom, went to you. You did your cryin'. Now it's time for you to pull it together, and be the rock for this family that you were bred to be. Anything less would be a disgrace to your daddy's legacy."

Suddenly, the muscles in Jonathan's back began to stiffen, and he stood upright after realizing that Gus was telling him the truth. The old horse was right. Jonas had been preparing him for this day for years, and he wouldn't want him wallowing in grief now that he was gone. Jonathan cleared his throat and wiped the remaining tears from his eyes.

"I guess it's all on me now," Jonathan said nodding his head confidently.

"Jonny, it's been all on you for years. Your daddy's passing ain't no reason to stray from the road you're on. He wouldn't want it, and I know you don't want that either. Your family's out there hurtin', son," Gus said while pointing at the door. "You're the head of this house-hold, and you need to be showin' them how to be strong like you."

"I know," Jonathan said before exhaling the deep breath he was holding in. "I'm going to go be with them," he added while stealing quick glances at his father.

"Go on ahead. They need you. And don't worry, I'm going to take good care of him," Gus said reassuringly after noticing Jonathan's darting eyes.

Jonathan reached out to Gus and pulled him close and wrapped his long arms around him. Momentarily locked in a bear hug, neither man said a word as the anguish passed between them, both know-ing that this would be their last opportunity to openly mourn. After both men felt as though they let it all out, they let go, and Jonathan headed for the door.

"Gus?" Jonathan called out to the old boss who had begun to smother the lamps.

"What?" he replied.

"Thanks," Jonathan said graciously.

"Aww, go on and get outta here, boy," Gus said with a dismissive wave, and Jonathan exited the room.

Gus McMiller displayed an incredible amount of stoicism as he found the strength to console Jonathan and convince him to comfort his family while in the presence of his dead best friend, a man he'd known his entire life and who he considered to be closer than a blood brother.

But that stoicism quickly disappeared when the bedroom door had closed, ensuring him that no one would see the mess he would become now that he was left alone with Jonas's lifeless body. He began to sob and hiccup uncontrollably while struggling to blow out the rest of the candles that were still illuminating the room. Once he finished, Gus spent the rest of the evening in the rocker next to the bed, quietly wailing in the darkness, grappling with the reality that Jonas was really gone.

Two days later, after a private service attended by only his family and a small group of field bosses and hands, Jonas was interred at the family cemetery along with his wife, father, mother, sisters, and brothers. As the morning sun burned brightly in the sky, the tiny crowd gathered around the large rectangular hole that was dug into the ground. Since no one was allowed to shed a tear or sob, there wasn't a peep as, one by one, each person in attendance stepped forward and threw a white carnation onto the mahogany casket lying six feet below. Everyone who passed by Jonathan and his family gave them a consoling nod and went on their way.

Following the burial, everyone communed back at the mansion where a mountain of food had been prepared. Jonathan sat quietly in the living room and listened as guests ate and drank while telling many tales of how Jonas uniquely touched their lives. He looked at the group of men who attended, all weathered employees of Azalea in some form or fashion, and became visibly upset. He couldn't stand to be around them any longer, so he excused himself from the room.

"What's the matter, Jon?" Debra asked after he burst into their bedroom and slammed the door. She had been lying in bed, resting her back after being on her feet most of the morning. Her right hand was lightly massaging her belly; the pregnancy was almost to term.

"It's this place," Jonathan said frustratingly. "It's like a prison. We have to get away from here."

"Oh, honey, what do you mean?" Debra asked with a strained look on her face.

"Azalea's no place for us anymore. We have to leave," Jonathan said as he undid the top buttons of his shirt. Even his clothing had begun to feel confining.

"Why, Jon? Azalea's beautiful."

"Yeah, it is, but what else is it good for? This is not our home anymore. It's a machine like those other factories that I built. Because of those slaves, no one is allowed within miles of here. My daddy was a pioneer who once ruled our trade. He had friends who respected him from all over, but not a single person who lives outside of those borders could've attended his funeral. That's a disgrace."

Jonathan exhaled before continuing. "I feel trapped here, and I don't want my funeral to be that way when it's my turn to go," he said vehemently.

"Well, then where, Jon?" she asked him impatiently. "Tell me where you would like for us to go."

For a moment, Jonathan said nothing. He just tilted his head toward the ceiling and thought. His mind took him to a faraway place where his children could grow up without being secluded, and receive their education from the most prestigious academies alongside children whose families' illustrious legacies flowed through their young veins; a place that was considered the pounding pulse for all of the commerce in the nation. A place where Jonathan could rub elbows with the likes of John D. Rockefeller, Andrew Carnegie, J. Pierpoint Morgan, and other titans of finance and industry.

"New York," Jonathan said confidently.

"New York!" Debra replied with wide eyes. "Jon, that's the city where they say the mothers eat their young."

"Oh, Debra, please," Jonathan said dismissively. "That's just old Southern folk talk."

"What in God's name are we going to do there?"

Jonathan gently laid a hand on her belly. He began to slowly rub in small circles. "We are going to live our lives the way it's supposed to be. I'm going to usher Tobias Incorporated into the next century. Our children are going to get the best schooling available. And you, my dear, are going to host grand parties at our home every other week if you wish." Jonathan's voice dripped with unbridled enthusiasm.

Debra grinned at his response. As reluctant as she tried to be initially, even she found New York's gravitational pull impossible to resist. The largest city in America, New York was a cultural melting pot brimming with possibilities. Her eyes met her stomach. "Jon, I want to have this child before we leave."

Jonathan smiled widely, showing all of his teeth. "Anything you want. I just wanted to make sure you were all right with moving away with me."

"Jon, I can't believe you just said that. I love you with all of my heart, and I would follow you to the ends of the earth."

Jonathan sidled up next to Debra and gave her lips a passionate kiss. "I love you too, Debra. I love you too," he said with warmth and sincerity. For the rest of the afternoon, he held her tightly in his arms until they both drifted off to sleep.

In the spring of 1877, almost two years to the day after Jonas's death, Jonathan moved his family into a brownstone mansion in Manhattan's tony Upper East Side, exchanging their views of Azalea's gardens and evergreen landscapes for New York City's jungle of concrete, steel, and streets made of cobblestone.

Protected by eight-foot wrought iron fences, the four-story mansion was nestled along a tree-lined oasis of Fifty-Third Street, just a block away from the hustle and bustle of Fifth Avenue. Though majestic and garlanded with ivy, the home didn't openly announce the Tobias's wealth like the gaudier mansions sprinkled throughout Manhattan that belonged to its old blue-blooded aristocracy. But inside, 19 West Fifty-Third boasted every amenity that a mogul of the "gilded age" could afford.

Marble floors greeted visitors at the entranceway and led them into the living area where plush Persian carpets stretched to the four corners of the elegantly decorated room. The staircase, also made of marble, spiraled in a subtle oval four flights up to the floor; and if ever the Tobiases opted to forgo the walk up the steps, they could ride in their elevator—which was one of the first to be installed in private homes.

Tables—polished to almost a mirror finish, chairs—wooden, rococo, or overstuffed leather; Jonathan had custom furniture made by the world's finest crafters imported from all over the globe. Silk wallpaper ran from the floors up to the ceilings from which silver and gilt chandeliers were hung. Every available corner in a room or spot on a wall was taken up by valuable ornaments or expensive pieces of artwork. Jonathan spared no expense in making sure their home was as precious as a museum's most prized exhibit.

He paid the same attention to detail when it came to his children's education, immediately enrolling Jackson and Thomas into the prestigious Cutler School. With the student body including names like Milbank, Rockefeller, Vanderbilt, and Bliss, the school's roll call read off like a who's-who list of New York City's elite. Lucy attended the Rye School for Young Ladies along with other little girls of her ilk. Only Jonathan Jr., who wasn't yet two years old, had the distinct pleasure of being in Debra's company as she prowled the furriers and clothing boutiques that were lined up and down Fifth Avenue every day. For a young woman with unlimited funds, New York City made the perfect fit.

That year, the Tobiases weren't the only family to relocate from Alabama to New York City. When Jonathan moved from Azalea, he brought the Tobias Cotton Emporium along with him. Sometimes he even waited at the train station to welcome his staff and their families once they arrived. Most of them were from the South, and Jonathan wanted to put them at ease as they made the transition from the country to the nation's largest city. He also put them up in New York's finest hotels until they were able to move into their new homes.

And even though Jonathan spent a ton of money on his house in Manhattan plus the expenses he paid to move his entire staff to New York, none of it would rival the amount he used for his grandest purchase.

After haggling with real estate brokers in the year prior to moving, Jonathan paid slightly over a million dollars for his corporation's new headquarters. An elaborate display of neoclassical architecture, the new Cotton Emporium towered eleven stories into the sky and cast an enormous shadow over Manhattan's business district. The massive building officially announced Jonathan's arrival to New York and gave warning to its moguls that a new player had now moved onto the block, and he was here to stay.

Most of the gawkers who travelled south down Broadway Avenue in those days were in awe at the sight of Jonathan's skyscraper, but the intimidating erection of granite and glass belied the harmony that was commonplace behind Tobias Incorporated's new fortress's walls. Any nonemployee lucky enough to get past the guards watching the front doors would find a dignified environment with many employees gathered around endless rows of mahogany rolltop desks conferring in hushed tones; even their footsteps were muted by the wall-to-wall maroon carpets that blanketed every floor. The decorum at the Cotton Emporium could have been compared to the most religious of sanctuaries except the only deity worshipped here happened to be the almighty dollar.

After an eleven-story ride up the elevator and a fifty-foot walk down a marble corridor would one come in contract with a pair of imposing eight-foot high arced double doors. They opened directly into Jonathan's office, and it was the only one that resided on the eleventh floor. Like a marionette puppeteer, he preferred to be seated alone at the very top of the empire he cultivated manipulating the strings.

Taking up two-thirds of the entire floor and unlike any other magnates of the era, Jonathan's office contained the barest of essentials. Only a broad desk made from shining black walnut faced the entrance, and a long matching conference table surrounded by large black leather chairs for each of his department heads furnished the enormous room. He wanted nothing fancy in his office that could serve as a distraction to the strategic meetings that were held there at the end of every work day.

The only distraction Jonathan welcomed came from the row of windows behind his desk that offered panoramic views of downtown Manhattan and New York Harbor. The sight was a constant reminder to the collection of men in the room that they were now sitting on top of the world.

The view also reminded them all of the long descent to the bottom, and if any man there couldn't keep up with the rest of the group, the bottom is where he would be. To Jonathan's delight, the unspoken threat kept Tobias Incorporated's executives on their toes at all times and the day-to-day operations at the Cotton Emporium running as smooth as a well-oiled machine.

During the last quarter of the nineteenth century, the United States transformed from a country of farms, small towns, and modest manufacturing into a modern nation dominated by large cities and state-of-the-art factories. And Tobias Incorporated was one of the many companies at the forefront, riding the surging waves of change.

By the year 1890, it became nearly impossible to find an article of clothing or any products made from materials that didn't come from a distribution warehouse bearing Jonathan's last name. Like Rockefeller in oil and Carnegie with steel, the name Tobias became synonymous with cotton and the textile industry. And just like his counterparts in the oil and steel industries, the casual mentioning of Jonathan's name caused his competitors to tremble with fear.

Their fear accompanied the knowledge that they were stuck in a field in which they could no longer compete and that Jonathan could come for everything they had anytime he pleased. But with the new antitrust laws barring monopolies essentially looking over Jonathan's shoulder, his competitors were given a reprieve. They survived on the crumbs Jonathan purposely left on the table. For now, they were safe.

A few years past the age of sixty, Jonathan realized the company would have to change hands one day. So with his stranglehold on the industry firmly intact, he was able to use his time to focus on Tobias Incorporated's future.

At a time when young men of their prestige and age were either chasing skirts or hamming it up with each other at New York's premier country and yacht clubs, Jonathan's sons shunned the playboy lifestyle, choosing to absorb his seemingly infinite knowledge like a pair of thirsty sponges instead.

After graduating magna cum laude from Brown University, both Jackson and Thomas could be found every day at the Cotton Emporium riding the backs of their father's heels. Since moving to New York as adolescents, they were almost permanent fixtures inside of the building, but now as the future heirs to the Tobias empire, they shadowed Jonathan at every meeting, acquisition, and major transaction, wanting to get a firsthand look at how their father wielded his control.

Having witnessed his company's growth from just a raw-cotton exporter into a multimillion-dollar corporate machine, Jonathan carefully monitored Jackson and Thomas as well. With more than just the family's legacy at stake, he stayed very close to his eldest sons to make sure they avoided the same pitfalls that befell him and Claude.

To Jonathan's satisfaction, no matter what kind of test he threw in their direction, Jackson and Thomas passed with flying colors, proving that nothing—no amount of money or the promise of sole control—could come between their unwavering brotherly love. It was time for the three of them to embark on a very important journey.

"Where are we going?" Thomas asked his father as he plopped down into his seat.

"You'll know soon enough, Tommy," Jonathan said as he sat back in his plush leather chair. They were at Grand Central Station, sitting in the observatory room of Jonathan's private railroad car waiting for Jackson to arrive.

Owning a private railroad car was the premium mode of travel for the rich at the turn of the nineteenth century. And Jonathan's car came outfitted with a kitchen, pantry, private office, three very cozy staterooms, an observatory room for gazing at the passing countryside, and a host of amenities. He even had a personal porter to attend to his every need.

A few moments later, Jackson entered the observatory and took a seat next to Thomas and faced his father. Jonathan looked at his sons and felt like he was seeing double. All of them could have been considered dead ringers for one another except that Jonathan's head of curls had long ago turned gray.

"Dad, what's going on? They told me at the office that you wanted me to come here," Jackson asked with a hint of concern in his voice.

Suddenly, the locomotive's whistle blew, and the train began to move. While Jackson and Thomas turned to each other with startled eyes, Jonathan remained at ease. He marveled at how their curiosities worked exactly the same. As their faces began to contort with confused looks, Jonathan's lips creased into a mischievous grin, knowing that it wouldn't be long before his boys knew the absolute truth.

There was a knock on the door, and Jonathan's porter entered the room carefully balancing a sterling silver tray loaded with jams, a plate full of biscuits, and three steaming mugs of chamomile tea. "Mr. Tobias, we're on our way now. Is there anything else that I can do for you sir?" the porter asked after placing the tray on the table between them.

"Everything is fine, Cole. Right now my sons and I don't wish to be disturbed. I'll call for you if we need anything," Jonathan replied.

"Yes, sir, Mr. Tobias, sir. Just ring the bell and I'll be here," the porter said before quickly disappearing.

As the train crossed the Verrazano Bridge into New Jersey, New York's majestic skyline became more difficult for Jackson and Thomas to see. And after realizing that they weren't going anywhere for a while, they both settled deeper into their seats. Jonathan took a careful sip of his herbal tea then cleared his throat to speak.

"Boys, when I look at the two of you together, I swell with pride. It reminds me of how much me and my brother could never get along. All I wanted was the best for our family, and all he wanted was total control. I thank God every day that the two of you haven't travelled down that same road." Again, the brothers gave each other a strange look because for as long as they could remember, no one in their family had ever made any mention of Claude.

Jonathan continued. "I understand you're confused. There's a lot that you don't know. But I promise by the time you reach our destination, the two of you will know it all."

"Where exactly is the destination?" Jackson asked.

"Azalea," Jonathan answered quickly.

Thomas's eyes widened. "Azalea? We haven't been there since we were kids. In fact, we haven't been back since we've moved to New York. Why are we going back there now?"

Jonathan leaned forward and looked Thomas directly in the eyes, and then he turned his gaze toward his eldest son. "I spent twenty-nine years running the corporation. I wish I could run it for another twenty-nine years, but I'm getting tired. And it's time that I hand over the reins. I truly believe you both have exactly what it takes to lead Tobias Incorporated well into the next century. I also believe that if you don't know where you've come from, you'll never know the right direction in which you should go.

"For good reason, I kept you both from Azalea all of these years, mainly because you were too young to understand or handle the severity of what's going on there. But now there would be no way the two of you could ever manage the corporation without knowing the complete truth." Jonathan paused to get another swig of tea.

As the speeding train swayed from side to side, and the scent of chamomile filled his nostrils, Jonathan remembered the similar train ride he took three decades earlier, a ride that forever changed his life. He knew that after making the facts surrounding Azalea known to his sons, their lives would never again be the same.

Jonathan put down his mug and saw that Jackson and Thomas were still hanging on to his last words. They were intrigued, and the impatient looks on their faces openly announced that they were waiting for him to tell them more.

After stealing a quick glance at the rolling hills and green meadows going by, Jonathan took a deep breath and slowly closed his eyes. Methodically, he mentally rolled back the hands of time. And when he found the exact spot on the timeline where he wanted to be, Jonathan opened his eyes and coolly began to speak.

"It all began in the year 1859 during what seemed like the coldest winter in years . . ."

BOOK TWO

CHAPTER 10

"I want to see it!"

They were the only words Jonathan managed to say, partially paralyzed by the story his father had just told him, stuck in the gray area that bordered between wonderment and disbelief.

Meanwhile, Jackson said nothing, opting to sit back in his chair and let the crux of the information he had just divulged weigh in on Jonathan instead. Carefully, he observed his son.

Jonathan glanced at his A. Lange & Söhne and saw the hands approaching 5:00 p.m. A whole seven hours had passed since the earlier meeting. They were still alone in the boardroom, and nothing had changed except for the entrees of food on the table between them, Jackson's had long ago disappeared but Jonathan's went untouched.

Jonathan leaned in close to his father. "Dad, do you realize what you've just told me? Tobias Incorporated has a secret workforce consisting of slaves. Not in Asia, not in Africa, not even in Mexico, but right here in the fuckin' US?"

"Yeah, son, that's correct," Jackson said while slowly nodding his head.

"Holy shit." Jonathan muttered as he slumped farther down into his chair. "Everything you've said sounds so surreal. It's not that I don't believe you, I just have to see it for myself."

"You need to," Jackson concurred. "There's no other way you could digest this without seeing it first. Come with me," he added as he rose from his seat.

Jonathan quickly got up and followed his father out of the boardroom and into Jackson's office across the hall. The soles of his oxfords scraped against the marble floor as he scurried to keep up with Jackson's pace.

Exquisitely decorated in black and gold, the cavernous office was an elegant but intimidating reflection of the man who resided there. For years, institutions such as Forbes, Fortune 500, and Standard & Poor continuously rained their praises down on Jack Tobias, and plaques and trophies representing his many accomplishments could be seen everywhere in the room.

A hidden door had been located directly between a pair of glass display cases, and if one didn't know about it, they would have easily mistaken it for a wall. Having frequented his father's office since childhood, Jonathan was one of the few people on earth who knew it opened into a dimly lit corridor. There was a door at each end of the hallway; one led to Jackson's personal elevator, and the other opened into his private suite. Neither man said a word as they rode up twenty stories to the roof.

When the Tobiases first migrated to New York in the late nineteenth century, travelling the streets in the evening had been a fairly easy feat. But now in the year 2007, trying to navigate the Manhattan gridlock during rush hour could force the most seasoned limousine driver to the brink of insanity. Fortunately, because of the advent of the helicopter, the Tobiases were able to avoid a major inconvenience that plagued the city's common fold between 5:00 and 7:00 p.m. each day.

Jackson and Jonathan exited the elevator, and the whining sound of the helicopter's idling engines filled their ears, and a rush of wind smacked them both in the face. At sixty stories high, the air atop the Tobias Tower was cool and crisp on any day, but it became a bit unbearable whenever it got whipped around by spinning copter blades.

The copilot held the door for them as they climbed inside and hopped into seats across from each other. Seconds later, they were floating seamlessly over New York's mountainous skyline. The nine-mile jaunt ended quickly as the helicopter prepared to touch down at Teterboro Airport across the Hudson River in northern New Jersey.

From Jonathan's window, he could see the long line of limousines filing in and out of the labyrinth of terminals and hangars. Airport to the very rich and important, Teterboro's hangars housed scores of expensive private jets and airplanes.

Once the helicopter landed, an all-black Lincoln Town Car was there at the pad to take them directly to their plane, and after a short drive, the car pulled onto Teterboro's longest runway. When Jackson and Jonathan stepped out of the car, White Gold One was there with the presence of a gigantic iron eagle eager to challenge the awaiting skies.

With a price tag of forty million dollars, the Gulfstream G7 was equipped to take a Tobias Incorporated executive anywhere in the world. It was the best private jet money could buy, and they owned a few of them. Jonathan followed his father aboard the jet where they were immediately ushered to their seats and buckled in by a platinum blond stewardess with hourglass curves. The plane began to taxi the runway.

"Meestir Jack, I will take care of all of your needs once we are in thee sky," she said in her heavy eastern European accent while flashing a friendly smile.

"Mr. Tobias, we're cleared for takeoff," the captain announced over the intercom as the jet began to pick up speed. The stewardess placed a satin pillow behind their heads before strapping into her seat.

Gravity forced Jonathan deeper into his seat as the jet quickly ascended into the sky. He closed his eyes and thought hard about everything his father had told him earlier, the past treachery and current tyranny that had been a closely guarded secret until today. Mentally, he tried to paint a picture of what Azalea would look like and envisioned a sadistic scenario of exhausted slaves being whipped and bound in chains. Somehow, the twisted thought brought a smile to his boyish face.

A soft chime on the intercom system signaling that they were now at cruising altitude brought Jonathan back to reality. He looked across the aisle at his father, who was having more than his seat belt unfastened, and shook his head.

Jackson felt Jonathan watching him and removed his hand from the stewardess's sumptuous thigh. "Ilsa, that'll be all for now. Go wait for me and I'll be with you shortly," he said before giving her a light slap on her ass.

"Okay, Meestir Jack," she giggled as she made her way back toward the jet's miniature suite.

Jonathan watched her saunter down the aisle until she disappeared behind a door in the rear. He turned to his father with a sinister smile. "Jesus, where did she come from? Dad, you go through more stewardesses than Delta and American Airlines combined."

"Jon, the closer you get to my age, you'll realize that variety is the spice of life," Jackson said as he loosened his tie. "Plus there's an unwritten rule that every man should fuck his stewardesses. The plane could go down at any moment, but at least you'll die happy. Don't tell your mother I said that," he added with a wry grin of his own.

Jonathan studied his father's face. Fifty-eight years on earth, thirty of them spent at the helm of the corporation, and he still managed to maintain a firm hold on his youth. As the unchallenged ruler of the cotton industry, Jackson Tobias III and his ilk lived exceptional lives, and now Jonathan knew exactly why.

"Speaking of Mother, does she know anything about where we're going?" Jonathan asked candidly.

Jackson's eyes widened a bit. "Absolutely not. She doesn't have a clue. Women are impulsive and emotional beings. They tend to say and do things they'll usually come to regret. The only woman to have ever known the truth about Azalea and our family was your great-great-grandmother. I don't have to tell you to keep what you've learned today and what you're about to see under lock and key."

"I still can't believe all of this," Jonathan said. He could barely contain his excitement, evidenced by the erection in his pants. "You had to feel the same way when grandfather told you about all of this."

Jackson reflectively stroked the side of his face. "Times were different then. I was barely into my teens when your grandfather brought me in. Blacks didn't have the voice in society that they have now. I didn't know any of them as you probably do, so when I learned of Azalea, I was quite numb. I was young and impressionable, and your grandfather explained to me that this was the way things had to be done. I never questioned his morals, and the older I became, I knew he was right."

"But you were just a kid. It must have been impossible to grasp everything you've told me. Shit, I'm a thirty-one-year-old Yalie, and I'm struggling with it."

"Oh, I didn't say it was easy. I didn't have the luxury of your grandfather explaining everything to me first. He was a strange man. Out of the blue, he took me there and let me see what was happening for myself. Gradually, I picked up on the history as time went on," Jackson said as he pondered his childhood.

"After all of these years, why now? Why am I learning about all of this now?" Jonathan asked pointedly. "Why didn't you bring me here as a child?"

Jackson rotated his ostrich-covered captain's chair in Jonathan's direction and looked him in the eyes. "Listen closely, this isn't for the faint of heart, and it's definitely not a place for kids. I had to watch and wait to see what kind of man you'd grow up to be. The only reason you're here today is because you've finally proved yourself to be worthy enough to see what you are about to see."

Jackson paused and impatiently looked toward the rear of the cabin, knowing what was waiting for him in bed. "Jon, get yourself a drink and relax. We'll be landing in a few hours, and we can pick up the conversation then," he added before getting up and leaving Jonathan alone in his seat.

As Jonathan sat there quietly, the list of questions he compiled for his father continued to grow inside of his head. Who else knew about Azalea? How in these days of modern surveillance do they manage to keep this obviously inhumane operation a secret? Is all of this really worth the trouble?

After looking out of the window and realizing that he wouldn't find any answers in the passing clouds, Jonathan decided to take his father's advice. He went over to the wet bar and poured himself three fingers of Johnnie Walker Black Label.

Furtively, Jonathan trained his eyes toward the rear of the cabin as he reached inside his jacket pocket and pulled out a tiny pill bottle containing twenty-five tablets of eighty-milligram OxyContin. He shook three of them into the palm of his hand before slowly walking to the rear and placing his ear against the door. Through the polished maple, Jonathan could hear the faint sound of Ilsa giggling and shook his head in disgust at the way his father flaunted his affairs in front of him.

Jonathan hurried back to the bar, popped the pills, and began to chew. Afterward, he slammed back the tumbler of scotch to rid his mouth of the medicinal taste. Within seconds, he felt a warm tingly sensation all over his body as the powerful opioid coursed through his veins. His eyelids became heavy, and Jonathan headed back to his seat. And with the world beginning to slow down around him, Jonathan pressed the recline button on the armrest and embarked on a journey he took at least three times a day.

Approximately three hours later, White Gold One landed safely at Tobias Incorporated's private airfield in central Alabama just as the sun began its decent. As the jet slowly taxied toward the hangars, Jonathan got a firsthand look at his company's extensive fleet of cargo planes. Emblazoned with the Tobias logo, an inverted triangle with a gothic letter *T* inside, on their tailfins, the behemoth C-130s raced down separate runways in a quest to deliver Tobias Incorporated's commodities around the globe.

Once the plane was securely docked inside one of the smaller hangars, Jonathan and his father followed the stewardess out of the plane, and they immediately noticed another Gulfstream G7 that was identical to theirs.

"Your uncle's here," Jackson said nonchalantly before his son could even ask.

Jonathan responded with a bemused look; his father was obviously a man full of surprises. He followed Jackson out of the hangar and into an awaiting SUV. During the silent ride from the airfield, all around them were open cotton fields stretching as far as the eye could see. Clearly, they weren't in New York anymore, now in the midst of what was known around the corporation as Cotton City.

With a radius of more than twenty-five miles, Cotton City was Tobias Incorporated's largest industrial complex in the nation. And with its round-the-clock workforce of forty-five hundred dedicated employees, it was the main employer to the three towns that surrounded it. Products for nearly every division of the corporation had been researched, developed, and mass-produced on its eastern outskirts inside a massive cluster of laboratories and factories. The rest of Cotton City was made up of cotton fields protected by an eighteen-foot-high electrified fence.

The SUV rolled past the facilities and didn't stop for another dozen or so miles until it reached the entrance of a privately accessed road. Two men in black suits watched from inside of a booth as the truck slowly approached the gate.

The submachine guns draped around their shoulders announced that they were there to ensure that no one without access could get inside. The driver slid his identification card through a reader and pressed his thumb against a fingerprint scanner and waited. Once the computer screen inside of the booth indicated that the driver had clearance, the gate slowly rolled back allowing them to enter.

Now inside of the perimeter, they rode on for miles. Jonathan turned to his left and to his right and saw nothing but cotton. He even looked out of the rear window and noticed that the assemblage of buildings they passed along the main road had now disappeared.

"This fucking place is huge," Jonathan thought aloud.

"You haven't seen anything," Jackson flatly replied.

They rode on for another mile and came to a stop at another eighteen-foot-high fence. The difference between this one and the fence that surrounded the entire complex was this one was hidden behind a wall of trees. Big trees, white oaks with broad trunks, towered up into the sky over seventy-five feet, signifying that they'd been there for years. Like an army's front line, they stretched along the fences perimeter in either direction.

A chill shot up Jonathan's spine when he realized the trees' true meaning. He was here, right outside of Azalea, and these were the very same trees that bore the symbol that kept the Union forces away. The story wasn't a lie.

There was another security booth at this entrance, and the card swiping and thumb print analysis was repeated again. The gate slid open, and the SUV slowly rolled inside. As they rode through a phalanx of trees, Jonathan's Blackberry began to ring. He pulled the phone from his belt clip and saw the name *Fels* flashing on the screen.

"Don't answer it!" Jackson said quickly.

"What?" Jonathan asked curiously.

"Don't answer that call," Jackson said sternly. "Make no contact with the outside world on any electronic devices while you're in here."

"Why?"

"Plausible deniability. You don't want anyone ever placing you here at any time." The phone kept ringing. "Turn it off," Jackson added to his son, who quickly complied.

By now, the SUV had just gotten past the extensive growth of oak and buttonwood trees. The sun had fallen farther, casting a burnt-orange glow across the western horizon. Jackson looked at his watch and grimaced. "Damn it, we're running late. Take us directly to the pound," he barked at the driver, and the vehicle began to pick up speed.

The winding road cut a path between a swath of ever-widening cotton fields. Jonathan looked around and saw nothing but neatly rowed stalks with limbs shooting wildly in every direction covered with blooming bolls of cotton amongst their leaves. He turned to his father and asked, "Where is everyone?"

"Be patient, you'll see," Jackson replied, and almost instantaneously, the SUV reduced its speed. They came to a stop at the entrance of another fence, only this time, there wasn't a booth with armed guards, just another identification card and thumbprint reader.

After the driver repeated the thumb and swipe routine, the gate opened, and he carefully steered the vehicle inside. As the gate closed behind them, Jonathan noticed signs along its perimeter displaying skulls with crossbones and lightning bolts serving as a final warning for everyone getting too close to the fence to beware. He realized that the fence was there to keep people in.

A hundred yards down the gravel road, the SUV approached the first in a row of one-story, flat-roofed brick structures. They were all identical, small and box-shaped with one door and one window in front and one window on the side. Each brick hut was positioned six feet from the next and sandwiched the tiny road from either side. Some had tattered garments hung drying between poles on clothing lines. They reminded Jonathan of the housing projects he visited in the slums of New Haven to feed his cocaine habit while studying at Yale. His palms began to sweat as he fought the urge to pop a few pills.

"What the hell!" Jonathan blurted out while trying to stifle a gasp. He ordered the driver to stop.

One of the doors had opened, giving them a view of the squalid conditions inside. Bare-bones at best, the floors and walls were covered in grit and grime. A shirtless child, no older than five, wandered to the doorway. No one said a word as they watched through tinted windows as the little boy frolicked back and forth. Suddenly, a black woman appeared and yanked him by the arm back inside and closed the door. The SUV drove on.

"What was that around their ankles?" Jonathan asked.

"GPS monitors," the driver answered, speaking for the very first time. His voice was coated with a thick Appalachian Mountain drawl. "We put 'em on them as soon as they learn how to walk. It tells us where they are at all times."

"Couldn't they just cut the anklet off?"

"They could, but it wouldn't make a difference. They all have been injected with a microscopic homing device. Believe me, ain't nobody goin' anywhere,' the driver answered with pride.

Jonathan looked over at his father, who sported a sinister smile. "Jon, look ahead," Jackson said, directing his son's attention toward the front windshield.

The SUV was nearing the main entrance of the compound, which was nothing but a gigantic sally port, and Jonathan looked on with wide eyes as it filled with people from the other side. Hundreds of them were being counted and ushered in by what he presumed to be Azalea's field bosses. Once the last person was counted, the huge electric gate slid shut, closing them all inside. They resembled a herd of cattle, rounded up and stuffed into a pen.

Jonathan observed the field bosses on the other side of the fence compare tally sheets and call the total head count in to someone at an undisclosed location. After a moment of waiting, the count was verified, and the gate on Jonathan's side of the sally port opened up allowing the crowd of men and women to walk toward them.

"My God," Jonathan whispered as throngs of weary faces, young and old, walked by.

None of them paid any attention to the SUV in the middle of the road. After spending a taxing fourteen-hour day out in the fields, all they wanted was to get to the disheveled brick huts they called home.

"Dad," Jonathan whispered, still not believing his eyes, "there are slaves out there."

Jackson leaned in close. "No, son, what they are is billions of dollars in unpaid wages. Billions. Never forget that." The words were candid but delivered sharply enough to pierce Jonathan's skin.

By now, the last of the slaves had walked by. The driver tapped the gas pedal, and the SUV pulled into the sally port; and after another swapping of the gates, the truck eased out on the other side. The field bosses who were in charge of the count were still there, and as the SUV slowly rolled past, the men all dutifully nodded at the vehicle knowing that someone very important was riding inside.

Dressed in black paramilitary fatigues, they looked just as rugged as Jonathan had imagined they would be, tall, muscular with weather-beaten faces with menacing glares enhanced by the sunken crow's-feet around their eyes. He looked them over and marveled at how much a century and a half of technology could change things. Instead of horses, the field bosses rode ATVs while carrying semi-automatic weapons. And the whips, which had been forever known as the tool that greatly affected and controlled the slaves, were now replaced by Tasers and high-voltage cattle prods.

The SUV sped on toward the main house, and no one said a word as the Range Rover effortlessly tackled the bumpy road that rounded the lake before pulling up to the front of the mansion. There were only a few minutes of sunlight left, and Jonathan quickly exited the truck in an effort to capture the centerpiece of Azalea's palatial beauty in all of its glory.

Jonathan stretched his long limbs as he stood in front of the mansion and breathed in the Southern air. The sights and smells were just as his father had described, and every detail of the story began to come alive. With its massive pillars, the mansion was both precious and grand and, ironically, reminded him of the Lincoln Memorial. The paint smelled fresh, and even though it hadn't been occupied in over a century, from the outside, the mansion showed no signs of neglect or deterioration that usually accompanied an edifice as its age neared two hundred years.

Jonathan followed his nose, which led him to series of gardens surrounding the mansion. Orchids, bluebells, dahlias, African violets, marigolds, and roses of all shades were everywhere. As he passed through each themed garden, he was in awe at how even in the diminishing light, the vibrant colors produced by the cornucopia of floral species still managed to gleam. When Jonathan finally circled the mansion, his father stood at the bottom of the steps waiting for him.

"Are you ready?" Jackson said while placing an arm around his son's shoulders. Rendered speechless, Jonathan nodded his head, and together, they marched up the steps and went inside.

The interior of the mansion was just as immaculate and well maintained as the gardens outside. After almost two centuries, the marble floor still sparkled, and the antique furniture his ancestors once used had been polished to a museum-quality shine. But as much as Jonathan wanted to see each room, he could tell by the way his father followed the driver down the main corridor that there would be no time for a grand tour tonight. Quickly, he fell in behind them.

Every ten feet along the corridor, Jonathan noticed the portraits of his family's male predecessors ornately framed on the walls. Starting with Jeb Tobias and ending with his grandfather, he eerily felt their eyes on him as he walked by. The rigid looks on their immortalized faces were a staunch reminder of the power that had just been bestowed upon him.

As they neared the end of the hall, the driver pulled out his key card and inserted it into a slot next to what appeared to be a closet door. It wasn't. The door slid open to reveal an elevator. The door closed once they all stepped inside, and after a brief standstill, the elevator began its decline. Jonathan noticed there were no buttons or keypads on any of the walls, which meant someone else was in control of the ride.

"Did it feel like they were watching you?" Jackson inquired.

"Who?" Jonathan replied.

"The portraits in the corridor. Their eyes, you can almost feel them watching you as you walk by them," Jackson said, referring to the feeling that swept over him during his first ever visit to Azalea. "They seem to easily convey the importance of me being here, reminding me that I was the bridge which would connect our past generations to generations to come. Jon, it will be your turn to be that bridge very soon. Don't let us down."

Jonathan knew his father's portrait was going to hang in that corridor someday, and that only with the continued success of Tobias Incorporated would his hang there too. He looked directly into his father's icy blue eyes and confidently said, "Dad, the last thing you have to worry about is me failing you."

Suddenly, the elevator door opened exposing a large room filled with men shuffling back and forth between computer stations and walls lined with surveillance screens. The air was thick with the smell of cigarettes and coffee, and the most pronounced sound in the room came from the continuous taps of fingertips punching data onto computer keys. This was Primary Control, the nerve center that monitored every inch of Cotton City, and to Jonathan's surprise was his uncle, Jerrold Tobias, standing in the middle of the floor sporting a tight-lipped grin.

Standing six feet four inches tall with the girth of an offensive lineman, Jerrold Tobias dwarfed his younger brother and nephew, but his solemn demeanor and affinity for handmade Brioni power suits belied his gargantuan size. He wore his gray hair well oiled and slicked back, and across his top lip ran a well-trimmed moustache that would have made Clark Gable proud. For a man who spent the majority of his time indoors, his skin had always managed to remain lightly bronzed. Patiently, he waited for the day when his face would grace the covers of *Forbes, Fortune 500*, or the coveted front page of the *Wall Street Journal*.

"Jack. What a surprise! I see you decided to inject us with some new blood around here. It's about time," Jerrold said as he looked his brother over. "Jonny, welcome aboard," he added while shaking Jonathan's hand and pulling him in close for a manly hug.

"I'm just trying to learn the ropes, Uncle Jerry," Jonathan said humbly.

"I couldn't agree more with your father that you're the right man for the job. I'm going to do everything in my power to make your transition as seamless as possible. After seeing all of this, I know you have questions, so don't hesitate to ask," Jerrold said before flashing a smile and exposing a perfect set of white teeth.

Jonathan eagerly looked at his father, who nodded in Jerrold's direction. "Your uncle's right. There's no better time to get some answers than now. Jerry, are the quarterlies available?"

"They're in the office on your desk," Jerrold replied.

"Jon, that's where I'll be," Jackson said before turning to leave.

Jerrold faced his nephew. "Okay, let's see if we can get to the bottom of a few things for you this evening."

"Just two questions, Uncle Jerry," Jonathan said as they began to slowly walk through the control room. "Who are these people? And how the hell do you manage to keep this operation from the outside world?"

Jerrold looked at Jonathan and smiled. "You're here, so it's obvious you've been told the whole story. Therein lay the answers to all your questions. These men you see in here, the bosses out on the plantation, and the guards you saw at the security booths are all descendants of your great-great-grandfather's employees," he said as Jonathan looked on in surprise.

"You see that fella over there?" Jerrold said while pointing a manicured finger at the man who drove them here. "His last name's McMiller."

The name instantly rang a bell inside Jonathan's head. "Gus?" he guessed.

"So you were listening," Jerrold said sarcastically while nodding his head. "That's his great-great-grandson. And just like Gus, he's the number-two man here. When I'm not around, he's in total control, keeping this outfit up and running. These men are well paid and were bred for the positions they hold. They have as much at stake here as your father or me. So don't worry, this operation is in caring hands.

"Now," Jerrold continued, "the answer to your second question would seem a bit more complicated, but it also comes with relative ease. Do you remember the contract?"

Jonathan's head went down for a second as he tried to retrace the major points of his father's story. "The one signed by Lincoln giving us exclusive rights to supply the government?"

Jerrold nodded yes.

"That deal's still in play?"

"Hell yes, it is," Jerrold said excitedly.

"Jon, you name it, we're everywhere. From moisture-freeing socks for our troops in the Middle East to the cotton cellulose used in rocket fuel that makes our aerospace program possible. Over the past century and a half, the government has developed quite a dependence on our production. But in that same span of time, our so-called competitors have become infected with a bit of jealousy—and we both know jealousy can cause the most scrupulous of people to do unethical things. For example, flying over our fields and dumping chemicals in hopes of destroying our cotton."

Jerrold looked at Jonathan's unbelieving eyes. "Oh, it's happened before. In 1924, some fool with a single engine dropped arsenic trioxide all over this place. My grandpa, rest his soul, said it looked like Christmas in July. Totally fucked up the harvest for that year. The next year, the bastard tried it again—but this time, we had authorization to blow his ass out of the sky. Since then, under legislative Act 62, subsection 39, article *d*, the air over Azalea has been declared a no-fly zone.

Jonathan smirked and slowly stroked his chin. "So basically, what you're saying is that a government-invoked competitive clause is keeping this place from being seen?"

"That's exactly what I'm saying. From the ground, Azalea's a heavily guarded fortress. No one's getting in here unless we let them in—"

"But a plane could fly in overhead and capture some spectacular aerial views," Jonathan said, finishing his uncle's sentence for him.

"Those pictures would go straight to the cover of *Time* magazine. Talk about a Pulitzer Prize," he added dryly.

"It would be pretty unfortunate," Jerrold said with a nervous chuckle. "But thanks to good old Uncle Sam, it's unlikely to happen. Only our planes can come near this place, and the airfield's way outside of Cotton City. No one flies over here. We're a virtual Bermuda Triangle," he added with a devilish smile.

Jonathan returned his uncle's smirk, but he was still trying to adjust to what he was seeing. He could grasp his father, the shrewd unfeeling person that he was, being part of something like this; but the thought of his Uncle Jerry, the docile giant who used to take him and his siblings ice-skating at Rockefeller Plaza every Christmas, being at the absolute heart of this operation was quite beyond belief.

Jerrold waved to the driver, who lumbered over to them. "Sean, I know you met on the way over, but I want to formerly introduce you to my nephew, Jon. One day, he's going to be the new number one," he said while placing a confident slap on Jonathan's shoulder.

While exchanging handshakes and formal hellos, Jonathan began to gawk at a nasty scar coursing down the side of Sean McMiller's face. He tried his best to avert his eyes, but he knew he was too late when Sean began tracing the lines of his scar with his index finger.

"Marines," Sean said with pride. "Force ReCon, Desert Storm. Five miles outside of Baghdad, I had the privilege to meet Bouncing Betty in person."

A puzzled expression appeared on Jonathan's face.

"It's a land mine. You step on it, and it shoots out of the sand six feet high and explodes. Hence the name," Sean said informatively. "Luckily for me, the damn thing was a dud, or I would have lost my fuckin' head. God bless bullshit Iraqi ordnance."

"You see, Jon, there's no need to be embarrassed," Jerrold chimed in. "Sean wears that thing like a badge of honor."

"Semper Fi," Sean McMiller bellowed in agreement.

Jonathan smirked and nodded his head just to stay politically correct while swearing to himself that he had never met a tougher-looking individual before in his life. He knew that by holding such a lofty position in the conspiracy, Sean McMiller was worth every penny he earned.

"Jon, I really need to speak with your father alone for a minute, so please excuse me," Jerrold said before turning to Sean McMiller. "Show my nephew around the entire facility. Bring him up to speed on everything that goes on here, and get him acquainted with all of our guys."

"Will do," McMiller replied.

Jerrold stepped in front of Jonathan and placed a hand on his nephew's shoulder and looked him directly in the eyes. "Relax, okay. I know it's a hell of a lot to grasp, but we don't expect you to get it all in one night. After I speak with your father, I have to head out, so I won't see you again until your brother's victory party. Go with Sean and get yourself familiar with this place and everything will be fine."

"Okay, Uncle Jerry," Jonathan said, finding comfort in his uncle's words before following Sean McMiller into the elevator and disappearing.

"You son of a bitch!" Jerrold yelled after he stepped into the office and closed the door. "How could you do this without consulting me first?"

"The last time I checked the charter, CEO followed my name, not yours," Jackson said coolly without looking up from the latest production statistics he had been poring over. "That's not to say the job you're doing around here hasn't been outstanding," he added as he finally faced his brother.

Jerrold's face turned a deep red. "Don't patronize me, Jack. Thirty-three facilities located in seven countries around the globe, and I'm the one in the trenches making sure everything runs smoothly while you remain spotless inside of those boardroom meetings. I don't need you to tell me what I'm worth to this corporation. Goddamnit, I deserved a say in this!"

"You could've had as many says as you wanted, but it wouldn't have mattered because the final decision will always be mine," Jackson said as he leaned back in his chair and calmly clasped his hands together. "If you have a problem with that, too bad. You should have taken it up with our father when he appointed me to this position. Better yet, you should've taken it up with yourself when you decided to double-cross me."

"So that's what this is all about? Sarah? You're still punishing me for something that happened thirty-five years ago. I guess you'll never let me live it down," Jerrold said while slowly shaking his head.

"And believe me when I say your children won't live it down either."

"You calloused bastard, leave them out of this. My sons have as much a right to this place as your precious Jonny!" Jerrold yelled. He tried to continue, but Jackson quickly threw up a hand.

"Oh, Jerry, shut up and quit your fucking whining. I didn't say my nephews couldn't be a part of this. They're Tobiases, and as you made clear, it's their right. But as CEO, I get to choose in what capacity, which means, barring something unfortunate happening to Jonathan, your offspring will never run this company. So get your sons in here and show them what it feels like not to be number one."

The words stung, and Jerrold struggled to control his anger. He wanted to leap over the desk but suddenly remembered the last time he physically challenged his brother; he ended up with a broken nose and three cracked ribs. He slowly exhaled and unballed his fists.

"I'm disappointed to see you've changed your mind," Jackson arrogantly snickered. "I could have used the exercise."

"One day, you're going to fall hard off of that pedestal you've perched yourself on, you son of a bitch," Jerrold said as he headed toward the door. "And I'll be right there to bear witness."

After Jerrold stormed out of the office and slammed the door, Jackson focused back on the quarterlies and muttered, "Don't hold your breath, big brother. You'd be a fool to hold your breath."

Later that night, the captain gunned the twin turbine Rolls-Royce engines while trying his best to beat a monstrous thunderstorm blowing in from Canada on a course straight for New York. The copilot glanced at the Doppler radar system and calculated that both jet and storm would arrive at Teterboro at precisely the same time. He informed the captain, who mashed harder on the throttle, and the Gulfstream G7 rapidly sliced through the pitch-black sky.

Meanwhile, inside of the cabin, Jonathan slumped in his chair and grappled with the reality of what he'd been introduced to throughout the course of the day. He had no idea that he would learn about the damning secret behind his family's power when he rolled out of bed this morning. In less than twenty-four hours, a mountain of power had been thrust upon him, and with it came a mountain of responsibility. Now that he was alone, the pressure of it all seemed like too much to bear.

Jonathan nervously twisted his head around the empty cabin and began to panic. He needed to talk to someone, but his father was back in the suite having another go at the stewardess. His right hand slightly trembled while digging into his pocket to retrieve his trusted vial of pills. In one motion, he popped a few OxyContin and used the back of his hand to wipe away the beads of perspiration from his brow.

"Whew, that's better," he exhaled when he got up to pour himself a drink, noticing the biting pain in his lower back was gone. After swallowing two straight shots of gin, Jonathan yanked his Blackberry from his belt clip and plopped back down into his seat. He turned the power back on then scrolled until he found the name *Fels* and pressed dial.

"Hello?' a woman's voice asked after the third ring.

"Felicia, it's me," Jonathan said as he undid the top two buttons of his shirt.

"Jonny?" she said half consciously. "Jesus, what time is it?"

"I don't know, a little after one," he answered while glancing at his watch.

"Where are you?"

"I'm on a plane headed back to the city."

"I tried to call earlier. Where were you?" she asked.

Jonathan nervously laughed. "Field trip with my dad."

"What?"

"It's a long story, but you probably won't believe it. I'm still trying to believe it myself."

"Well, you called me," she said sarcastically.

"Don't be a smart-ass. I'll be there in an hour. Have some lines ready. You'll need to be wide awake when you hear about where I've been tonight."

CHAPTER 11

For the Society of American Humanitarian's annual banquet and awards ceremony, the great hall of the Smithsonian Museum had been transformed into an elegant ballroom suitable enough for kings and queens. The night's theme was *success*, and every detail inside of the ballroom, from the place settings to the forty-foot silk draperies adorning the walls, had been exquisitely decorated in coordinated hues of silver and gold.

Beneath the sparkling light of Swarovski crystal chandeliers, a little over nine hundred of the nation's most altruistic citizens dined on a variety of five-star entrees accompanied by a host of vintage wines and champagnes. No expense had been spared, money was no object, and there was enough of it in this ballroom to support a small European country for the next five years.

Every member of the SAH was in attendance this evening—doctors, lawyers, educators, entertainers, current and former pro athletes, politicians, and the corporate leaders of the world's most lucrative industries—all to honor and be honored for their philanthropies and the manner in which they gave back. They were from different walks of life, but they had two things in common: they were either very wealthy or influential, and they wanted to use those gifts to help uplift the unfortunate people of the nation. Sure, there was Unicef and USA for Africa and other world help organizations, but the SAH was solely dedicated to getting things done right here.

Even the president of the United States graced the ballroom with his presence, unable to pass on the ceremony's invaluable photo opportunities since his approval ratings started to dip. He was the evening's guest of honor. But at the moment, everyone's attention was focused on the handsome young man, who, despite the annoying stream of camera bulbs flashing into his eyes, humbly accepted the award for Highest Philanthropic Achievement of the Year for his tireless work with underprivileged children. After giving a brief statement of how he wished he could share the award with every member of the SAH, he received a thunderous applause as he exited the stage.

"Ladies and gentlemen, let's hear it again for our Mr. Mitchell Breston," said Howard Astor, the president of the SAH, who eloquently handled the hosting duties for this evening. "It is always a wonderful thing to see a young person like him who truly gets it. He had everything going his way. With one phone call, he could have any wish fulfilled, but he'd rather give huge chunks of himself to a host of worthy causes than cash in on his Hollywood looks and fame. And I've heard in some circles that chivalry is dead, but Mitchell Breston is proof that it's still living. The audience erupted again.

Howard Astor cleared his throat and continued. "With that said, there aren't many words in the lexicon that would do any justice to describe our next honoree, but I promise I will give it my very best. Fifteen years ago, a young gentleman fresh out of Harvard Law approached me at a seminar we held in Boston about equality in the workplace and asked was there anything he could do. At the time, he was just a skinny kid still wet behind the ears, but I could tell by his firm handshake that inside of him resided a ferocious tiger ready to take on the world. I told him the only answer I felt was appropriate at the time. I said, 'Son, I can't tell you what to do, but whatever you decide, just do your absolute best.' He listened. Boy, did he listen," Astor said as he looked up and smiled.

"Ever since that evening in 1992, this young man has been answering his calling by aggressively championing the rights of his fellow citizens. Whether large or small, he attacked the problems head-on with the same voracity and produced an unending string of victorious results. A subpoena served by him signaled the death knell for bias in the workplace where, unfortunately, racism, sexism, and anti-Semitism continue to thrive. And judging by the damages awarded by the juries in his class-action lawsuits, now when those prejudices rear their ugly heads, it would be disastrous for a CEO to turn a blind eye.

"Oh yes, he's made one hell of a difference. And although today that tiger inside of him is more visible than ever, he still remains as humble and approachable as that young kid I met fifteen years ago on that frosty New England night. Therefore, with great pleasure, I would like to present the Society of American Humanitarians' most esteemed award, the Thurgood Marshall Memorial Bust, recognizing a commitment to excellence in the field of Civil Rights and Liberties, to J. Alton Pierce of the Law Offices of Chesney, Bregman, Pierce, and Associates. Ladies and gentlemen, let's give him our much overdue praise!" Howard Astor announced, and the spotlight shined on J. Alton Pierce as the audience gave him a standing ovation.

After receiving a congratulatory kiss from his fiancée, Alton rose from his seat and flashed his most gracious grin as he walked the main aisle that led from his table up to the stage. The resounding applause continued until he stood beside Howard Astor at the podium. It grew louder when two beautiful valets carefully rolled out the delicately sculptured crystal bust of the nation's first African American US Supreme Court Justice and unveiled it for all to see. Only after Howard Astor embraced Alton and left him alone in front of the microphone did everyone retake their seats.

Alton was all smiles. "Thanks, Howard, for reminding everyone that I once was a scrawny young kid," he casually mentioned and received a hearty chuckle from the crowd. "I am truly honored to be up here tonight accepting this award, and to stay humble, there are some very important people here I would like to thank.

"First, I want to thank my beautiful fiancée, Lara, for being the supportive sun that brightens every day of my life. Next, I would like to thank my partners, Amy Bregman and Dick Chesney, two people who I know would gladly follow me into a dark alley on any given night. But more importantly, thanks to all of you. This evening would not be possible without your help."

The crowd began to applaud, but Alton quickly raised his hand and continued. "As you all could probably guess, I'm the descendant of a man who was once a slave, and I want to share with you his story, a story my father told me when I was younger, which stuck with me throughout my life and made me the man I am today.

"Jasper Pierce was a Nguni Zulu who was captured along the western coast of South Africa, and since the majority of the traders operated on West Africa's Ivory Coast where the people were less stout, his towering muscular frame was a rarity, and needless to say, he fetched a high price on auctioning day. When his owners brought him back to their plantation, they immediately took notice of his physical prowess and used him to oppress the rest of the slaves.

"Under the constant threat of death, he was given a whip and was forced to use it to keep everyone else in line. For his service, his handlers had given him extra scraps of food. But one night while lying alone in his shack, he was struck with a dose of morality. Even though he was doing what he was told, somewhere inside, it felt wrong, and Jasper Pierce decided that it was now time to leave.

"The next morning, he escaped, killing a man in the process, and ran for what seemed like an eternity. For five months, living off the land and using the sun and the moon as his guide, he headed north looking for the land of freedom. Finally, he found it. Once he set foot in Chicago, he was taken in by a local blacksmith named James Tunstill, who gave my great-great-grandfather a job and taught him how to read and write. A few years later, he married a woman named Bessie Adams and started his own family."

Alton paused to look around and saw an audience captivated by his story, a familiar sight he experienced every time he'd give a heart-felt closing argument to a panel of convinced jurors. He continued.

"As time passed, Jasper Pierce seemed to have it all, his freedom, employment, a family with a roof over their heads, and a life that had finally become sweet. But deep in the pit of his stomach, he struggled with a tiny feeling that had been nagging at him for years. It was the same feeling he had at the plantation, which prompted him to leave.

Only this time, the emphasis focused on those he left behind, telling him that something had to be done to help the young, the old, the sickly, and weak people.

"Following his inner feelings, Jasper Pierce joined the American Antislavery Society and aggressively battled slavery for the next twelve years. He even put his life on the line by aiding the Underground Railroad by giving food and shelter at his home to scores of escapes as they passed through the Windy City. And when slavery was finally abolished, he joined the Liberty Party, which pushed for the Fifteenth Amendment, giving blacks the right to vote. Valiantly, he fought for the equal treatment of African Americans well into his senior years, never giving up until his death at the age of eighty-three.

"I was told the long version of that story early on in my life, but it took a while for me to understand its meaning. Giving: taking the good fortune that's bestowed upon you and using it to help someone else. My great-great-grandfather was fortunate enough to take his freedom, but when others kept on running, he turned around and made a stand for those who couldn't do it for themselves.

"As I look around this beautifully decorated ballroom, I see a room full of people who share the same unique trait. And that, ladies and gentlemen, is what makes all of us here tonight great. Thank you!" Alton said with a bright smile and a wave, which caused the audience to burst into a fervent bout of applause and cheers.

After a quick photo session with the SAH's board of trustees and a brief meet-and-greet with the commander in chief, Alton was back at his table where the mood could only be described as pure bliss. The Cristal flowed freely while Alton and his party of five hoisted toast after toast as a continuous line of well-wishers stopped by their table to shower him with praises.

"Alton, tonight is your night. You're on one hell of a roll!" Dick Chesney said as he reached over the table to give his partner a high five. "I know the perfect place for that statue. We can put it in the consultation room. It'll give the firm an air of prestige."

"Oh, Dick, please. Every time you show up to the office, that distinctive air will leave," Amanda Bregman snorted with a wry smile.

"Amy, I got class. I own my own jet," Dick haughtily said in his defense. "That statue will guarantee us some of these wealthy clients.

Ever heard of the words *in-house counsel*? I don't know about the rest of you do-gooders, but I become an attorney to get rich."

"Do you ever stop thinking about money?" Amanda said. "Alton should have his award at home where he can be reminded of his accomplishments."

"Listen, you guys, I really don't care about trophies and accolades. The people affected by what I do mean more to me than all of that," Alton said sincerely. "Dick, put it wherever you please."

"Ha!" Dick triumphantly exclaimed in Amy Bregman's direction.

The slender attorney with mouse-like features turned to her husband. "Do you see what I go through while you're at home with the kids? Look at his date," she said, gesturing toward the tanned redhead sitting next to Dick Chesney dressed in a tight-fitting sleeveless Karl Lagerfeld gown. "The poor thing won't last ten days."

"I can hear you, Amy," Dick suspiciously said before slamming back the rest of his champagne. "And since you're keeping tabs, she'll be gone in less than a week," he added arrogantly.

Meanwhile, Alton had ventured off into a world of his own. Gazing into Lara's eyes, he became oblivious to Dick and Amanda's routine. Just seeing her dressed to the nines in that Carolina Herrera gown reminded him of when they met at a private fund-raiser sponsoring inner city mentoring centers that would offer alternative opportunities to the underprivileged youth of Washington, DC.

That night, Alton's eyes tracked the hostess's every move as she racked up pledge after pledge while working the stage. From his table, he could already see that Lara Gatewood was a living work of art blessed with a flawless French-vanilla complexion, full kissable lips, a head of silky black hair, and eyes blue enough to swim in. He told himself that if God had made her any more beautiful, it would have been a sin.

Now, four years, a shared townhouse in Georgetown, and a four-carat yellow diamond on her left ring finger later, Lara was still able to enchant him the way she did on that night in the spring of 2003.

He leaned in close to her ear. "You look spectacular tonight, but I can bet that gown's got nothing on what you're wearing underneath it."

Beneath the table, he placed a hand onto her knee, and she playfully pushed it aside. "Look, mister, you're just gonna have to wait and find out," she said with a sensual grin.

At the moment, she wanted him just as much as he wanted her. An erotic fire had simmered between her legs from the second Alton stepped onto the stage and the spotlight cast a radiant glow against his brown skin. Now that he was back sitting next to her where she could see every chiseled detail of his face, Lara began to regret attending the ceremony without wearing any panties.

In the wee hours of the next morning, after a heart-thumping bout of hard partying at private parties held in and around Washington, DC, Alton and Lara were being chauffeured home in the back of a stretched white Cadillac limousine. As the modern day carriage cruised up I-95 from the Governor's Mansion in Richmond, Virginia, the midnight sky had turned a pale blue-gray as the rising sun flirted with switching on the lights to start the day.

"Baby, you were absolutely the most beautiful woman at every party we've been to tonight," Alton said before peppering Lara's lips with soft kisses.

"That's the champagne talking," Lara purred while looking up into her fiancée's eyes. Her endless legs were stretched out along the leather bench as Alton cradled her in his arms across his lap.

"Oh no, the effects of the bubbly wore off long ago. Besides, I don't need any alcohol to see that there's no better looking woman in the world than my future wife," Alton responded with a wet kiss, but when he came up for air, he noticed a distant look on Lara's face. What's the matter?"

"Nothing," she lied.

"Don't say it's nothing. I can see it in your eyes. It's him again, isn't it?" he asked with concern.

Lara uprighted herself and averted her eyes from his troubled glare. "Okay, Alton, lately he's been on my mind," she said before exhaling dejectedly.

"Shit," Alton snickered while shaking his head in disappointment. "How someone can send you an e-mail claiming to be your father and you believe it is completely beyond me. I've seen these kinds of scams happen all of the time. Why are you being so naïve?"

"I'm not being naïve. There's something different about this," she stated while subconsciously fixating onto the diamond bracelet she'd been given on her eighteenth birthday.

"So that means you're still going to meet with him in New York next week?"

"Yes," she answered softly.

"Then I'm going with you," he said stubbornly.

"No, Alton, you can't!" she said as she whipped her head around to face him.

"What the hell do you mean no!" he snapped. "You're my fiancée. There's no way I'm going to let you see some strange man alone."

Lara grabbed a hold of Alton's hand and gently squeezed. "Baby, listen to me. I've been searching for traces of my family for as long as I can remember, and since I was a little girl, I've done it on my own. I told myself long ago, discovery or disappointment, whatever I find, I would handle it alone."

"You know it doesn't have to be that way," Alton said softly. "We're a team."

"I know we are," Lara said as she began to massage the back of Alton's neck. "But this is something I have to do for me. I just need for you to respect my reasons. Please."

Quickly, Alton thought of her many tales of heartbreaking dead ends. "I will," he said reluctantly. "I hope he's not some desperate ex-boyfriend trying to recapture your heart."

Wishing she'd never told him about the brief e-mail exchange with a man who claimed to be her long-lost father, Lara knew she had to do something to get her trip to New York off Alton's mind. Slowly, she unclasped her bodice and slipped out of her gown, revealing her athletically toned naked body, and Alton's rigid lips creased into an eager smile.

"I've been waiting to give this award to you all night," she whispered into Alton's ear before sliding down onto her knees, unzipping his pants, and taking his throbbing erection into her mouth.

Alton bit his bottom lip in ecstasy as all of the muscles in his body tensed while Lara's head bobbed slowly up and down on his cock. Miraculously, he resisted the strong urge to come and pulled her up to him and met her mouth with a passionate kiss. As their tongues sensuously touched, he held onto her tightly because her warm body felt so good in his arms.

With his strong but gentle hands, Alton laid Lara across the backseat before peeling out of his clothes. And protected by the privacy of mirror-tinted windows, they made intense love to each other for ninety miles—until the limousine pulled up to the front of their home.

Being uniquely rich in contemporary culture while staying true to its storied traditional history makes Washington, DC, one of the biggest tourist draws in the entire country. But unbeknownst to millions of its unsuspecting visitors, lurking in the shadow of the Washington Monument and hiding in the dark corners of Capitol Hill, was a multifaceted monster camouflaged by the city's ever-present political machine. Made up of cronyism, blackmail, scandal, and greed, it was as certain as death and taxes, and almost always waited until the fall election season to appear.

So on the drizzly Monday morning after the awards ceremony, Alton was not surprised when he picked up a copy of the *Washington Post* and saw the monster's latest casualty. James Granderson, an incumbent six-term US senator for Connecticut who had to suddenly drop out of the race for reelection once his name became embroiled in an internet child-pornography sting. He read most of the unsavory details while munching on a light breakfast of creamed cheese on raisin toast before shrugging the article off as "politics as usual" and heading off into the city.

It was a typical late October morning outside the Law Offices of Chesney, Bregman, and Pierce. Gray skies, opened umbrellas, and brown leaves stuck like refrigerator magnets to the wet pavement. After a hard-earned 200-million-dollar settlement from a class-action lawsuit against the tobacco industry, the partners purchased a defunct public library at the corner of Georgia Ave. and U Street. They sunk in a large portion of their commission and had every inch of the outdated building gutted and retrofitted to mirror the twenty-first century, transforming it into an elaborate testament to the firm's very first victory.

Alton pulled up to the front of the building and left the Mercedes S55 running for the valet parking attendant. Like clockwork, the doorman ran to the car holding a huge umbrella to make sure Alton and his valuable briefcase didn't get wet.

The mood was exceptionally light and cheery for a Monday morning, and a barrage of "good mornings" and congratulatory smiles met Alton once he set foot into the lobby. He politely returned their greetings before stepping into an elevator and heading up to the fourth floor, which housed the partner's suites.

"Mornin', boss," said Alton's personal secretary before taking his coat and briefcase. "Your team's in the conference room waiting for you. The interview with *Black Enterprise* magazine is still on for ten-thirty, and Judge Anderson's clerk called—the noon deposition has been postponed. So for lunch, maybe you can take me out to eat," she rattled off in rapid succession as they made the short walk from the elevator to his suite.

"I don't think so," Alton quickly replied. "Robin, you know my fiancée would have a problem with that."

"Who, Ms. Mystery? Lara has nothing to worry about. I don't want you," Robin said defensively, trying to hide the crush she'd been holding so close to her heart for the last ten years.

Alton walked into his expensive office and took a seat behind a glossy teakwood desk that wrapped around him like a gigantic horseshoe. The desk matched the rest of the furniture in the room. The cutting-edge interior decoration was a pricey "thank you" from a group of parents satisfied with the judgment from their children's Medicare malpractice suit. Alton's only decorative input in the office was his prized Japanese bonsai trees and a framed copy of his law degree.

"Oh, I almost forgot to say congratulations," Robin said as she bought him a steaming mug of espresso. She was remarking about the bust of Thurgood Marshall sitting on a stand in a corner of the room.

"What's that thing doing in here?" he asked curiously.

"I don't know. The delivery guys brought it in this morning."

"I see that, but Dick wants it in the consultation room."

"Dick? What about you? You earned it. Besides, I think it's cute."

Alton sighed and gave Robin a dismissive wave. "Look, I care, but not about that shit. Being successful doesn't make me a glory hound. So if Dick wants to use it to bring in more money, so be it."

Robin threw up her hands in retreat. "Okay, okay. You've made your point. It'll be out of here when you get back from your meeting," she said before sauntering out of his office and closing the door.

Alton couldn't help laughing to himself at Robin's antics, knowing that if she had worked for someone else, her suggestive behavior would have gotten her fired long ago. But throughout the last decade, Robin Alvarez had been more than competent at her job while remaining immensely loyal. A large portion of his success could be attributed to her. After working very closely with each other for so many years, he couldn't blame her for feeling about him the way she did. And as beautiful as Robin was, Alton could distinctly remember the lonely nights before he met Lara when he almost fell weak to the temptation.

The passing thought of Lara immediately caused Alton to focus all of his attention onto his fiancée. He took a quick sip of espresso before swiveling around in his high-back chair and staring out of the large plate glass window. From his office, Alton could admire the panoramic view of Rock Creek Park and its picturesque multicolored treetops signaling the inevitable change of seasons.

"Ms. Mystery, huh," he said to himself and snickered out loud since the moniker Robin had given his woman could not have been further from the truth. Lara had told him everything about herself from her life growing up as an orphan in a prestigious all-girl London academy to waking up on her eighteenth birthday and discovering a twenty-million-dollar trust fund in her name—which she immediately followed its paper trail here to the United States.

Knowing that the wealthy only traveled in certain circles, Lara admitted to Alton that at first the only reason she became involved with philanthropy was to try and find a lead. The only clue she possessed was the heavily jeweled bracelet that accompanied the fortune she received on that life-changing day.

For seventeen years, she openly wore the bracelet to every charity function with the faint hope of someone recognizing it and giving her any kind of reaction. And for seventeen years, Lara never found what she was looking for until a little over a month ago when a man claiming to be her father sent her a picture of a necklace that identically matched the bracelet, and now they were set to have their first meeting.

With absolute certainty, Alton knew that with one phone call to his friend, Buck Jennings, he could find out anything he wanted to know about his fiancée; but he also knew that if he asked Lara herself, she would tell him the truth. Putting Robin's misgivings aside, Alton decided that not trusting Lara would be a huge mistake, realizing that if he didn't trust her, he didn't love her. And he loved that woman with every resounding beat of his heart.

Alton turned away from the window and finished off the rest of his espresso, injecting himself with a much needed jolt of caffeinated energy. And after a quick trip to his private bathroom to gargle a little mouthwash and get some time in front of the mirror, he quickly headed out of the office to meet with his research team.

If someone had made an analogy comparing the Law Offices of Chesney, Bregman, and Pierce to a plate of food, the meat and potatoes would have to be represented by the second floor. The place where extremely long hours were logged and cases were built, it teemed with young associates looking to gain the necessary experience before moving on to other law firms or striking out on their own. The partners didn't mind the revolving-door policy because it kept the firm injected with fresh blood.

"Okay, everybody. Weekend's over," Alton said as he entered the conference room snapping his fingers, and immediately, everyone at the table opened their notebooks and began to shuffle pages. Alton took off his suit jacket and draped it over a chair before taking a seat. "All right, what do ya got for me?"

"Five, sir," said a bookish young attorney who sported a pair of horn-rimmed glasses. "Factoring in the components you've given us, including region, racial and sexual demography, and rate of employee turnaround, our query produced five companies that fit the criteria."

"Let me hear our options," Alton said casually.

Michelle Kim, the longest tenured attorney in the group, passed Alton a list of the targeted companies before reading off the names from an identical list of her own. "We have Dyson Energy Corp, a coal mining outfit in Beckley, West Virginia. MicroSolutions based in Silicon Valley, California. They provide cutting edge nanotechnology for America's top three computer companies. Foodmark in Biloxi, Mississippi. It's the second largest plant for the nation's largest meat-packing company. Tobias Industries, an industrial complex near Montgomery, Alabama, centralizing in cotton-related textiles. And finally, Amalgamated Steel Mills located outside of Pittsburgh, Pennsylvania, a major supplier of sheet metal to the automotive industry."

"Which one is the slam dunk?" Alton asked after scanning the short list.

"It has to be Amalgamated Steel Mills," Kim answered. "The numbers stack up against them. In an area where the minority race makes up over 50 percent of the population, they only account for 2 percent of Amalgamated's entire staff. Also, less than 1 percent of their staff is female. That's a breeding ground for sexual harassment."

There was a quick laugh from Chuck Boras, a young hotshot attorney new to the firm. "I don't think the kind of chick that get's sexually harassed works in a steel mill."

Alton slowly leaned forward in his chair. "That kind of thinking is why we're here. Studies show it's not pretty blonde bombshells that get harassed. No, it's the so-called undesirable women that get it because men think they're doing these women a favor with their salacious advances. Then when these woman complain, because it's their God-given right to complain, it's people like you who tend not to believe them. So shut the hell up and maybe you'll learn something," he said while staring daggers at his young subordinate.

Boras lowered his eyes and humbly nodded a yes.

"Michelle, which one of these companies is the biggest? I never heard of any of them before. They seem like a bunch of independents," Alton said.

"It has to be Tobias Industries. They're a division of Tobias Incorporated, and they are huge. For better use of the word, I would say they have a monopoly on the cotton industry. They're smart too. They leave just enough business on the table for their competitors to keep them from coming under government scrutiny."

"Well, if they're so smart, how did they end up on this list?" Alton asked curiously.

"At first, I asked myself the same question. From outside appearances, it looks like they're doing the right thing. But after cross-checking their minority roster with the census records of four of its neighboring counties, it seems that Tobias Industries might be overdoing it."

"Hmm," Alton said with a raised eyebrow. "You're suggesting that they have ghost employees?"

"It's serious," said Kim, "but without solid evidence, it's a very difficult case to prove."

"I know, just get started with Amalgamated while I take Chuck with me and devote some energy into this Tobias thing. Send a few people up to Pittsburgh to canvass. Tell them not to come back without any complaints," Alton said, emphasizing his orders with a stiff index finger.

"I know the drill," Kim said, confirming that she and her boss were on the same page. "We'll get right on it."

From across the table, Alton caught a look of dissatisfaction on Chuck Boras' face. "What's the matter? Don't you want to get some time in with me?" he asked facetiously. "Oh, I get it. You want to be with the rest of the team and rack up a victory with a case that's pretty much a breeze."

"Well, I, uh, don't see the logic in going after a claim that's nearly impossible to prove," the young man opined honestly.

Alton looked into Boras gray eyes and saw a younger version of Dick Chesney. "Chuck, why did you become an attorney? Did you want to help people or was it the money?"

Silence.

"Don't worry, there's no right or wrong answer. Just tell me the truth," Alton added.

"The money, of course," Boras responded smugly.

"Good, now we're getting somewhere," Alton said with an impish grin. "What if I told you that you really can't have what you want, which is the money, without doing the other. That is, unless you're an attorney working for the companies we go after, which you're not because you're sitting here with us and because they don't hire attorneys who don't have a name.

"Now," Alton continued, "I know what you're thinking right at this second. 'How do I get a name?' Well, I can tell you how not to get one—developing a reputation for only going after cakewalk cases. In corporate litigation, the only way to get a name is to win cases that make a difference. Corporate America is like high school at recess. You beat up the biggest bully, and the other bullies will fall in line. It took Enron to get CEOs to stop stealing. Win a case that shakes up an industry, and I can guarantee you'll be able to punch your own ticket. And maybe, just maybe, one day, you'll find yourself in a courtroom defending a Fortune Five Hundred against me."

Alton paused for a second to let his words sink in and saw that Chuck Boras had liked what he was hearing. "So, Chuck, are you ready to go out there and get yourself a name?" Again, silence. "Come on, don't be bashful now. Answer me."

"I guess so," Boras mumbled while nodding his head uncomfortably.

"Nah, don't give me that shit. Say it like you really mean it," Alton said, slightly raising his voice as he egged the younger man on.

Instantly, a vision flashed inside of Boras's head—a vision of him receiving million-dollar retainers, soaring cross-country in his own private jet, and golfing with his executive clients on balmy weekends. Quickly, he stood while slamming his hand hard against the table and excitedly said, "Yes! Yes, goddamn it, I want it! I want my fuckin' name!"

Alton smiled and began to vigorously clap his hands. "So you're on board?" he asked.

"You better believe I'm on board," Boras answered with a pumped fist.

"Look, everybody, Chuck's on board. Give the man a hand," Alton said sarcastically as the six other people around the table joined in on the sartorial bit. And for a split second, Chuck Boras felt like he was on top of the world, until the clapping stopped and Alton deadpanned, "Now that you're on board, I want everything there is to know about Tobias Incorporated on my desk by five o'clock this evening." Alton's final order was an abrupt end to the meeting.

Later on that night when only the throaty hum of industrial vacuum cleaners filled the building, Alton sat hunched over his desk skimming through the information Chuck Boras had compiled. He had to hand it to the young attorney for diligently gathering so much pertinent data in such a limited amount of time. Boras had even tried to stay late to look for more info, but Alton took pity on the eager attorney's soul and sent him home.

Pausing every few pages to take a bite from a ham-and-cheese sandwich, Alton had gotten acquainted with the people behind Tobias Industries. With each turn of the page, he learned more and more of the Tobias legacy and their complete dominance of the cotton industry since the turn of the twentieth century. And though their generational history read off like a who's-who list of a British monarchy, with each man using his time at the helm of the corporation to revolutionize the industry, Alton focused his attention on the empire's current ruling family.

Jackson Tobias III, born in 1949 to Meredith and Jackson Tobias II, took over as CEO in 1977 without even possessing a college degree. At age twenty-nine, he was the youngest Tobias to ever run the company, but he was also the shrewdest. He spent his entire tenure as CEO developing a reputation for devouring competing companies. There was a saying in discreet circles that if you wanted to find a photograph of Jack Tobias, all you had to do was look up "corporate raider" in the dictionary.

Jack Tobias had four children who lived with him and his wife, Belinda, at their estate in Greenwich, Connecticut. There were two sons and two daughters, but Alton only focused on the men because throughout their history, no female Tobias had ever worked for the company.

First, there was William Jefferson Tobias, a thirty-seven year old married father of two, who once had a very promising college football career until he lost half of his right foot during the first Gulf War. When he returned home from Kuwait, William never became involved with the family business, opting to enjoy the rich playboy lifestyle until he found God at the age of thirty. Two years ago, he threw his hat into the political arena, and currently, he was running against James Granderson for a seat in the United States Senate.

Somehow, the name James Granderson had set off an alarm inside Alton's head. He swiveled to his left and punched the name into the computer, and up came a series of bylines: "Connecticut senator disgraced in kiddie porn sting!" "Mired in scandal, James Granderson is forced to drop from close race!" "Sick desires cost Granderson his senate seat!"

"Coincidence?" Alton asked himself out loud. "I think not," he added sarcastically before reading on.

Jonathan Taylor Tobias was the youngest of Jack Tobias's children, but with William soon to claim his spot as Connecticut's new senator, he was the obvious heir to the throne. Alton noticed that there was very little information on the CEO-to-be, none of the reckless behavior that usually accompanied young blue-blooded Americans and their family's immense fortunes. After finishing Yale with a master's degree in corporate finance, he spent every free moment shadowing his father in an effort to obtain all the information Jack Tobias had to offer about running the company. Alton knew that no one could be that clean cut and decided that the report on Jonathan Tobias was incomplete.

It was close to midnight by the time Alton finished sifting through the pile of paperwork, so he dimmed the lights and poured himself a snifter of brandy. Following the drink, he leaned back and lit a Cuban cigar, preferring to mesh its sweet aroma with the cognac's aged woodsy taste. Alton then put his feet up onto the desk and closed his eyes and allowed the report on the Tobias family to permeate his thoughts.

It didn't take long for Alton to determine that he didn't like the Tobiases at all since they controlled billions in purported wealth, and not a single penny had ever been donated to charity. He figured that with all of their contributions to the cotton industry, they probably considered themselves God's gift to the free world. To Alton, they were just another powerful family who believed they could do no wrong. But they made the list, and having ghost employees meant there was something going on at Tobias Industries that they were breaking the law to hide. Alton had no clue what it was, but he reached for the phone to call the only person he knew could find out.

"What can I do for you, Alton?" Buck Jennings asked after the first ring.

"I just wanted to see what my favorite ex-spook was up to," Alton responded innocently.

Jennings laughed. "Don't give me that shit. You only call when you're on someone's case."

"Okay, Buck, you got me," Alton conceded. "Ever heard the name Tobias before?"

"Military or civilian?"

"Civilian. Abundantly rich civilian with their hands in everything, including the military," Alton answered.

"Can't say that I have. What's up?"

One of their companies has been flagged by us for having employees on their roster that census bureau records say don't exist."

"Where?" Jennings asked.

"Alabama. I need you to get someone in there and confirm my suspicions and find out why."

Momentary silence. "It's going to take some time. That kind of information won't come overnight. It may be months before my plant can get in deep enough to find anything out," Jennings said after giving Alton's proposition some thought.

"You know I don't give a damn about time constraints. I know you'll be thorough and bring me an airtight case," Alton said, giving his ace investigator a vote of confidence. "Take as much time as you need."

"Before you go, leave a copy of the report you have on them with the guard at the front desk. I'll drop by and pick it up sometime tonight," Buck Jennings told Alton before the line went dead.

Alton returned the phone to its base and thought about Jack Tobias at his sprawling estate, nestled in bed while peacefully sleeping. Alton took a few puffs from his cigar and hoped the CEO was resting easy because he could foresee many restless nights in the unsuspecting man's future, knowing that it would only be a matter of time before Buck Jennings's operative returned from Alabama with the truth.

CHAPTER 12

G lowing unobstructed for miles around, the midmorning sun easily illuminated the northern tip of the New Jersey Turnpike. And as drivers adjusted their visors or scrambled for sunglasses to avoid its blinding glare, Lara Gatewood miraculously managed to fix her makeup while steering her Range Rover through exit 15E as she made her way to New York City. She was thankful that her appointment was for a noon lunch at the Plaza Hotel, which allowed her to miss the rush hour traffic heading into Manhattan because it was ten times worse than the daily gridlock in Washington, DC.

Lara knew that applying makeup while driving was dangerous, but she wanted to make sure she looked her absolute best. Everything had to be perfect since she was so sure this time would not be like the others. As the SUV rolled east into the Lincoln Tunnel, the butterflies in her stomach told her that the man she was about to meet would be her father. After navigating through a maze of skyscrapers, she arrived at Grand Army Plaza at Fifth Avenue and Fifty-Ninth Street and left her vehicle with the valet parking attendant.

As Lara ambled through Palm Court, men sulked when they saw the glowing rock on her left hand and realized she was already taken. She wore a navy blue pantsuit in an effort to be modest, but the pedestrian outfit was unable to hide her flattering curves. Lara received envious stares from almost every woman she passed as she made her way northeast to the Edwardian room.

Although the lunchtime traffic completely crowded the restaurant, the atmosphere was notably serene as the violin's harmonious tunes blanketed the dining room. Lara gave her name to the maître d' and was escorted to a booth with a Central Park view. She ordered an Evian and waited.

After gazing out the window for a few moments, she spotted a man heading directly for her table. From what she could see, he was tall with a full head of salt-and-pepper hair and built as though, at one time in his life, he had played sports. He was very handsome and received a considerable amount of head turns from the older women in the restaurant. Being biracial, Lara figured this man could potentially be her father since she never knew which one of her parents were black or white. He came to her table and stopped.

"Lara?" he asked cautiously.

"Yes," she answered slowly while desperately trying to quell the frantic beat of her heart.

For a frozen moment, while he stood and she sat, they searched each other's faces for any clues that they shared an identical bloodline. Lara saw a few resembling features on his face, and he could somehow see her mother on hers, but it was their unmistakable blue eyes that indicated there was a strong chance that he was her father and she was his daughter. Lara broke the silence.

"Are you going to sit down?" she asked, and he obliged.

"This isn't easy," he said after more silence and awkward staring.

"I know," she agreed. "This is not how I thought it would be at all."

"What do you mean?" he asked.

Lara clasped her hands together and began to twiddle her thumbs. "I've been holding on to a dream since I was five years old. It's silly now that I think about it, but my parents would burst into the school and inform the headmistress that there was a huge mistake at the hospital where I was born. Somehow, the nurses gave them the wrong baby, and after the mix-up was explained, my parents were allowed to take me home."

"I'm sorry," he said softly after thinking of the incalculable number of orphans who held onto the very same dream.

"You don't have to be," she reassured him. "You're here now, albeit after thirty-five years."

"I guess I deserve that," he said, taking her biting remark in stride, "and I'm smart enough to know I should expect more."

"What's your name?" she asked.

"John," he lied. "Jonathan Bradford."

"And my mother's?"

"Sarah," he replied.

"Are you two married?" she asked upon noticing his wedding band.

"I'm married, but not to her."

"Where is she?"

"Sarah . . . she, uh, is not with us anymore," he said pensively.

Lara tried her hardest to mask the disappointment of never being able to know her mother. "What happened to her?"

Jonathan Bradford lowered his head and began to speak. "The summer of 1970 was extremely hot, so a few college buddies and I decided to leave the country and embark on a European vacation. We planned to start in England, work our way through the entire continent, and finish up in the Greek Isles. For a group of young WASPs living off our trust funds, the trip was supposed to be a carefree journey, but for me, it became something altogether different.

"It was our third night in London, and Miles Davis had just happened to be performing at one of the local nightclubs, so the guys and I decided to go. The Xanadu was a cozy little place only big enough for about fifty people, and out of respect for the performers, the waitresses were only allowed to serve drinks in-between sets. We ordered a round of vodka martinis and our waitress called on another server to help bring us our drinks, and that's when your mother first caught my eye.

"She was beautiful, tall with cinnamon skin, a bright smile, and a set of large curious eyes. I had to know her name. She told me it was Sarah. And for the rest of the night, I was oblivious to the King of Bebop and his legendary trumpet. All I wanted to do was think about her."

He continued after a quick sip of water. "After the show, I managed to ditch my friends and waited outside of the Xanadu for Sarah to come out. It took a little bit of prodding, but she agreed to go out with me on a date. The next day, she gave me the grand tour of the city. She took me everywhere. We visited Parliament, Buckingham Palace, and we even shared our teatime along the Thames. That day, we really enjoyed each other's company, and by nightfall, we promised to do it all over again. And for the next seven days, that's exactly what we did. When my friends decided it was time to move on to Paris, I convinced them to go on without me. I told them I would catch up in a few days, but they never saw me again.

"We moved into a flat in Notting Hill and completely shut ourselves off from the worlds we knew before we met. We knew no one would agree with what we were doing, but we had each other, and all that mattered was our love. With the insane amount of passion we shared, it didn't take long for Sarah to become pregnant. She was at her happiest during that time, always singing lullabies around the apartment while rubbing her stomach. She used to say the baby would be special because it was made from only the best parts of us. From what I can see, Sarah was right," he said before looking up and noticing that Lara was crying. "Are you all right?"

"I'm fine," Lara said as she dabbed a handkerchief at her eyes. Go on. Please."

"New Year's Eve had rolled around by the time the pregnancy had come to full term, and Sarah had convinced me that we should go out. She said it would be our last time out as a pair, so we got all dressed up for a night on the town. People were everywhere, and the roads were congested with traffic. New Year's Eve in London is much worse than it is in Times Square. We dined at our favorite restaurant and went to the waterfront to enjoy the fireworks show.

"It was well after midnight when we decided to leave. The traffic on the expressway was ridiculous. I knew nothing good could come out of a few thousand cars travelling in the same direction, especially with half of them speeding and the other half driving drunk. Somehow, we were able to safely make it back to Notting Hill. However, just a few blocks from home, we collided head-on with an American tourist driving on the wrong side of the road.

"The next thing I can remember was waking up a week later inside of a hospital with two broken legs asking for Sarah. The doctors told me that she was gone. They said she died from intense trauma to her head, but they were able to save the child."

Jonathan Bradford looked to the ceiling and reflected on that god-awful night. "I wanted to get a hotel room for the evening to avoid the traffic, but Sarah insisted on us waking up in our own bed. I could never say no to her, but that night, I truly wish I did."

After her father finished the story, a momentary quiet resided between them until Lara asked the question she wanted answered the most. "What happened to me?"

Jonathan Bradford sighed. He knew this was coming. "Lara, please," he begged off. "It's complicated."

"Did you just say complicated?" Lara asked as her face reddened. "I'm named after a boarding school. I didn't have many friends growing up because I wasn't black enough for black people or white enough for white people. The last thing I want to hear now is the word complicated. It's practically my middle name."

"I know this is hard for you, but this is just as hard for me too," he said before signaling the waiter over and ordering something stronger than water.

"I don't think you know what it feels like to watch everyone go home to their families for the holidays and be stuck in some school all alone. I want to know how I ended up that way," she said as her intense glare pressed him for an answer.

He downed the glass of scotch in one swallow and began to reminisce again. "I wasn't alone when I woke up in that hospital. The authorities must have contacted my family because my mother was sitting next to me. It was the first time we saw each other or spoke in almost two years. She expressed her displeasure with my disappearance, but she was thankful that I was alive. She kept blathering on about how much I angered my father and that he sent her to London to bring me home.

"Mother was there when the doctors told me they saved you, and she was there when they rolled me into the nursery. You were so oblivious to the ugliness of the world as you slept peacefully in your crib. Mother said you were a disgrace to our family's heritage and that there was no way I could bring you home. She must have asked me ten times how could I have a black baby. I told her that I loved your mother, and she dismissed it as just a phase.

"There was no reasoning with her. Sometimes she could be worse than my father. I think that's why he sent her. But after arguing for two days, we were able to compromise. If I agreed to go back to America with her, she wouldn't tell anyone about you, and I could return for you once you turned eighteen. We enrolled you into Gatewood Academy, and I went with her back home," he said before searching Lara's face for any kind of reaction.

"So I became your dirty little secret?" she asked as her body went rigid in anger.

"No, no," he quickly responded. "It was never meant to be that way at all."

"I turned eighteen seventeen years ago. What am I supposed to think?"

He shook his head dejectedly. "You don't understand the kind of family I've come from. *They* are very powerful, and at the time, I was very weak and young. They believe in only one way of doing things—theirs. My father threatened to disown me if I didn't marry and have children with his partner's daughter. I knew that if I refused him, I would end up with nothing, and you would end up with nothing as well. So I did it just to please my father. I married a girl I hardly knew.

"I always knew I'd come back for you. And I monitored your progress at Gatewood from afar. As your eighteenth birthday neared, Mother approached me about our agreement and warned me that revealing a secret of that magnitude would break my father's heart. She convinced me to at least wait until he passed on. By then, my standing had grown very powerful within the family's corporation, and I arranged for you to receive your trust fund."

Lara began to cry again. "I guess the real reason why you're here is that your father is gone and there's no reason to hide?"

It bothered him to see what the truth was doing to her. "Lara, believe me when I say I'm not proud of what I've done. I'll give anything to make up for the lost time. Money is no object," he said before reaching into his coat pocket and pulling out the necklace that matched her bracelet. "This is yours now. It belonged to your mother. I don't blame you for being upset with me, and I would understand if you never want to see me again."

Lara didn't respond. Her attention remained focused on the sparkling piece of jewelry in her hands. As she held the heavy necklace, she could feel the green-eyed leers from the other women in the restaurant who assumed she was just another affair receiving an expensive gift from her adulterous sugar daddy. Lara scoffed at their suspicions and reached across the table to grab a hold of her father's hand.

"I've waited my entire life for this," she said while peering into his morose eyes. "It may not be the fairy tale I'd hoped for, but this is exactly what I wanted. Don't bring your money into this because it's clearly not the answer. It never was. All we can do right now is build a relationship from here. I'm willing if you are. If not, you should get up and walk away."

As Lara spoke, Jonathan Bradford thought he was sitting across from her mother. Her passion and conviction reminded him of a few traits that once belonged to Sarah. They were part of what made him fall in love with her, and he'd never thought he would ever see them again. He leaned forward and enveloped his big hands around hers. "Lara, I'm here now," he said sincerely, "and I'll be here for as long as you want me to be."

She stood and then he stood, and they both wrapped their arms around each other in a tight embrace. Lara squeezed her eyes shut and ignored the gawkers peering in their direction. This moment was thirty-five years in the making, and she refused to let it be ruined by someone else's ignorance.

"This was one hell of a lunch," he said once they returned to their seats. "And we didn't even eat anything."

"I'm famished," Lara said as she picked up her menu. "Do you want me to order for you?"

"No, no, I'm fine," he said while glancing at his watch. "I have to be going anyway. A pressing business matter needs to be tended to."

Lara lowered her eyes and nodded her head. "I understand."

"Lara, this isn't it, believe me," he said after noticing a hint of disappointment on her face. "We have a lot of catching up to do, and I promise we will. You know how to reach me now. I'll be there whenever you call. Please don't be upset."

"I'm not," she reassured him. "I know this is going to sound a little clingy, but after searching for all of these years, I don't want to see you leave."

"I can understand, but allow me to earn your trust. Remember, I found you," he said before placing a few hundred dollar bills on the table. "Enjoy your lunch."

They embraced once more, and Lara struggled with letting him go. Something inside of her told her that if she did, she would never see him again. Finally, after overcoming her insecurities, she unlocked her arms and allowed her father to walk away.

Later that afternoon as the autumn sun began to set, a black limousine rolled through the open gates of the Tamarack Estate. Named after the blue-green pines that blanketed its land, Tamarack was the largest piece of privately owned property in Greenwich, Connecticut, a town that boasted the nation's highest per capita of billionaires.

Hidden strategically beyond the lush evergreens encircling the estate were a labyrinth of riding trails, squash and tennis courts, a Ferris wheel, and a USGA-rated eighteen-hole golf course that separated two gigantic lakes. Tamarack was so immense it had its own zip code, and would have made the perfect country club for Greenwich's mega-rich except that it had been Jack Tobias's primary residence for the past thirty years.

The limousine sped up as it tackled the steep hillside that leveled off near the extensive gardens surrounding the estate's Victorian mansion. And even though the exotic flowers were beginning to die off for the winter, coupled with the sculptured Venetian fountains scattered throughout the gardens, Tamarack's landscaping still managed to rival the sumptuous grounds encompassing the Castle Versailles.

The driver stopped the car at a pair of arched double doors and allowed Jerrold Tobias to exit before parking on the lawn beside a row of luxury cars and limousines. The doors immediately opened for Jerrold, and once he stepped inside, a servant was there to take his overcoat. Red, white, and blue balloons were scattered everywhere. Another servant appeared holding a tray of champagne, but Jerrold refused and walked toward the steady stream of music emanating from the mansion's banquet hall instead.

Throngs of people poured in and out of the banquet hall, and hanging from the ceiling right above the live band was a red-and-blue banner with huge white letters bidding William Tobias congratulations. The entire party was marked with an air of overdrawn festiveness, and Jerrold assumed that it was probably because the room was filled with opportunistic lobbyist and boosters who were eager to align themselves with the newly appointed senator. Jerrold donned a sham smile and looked for a familiar face.

"Ah, there he is!" Jackson yelled once he caught sight of his brother walking toward him.

"You know I wouldn't miss this for the world," Jerrold said as he joined Jackson and a small huddle of men. He didn't know any of them except for his two nephews, but knowing his brother, these were a few of the country's most powerful men, and they were amassed in the semicircle for that very reason. To Jackson Tobias, no one else mattered in the room.

One of them looked old and decrepit and wore an oxygen mask while sitting in a wheelchair with tanks on either side. Jerrold figured that rather than dying peacefully, the poor old man probably threw millions at advanced medicine just to prolong his important standing in the world. Jackson introduced them, and Jerrold politely shook their hands.

A round of champagne was signaled for, and once everyone in the group received a glass, Jackson raised his hand up for a toast. "To Billy, my oldest boy," he said with pride. "You've made us all proud with what you've accomplished today. This day, this little celebration, marks the beginning of a journey that hopefully, with some help from our friends here, will culminate with you in the White House. So remember, son, when you're sitting behind that big oak desk in the Oval Office ruling the free world, don't forget about us."

"Amen," one of the men blurted, and all of them laughed before gulping down their champagne.

After the toast, the small party within the party broke apart, and everyone went their separate ways while Jackson, Jerrold, Jonathan, and William stayed behind.

Jerrold placed his big hand on William's shoulder and smiled. "Your father's right, Billy, you are in a position to do this family some good. Good for you."

"I didn't do much," William said humbly. "The numbers were in Granderson's favor, but he was forced to drop out of the race."

"It doesn't mean you're not the right man for the job. Sometimes, in order to win, all you have to do is show up," Jerrold offered as he winked an eye.

"Yeah, Billy, nobody gives a shit how you won, the bottom line is that you did," Jonathan chimed in after exhaling a sigh. "So drop the aw-shucks routine and start acting like you won this thing at the election polls."

"Listen to your brother," Jackson added. "You have to really kick some ass once you move to DC. If you don't exude any confidence along with a little arrogance, all of this will have been for nothing because that fuckin' town will eat you alive."

"Okay, Dad, don't worry. I won't screw this up," William said with a reserved smile.

"All right, Billy, I'm not telling you to be a tight-ass," Jackson said after noticing his son's constraint. "I'm okay with you hiring a couple of hot young pages to bang from time to time."

William let out a nervous titter. "Those days are long behind me. I have a wife and children, and as a matter of fact, here they come right now," he said upon spotting his family walking in their direction.

Jackson's lips creased into a wide smile when he turned and saw William's wife, Elaine, and his twin granddaughters, but it quickly disappeared after seeing his own wife, Belinda, and Fels trailing behind them. After toiling in a rocky marriage for nearly forty years, Jackson had a laundry list of reasons why he abhorred Belinda, but he despised Felicia Wennington for the unwanted attention she brought to his family.

Being the great-granddaughter of Marshall Wennington, one of the early engineers of New York's financial district, she was the sole heir to her family's outrageous fortune. Jackson had absolutely no problem with her prominent background, it was her behavior, the hard partying, the DUIs, and her photograph consistently being featured on page six that was solely responsible for his ire. Even now, Felicia managed to steal the spotlight from William as she sauntered through the banquet hall wearing a tight-fitting pantsuit in her signature color, Tiffany blue.

Belinda Tobias approached her sons and kissed them both on their cheeks. "My darling boys have grown up to be such handsome men," she said before turning to Jackson and planting one right on his mouth.

Embarrassed by the public display of affection, Jackson gently pushed her aside. "You've been drinking again, haven't you?" he asked after smelling the alcohol on her breath.

"Who, me?" she asked giddily. "This is a celebration, isn't it?"

"You know goddamned well you're not supposed to be drinking. Especially not tonight," Jackson said through clenched teeth while angrily furrowing his brow.

"Oh, now you want to pretend like you care about me," she slurred sarcastically. "Don't worry. I'm not going to ruin your precious little party. I came here to say good-bye to my son. I know I'll never get to see him once he leaves. You've already taken Jonathan away from me."

"Mother, I'm right here," Jonathan said softly in an effort to console her.

"Jonathan, your father knows exactly what I mean. I haven't had a minute alone with you since you started working for the company," she said before turning to Felicia and Elaine. "I know it's too late for you Elaine, but Felicia, you need to get away from this family before you turn into me. Look at me. This is what happens when you marry a Tobias and all of their prestige. You get fat, and you get left alone. Everyone thinks this is such a perfect family, but that's a goddamned joke—"

"Lower your voice, woman!" Jackson hissed in an attempt to quell her ranting before she drew the attention of the writers who were invited to cover William's unofficial victory party. "How dare you come in here tonight and insult this family. What gives you that right?"

Belinda Tobias slightly teetered from side to side as she struggled to keep her balance. "I can say whatever I want. This is my family too."

Jackson's cheeks began to crimson. He long ago tired of feeling sorry for Belinda since she turned into a raging alcoholic because he no longer found her attractive when she couldn't shed the weight after delivering their last child. "This is only your family because I allow it to be, and you're almost at the end of that rope. Will someone please take this drunk to her room before she completely embarrasses us all?"

Belinda gasped at Jackson's remark, but Jerrold stepped in between them before she had a chance to respond. "All right, you two, that's enough. This shouldn't be happening right now, especially in front of your grandchildren," he said before looking directly into his sister-in-law's eyes. "Belinda, you do look a little flushed. I have no doubt there are some people here who would love to use that as a reason to ruin this night for your son. So why don't you go to your room and rest for a while. When you're feeling better, come on back down to the party. Will you do that for Billy?"

Her eyes rolled upward as she mulled over Jerrold's request. "For Billy?" she asked cautiously after a momentary thought.

"Yes, only for Billy," Jerrold replied.

"Well . . . all right," she said. "But just for a little while, right?"

"Yeah, Mother, everyone will still be here," Jonathan said before turning to Felicia. "Fels, go with her and make sure she makes it to her bedroom, okay."

Once Felicia led Belinda out of the banquet hall, Jackson discreetly breathed a sigh of relief. He advised William that it would be wise for him to work the crowd with his wife and children before taking the stage and delivering his victory speech. Jackson was in a hurry to get the party over with before Belinda returned because she was the one thing in his life that he couldn't control. He kissed his two granddaughters on their foreheads before ducking out of the party early and having Jerrold and Jonathan follow him to his home office.

"We dodged a bullet," Jackson said after they all entered the soundproof office, and he locked the door. "Jerry, it's a good thing she listened to you. The last thing Billy needs is an embarrassing start to his first term. You can see that he has confidence issues as it is."

"I wouldn't worry about him, he'll get the hang of it soon," Jerrold said as he walked over to the wet bar to pour himself a drink. "What I don't understand is why you don't try to get your wife some help," he added after sitting in one of the cushy leather chairs positioned in front of Jackson's desk.

"I've tried everything," Jackson said with a dispirited wave. "Inpatient, outpatient, retreats, fuckin' acupuncture. You name it. None of it works. I think Belinda prides herself on being my only blemish. As long as she stays out of my way, I don't give a damn."

Jerrold slowly craned his neck to the right and looked at his nephew. "Jon, what about you?"

For a moment, a lifetime of disturbing memories passed through Jonathan's head. He envisioned his mother passed out on numerous occasions or wandering the estate in the middle of the night pissy and drunk. He often wondered if those same images had directly led to his own drug abuse. Since boyhood, he had always wanted better for his mother, but he knew now was not the time to tell the truth. "I don't really care at all," he said with a straight face as he painfully echoed the sentiments of his father.

"What are you, a psychiatrist now?" Jackson said sarcastically. "I didn't come in here to discuss her," he added before placing a black Halliburton briefcase onto the desktop.

Jerrold leaned forward and pulled the titanium briefcase off the desk and onto his lap. He unfastened the latches and flipped open the lid to reveal neatly rowed stacks of brand-new hundred-dollar bills. "This looks like more than one million," he said after glancing at the money and reclosing the case.

"It's one point five, all untraceable," Jackson said as he lit up a cigar. "The extra five hundred is a bonus for a job well done. Tell your internet guys not to spend it all in one place."

"Shit," Jonathan snickered. "Dad, those geeks are going to spend all of that on computer programs and comic books."

Jerrold abruptly rose from his seat. "Well, I promised those geeks that I would have their money to them by eight o'clock tonight. I better get going if I'm going to make it back to New York on time."

"Oh," Jackson said as if a thought had suddenly crossed his mind. "I tried to reach you earlier but your phone kept going to voice mail. Was everything all right?"

For a split second, Jerrold hesitated because Jackson's concern completely caught him off guard. "Yeah," he said nervously. "Around noon, we were stuck behind a car accident, so I shut off my phone and stole a little bit of shut-eye. I was only out for about an hour. If it was important, you could have called the driver on the car phone. He would have woken me up."

"It's no big deal," Jackson said nonchalantly. "I just wanted to get this done early before all of those people showed up at the house."

"Then I'll leave by the back way," Jerrold said before turning to leave, totally unaware that Jackson's suspicious eyes were tracking him until he walked out of the door.

Back at the Plaza Hotel, Lara was stirred from her sleep by the relentless vibration of her cell phone. The clock on the night table read 9:00 p.m., and the room she booked after lunch had turned pitch-dark. Lying face-up across the king-sized bed, Lara slowly ran her hands over herself and realized that she still had on all of her clothes, and her cheeks felt icky from crying all afternoon. She rolled over and grabbed her phone. There were twelve missed calls, and all of them were from Alton.

"Lara!" he said excitedly, barely after the first ring. "Where are you? Are you all right?"

"Yes, Alton, I'm fine," she said. "I'm still at the hotel."

"What's going on? Why are you still there?"

"I'm not sure. I think I just needed to rest or be alone. Whatever the reason, there was no way I could drive home. I couldn't stop crying, so I got a room."

Immediately, Alton began to think the worse. The last thing he wanted for Lara was another heart-wrenching false alarm. "Did he even show up?"

"Yes."

"What happened that made you so upset?"

"Nothing happened," she responded. "I never said I was upset."

"But you said you couldn't stop crying," Alton said, clueless.

"I know, but that's not the reason why," Lara said. "I couldn't stop crying because I met him. I finally met my father."

Momentarily, the other end of the line went silent while Alton processed what she said. "Are you sure?" he asked hesitantly. "Lara, I don't mean to be a party pooper, but I know what you've been through."

"I know and I understand, but this is really it. I never felt this way before," she said before totally recounting, word for word, the entire encounter with her father.

"Wow," Alton said once Lara finished her story. "So how do you feel?"

"I don't know, Alton, just crazy inside," she said, unable to describe the strange mixture of emotions currently overwhelming her.

At that very moment, like all others, Alton wished he could be next to Lara. He wanted to put his arms around her just so she could feel him and know she wasn't alone. "What room are you in? I'm coming to New York."

"No, Alton, don't do that," she whined. "This is just fine. Hearing your voice is exactly what I need right now."

"But I can do even better with my lips and my hands."

"I know you can," she said after a giggle, "and I'm going to hold you to that as soon as I get home. All I want to do right now is get out of these clothes, take a hot bath, and go back to sleep. I'll be there first thing in the morning to fall into your arms."

"Well then, tonight, I'm going to sleep by the door."

"Alton?"

"Yes, my love," he answered attentively.

"I love you."

"I love you too," he responded.

"No, I really, really, love you," she slowly said in a tone laced with so much emotion her words could have only come from the deepest depths of her heart. They blew each other a good-bye kiss before disconnecting their phones.

At the close of business the following Monday, Jonathan entered Jackson's office at the Tobias Tower and dropped a stack of papers onto his father's already crowded desk. They were detailed progress reports from six different executive meetings Jonathan had chaired in Jackson's place. He plopped into a black leather chaise lounge and loosened his tie.

"I see being the boss is not as easy as you thought it would be," Jackson uttered without even looking in Jonathan's direction.

"Shit," Jonathan said wearily, "it's like babysitting a bunch of bickering children. Everyone's trying to one-up each other just to impress you. The routine got old by the third meeting."

Jackson laughed as he took off his reading glasses and swiveled his big chair around to face his son. "Oh yes, Jon, being at the top is a dirty job, but I want to be the only one doing it. I've been CEO for thirty years now, and the meetings have always been the best part of it for me. I enjoy watching subordinates backstab and squirm for my approval. Besides, the competitiveness is healthy for the corporation. You'll get used to it."

"Dad, did you mean what you said the other night at the party?" Jonathan asked after a quiet moment.

"About your mother?"

"No, about getting Billy into the White House. He can't even tie his shoes without looking to you first."

"There are two types of people in this world. Those who give orders, and those who follow the orders given to them. Unfortunately, your brother falls into the latter category, but that doesn't make him useless to us."

"I know, Dad," Jonathan reluctantly agreed, "but president? I can't see anyone in America voting for him. He couldn't even get the votes in his own state."

"It surprises me that even after all you've seen, you still underestimate this family," Jackson said before walking over to a display case and returning to his desk with two crystal containers. "Jon, come over here."

Jonathan dragged himself to one of the chairs in front of Jackson's desk and sat down. He looked at the two bottles with their many sculptured facets and assumed the liquid inside of them contained alcohol. He cleared his throat in preparation for a drink, but once Jackson removed the lid from one of the bottles, a pungent odor shot up his nose.

"What the fuck is that, gasoline?" Jonathan shrieked as he snatched his head away from the desk.

"It's E85. Do you know what that is?" Jackson asked as he replaced the lid.

"Yeah, it's a clean burning fuel—ethanol, I believe, derived from corn," Jonathan said. "I've heard it was designed to combat global warming."

"That's right," Jackson said as he removed the second lid and passed the bottle over to his son. "Now smell this."

Wanting to spare the remaining hairs in his nose, Jonathan carefully inhaled as he brought his face closer to the bottle; but after a few whiffs, he looked to his father and shook his head. "I don't smell anything."

"I know," Jackson said with a sinister grin. "What you are holding in your hands is a liquid that's going to revolutionize the modern world as we know it. It's called CX9, and it's made from a genetically altered strain of cotton. CX9 is almost as pure as water, it burns longer than gasoline, it's safer than hydrogen cells, and its emissions are cleaner than E85, so the tree huggers will love us. Compared to its profits, CX9 costs nothing to produce, and only we have the formula. This is our baby, son. And it's going to make this family trillions."

Jonathan placed the lid back onto the bottle and held it up to the light. As he gently swirled the clear liquid inside around, it didn't take long for him to grasp that CX9 had the potential to thrust the

Tobiases into immortality. "I'm speechless," he said after placing the bottle back onto the desk.

"That's okay, Jon. I had the same reaction when our physicists first came to me with their findings. And I'm willing to bet that once we enter CX9 into the market, we will get that same response from the rest of the world."

"So when do you plan to unveil this innovation," Jonathan excitedly said after receiving a greed-inspired jolt of energy. "E85 is making some headway. I don't think we should keep this ace up our sleeve for too long."

"Wait a minute, Jon," Jackson said with a raised hand. "Let's not lose our purpose in a mad dash to the bank. We've been ready with this fuel for the past two years now, but history repeatedly told us that every great feat has always depended on one thing: timing."

"I have closely monitored the corn farmers' quest to peddle E85, but as close to a magic bullet as it may be, their product is not without flaws. The funny thing about competition is that it breeds awareness. If you know someone's out there, you tend to watch your back. But if you believe you're all alone, you relax. The corn farmers believe it's just them and no one else, which is exactly the way I want it."

"So we wait?" Jonathan asked.

"That's right, son," Jackson quickly responded. "But not for long. As soon as they've sunk every penny into their investment, we will swoop in with CX9 and pull the rug out from underneath of them. I have someone over there who will inform me of that time. The blow will be so overwhelming I can all but guarantee the farmers will never be able to recover, and they'll be forced back to the super-markets where they belong."

Before Jonathan could say a word, Jackson continued. "That's only the beginning. Next, at no charge, we'll fuel the entire military until the end of their campaign in the Middle East. You probably think it's foolish, but the war would end a lot sooner if half of the military's budget wasn't spent on energy. The generous offering from Tobias Incorporated will be in the name of fighting terrorism because we both know Al-Qaeda is funded by Arabian oil."

"And Uncle Sam will be grateful," Jonathan added with a wry smile as he nodded his head in agreement.

"Once the military and the government align themselves beside us, we will introduce CX9 to the public sector and significantly reduce the price of fuel in the nation. That's when Billy will begin his push toward the White House."

Jonathan leaned forward. "So basically, you're willing to gamble that the average American voter will be grateful to the man whose family brought them cheaper, clean burning fuel to the gas pump."

"This is a working-class nation we live in, and it still matters if you can save people a few bucks. Remember, only fools gamble, Jon. I deal solely in guarantees," Jackson said convincingly. "Furthermore, since we both know Billy can't tie his shoes without looking to me first, when he becomes president, I'm going to instruct him to begin a campaign to restrict foreign oil from coming into the United States. Those goddamned sand niggers in Saudi Arabia earned ninety billion in profits last year. I don't see any reason why that money shouldn't be funneled over to us."

Again, Jonathan picked up the bottle and marveled at the precious liquid inside. He began to ponder everything Jackson had just said. And as farfetched as his father's aspirations had sounded, after all that he learned about his family in the past two months, Jonathan knew that there was absolutely nothing in this world that could stop Jackson Tobias from getting exactly what he wanted.

CHAPTER 13

Early the next spring, a brisk wind blew in from Lake Michigan and blanketed Chicago with a frigid air that reminded some of the city's lighter dressed citizens of the harsh winter that had just passed by. Fortunately for Alton, having spent his entire childhood there, he remembered the seasons' unwillingness to change and was appropriately dressed for the weather.

It was Easter Sunday, and Alton had flown north with Lara to visit his parents for the weekend. They stayed at their roomy suburban home, and since they weren't married yet, Alton's old-fashioned parents made them sleep in separate bedrooms. The three nights spent apart from each other didn't bother the lovebirds because with Alton's extended family stopping by to meet his fiancée for the first time, sex was the last thing on their minds.

Lara had never been to Chicago before, and all weekend long, Alton served as her personal tour guide, taking her to all of the Windy City's historical and hot spots. But since this was their last night in town, Alton wanted her to see his humble beginnings, which meant bringing her to the city's rough-and-tumble South Side.

After giving Lara the grand tour of the tiny two-bedroom house he grew up in, he took her around the corner instead of heading back to their car. They held hands while walking down a block lined with burned-out four-story apartment buildings. Alton could feel Lara's grip tighten as they approached a group of men listening to loud rap music and drinking beer. When Alton got close enough, one of the men turned the blaring radio down.

"Hey, everybody! Look! It's Al!" the man yelled to his pals before turning back to Alton with a welcoming smile.

Instantly, everyone began to shower Alton with "hey" and "how are ya doing?" and finally, "where ya been?" Alton took their salutations in stride and returned an equal amount of love. Lara saw that they were happy to see him, so she loosened her grip on his hand and began to relax.

"So what brings you around?" asked the first man. "And who's this pretty thing on your arm?"

"You know damn well I would never come to the city and not check up on my boys," Alton answered. "And this lovely thing on my arm is my beautiful fiancée, Lara."

Alton's answer drew a chorus of whistles and cat calls that made both him and Lara blush. He then turned to his fiancée. "Lara, I want to introduce you to the fellas. The guy with the big mouth is Mike, and I've known him since the second grade. And this is Bobby Do Right because when we were kids, he always stayed in trouble. Every day before he left the house, his mother would yell, 'Bobby, please do right!'" Everyone laughed.

One by one, Alton introduced what was left of his childhood friends. A lot of them were dead by now, and a few were still locked up. It didn't matter to Alton what paths their lives travelled along because he vowed to be there for them if they ever needed him. These were the neighborhood toughs, and they always had his back while he was growing up.

"Yeah, guys, I just wanted to show her the old neighborhood before it gets tore down," Alton said before turning to Mike. "Remember, we're on for the first of June, so have your people ready. That goes for all of y'all," he added, remarking about the revitalization project he heavily funded in hopes of transforming the dilapidated neighborhood back into the thriving community it was before gang culture had invaded. It would bring much needed employment to the area and give some of its at-risk youth an opportunity to learn a skill.

After catching up a bit, Alton shook hands and embraced everyone before leading Lara back to the car. Nightfall was quickly approaching, and Alton had to get Lara back to the suburbs because his parents had invited the entire family over to have dinner before they flew back to DC.

"God, those guys looked scary," Lara said once they were out of earshot.

"They are scary, but they have good hearts. They looked after my parents when I went away to college. I could have easily been one of them, but they saw potential in me and wouldn't let me join the gangs."

"Thank God for that," Lara said as she leaned over the armrest and kissed Alton on his cheek.

"I do thank Him. Every time I come back here," Alton replied with a sigh of relief. "The South Side is the reason why I fight so hard in the courtroom because each victory takes me a step further away from this place."

As Alton drove past each crowded corner in the seemingly unending ghetto, Lara gently massaged the back of his neck. She was grateful for the field trip and the window it offered into her fiancé's meritorious soul. Lara wished she could take him to London and do the same, but there was no way she would ever go back to that boarding school again.

Meanwhile, approximately 650 miles to the south, Kyle Bingham waved good-bye to his coworkers as he climbed into his pickup. Right after starting the engine, he rushed to turn on the air-conditioner because the humidity in Alabama made the air extremely sticky although it was early spring. He stepped on the gas and sped out of the parking lot and tried to put as much space between him and Cotton City as he possibly could. It didn't matter because he would be back there tomorrow completing the same routine.

Once Bingham made it to his apartment on the outskirts of Montgomery, he went straight to the bathroom to brush his teeth. He wanted to get the foul taste of chewing tobacco out of his mouth, and after scrubbing his teeth and gums to the brink of bleeding, he kicked off his boots and flopped his tired body across the bed and exhaled wearily.

While staring up at the broken ceiling fan, Bingham openly cursed his boss because in all of his years of working for Intel-Ops, this had been his most difficult assignment to date. The current difficulty was not the bloodthirsty rebels he encountered as an attaché in hostile third-world countries or the suspense of being a corporate mole while pilfering a company's trade secrets; no, the culprit was boredom.

Approximately five months ago, armed with the personal and technical background Buck Jennings had created for him, Kyle Bingham applied for an open midlevel troubleshooting position at Tobias Industries. He interviewed well, and the personnel department particularly liked that he recently completed three tours of duty in the Iraqi War; and following a thorough investigation, they were convinced he was the right man for the job.

His assignment was simple: verify that Tobias Industries didn't have the minority staff the company's roster claimed worked there and find out why. After his first tour of the facilities, it wasn't hard for Bingham to discern that the industrial complex was short on minority employees. Sure, there was a black face scattered here and there, but the disparity could have easily warranted an investigation by the Senate Ethics Committee. It was the second part of the task that was difficult to prove.

For months, Bingham had seamlessly blended in with the minions at Cotton City in an attempt to locate the truth. His innocent features and blithe demeanor made him very approachable at work. Everyone welcomed him with open arms, the ladies thought he was extremely handsome, and being a decorated war hero easily made him one of the guys.

He quickly made a few friends at the industrial complex, but the relationships were fruitless. No one there knew of anything strange going on at Cotton City, and no one really paid attention to the disparity between blacks and whites because, essentially, this was still the South. Even the few black employees he spoke with had no problem with being grossly outnumbered, they just felt lucky to have landed such a fine job. Overall, everyone had the same thing to say about their employer: Tobias Industries offered excellent benefits, and they paid very well.

Being a troubleshooter gave Bingham access to almost anywhere he wanted to go at the facility, and he used it to his advantage. Daily, he conducted thorough inspections of each laboratory, warehouse, and factory, and still he came up empty. The only place he was denied access had been a secure road that disappeared deep into the cotton fields outside of the facility. The road was completely off limits to every employee at Cotton City except for a few higher-ups.

Lying in bed, Bingham remembered being told the road led to a facility that was strictly being used for government testing. Before coming to work for Jennings at Intel-Ops, he worked as a handler for the CIA, so he knew the story about government testing was a ruse. With each passing moment, Bingham began to surmise that the answers he was looking for lay at the end of that road. Judging by the security at the road's entrance, whatever it led to had to be heavily guarded as well; but if Bingham had any desire to complete the assignment and escape the doldrums of being stuck in Alabama, he had to throw caution to the wind and force the issue.

The following night at Cotton City, right before the 10:00 p.m. shift began, a throng of mill workers poured into the parking lot. They were the two-to-ten workers, and every day when the whistle blew, there was a mad dash to Triple Sixes. Not the typical watering hole, Triple Sixes was an adult playground with pool tables, bowling lanes, and strippers who danced twenty-four hours a day. It was Southern excess at its naughty best, and it made the perfect sanctuary for Tobias Industries weary employees to gather and gossip while tossing back a few beers.

Tonight was like any other, Bingham walked in step with a group of coworkers as they headed to their vehicles. The plan was to get in his truck and follow everyone over to Triple Sixes, but when he got to his pick up he realized that he didn't have his keys. After promising to catch up with his friends at the bar, he walked back toward Cotton City's cluster of brick buildings.

The clamor created by the pulverizing machines was deafening, but Bingham had grabbed a set of earplugs when he stepped inside of the oil mill, and the sound of half-ton pneumatic hammers smashing billions of cotton seeds into pulp disappeared once he inserted them into his ears. No one in the processing plant paid any attention to him as he made his way to the rear exit of the building where he swiped the security card he lifted from one of his coworkers through a scanner to get outside.

The distinct sound of crickets and cicadas greeted Bingham after he climbed the fence behind the oil mill and stepped into the darkened cotton fields. He donned a pair of night-vision goggles and carefully navigated through a phalanx of spindly cotton plants as he crept over to the fence that ran alongside of the secure access road. Once there, he aligned himself with the access road and followed it deeper into the cotton fields, totally unaware of what awaited him at its end.

Under the cover of night, Bingham hiked for what seemed like miles, or at least until the oil mill and all the other buildings that made up Cotton City had disappeared. After walking what he estimated was another five miles, he slowed his pace when the road came to a stop at a booth hidden behind an extensive growth of trees. Quietly, he moved in closer for a better look and counted three armed men sitting in front of a huge eight-panel video screen. While staring intently at the steady stream of surveillance footage, they were all oblivious to the man peering through the window at them, and before anyone could notice, he crept back into the darkness where he couldn't be seen.

Bingham didn't stray too far away from the booth because he noticed directly behind it stood an eighteen-foot-high chain link fence. He aimed his miniature infrared flashlight at the fence and saw that it stretched on in either direction, creating a new perimeter. Since secretly crossing barriers into unfamiliar territory had been a job requirement at Intel-Ops, Bingham didn't hesitate at all before scaling the fence and climbing down on the other side.

Immediately, he noticed the road that led him to this point continued on. He followed it. There was no fence on either side of the winding road, and it wasn't long before Bingham found himself in the middle of another cotton field. He glanced at his watch and saw forty minutes had gone by since he told everyone that he was going back to look for his keys. He was faced with two options; either turn back now and meet up with his unsuspecting coworkers at Triple Sixes or follow the road to wherever it might lead. He kept going.

Not long after deciding to go on farther, Bingham faced another dilemma when he approached a fork in the road. His head filled with obscenities as the road split in two. Time was beginning to become a factor, and he didn't want to waste too much of it making a decision. He couldn't afford to make the wrong turn and get lost. The last thing he wanted was to be caught wandering this place come daylight.

Finally, after giving it some thought, he decided to take the road on the left but pledged to turn around and head back to Cotton City if he didn't find anything significant within a few miles.

Bingham's snap decision-making skills quickly paid off when the road he chose came to an abrupt stop at another fence. A feeling in the pit of his stomach told him this might be the break he was looking for. There was no booth or any armed guards in sight, so he proceeded with caution. As he approached the towering fence, Bingham dug into his pocket for his keys and tossed them toward it and watched blue sparks fly as the two metals touched. It was electrified.

He pulled on a pair of insulated rubber gloves and began to climb. He was very mindful of where he placed his hands and feet because if anything other than his gloves or the rubber soles of his boots touched the fence, the voltage would suck him in and burn him to a crisp like a piece of toast.

Once Bingham successfully made it to the other side, he retrieved a small digital camera from his belt clip and began to record. He had a hunch there had to be something here worth documenting to make someone go through the trouble of erecting an electrified fence in the middle of nowhere to protect it. Slowly, he panned the camera left and right and saw nothing but brush. The darkness was downright eerie; not a sound could be heard except for the occasional coo from an owl nesting the trees, but he pressed forward while managing to stay close to the gravel-strewn road.

After trudging through another thirty yards of dried leaves and twigs, Bingham approached what appeared to be a small one-story brick shack. It was a perfect square, twenty by twenty feet; and when he panned the camera toward the window, he spotted bars welded onto the outside. He inched closer with caution while steeling himself for whatever he may find, but nothing could have shocked him more than when he heard the distinct wail of a baby crying.

Bingham couldn't believe his ears. An infant was the last thing he expected to find out here on this night. Perspiration quickly dotted his forehead as he crept over to the open window to get a glimpse inside. Now directly underneath of the noise, he rose to his feet at a snail's pace and almost gasped when he peeked into the window before quickly ducking back out of sight. His heart began to race as he reached for the video camera at his side. Again, he slowly rose to his feet, took a deep breath, aimed the lens into the window, and pressed record.

A few minutes later, the wailing stopped, and Bingham felt as though he had enough footage, so he closed the lens and carefully fastened the camera back to his side. Instantly, a tingling sensation of nervousness began to pervade his usually steely resolve, and now he wanted to get away from this place as fast as he possibly could. Furtively, he slinked away from the edifice before blending in with the trees and vanishing into the night.

It took a little under an hour for Bingham to make it back to the oil mill, and now he sat behind the steering wheel of his pickup guzzling down a bottle of water. He was exhausted, totally drained both physically and mentally, and all he wanted to do was go back to his apartment and get some sleep. But as much as he wanted to drive straight home and dive into bed, he knew there was one more stop he had to make before he could rest his fatigued eyelids. He hissed loudly before yanking the gear into drive and driving toward Montgomery.

Twenty minutes later, Bingham pulled up to a house he rented on a quiet street in the city's suburban section and parked his truck inside of the two-car garage. The house was completely empty, void of any furniture except for the lone folding table and chair in a small bedroom upstairs.

He quickly navigated through the darkness as he made his way to the bedroom and retrieved a metal lockbox from the closet. He opened the box and placed its contents—a laptop computer and an encrypted cellular phone—onto the table. He powered up the laptop, and light from the screen turned the tiny bedroom electric blue. He downloaded the footage from his camera onto the computer and pressed send.

Suddenly, the phone on the table began to vibrate. Bingham answered it on the third ring. It was Buck Jennings.

"Can you please explain to me what the hell I am looking at on my computer screen?" Jennings asked from the other end of the line.

"I don't think I can answer that question honestly, but I can tell you what I saw," Bingham replied.

"I've got all night," Jennings deadpanned.

"I was afraid you were going to say that," Bingham said before sighing and recounting the events of the evening.

Jennings stopped him at the part where he got to the electrified fence. "So you mean to tell me that outside of that industrial complex was a cotton field which surrounded another cotton field which led to this area on the screen?"

"Yeah, sounds farfetched, but that's what I'm saying," Bingham answered.

"So what happened next?" Jennings asked after a momentary thought, and Bingham picked up the story from where he had stopped him.

"Once I cleared the fence, I had to cross a fifty-yard thicket of bracken before I got to the little brick hut on your screen. I moved in closer when I saw the bars on the windows, but the sound of a baby crying was truly the last thing I expected to hear. That's when I peeked into the window and saw what you are now seeing."

"Holy shit, man, this had to be one hell of a head trip," Jennings soberly offered, totally unsettled by the sight of a young mother breast-feeding a suckling infant while what appeared to be the rest of her family slept on mats strewn across the floor.

"The camera doesn't do what I saw any justice," Bingham said reflectively. "You had to smell the stink coming out of that window. That shack looked pretty old, I would guess pre-sixties, and I doubt if it had running water. I saw an outhouse, but those people were padlocked inside."

Jennings exhaled in disgust. "That's just sickening."

"No, what's sickening is that there are at least two hundred of those brick huts out there."

"How the hell doesn't anyone there know about this?"

"I told you, there is only one way in and one way out, and no one's getting access to that road but a select few."

"Maybe this is some type of government experiment," Jennings offered before realizing that what he just said was an absolute stretch.

"Come on, Buck, we both know America is fucked up, but Uncle Sam would never sanction shit like this."

"Hey, I'm just trying to make some sense of it all. This shit is crazy."

Bingham yawned. "You sent me here to find something substantial, and I think I did. What do you want me to do next?" he asked with the faint hope Jennings would tell him his assignment was complete.

The line went silent as Jennings contemplated for a moment. "Listen, Kyle, I know you want to get the hell out of there right now, but we just don't have much to go on. Get me more detailed footage of that place. This time, begin recording as soon as you get to Cotton City. I want a streaming link between this brutality and Tobias Industries. Don't leave those sons of bitches any room to weasel out of this," Jennings said before hanging up the phone.

The next day at the end of the two-to-ten shift, Bingham again found himself climbing over a fence and slinking into the cotton fields behind the oil mill. He checked the small fiber optic camera sewn into his baseball cap to see if it was still recording before heading into the darkness back to the hidden encampment he discovered the night before.

The night air was extremely sticky, and it wasn't long before the sweat began to pour down Bingham's face. He ignored the oven-like conditions and hiked on toward his destination while meticulously craning his head from side to side in an effort to capture as much footage as he possibly could. He wanted to make sure this was the last night he would ever have to spend in Alabama again.

This time, Bingham knew exactly where he was going, and he made it to the encampment rather quickly. He didn't hesitate to give himself a personal tour of the place once he got there—surreptitiously crisscrossing the entire compound in an attempt to survey every hut in the enclosure.

He counted ten rows, each twenty huts long with very little space in between them. Each hut shared the same dimensions, barred windows on every side and a huge padlock that kept the steel doors from being opened from the inside. The place was a virtual prison.

One by one, Bingham filmed each hut; and with each one, his disgust and enmity for Tobias Incorporated steadily grew. The conditions were deplorable. Sometimes there were as many as ten people of all ages packed inside the tiny huts like human sardines. Every time he peeked into a window, he held his breath because the putrid smell of urine and feces made it damn near impossible to breathe. He often wondered how people could sleep so peacefully under such inhuman circumstances.

As an operative for the CIA, he was present during the ethnic cleansings of Rwanda, Somalia, and Croatia and witnessed firsthand their genocidal atrocities. Bingham had become numb to seeing thousands of bodies strewn in the streets of those countries like unwanted garbage, but the sight of what appeared to be hundreds of black families literally imprisoned in the middle of America's heartland absolutely shook him to the core.

There was an outhouse positioned at every fifth hut, and immediately, he noticed the door on one of them wasn't locked, so he went inside to get a closer look. Florescent lights droned overhead and illuminated the interior, allowing him to remove his night-vision goggles, but the combined odor of human waste and stagnant moldy air almost knocked him back through the door. The outhouses were twice the size of the huts with no windows for ventilation. He covered his nose with his T-shirt and tried to tough it out.

A six-foot cinderblock wall divided the outhouse into two parts. One side was lined with stainless steel toilets and high up on the walls of the other side hung scummy shower heads. The conditions inside of the outhouse were no different from what he saw of the huts; the filth on the toilets must have taken years to accumulate, and the mold in the shower area looked like grass growing on the walls. Bingham looked down at the floor and winced when he thought of the billions of parasites swimming in the water that pooled around the drains. The environment was toxic, and he hurried outside to get some air.

Now outside, he leaned back against the door and tried to gather himself together. Bingham gagged and coughed in an attempt to fill his lungs with oxygen, but the humidity outside didn't make things any easier. As he doubled over, hoping he gathered enough footage to put an end to this viciousness, he realized that he wasn't wearing his night-vision goggles.

In his rush to exit the outhouse, Bingham forgot to put his goggles back on, and now that he was engulfed in total darkness, he couldn't see the two burly men standing in front of him. He reached for his goggles, but the men squeezed the triggers on their Tasers, and the last thing Bingham felt was a paralyzing jolt of electricity before falling lifelessly to the ground.

"Wake up, Kyle," a man's voice bellowed, rousing Bingham from a drug-induced stupor, "if that's really your name!"

Slowly, Bingham raised his head and opened his eyes. It took a second for him to adjust to the bright light, and when he did, he counted at least five other men in the room. He couldn't see who was behind him because he was strapped into a steel chair, but he knew someone was there. The men were dressed in black combat fatigues. Two stood by the door while the rest were occupied with rifling through his belongings, meticulously itemizing each article of clothing before tearing them into shreds.

"Found something," one of the men proclaimed when he took apart Bingham's baseball cap and discovered the hidden camera. He held up the mess of wires and synthetic material before walking past Bingham and handing it over to the man sitting at the desk behind him.

The room was antiseptic; white tile covered the floor and ran all the way up to the ceiling. In one corner, there stood a huge stainless steel cabinet, and in the other was a metal gurney equipped with ankle and wrist restraints. Bingham didn't have to guess what this room was used for. He knew he'd have to pay a price for getting caught. He put on his best poker face and mentally prepared himself for what would happen next.

After the men finished going through his things, they approached Bingham and turned his chair around so he could face the man sitting at the desk. There was a veil of cigarette smoke between them that made it hard for Bingham to see the man's face, but when the smoke cleared, he immediately took notice of the inch-thick scar that ran from the man's left eye down to the base of his neck. It was as if the man's head had been blown apart and sewn back together.

Sean McMiller stubbed out his cigarette and drummed his fingers against the desktop while studying Bingham's face. He looked for any signs of fear and Bingham showed none of it. McMiller knew he was dealing with a pro. "Who sent you?" he asked pointedly. Bingham said nothing while remaining stone-faced.

McMiller admired Bingham's stoicism, his ability to stay poised while being strapped to a steel arm chair buck naked. "Listen, Kyle, I kind of like you, so I'm not going to bullshit with you at all. This is your last stop. You're not going to make it out of this room alive," he said nonchalantly. "How painful you die is completely up to you, but you will tell me what I want to know."

Instantly, a chill went up Bingham's spine, and he could literally feel the hair standing up on the back of his neck. The man's words were so calloused he knew he was hearing the truth. From behind, Bingham could hear the steel cabinet being opened, so he took his mind to a happy place in his life and tried to stay there.

McMiller calmly lit another cigarette and took a long drag before blowing out a billow of smoke. "So who sent you?"

Silence again.

McMiller shifted his eyes to one of the men standing behind Bingham and quickly gave him a nod. Suddenly, without warning, the man walked over to Bingham and cut off his right pinky finger with a pair of pruning shears.

Bingham's eyes widened to the size of fifty-cent pieces as he resisted the urge to scream. Immediately, sweat began to pour, and his heart began to race at a staggering pace. He tried to remain at his happy place in a desperate attempt to ignore the pain.

McMiller pulled on his cigarette again. "Who sent you here?'

No answer.

Another quick nod, and the man with shears cut off Bingham's left pinky finger. Pain shot up against Bingham's left arm, and he pursed his lips as his breathing began to increase. He thought of his happy place, but it was almost impossible to focus on his wife and newborn son while blood spewed from his hands onto his legs.

McMiller remained unfazed by the man in front of him writhing in pain. He had seen and done much worse many times before. "Who sent you?" he deadpanned.

Sweat ran into Bingham's eyes, causing him to blink incessantly. His body shivered and his lips quivered, but he still refused to answer.

McMiller gave Bingham a half smile; part of him was impressed with the man's resolve, but the other part knew resistance was futile. He wished Bingham would just give up a name so he could die in peace. "Come on, Kyle, let's make this easy," he pleaded. "Your valiance is totally unnecessary."

Bingham didn't respond, and McMiller gave a nod to the man with the shears. Bingham braced himself to have another one of his fingers lopped off, but the man went over to the steel cabinet and returned with a blowtorch. The man turned the nozzle at the base of the torch's neck, and from its mouth breathed an intensified flame. As casual as kneeling to tie his shoes, the man dropped to one knee and aimed fire right at Bingham's feet.

There was no more happy place, no sanctuary Bingham would run to in the corner of his mind, just the smell of burning flesh. He tried his absolute best to remain strong, but when he looked down and saw the flame sear, blister, and rip through his skin, he opened his mouth and let forth a bloodcurdling scream.

A week later, it looked like a typical spring morning in Washington, DC. The sky was a baby blue with the sun shining brightly overhead. Proof of the pleasant day could be evidenced by the legions of people dressed lightly, out walking Georgetown's tree-lined streets.

Fine Print was a tiny vintage bookstore nestled between an antique jewelry shop and a French café near the corner of Connecticut Avenue and K Street. It specialized in first editions of any genre, and its leather-bound books fetched a pretty penny and attracted buyers of the eclectic kind. Customers were few and far between.

As he sat behind the counter reading the *Washington Post*, Buck Jennings didn't expect to see many customers today, so he was kind of surprised when he heard the bell over the front door jingle. He looked up and noticed a tall middle-aged man dressed in a business suit. The man was lightly bronzed and wore his hair slicked back exposing his graying temples. Jennings paid him no attention as he browsed through the aisles.

Suddenly, the man appeared at the counter. "Hello," he said with the toothy smile. "Nice day, isn't it?"

"Yeah, it is," Jennings said without taking his eyes away from the funny paper. "Can I help you with something?" he added after realizing the man wasn't going anywhere.

"Yes, I'm looking for anything written by William Makepeace Thackeray, circa 1833."

"That's a pretty rare request, if I must say so myself," Jennings said as he closed his newspaper and came from behind the counter. "I don't get too many seekers of Thackeray. His style of prose was way before his time," he added while walking toward the rear of the store.

"It's for my son," the man said as he followed behind Jennings. He's graduating from Stanford with a master's in English Literature. I thought Thackeray would be the perfect gift. Maybe he will amass a library as grand as this one day," he added, remarking about Fine Print's extensive collection of first-print books.

The books in Fine Print were stacked neatly inside of mahogany bookshelves that raised three stories high up to the ceiling. Jennings knew every square inch of his store, and he remembered Thackeray's were located high up on the third row of bookcases. He grabbed the stepladder and began to climb.

The man watched until Jennings reached the third row of bookcases and was almost as high as the ceiling. That's when he dug into his suit jacket and retrieved a small caliber pistol. "Have you located the book yet?" he looked up and asked as he calmly screwed a silencer into the gun's barrel.

"Not yet, but I think I'm getting closer," Jennings yelled down, oblivious to what was going on underneath him.

"Hey, Buck!" the man called up to Jennings after he took aim.

Instantly, Jennings furrowed his brow as he wondered how this man knew his name. "Yes?" he answered without letting on that he was surprised.

"Why did you send Kyle Bingham to Azalea?"

"Who?" Jennings replied.

"Bingham, you know, one of your operatives here at Intel-Ops!"

Jennings felt his heart skip a beat, but he managed to stay calm. "Hey look, pal, I don't know what you're talking about. You have me mistaken, but we can figure this all out once I climb down!"

"No!" The man yelled. "Stay your ass right up there where I can see you!" Jennings looked down and saw the man holding a gun. He stayed put.

"Listen, you can drop the charade! Bingham told us everything. If it's any consolation, it took a hell of a whole lot to get it out of him. We know you sent him. Now we want to know why."

"He told you everything, huh?" Jennings asked disappointedly.

"That he did," the man answered. "You can ask him why when you see him," he added arrogantly.

"I don't think I'm ready to have that conversation yet," Jennings said as he grabbed the top of the bookcase and yanked it toward the floor.

The man barely had a chance to yelp before the five-hundred-pound bookcase came crashing down on to him and all of its books.

After Jennings climbed down the stepladder, he dug through the rubble of books to see if the man was dead. He was. Jennings hurried to the front of the store and pulled the shades before locking the door. He grabbed his pistol from behind the counter and slipped out through the back door.

Later that afternoon, when he was absolutely sure he wasn't being followed, Jennings walked into the Law Offices of Chesney, Bregman, and Pierce. He got off the elevator at the fourth floor and headed straight to Alton's suite. He gave Robin Alverez a little small talk before letting himself in.

"Buck, this is a surprise," Alton said once Jennings entered his office. He got up to shake his hand.

"Look, Alton, I didn't mean to barge in on you on such short notice, but the shit is beginning to hit the fan around here."

"What do you mean?" Alton asked.

Jennings pulled a disc from his shoulder bag and inserted it into the DVD player connected to Alton's wall unit. Over the next few minutes, they watched, in silence, the footage Bingham had gathered from Cotton City. When they were done, Jennings had Alton's full attention as he relayed everything Bingham had told him.

"I wanted to come with more than this, but my man got made," Jennings said before pouring himself a drink.

"How do you know that?" Alton asked.

'Because someone from Tobias Incorporation tried to kill me today."

"Jesus Christ."

'Yeah, you got that right," Jennings said with a sigh. "You struck a nerve. These people obviously have a lot to lose. It's only going to get worse as you push forward."

"I know," Alton said apprehensively. "But what can I do? These people have to be stopped!"

"You have to be careful. They don't know anything about you. As long as it stays that way, you'll be safe. Don't tell anyone about this you don't trust. These people are determined to keep a lid on this. I lost one of my best men. Now I have to find a way to tell his family."

"What about you?" Alton asked with concern. "You're on their radar now."

"That's why I'm here," Jennings responded. "I wanted to give you this shit before I went underground. I'm going to take a little vacation, hop a few third-world countries until things are safe. I'll be sloppy so maybe I can buy you some time if I lead them on a wild-goose chase."

"Thanks, Buck."

"Don't thank me. This is all a part of the job. Be careful, and remember to work behind the scenes. Make these sons of bitches pay for what they've done," Jennings said before turning to leave. "One more thing, the guy at my store called the place on the disc Azalea. You might want to look into that," he added as he walked out of the door.

Immediately after Buck Jennings left, Alton called Dick Chesney and Amy Bregman to his office. Before they arrived, he managed to pour himself a drink. He was visibly disturbed by what he had just heard and seen.

"Alton, are you all right?" Dick asked.

"No, Dick, I'm not," Alton replied. "Why don't the two of you take a seat?"

Alton pressed play on the remote, and the images from Bingham's initial recording appeared on the TV screen. First was the extensive brush surrounding the encampment, and then came the compound itself with its small huts, bars on the windows, and locks on the doors.

Dick and Amy were completely caught off guard when they heard a baby scream. Their eyes widened a bit as they watched a young mother breast-feed the child while at least six other people were sprawled out across the floor asleep. The camera zoomed in on the filth and mice scurrying around on the floor before everything went black.

"What was that?" Dick asked as he sat up in his chair.

"That is Corporate America," Alton said while loosening his tie. "Have you two ever heard of Tobias Incorporated?"

They both nodded. "They're only the biggest textile conglomerate of the last century," Amy said sarcastically. "What do they have to do with this?"

"Late last year, I locked on to them because I suspected their minority roster was made up of ghost employees. I had Buck send someone down to Alabama to investigate. He got hired as a trouble-shooter at Tobias Incorporated's main industrial complex, and that's where he discovered this," Alton said as he pointed to the images replaying on the TV screen.

"Out of nearly five thousand employees, the African American employees can almost be counted on one hand. It's probably because they are imprisoning these people down there. I'm told there are at least two hundred more of those huts out there.

"What do you think it is?" Dick asked.

"I don't know," Alton said. "But whatever it is, it stinks."

"So what do you want to do, bring Buck's man in here, swear him up, and depose him?" Dick said. "I don't think bringing a case against Tobias Incorporated is going to be that easy."

"It's going to be harder than that," Alton deadpanned. "Buck's man is dead. And someone from Tobias Incorporated tried to kill Buck at his bookstore today."

"Holy shit, Alton, what have you gotten us involved in?" Dick said in a tone laced with panic.

"Nothing," Alton said confidently. "I'm going after them alone, and I'm doing it secretly. I just wanted you two to know what I'm up to in case anything happens to me."

"Amy, what do you think about all of this?" Dick asked.

Her eyes were glued to the TV screen. She was the granddaughter of Holocaust survivors, and the footage reminded her of her grandparents' horrific tales of the Nazi camps in Auschwitz. Tales of hunger, death, and desperation. Her blood began to boil.

"Amy! Amy!" Dick called out while snapping his fingers to get her attention.

"What," she shrieked as she turned to face him.

"How do you feel about what Alton's doing? People are getting killed. I say he should burn the disc and forget about all this shit."

"I'm supportive. Dick, someone has to put an end to this. I would be dishonoring my grandparents if I stood by and did nothing," Amy stated firmly before turning to Alton. "I'm totally on board."

"Thanks, Amy," Alton said before facing Dick.

Dick twisted his face and thought for a moment then he exhaled heavily. "Okay, Alton, I'm in," he said reluctantly. "But you're going to owe me big time if someone tries to kill me."

"Nobody's going to come for you," Alton reassured him. "No one knows that we know anything. I'm going to give each of you a copy of this DVD. Put it in a safe place, and don't say anything to a soul."

The next morning at the Tobias Tower, Jackson Tobias found himself in a boardroom chairing over an executive meeting. Regally, he sat at the head of the table and listened intently as each department head read off last quarter's profits and forecasted projections for the next fiscal year from a stack of spreadsheets.

As the succession of executives droned on about the success of their divisions, Jackson's Blackberry began to vibrate. He retrieved the phone from inside of his jacket and read the message on the screen.

Suddenly, he rose to his feet. "Ladies and gentleman, I hate to be rude, but could you all please leave?" Jackson calmly said, bringing the meeting to a grinding halt.

Everyone stopped what they were doing and looked directly at him.

"Nooowww!" he yelled as he slammed his hand against the table, and instantly, the entire boardroom cleared.

All alone in the empty room, Jackson slumped back into his seat. He wiped away the sweat that was beginning to dot his forehead. Anxiety slowly saturated through his body, and he felt a slight quake in his knees. He looked at the message again.

"Someone knows about your dirty little secret in Alabama, and for the right price, I'll tell you who it is."

CHAPTER 14

"**C**ome on, Jonny," Felicia breathed as she bent over the railing that bordered the wide terrace outside of Jonathan Tobias's twenty-million-dollar midtown Manhattan penthouse. "Say yes."

Jonathan, pretending he didn't hear her, just kept thrusting into her from behind. Every few strokes, he would either reach around and cup her breast, smack her hard on the ass, or grab and pull fistfuls of her long blonde hair. He didn't want the moment to end.

"Yeah, baby, say it to me," Felicia yelped between pants. "Tell me that I'm going to be your wife before you come," she added as he continued to pump away.

They loved having sex this way; fifty stories above the city and high on ecstasy. Being outside on the lofty terrace made him feel like Zeus making love to Aphrodite in the clouds over Olympus.

"Yesss! Oh, yesss!" Jonathan hissed as every muscle in his body began to tense. He held on as long as he could before succumbing to the carnal excitement swelling inside of him and filling Felicia's erogenous zone with his love.

They fell into a cushy chaise lounge, naked and wrapped in each other's arms. They both took in deep breaths while looking up at the silver moon hovering in the sky among the stars. Felicia leaned over and grabbed a gold-plated sugar bowl from the glass tea table beside her and handed it to Jonathan. It was filled with cocaine. He took two quick sniffs and passed it back to her. She took two sniffs as well, and together, both of their hearts began to race.

"Jonny, we're going to have the biggest engagement party New York has ever seen," Felicia said while wiping a little excess powder from her nose. "Everyone who's anyone is going to be there to celebrate us. I can see it now, can't you?" she added with heightened enthusiasm.

"I see it too, babe," he answered with an equal amount of zeal. But it was a lie; his mind had been somewhere else since learning his family's secrets were halfway out of the bag. The only thing he was seeing was CX9's potential billions going up in flames. The past week was spent in such a daze he didn't even remember saying yes when Felicia asked him to marry her.

"I had my publicist take out full pages in *Gotham*, *New Yorker*, and every newspaper in town to announce our engagement. By this time tomorrow, the whole city's gonna know."

Jonathan sat up. "Damn it, Fels. Why didn't you tell me about this first? Right now is not a good time for my family and your publicity."

"Hey! What the hell do you mean by that?" she asked indignantly. "My publicity?"

"You know, the tabloids and paparazzi," he said with a shrug. "I don't feel like hearing my father's shit. Especially right now."

Felicia hissed. "Why do you always have to bring him into everything? Are you marrying him or me?"

"I'm marrying you. But you know damn well that my father hates you."

"I know, but I don't give a shit. I'm not attached to his strings. That's what he hates."

"Amongst other things," Jonathan said as if he personally read the laundry list of things Jackson disliked about her.

"Who cares?" she said while rolling her eyes. Just lie back and let me deal with your father when the time comes."

As Felicia buried her head between his legs, Jonathan tilted his head toward the sky and thought of the woman he would soon marry. With all of her flaws, Felicia Wennington had captured his heart long ago. She too suffered the angst of having to appear perfect for the sake of her prestigious family. But she never gave in; while he hid behind his two-hundred-dollar haircut, oxford shirts, and Brooks Brothers suits, Fels let her true self hang out for the world to see. He loved that she wasn't the phony he and most blue bloods were, but more importantly, he loved her because she was the only person brave enough to consistently defy his father.

Two nights later, Jonathan found himself sitting next to his Uncle Jerrold glancing across the desk at his father. They were in Jackson's home office at Tamarack, and this was the first time the three of them were together since the debacle at Azalea.

"How the hell could you let something like this happen?" Jackson said while staring daggers at Jerrold. "Azalea's your baby, so you're responsible for the blame."

Jerrold bit his bottom lip and slowly shook his head. "Jack, we need to think about solutions rather than playing the blame game."

"I'm the one being blackmailed, so it's safe to say I can lay the blame wherever I please. Don't you agree?"

"Jack, what do you want me to say? What happened in Alabama was an aberration. It'll never happen again," Jerrold said in his defense.

"Aberration? How can you sit here and say a thing like that?" Jackson barked back at him. "Almost 150 years, and no one outside of the fold has ever come close to Azalea. That's someone not doing their fucking job, not an aberration!"

"Dad," Jonathan said in an attempt to speak up, but Jackson quickly raised his index finger.

"Don't you say a goddamned word Jon," Jackson snapped as his face gradually turned red. "I'll deal with you in a minute."

After inhaling a deep breath, Jackson turned back to his brother. "Damn it, Jerry," he said calmly. "I don't mean to slam down on you, but if anyone should know what's at stake, it's you. Billy's beginning to make some headway down in DC. He's getting a name for himself in the Senate. The timing could not be worse. In less than a year, I plan to unveil CX9 to our friends in the military, but if word gets out about Azalea, we won't be able to give CX9 away for free."

Jerrold exhaled. The tension was thick inside of the office. "So what do you propose we do?'

Jackson leaned back into his chair. "Well, the way I see it, the only reason someone contacted me is because they're looking for a payday. I say we give them what they want. It can't possibly be worth more than what we stand to lose if the truth gets out. Besides, it's the only way we're going to find out who's the nosey fuck that's so goddamned interested in our business."

Jerrold and Jonathan both nodded their heads, indicating that they agreed. Jackson continued, "Jerry, I'm through with crying over the spilled milk. Now it's time for you to clean it up."

"Okay, Jack, you've made your point," Jerrold said as he rose from his seat. "Don't worry, I'm going to take care of everything."

"You damned well better," Jackson deadpanned before his brother walked out of the door. "You're the one who's responsible for this mess."

Jonathan decided not to say anything once they were left alone in the office because he knew his turn was next.

Jackson stubbed out his cigar and pulled a file folder from a drawer and placed its contents on top of the desk. "Explain this."

Jonathan thumbed through the stack of newspapers and magazine ads announcing the engagement of Jonathan Tobias and Felicia Wennington.

"Tell me this is a joke—because if it is, I'm not laughing."

Jonathan shook his head. "It's not a joke. Fels and I are getting married."

"So this is how I was supposed to find out?" Jackson said as he placed his big hand on top of the pile of newspapers and magazines. "What's the matter with you? Aren't you aware of the timing? The last thing this family needs is to be in the headlines."

"Why is everything always about the family? Why can't I make a decision for me?"

"Because there would be no you without this family."

For that, Jonathan had no response.

"I thought she was just something you liked having fun with," Jackson said boorishly.

"No, Dad. I love her."

"Why, Felicia's nothing but rich white trash. Good for nothing but unwanted attention. With all of the press she gets, one would think she was personally responsible for the Wennington Seat on Wall Street. You want to bring that kind of poison into our family?"

"She's not poison, she's unique," Jonathan said in her defense. "You don't understand who she really is."

"I understand exactly who she is, a druggy and an alcoholic who stays in trouble. And how you would want to marry someone like that is completely beyond me."

"I can't see why not, you did," Jonathan said defiantly.

Before Jonathan realized what he had said, Jackson's right hand was tightly clenched around his neck. "Your mother is sick! Sick, you got that? Don't ever disrespect her that way again! Do you hear me?"

"Yes," Jonathan wheezed as he struggled to breathe in air.

"Do you hear me?" Jackson roared as his face turned red.

Jonathan opened his mouth to respond, but nothing came out as his eyeballs began to roll toward the back of his head. Jackson let him go and sat back down in his chair.

As he tried to regain his composure, Jonathan doubled over in his seat and grappled for air. He couldn't stop himself from coughing.

"You can see your mother is a sore topic for me. She should never be compared to Felicia," Jackson said calmly as he watched his son gag. "I chose you to succeed me because I trust your judgment. I truly hope your decision to marry Felicia doesn't give me cause to reconsider. Now get the hell out of my office."

Miraculously, Jonathan picked himself up and left immediately.

Outside of his father's mansion, Jonathan loosened his tie and dug into his pocket for his keys. He wiped the sweat from his brow with his forearm as he tottered over to his Mercedes. He got behind the steering wheel and let the engine run while gathering himself for the drive back to the city.

Suddenly, a black limousine pulled up beside Jonathan's car and rolled down its rear window. It was Jerrold. "I see he tore you a new one," he said once he got Jonathan's attention.

Jonathan exhaled a deep breathe and slowly shook his head.

"What did you do?"

"I decided to get married."

"Let me guess, your father doesn't agree with your choice of bride?"

"Hates her guts," Jonathan said dejectedly.

"My brother the control freak. Jack's been that way since we were kids. So what do you plan to do?"

"Get married," Jonathan said gallantly, but he remembered the feeling of his father's fingers tightening around his neck. "I guess."

Jerrold smiled sinisterly. "I like a man who stands by his convictions, even in the face of adversity."

"You give me too much credit, Uncle Jerry," Jonathan offered humbly.

"Your father means well, but sometimes he can come off like a bully. Especially when it comes to protecting his family," Jerrold said sympathetically. "I think he forgets you are still a young man. Let me talk to Jack. I can remind him that he once was a young man too. Your first night at Azalea I told you I'd be there to help you along. So remember, if there's anything you need assistance with, anything— my brother, the company, or you just want to talk, you can always call me."

Jonathan began to nod his head. He needed an ally within the company, within the family, and he was grateful that his uncle offered to be that man. "Thanks, Uncle Jerry."

"Don't mention it. Now go on home and get some sleep," Jerrold said when he noticed the red marks on Jonathan's neck.

In the ensuing weeks, Alton totally submerged himself in his work. He farmed his entire caseload out to his most proficient associates at the firm in an effort to dedicate all of his energy to pursuing Tobias Industries. He practically lived at the office, putting in eighteen-hour days and coming home with just enough fuel left to eat a quick meal before going to sleep. The next day, he would do it all over again.

Alton's behavior drove Lara crazy. They used to talk about everything; now he was secretive. She would often inquire about his work, but he would always say that he couldn't answer out of concern for her own safety. Lara ignored the tiny voice in her head whispering that there may be another woman because, deep down inside, she knew Alton was telling her the truth. She wished things didn't have to be this way with their wedding approaching, but she was thankful for the other man in her life she could turn to.

As promised, Jonathan Bradford made himself available for Lara after their first meeting. They would call each other at least once a week and meet for lunch at the Plaza Hotel monthly. They always sat at the table where their first encounter took place, the one with the view of Central Park.

Every time they met, Bradford came bearing gifts. It was usually a million-dollar bearer bond and an expensive piece of jewelry. Lara loved the jewels, but she told her father it would be best if she donated the money to charity. Upon hearing what his little girl wanted to do with the money, Bradford saw to it the value of the bonds increased, and today, it was a treasury bond worth ten million dollars.

"This is a lot of money," Lara said with wide eyes over tiramisu and cappuccino.

Jonathan Bradford smiled meekly. "A lot of money will do a lot of good deeds. You'll do what's best with it." Lara reached across the table and placed her hand on his.

"Lara, it's a beautiful day outside. Let's not waste it. How about a stroll in the park?"

He was telling the truth. It was a beautiful day outside. The temperature was balmy, and the noon air still smelled morning-fresh as a few sun rays managed to squeeze around a skyscraper and brighten the intersection at Fifth Avenue and Fifty-Ninth Street. They held hands as they crossed the intersection and entered Central Park.

The park was crowded, and people were everywhere: joggers in spandex looking to burn off unwanted calories, tourists taking pictures, vendors hawking soft pretzels, and a bevy of doe-eyed couples out enjoying the afternoon. Birds chirped noisily while flitting from tree to tree. Lara and her father strolled through the picturesque scene until they reached a bench at the edge of a pond and took a seat.

"Dad?" Lara had begun to call him that lately. "Can you tell me about my brothers and sisters?"

The question completely caught Bradford off guard. Since they'd been in contact, Lara had never broached the subject. He stood up and tossed a pebble into the water before turning back to face her. "Why?" he asked softly.

Lara shrugged slightly. "I don't know. Lately, I've had some time on my hands since Alton's been so busy. I've been wondering what they were like."

Bradford sat back down on the bench and looked at his daughter. He took a second and studied Lara's features; the icy blue eyes that came from him, the high cheekbones and angular face donated by her mother, and the unblemished almond-colored skin derived from the both of them. He made a beautiful daughter, but he knew the essence of Lara's beauty came from within. He decided to tell her the truth.

"They are not you. If I could use one word to describe them, it would be *entitlement*. They've never worked for anything but believe they deserve everything. When I look at them, I see all of my failures as a parent."

Lara's eyes lowered a bit. "I didn't mean to bring up such a sore subject."

"It's all right," Bradford said with half a smile. "Sometimes it's good to vent. Do you know what's funny?"

"What?"

"You're nothing like them, and it's probably because I wasn't around."

"Believe me," Lara said. "I'm not so perfect."

"I'm serious. If there's anyone who should feel they were owed anything, it's you. Yet you are the most reserved person I know," he said before leaning over and giving Lara a one-armed hug.

A silent moment passed between them as Lara gathered herself. She had an important request for her father. It was months in the making, but she was afraid to ask because she would be devastated if he told her no. Today, on a bench in Central Park, she'd finally worked up the nerve.

"Dad, I know because of your current status within your family's company, you've been adamant about keeping our relationship a secret." She spoke slow and carefully. "I'm fully aware that you are not ashamed of me and that there are some in your family who would use me as an excuse to bring you down. But I'm about to be married to the kind of man that only comes around once in a lifetime, and on my wedding day, I would like for you to walk me down the aisle."

Jonathan Bradford looked to the sky as he considered Lara's offer. He knew he would be finished if his secret ever got out. He began to think of everything that could go wrong if he walked Lara down the aisle when, suddenly, out of the corner of his eye, he spotted a group of elementary-school-aged girls dressed in identical uniforms. They walked in a two-by-two line formation and were trailed by a pair of nuns. Immediately, he thought of a little uniformed girl with a broken heart and the vow he made never to hurt her again. He turned to his daughter.

"I would absolutely be honored to give you away."

"Will you?" Lara gushed as her eyes welled with tears. "Do you mean it?"

"Yes, I mean it. I was wondering when you were going to ask," he said with a nervous laugh, knowing he was risking career suicide.

"Oh, thank you, Dad! Thank you!" Lara said as tears of joy poured from her eyes.

Later on that week, a black SUV pulled up in front of the mansion at Azalea. It was Jerrold Tobias as he had just flown in from New York. The sun was beginning to wane over the horizon, and it painted the sky burnt orange. The view was spectacular and enticed Jerrold to light a cigar and admire the sunset from the front porch. But there was pressing business at hand, so he pocketed his Cohiba, turned his back to the sun, and went into the house.

As he made his way to Primary Control, Jerrold remembered running through the mansion's marbled hallways with Jackson as a child. He sighed, realizing those days were long gone. Azalea represented nothing but dollars and cents now. He stepped off the elevator and into the command center hidden deep below the mansion and summoned Sean McMiller to his office.

"What's going on, boss?" McMiller said after lumbering into the office and closing the door.

"I just left Jack, and he gave me the information we've been looking for," Jerrold said as he slid a thin file across the desk. "Said it cost him a hefty sum."

"How much?" McMiller asked as he perused through the small stack of papers.

"Don't ask."

"That much, huh?" McMiller said with a laugh.

"Yeah, and he's blaming me."

"What else is new?" McMiller said casually. "If there's anyone to blame, it's me. I let you down, boss. It won't happen again."

"Ahh, Sean, don't worry about it. This is something we can fix," Jerrold reassured him. "Besides, I like to see that fuckin' Jack sweat."

"So, Alton Pierce, he's the guy behind all this shit," McMiller said as he placed the file back onto the desk. "Who is he?"

"Some hotshot civil attorney from DC with a goddamned hero complex," Jerrold said as he leaned back in his chair and lit his cigar. "The word is he's good. And he hates corporate injustice."

"Shit. He must have a big hard-on for us."

"That he does," Jerrold said between exhaling puffs of sweet-smelling smoke.

"So what are we going to do about him?" McMiller asked before making a slashing gesture with his thumb across his throat.

"No, not yet," Jerrold said while slowly shaking his head. "He doesn't have anything on us except for some footage on DVD. And legally, he knows he can't prove it came from this place. Right now, we watch and wait."

"I don't like the idea of not taking care of an open wound. You know they can get infected and cause serious injury if left unattended," McMiller said as he ran his thick fingers along the crevice on the left side of his face.

"Listen, Sean, we'll deal with this Pierce gentleman in due time. For now, he gets nothing but surveillance. I don't want him touched, but I do want his computers piggybacked and his office and phones wired for sound. I want to know everything about him, what he eats, and how hot he likes his tea. I want to know what's on the inside of this prick's head."

McMiller rolled his eyes. "Wouldn't it be easier to just kill him?" he asked impatiently.

"Yeah, but if I wanted that, he'd already be dead," Jerrold responded. "For argument's sake, say Pierce disappeared, committed suicide, or has an accidental death—then what?"

McMiller remained silent.

"I'll tell you," Jerrold continued. "Someone else he knows will come along and pick up where he left off, and we'll find ourselves faced with the same damn problem again. Nothing happens to Pierce until we convince him to back off our case."

"How do we do that? He doesn't sound like someone who'll take a payoff."

"We observe," Jerrold said before puffing on his cigar. "We learn what he loves and, subsequently, what he fears."

"He doesn't strike me as someone we can just scare."

Jerrold snickered. "Sean, everyone's afraid of something. When a man appears to be fearless, you threaten to take away what he loves, and ultimately, you'll expose what he fears the most."

Meanwhile, alone in his office, Alton sat behind his desk staring at a blank computer screen. He was frustrated. Three whole weeks had passed since he had learned of the atrocities taking place at Tobias Industries, and yet, he hadn't accomplished anything. The clock on the wall read 1:00 a.m. It was shaping up to be another night that would end with his eyes burning red from reading and re-reading a mountain of papers and him still light-years away from building a case.

Alton's cheeks ballooned before exhaling dejectedly. He had dug up every unknown fact about Tobias Incorporated including the company's origin as a cotton plantation called Azalea at the start of the nineteenth century, the peculiar contract Abraham Lincoln drafted in 1862 granting them the exclusive right to supply their textiles to the US government indefinitely, as well as the equally peculiar competitive clause in 1925 prohibiting any aircraft from flying over the airspace above Cotton City. The information led Alton to believe that the Tobiases had been hiding something for at least a century. Still, he had absolutely no clue what it could be. And to compound the matter, with Kyle Bingham dead, he had no way to legally tie Tobias Incorporated to the DVD.

"Alton?" Robin Alverez said as she peeked into his office. "It's late. Do you need anything before I leave?"

He looked up and saw her standing in the doorway. "No, Robin, I'll be all right."

"Are you sure? I have an air mattress in my car if you need me to stay here tonight."

Somehow, despite his despondency, Alton managed a laugh. "You must want Lara to castrate me."

"I don't think she would mind," Robin said facetiously. "She hasn't seen you in almost a month."

"How do you know she hasn't seen me?"

"Because you've been locked in your office for the last three weeks."

"Robin, she understands," he said defensively. "Lara knows that in my line of work, people need me."

"Yeah, I know that, Alton, but did it ever occur to you that she may need you too. I know if I had to go to sleep alone for twenty-one days straight because my fiancée wanted to work late, I'd be pretty pissed."

"It's not like she's not busy with the wedding and all. Besides, the relationship with her father keeps her occupied."

"I almost forgot about that. How is it going?" Robin inquired.

"Fine, I guess," he said while shrugging his shoulders. "She doesn't tell me much, but I respect her privacy."

"Have you met him yet?"

"No, our schedules conflict because a lot of his work's abroad, and when he's stateside, he doesn't have much time to spare. But he's giving Lara away at our wedding, so I'll get to meet him when we start the rehearsals next month."

"So there's still going to be a wedding?"

"Why wouldn't there be?" Alton asked curiously.

"I didn't think you would have much time to get married since you're spending so much of it on this case," Robin quipped.

"Come on, Robin, lay off me," Alton pleaded. "Tobias Incorporated's treating people worse than animals, and someone has died bringing that information forth. What am I supposed to do, take a break?"

"Yes!" Robin said vehemently. "You are putting entirely too much pressure on yourself. In all of our years working together, you've never been like this. Have you looked in the mirror? You look like shit."

Alton had nothing to say because he knew Robin was right. He hadn't had a decent meal and a good night's sleep in weeks. Alton stopped pondering and got up. He then went over to Robin and kissed her on the cheek.

"What was that for?" she asked.

"Because you're right," Alton admitted. "I need to take my ass home. It's not like I'm getting anything accomplished around here anyway."

"Good," she said after breathing a sigh of relief. "And stay there for a few days—everyone will be better for it. Maybe a break will open your eyes to whatever it is you're not seeing."

"Maybe," Alton concurred, "because I definitely need to catch a break in this case."

"You will. I have all the faith in the world in you," Robin said as she embraced him before turning toward the door. "Are you coming?"

"Not yet. Go on ahead," he said while waving her away. "I have a few things to do before I leave."

Once Robin left him alone, Alton shut off his computer and headed into the bathroom. He grabbed a washcloth, walked over to the sink, and turned on the faucet. He looked at himself in the mirror while wiping his face with cold water. He agreed with Robin. He did look like shit.

Alton opened the medicine cabinet and retrieved a bottle of Visine to wash the redness from his eyes. He looked to the ceiling to add a few drops to his eyes when, suddenly, someone closed the bathroom door. Immediately, he went over and tried to turn the knob, but it was locked. Then the lights went out.

"Robin!" he yelled while struggling to open the door.

No one answered.

"Hello!" he bellowed to no avail.

Alton's mind was beginning to wander to the darkest corners of his imagination. He had no idea who or what was on the other side of the door. He felt around the pitch-black bathroom in an effort to find a weapon but only came up with a wooden-handled toilet brush. Alton clutched it like it was a miniature baseball bat and waited and waited. Nothing happened. For the next few minutes, he stood by the door with toilet brush firmly in his hands anticipating an attack, but suddenly, the lights came back on.

"Hello!" Alton called out again. No one answered, and he braced himself before trying the door again. This time it opened. Still clutching the toilet brush with all his might, he slowly stepped out of the bathroom and into his office.

It was empty. Alton saw no one as his eyes darted around the room, but he did notice that the chair behind his desk had been turned around to face the window. He could see from a shadow cast against the wall that someone was seated in his chair. He took a deep breath and held it.

"Hey!" Alton called out sternly. "I have a gun. Turn around slowly, and I won't shoot."

The person in the chair didn't move, and Alton inched a few steps closer.

"Look, goddamnit, I said turn around!"

Still no response. But by this time, Alton had reached the desk. He grabbed the chair, quickly spun it around, and felt his heart dip into his stomach.

"Fuck!" Alton said as he let the toilet brush fall to the floor.

Sitting lifelessly in Alton's chair was the crystal bust of Thurgood Marshall with a red bull's-eye painted on his forehead. But it wasn't' the desecration of the Supreme Court Justice that startled Alton; it was the envelope taped to its chest. In red marker were the words "FOR ALTON." He snatched the envelope and read the note inside.

YOU KNOW ABOUT US. NOW WE KNOW ABOUT YOU.

BACK OFF OR YOU WILL BE NEXT.

Alton put the note down and reached for the telephone and speed-dialed Robin.

"Hello?" she answered.

"Robin! Thank God!" he said excitedly. "Where are you? Are you all right?"

"I'm fine. I'm almost home. What's going on?"

"They were here," Alton said frantically. "And I thought you might have run into them on your way out."

"Who?"

"The Tobiases or the people who work for them. I don't know, but they locked me in the bathroom and left a warning for me in my office!"

"Where are they now?"

"I don't know. They seem to have left."

"I'm calling the police," she said with concern.

"No, Robin, don't," Alton quickly said.

"Well, what are you going to do?"

"I'm going home. Lara's there all alone."

Alton made it home in record time after speeding through the lights in the city and rushed directly upstairs to his bedroom where he found Lara in bed, sleeping peacefully. As he watched her lay comfortably beneath the covers, he exhaled a sigh of relief. Alton decided not to wake her. Instead, he stood guard over her, peeking out the window from time to time until fatigue finally won out, and he crawled into bed fully clothed, wrapped his arms around his fiancée, and drifted off to sleep.

The next morning, Alton wasted no time before summoning Dick and Amy to his office. They sat quietly as he recounted the details of the night before. Neither of them blinked an eye until he finished.

"Jesus, Alton. Are you sure that you're okay?" Dick asked protectively.

"Yeah, I'm fine," was Alton's response. "Dick, are you absolutely certain you told no one about this case?"

"Hell no! Alton, I didn't want you to get involved with this shit in the first place. Why would I tell anyone? I don't want to get killed," Dick said nervously. He was visibly shaken.

Alton cast his gaze in Amy's direction. His eyes asked the question.

Amy pursed her tiny lips and shook her head. "Nope, I didn't say anything to anyone. Not even Adam, and you both know I tell my husband everything."

"I know," Alton agreed. "But someone had to say something."

"Well, it wasn't one of us," Dick offered quickly.

Alton exhaled. "If neither one of you said anything, there could only be one other logical answer. They must've tracked down Buck. Shit, I could have sworn he wouldn't get caught," he said before placing his head in his hands, distraught.

"Damn," Dick said solemnly. "Alton, they are on to you now. What're you going to do?"

"I'm going to buy a gun. And I swear, I am not going to leave this office until I find a way to make these bastards pay for what they're doing."

Alton tried to look confidently at his partners, but there was a glaze of uncertainty in his eyes. Suddenly, a case against Tobias Incorporated seemed almost impossible to mount. The pressure was beginning to build, and Alton knew that if his words were going to ring true, it would damn near take a miracle since his most resourceful ally was likely dead. The battle instantly turned uphill, and now he would have to go it alone.

For Jonathan and Felicia's engagement party, throngs of onlookers flocked to the South Street Seaport just to catch a glimpse of the entertainment industry's most famous celebrities and a bevy of New York City's social elite. From behind the velvet rope, they watched each star walk the red carpet before stepping onto a private pier where the hottest techno artist blared his music. The party served up only the best cuisine—cocktail shrimp the size of fists, sushi from New York's premiere Japanese restaurant, and of course, an ice-sculptured mountain cascading with Cristal champagne. "Only the best for the best" was Felicia motto, and so it was on this occasion.

Suddenly, a Tiffany blue–colored Bentley GT pulled up to the red carpet, and the crowd began to scream ferociously. The guests of honor had arrived. A frenzy of whistles and catcalls greeted Jonathan and Felicia once they stepped out of the car, and both were nearly blinded when they stopped to pose for pictures.

"Fels, show us your ring!" yelled a paparazzo, and she extended her left arm to put the sparkling gigantic rock on display for the cameras and everyone else to see.

"Jon, look at them. They absolutely love us," Felicia whispered into his ear as they walked the red carpet.

"No, they are in love with you," he said with a grin as they turned to take another series of pictures before being ushered into the party.

Once inside, the couple was welcomed with a standing ovation and led to a table at the center of the stage. From there, as the music thumped, they presided over the party like a newly coroneted king and queen.

After discreetly slipping three Ecstasy pills into her champagne glass, Felicia could actually feel the music pulsating through her body. She suddenly found the dance floor impossible to resist.

"Come dance with me," Felicia said to Jonathan while gently tugging at his arm. Jonathan placed his hand on his stomach and shook his head.

"Pah-leeze," she begged.

"Fels, go on without me. I'm not feeling too well," he said with a slight twinge in his eyes. "It must have been something I ate at your parents' before coming over here. My stomach is doing backflips."

"Jonny, you can't be serious," Felicia said. "You can't get sick, not here, not tonight. This is *our* engagement party, and you are so fucking ruining it right now!" she added before rolling her eyes and marching off to the dance floor.

Jonathan seethed while watching Felicia mingle and dance the night away. He wasn't sick at all; it was the phone call he received earlier from his father that kept him glued to his seat. In less than a week, Tobias Incorporated had plans to unveil a new division called Solutions4Energy. It was the precursor for CX9, and Jackson had warned him not to do anything to embarrass the family. Jonathan wanted to do some coke, pop some Ecstasy, and join his fiancée, but he knew nothing was sacred in the age of information—especially with media helicopters hovering overhead in an attempt to pilfer footage of the festivities.

The party went on for hours, everyone dancing like there was no tomorrow. The music pounded until 3:00 a.m. when carts of glowing champagne bottles with sparklers affixed to them were wheeled in, parting the dance floor like the Red Sea. Everyone was handed a gilded bottle, which they raised on high in deference to Jonathan and Felicia. And like gunfire, corks began to pop in rapid succession as champagne spewed wildly into the air. The partygoers roared and reveled in awe as a barrage of fireworks burst into a rainbow of colors lighting up the lower Manhattan skyline. As promised, the party ended with a bang.

By this time, the crowd outside had grown twice its size. They wanted one last photo of their favorite celebrities as they left the party. The endless flashing from the paparazzi's cameras and the fireworks detonating in the sky above transformed the southern tip of Manhattan into a Hollywood-like reality.

The engagement party was a complete success, and by its end, Felicia was totally wasted. She could barely hold herself up as she and Jonathan exited the pier. Jonathan held her hand as they walked the red carpet on the way back to her car. Felicia used her other hand to wave at what she perceived were her adoring fans.

"Give me your keys," Jonathan whispered discreetly in her ear.

"What?" she asked.

"Your car keys, give them to me."

"The valet has them, why?"

"Because you are not fit to drive. You can barely walk."

"There's nothing wrong with me," Felicia said defiantly. "You're the one that was sick. That's my car, and if you don't want me to drive, then I suggest you hail a taxi."

Jonathan bit down hard and tried to ignore Felicia's remark. He struggled to keep from smacking her in the face.

They posed for more pictures once they reached the curb, and Felicia waved to the crowd before climbing into her Bentley. The crowd went crazy, and like his father, Jonathan wondered what the hoopla was all about. He climbed in and fastened his seatbelt.

Felicia buckled herself in before turning to Jonathan. "Are you sure you want to ride with me since I am so goddamned drunk? Jesus, you sound like your father. And for the record, I know you weren't sick, you fuckin' pussy," she hissed while putting the car into gear.

"Felicia!" Jonathan yelled.

"What?" she turned and asked, but it was too late. Her foot mashed the gas pedal and the car went reeling backward. Totally shocked that she mistakenly put the gearshift in reverse, Felicia tried to regain control of the vehicle, but it jumped the curb and smashed into a crowd of people before slamming into a light pole.

Jonathan checked on his fiancée then unfastened his seatbelt and climbed out of the car to survey the damage. Panicked screams for help polluted the air as good Samaritans rushed over to care for the injured. The Bentley mowed down a total of six people, and huddles of onlookers were scattered along the sidewalk checking to make sure they were still alive. As if on cue, a chill wind blew in from off the Hudson River to compound the misery; but in the distance, Jonathan could hear the consoling wail of ambulance sirens.

By the time Jonathan made it back to the car, Felicia had at least twenty cameras shoved into her face. All of them were rapidly clicking and flashing away at the stupefied look in her eyes. Envisioning tomorrow's headlines, Jonathan's head began to throb, because in his wildest dreams, he couldn't have imagined a more disastrous way to end the evening.

The following Monday morning, a fierce electrical storm pelted Manhattan with sheets of rain. The top half of the city's skyscrapers disappeared into an armada of low-hanging clouds. The torrential downpour made visibility nearly impossible and reduced rush-hour traffic to a crawl. Hordes of pedestrians clung desperately to their umbrellas in an ill-fated attempt to stay dry.

Meanwhile, inside of a parking garage two blocks north of the Tobias Tower, Alton sat behind the steering wheel of his Mercedes while trying to gather his nerves. He woke up early, as Lara lay asleep, and made the three-hour drive from DC to New York. Now that he was here, he flirted with the idea of turning around and driving back home.

Cradled in his hand was a nickel-plated .38 special, that gleamed under the glow of the car's interior light. Alton never owned a gun before, and he marveled at the power it gave him. He no longer felt afraid since he began carrying the firearm. Alton had a new best friend, which he never left home without. But at the moment, he had second thoughts about leaving his friend in the car.

After locking the gun away in the glove compartment, Alton braved the elements while making the short trek to the Tobias Tower. From a block away, he could see the office building; and the dark clouds, crackling thunder, and lightning overhead transformed the towering slate and mirrored glass structure into an intimidating and menacing sight. When he reached his destination, he fell in step with Tobias Incorporated's legion of employees and went inside.

The gloomy conditions outside completely disappeared once Alton entered the building. He was greeted by an oasis of Italian marble offset by a six-story atrium capable of sustaining the lobby's array of soaring palm trees. Positioned in the center of it all was a fountain large enough to be considered a pond.

When Alton craned his neck from left to right, he could see people heading to a wall of elevators in droves. He shook his head slightly and wondered if any of them knew of the unspeakable evil that created their jobs. Instantly, Alton realized there would be in infinite amount of collateral damage should he successfully bring the corporation to its knees. He cursed the Tobiases as he stepped onto an elevator and rode up to the fortieth floor.

Jackson Tobias entered his swanky office from his private entrance by 8:00 a.m. and picked up the telephone. He buzzed his secretary and told her to hold all of his calls as an important meeting was about to take place, and he didn't want to be disturbed. Oblivious to the thunderclaps that seemed to reverberate right outside his window, he casually leaned back in his chair and waited patiently for his appointment to arrive.

Suddenly, the double doors to Jackson's office swung open, and a man stormed in unannounced. It was Alton, and Jackson's secretary walked in behind him.

"I'm sorry, Mr. Tobias, I told him that he couldn't come in here without an appointment. But he wouldn't listen. I telephoned security," the older woman said nervously.

Jackson calmly threw up a hand. He knew exactly who the younger man was. "It's all right, Marie. Just wait outside until they get here."

The secretary left them alone in the office, and for the next thirty seconds, the two men engaged in an old-fashioned stare down. Alton's heart beat at a frenetic pace, but he tried to remain calm while leering at the number-1 beneficiary from the atrocity hidden deep within the land surrounding Tobias Industries. Jackson furrowed his brow like a wily old gunfighter and held Alton's gaze while the soaking-wet attorney dripped water onto his floor.

"You made a mistake by coming here," Jackson said, casually breaking the silence. "You keep looking under rocks, and one of these days, you'll end up bitten by a snake."

"I'm not afraid of you. I know what your family has been doing, and sooner or later, the whole world's gonna know," Alton stated as a shot of adrenaline coursed through his entire body.

"Son, this isn't one of those pushover corporations you've built your career marching on," Jackson responded with a wry smile. "You're way out of your league."

"Why, because I believe in the law? Because I don't have people killed?" Alton's words were laced with religious-like indignation. "As much as I would like to pull you from behind that desk and kick your ass, I know of a better way to make you pay for your sins."

Without a knock, the double doors opened, and in came two refrigerator-sized security guards. They stood on either side of Alton and took a hold of his arms.

Jackson rose from his seat and walked over to them. From where Alton stood, he could see the CEO of Tobias Incorporated was much larger than he appeared in the photos from his computer files. He was grateful that the impromptu meeting didn't come to blows.

Jackson looked down at Alton and leaned in close. "Well, it seems as though time is up," he said flatly, and the guards began to usher Alton out of the office.

"Speak for yourself, Tobias!" Alton yelled as the two guards forced him toward the door. "Take a good look at me! This is exactly how you'll look when the government leads your high and mighty ass out of here in cuffs!"

The rain had stopped by the time the security guards escorted Alton out of the building. And once he made it to the sidewalk, he reached into the breast pocket of his trench coat and retrieved his cellular phone.

Dick answered on the first ring. "Alton, you okay?"

"Yeah, I'm fine," Alton answered while glancing behind him. He wanted to make sure he wasn't being followed, but it was impossible because the storm's ending brought scores of people outside.

"I was ready to call the police if you would have waited one more minute to call," Dick said excitedly. The events of the last month had made him totally paranoid.

"I told you I'd be fine. I think if they wanted me dead, it would have happened a long time ago," Alton said confidently. "I just wanted to ruffle their feathers a little bit. Maybe they might do something stupid."

"Alton, you must have some kind of death wish. Shake the wrong tree, and a leopard might fall out."

Alton chuckled at Dick's remark.

"What's so funny?" Dick asked.

"Nothing. Jack Tobias said something to that extent a few minutes ago," Jonathan said before taking one more glance behind him and hanging up the phone.

Alton made it back to the underground garage in less than a minute after putting away his phone. And by now, Lower Level Three was jam-packed with vehicles. The lighting was dull, and the stagnant air smelled like moist asphalt and old motor oil. The whole scene made him feel trapped, and suddenly, barging into Jack Tobias' office didn't seem like such a good idea anymore.

Looking all around him now, Alton exercised extreme caution as he walked toward his car, but a black van parked next to his Mercedes stopped him dead in his tracks. A rush of trepidation turned his legs into cement as he eyed the van suspiciously. He wanted to turn around and go back the way he came, but Alton ignored his better judgment and decided to face his fear. Still, at that moment, he wished he had his gun.

Alton crouched down and looked underneath the cars to see if anyone was hiding behind the van, but he saw no feet. He slithered over to the van furtively and studied the area. He found nothing. The space between his car and the van was empty. There were no goons waiting to toss him inside of the van, and no armed gunmen with silencers to shoot him dead. Dick's paranoia was becoming contagious.

After realizing he was alone, Alton climbed into his car. The first thing he did once he got inside was open the glove compartment and retrieve his gun. Miraculously, the fear he felt when he stepped into the garage instantly disappeared when he wrapped his fingers around the firearm. Alton fired up the car's engine and placed the pistol on the passenger seat before riding up to the surface and embarking on the long drive home.

Back at the Tobias Tower, Jackson had just retaken the seat behind his desk when Felicia Wennington walked in sporting a neck brace and a pair of wraparound sunglasses to hide the purple bruise surrounding her left eye. She took a seat on the other side of her future father-in-law's desk and crossed her legs.

"What's going on, Jack?" she asked while smacking loudly on her chewing gum. "It feels like I've been summoned to the principal's office. What did I do now?"

Jackson's icy blue eyes bore into her. "Lately, it's been what haven't you done."

"Are you referring to the accident?"

"Is that what you are calling it now? Your blood-alcohol level was twice the legal limit, and you tested positive for three different drugs. That was no accident, sweetheart, it was all you."

Felicia shifted nervously in her chair. Being alone with Jackson Tobias made her very uncomfortable. "It wasn't my fault. The car just jumped the curb," she offered in her defense.

"My son told me everything," Jackson scoffed. "So you can save the excuses for your attorney and the six people you ran over."

"No one was seriously hurt," she said dismissively. "It's not like they won't be heavily compensated. This will go away soon, I promise."

"Like the last DUI? And the shoplifting incident in Paris before that? Oh, and let's not forget the multiple overdoses at four different nightclubs, or the Vietnamese infant you tried to adopt that you left at the Waldorf Astoria for twenty-four hours alone," Jackson said while looking up at the ceiling as if he was reading from a cue card. "There's plenty more. Shall I go on?"

Felicia's rose-colored lips remained pursed.

"What boggles me is that you're thirty-two and have been blessed with one of the most prestigious names in finance, yet you parade around this city like a goddamned fifteen-year-old. I know your father, he's a good man, and you're wearing him down to the bone. I refuse to let that happen to my son."

A disconcerted expression appeared on Felicia's face. "What do you mean by that?"

"Your antics are no longer cute. This latest incident has dragged Jonathan's name into the headlines. And the last thing this corporation needs is the negative publicity that seems to accompany you wherever you go."

"Jack, I don't understand what you are trying to say. What do you want from me?" she asked softly.

After leaning forward and placing his folded hands onto the desk, Jackson looked down upon her with eyes that were cold and unforgiving. "Felicia, let me put it to you plainly. You're out. The wedding's off. You are no longer welcome in this family. And I don't ever want to hear yours and Jonathan's name mentioned in the same sentence again."

Felicia was taken aback. "What!" she shrieked. "Are you forgetting that I woke up with Jonathan this morning? He never said anything about ending the wedding."

"That's because he doesn't know it yet," Jackson informed her. "It's a shame because my son really loves you. And when you break your engagement with him today, he's going to take it pretty hard."

"Why would I do something like that?" Felicia asked after chuckling lightly.

Jackson casually reached into his desk drawer and pulled out a medical file. He opened it and slowly pushed it toward the opposite edge of the desk for Felicia to see. She leaned forward and read her name.

"It's your medical report," he told her, "taken from the hospital after your quote unquote accident the other night. If you look at the bottom right corner where it is highlighted, you'll see the results of your blood toxicology exam."

Felicia's eyes roamed to the bottom of the page, and she saw a blood-alcohol level of 2.4, and positives for methamphetamines, marijuana, and cocaine.

Jackson continued, "When Jonathan informed me of the accident, I used my resources down at the hospital to have these records pulled. You've proven over the years that you don't give a damn about your image, but as you can see, even for you, this doesn't look good."

Felicia's silence indicated that she concurred. He went on.

"The way I see it, you have two options. You can do as I say, and this file will see the shredder. Or you do as you want, and this will end up on the district attorney's desk. And I swear by my mother's grave, I'll have him prosecute you to the fullest extent of the law." Jackson paused to let his words sink in. "That's six aggravated assaults by vehicle, good enough for at least three years each. Choose wisely or spend the next eighteen years behind bars," he added flatly before leaning back in his chair and lighting a cigar.

Felicia removed her sunglasses, and through a cloud of cigar smoke, Jackson could see a lone tear streak down her face. After helplessly absorbing Felicia's negligent behavior over the years, it felt good for Jackson to see her cry. He found it impossible to hide the glint of satisfaction in his eyes.

"Oh God," she said in between sniffles. "You're enjoying this."

Jackson blew a billow of sweet-smelling smoke. "As a matter of fact, I am," he said sarcastically. "Frankly, seeing you like this makes me regret not having this talk with you a long time ago."

Felicia stiffened in her chair as her body began to saturate with anger. The tears no longer flowed from her eyes. "You're just like that son of a bitch," she said as her lips quivered.

"To whom are you referring to?"

"My father. He also found pleasure in other people's misery, especially mine. He used to look at me the same way when he snuck into my bedroom to molest me when I was a child," she divulged, painfully remembering the darkest days of her life. "It started when I was nine and went on for five long years. I would piss in my panties every time he crawled into my bed. I hoped it would stop him, but he didn't care. Nothing could deter him from forcing his way inside of me with that same omnipotent glow in his eyes."

"That's right," she continued. "Calvin Wennington, grandson of Marshall Wennington and Wall Street golden boy, was a fucking pedophile who sodomized me every night before finishing in my mouth. I was a little girl. He was supposed to protect me, but instead, he became my own personal monster. I tried to tell my mother, but I guess the bitch figured my innocence was a fair exchange for European shopping sprees and her collection of diamonds. No one helped. Thank God I was their only child."

Felicia dug into her handbag for a cigarette. "Suddenly, after I turned fourteen, he stopped. I guess I was too old for him to fuck. But it didn't take long for me to figure out what old Cal was up to. I wasn't a kid anymore. I had a voice now, and he knew that the windfall profits he generates along Wall Street would dry up if I ever told anyone what he'd done. So to keep me quiet, he puts up with all of my bullshit and gives me anything I want."

"Have we reached the point of the story when I'm supposed to give a damn?" Jackson asked.

"I'm getting to it right now," Felicia responded while bringing the lit cigarette to her lips. She took a long drag and blew out. "Jesus, you're just like him, impatient, arrogant, and you have a secret that you don't want to get out. Pillow talk is so underrated."

There was a subtle but sudden shift of power in the room. Jackson made a valiant attempt to don a straight face, but Felicia was still able to recognize the yield in his eyes.

"You look surprised," she said with a chuckle. "You had to know Jonathan would confide in me. He's defied you for years by sticking by my side. Come on, Jack, you had to suspect he would tell. But then again, you're so fucking arrogant you believe Jonathan blindly obeys your orders. Well, you were wrong. The funny thing is, I wouldn't have opened my mouth. If you hadn't called me in this morning, you would have never known that I knew, but I do know—about it all.

"And to think you just tried to threaten me with prison. You're in no position to make threats when I have enough dirt on you to send you away for a thousand years," she chided while wagging her index finger. "Now the way I see it, you have two options. Keep fucking with me and watch that super fuel you plan to take over the world with get flushed down the toilet. Or you can let me marry your son, and I'll leave that twisted little operation you got going on in Alabama alone. The choice is yours."

Felicia's show of strength rendered Jackson speechless. Without taking his eyes away from her, he angrily smashed his cigar into the ashtray. She had her answer.

"I knew you would see things my way," Felicia said with a wry grin. She stood and put her sunglasses back on. "Well, Jack, I'm glad we had this talk. Maybe now you'll find a way to respect me. Oh, before I forget," she added before snatching up the medical file from Jackson's desk and turning to leave.

Jackson seethed as he helplessly watched Felicia sashay out of his office. The meeting left a bad taste in his mouth for sure, but it was actually the blood from biting down on the inside of his cheek that rendered him speechless. He vented by hurling the ashtray at the wall.

Jackson picked up the phone and summoned his son to his office, and five minutes later, Jonathan walked through the door. He tried to take a seat, but Jackson ordered him to stand. Jonathan noticed the broken bits of ashtray on the floor, and he knew he was in trouble.

Jackson leaned back in his chair and surveyed his son. Blessed with a charming smile and boyish features surrounded by neatly cropped sandy blond hair, Jonathan was indeed a handsome man. It also helped that he was tall and gracefully built like an Olympic free-style swimmer. Jackson remembered holding Jonathan in his arms as a child with the hopes and dreams of his son ushering the company into the future as Tobias Incorporated's CEO. Up until a few minutes ago, those hopes and dreams were still alive. Now they were long gone.

"I had an unexpected visitor today," Jackson offered calmly. "It was Alton Pierce, and he busted in here about an hour ago threatening to nail my ass to the wall. He's a ballsy fucker, I'll give him that much. What with his heroic background, I expect that kind of behavior. But what I didn't expect was to hear about Azalea from Felicia."

Jonathan's jaw slackened, and his mouth slightly opened up.

"Basically, she threatened to expose the plantation if I didn't leave the two of you alone. How fucking romantic."

A pair of battleship anchors couldn't keep Jonathan's eyebrows from shooting upward.

"Your fiancée gave me an ultimatum—can you imagine that? Felicia gave me an ultimatum. Me! An ultimatum!" Jackson roared from the bottom of his lungs. "Do you know how she was able to do that? Because you couldn't keep your goddamned, no-good mouth shut!"

Jonathan's heart sank to the pit of his stomach. He swallowed hard because it took every ounce of restraint to keep from throwing up his breakfast onto the floor.

"You told her everything. What the hell is the matter you?" Jackson asked frustrated. "Your entire life, I worked my ass off to afford you everything you've ever wanted. Provided the best schools money could buy, and I put a stable roof over your head. And I've gone great lengths to make sure this corporation would be secure in your hands when I'm gone. And this is how you show your appreciation?"

Jonathan had nothing to say.

"Let me explain something to you. The thing about a secret, it's like a cancer—once it gets out, it can spread and destroy everything. You gave away all of our family's secrets and put us all at risk. I expected this from one of Jerrold's idiotic sons. That's the main reason why I lobbied for you to become my successor. Boy, did you prove me wrong. I can't remember another time in my life where you disappointed me more."

"Dad," Jonathan managed to say solemnly. "I just want to say that I'm—"

"Sorry?" Jackson interrupted. "Oh, it's way too late for that. The best thing you can do right now is get the fuck out of my office. Right now, I can't stand to look at you. Come to think of it, you need to leave the building altogether before I call security," Jackson said while reaching for the telephone.

Later on that evening when Lara returned from her job at the Center for Charitable Contributions, she was greeted at the door by a path of rose petals that led to the dining room where Alton had a romantic candlelit dinner prepared.

Her favorite Nora Jones album played softly on the sound system as the aroma from an assortment of delectable delights wafted from the table and pleasantly imbued the air. Porterhouse steak— served medium rare just to her liking, and roasted asparagus tips lightly buttered and salted to perfection alongside broiled lobster tail and sherry butter dipping sauce. Alton gently took Lara by the hand and guided her to her seat before fixing her a plate.

"Wow. All this for me?" Lara asked with a smile as she sliced at her steak. "What's the special occasion?"

"There isn't one," Alton said as he filled her glass with red wine. "This is just because."

"So I should expect this kind of treatment once we're married?"

"You bet. I'll do anything to please you."

"Are you sure? Because I could've sworn our marriage would be like it was this morning. Today was the tenth day in a row that I've woken up to an empty bed, and I've lost count of how many times I've gone to sleep that way."

"Lara, please," Alton said as he rolled his eyes toward the ceiling. "This is a high—"

"I know, I know. A high-profile case," Lara chimed in sarcastically, suddenly turning the romantic mood into an afterthought.

"Come on, Lara, I'm serious," Alton pleaded. "It is high profile, and it's going to take every moment I can spare. These people I'm up against are extremely dangerous. I have to be very careful."

"If they are, why are you going after them?"

"Because they need to be stopped," Alton stated emphatically. "You would understand if you knew what these people were doing."

"Then tell me, please," she quipped.

"You know I can't do that. It's for your own protection."

"Alton, I'm a big girl. You don't have to water anything down for me," she said before biting into a piece of lobster tail. "I thought we were a team."

"We are, my café au lait, but people have been getting killed," Alton said before sucking his teeth. "See, I told you too much already. The more you know, the more you are at risk."

"Have you ever considered that I'm already at risk with you living here? Besides, we're getting married soon. That means your issues become my issues. I don't care how dangerous it may be, I have a right to know," Lara said with a pensive look in her blue eyes.

"Don't look at me that way," Alton whined playfully. "You know I can't say no to those eyes."

"So tell me," she demanded. "What are these people doing?"

Alton took a generous swallow of wine after coming to the realization that Lara had made her point. The case was putting her and anyone else close to him in danger, and ultimately, she had the right to know. "There's a textile conglomerate out there called Tobias Incorporated. Have you ever heard of them?" Lara shook her head and Alton continued. "Well, they're huge. Their hands are in everything from cottonseed oil to components that produce rocket fuel. They are in excellent standing with the government, and they rake in billions of dollars every year.

"You would think that with so much at stake, Tobias Incorporated would be squeaky clean. But they're not. Located deep inside of their largest industrial complex in Alabama is a hidden encampment where at least nine hundred blacks are being held in captivity. Their ages range from infant to elderly, and from what I've seen on a DVD that was smuggled out of there, the conditions were third-world filthy. What else I've learned is that the higher-ups in the corporation will do anything to keep this place a secret. Even commit murder."

Lara's fork clanked against her plate. "A billion-dollar corporation holding people captive? What for? That doesn't make sense."

"I thought the same thing, but it's true. The people are locked in tiny brick huts with no running water, and the entire encampment is cordoned off by an electrified fence."

"That's just sick," Lara said with a grimace stamped on her face. "Why haven't you nailed them yet?"

Alton threw up his hands and sighed. "Lara, that's what I've been trying to do. It's hard. I can't just call 911 and tell the cops something strange is going on there. These people are very crafty. It seems as though they've been doing this for decades. I need to have solid evidence if I plan to bring a case against them. Otherwise, they can use their legal team and loopholes to keep me at bay."

"How are you on that front?" Lara asked before resuming her meal.

"Not where I want to be," Alton answered despondently.

"So until then, those people down there have to suffer?"

"You already know how that makes me feel," Alton said after sensing the despair in Lara's eyes.

"I know, baby," Lara said softly before getting up and walking over to her fiancé. She sat on Alton's lap and gently cradled his head. "Don't beat yourself up. I know you're doing all that you can," she added before reassuring him with a kiss.

"Lara, I did something crazy today," Alton said while peering up into her eyes. "I drove up to Tobias Incorporated's headquarters and confronted their CEO."

"Why did you do that?"

Alton quickly sighed and shook his head. "A few weeks ago, someone representing them snuck into my office after-hours, they cut the power, and locked me in the bathroom. When I finally made it back to my office, that bust of Thurgood Marshall was placed in my chair. But that's not all. There was a bull's-eye painted on its face and an envelope attached to it with a note telling me to back off or I would be next."

"Oh my God," Lara said as her hand covered her lips. "Are you all right? Why didn't you say something to me?" she asked while peering into his eyes.

"I'm fine. I didn't say anything because the last thing I wanted to do was scare you."

"What if they come back?"

"I'll be ready this time," he said brazenly. "I bought a gun."

"A gun?" Lara shrieked. "You bought a gun. You're threatening people who could have you killed. Alton, what are you turning into?"

"I don't know," Alton said after shrugging his shoulders. "Going to New York this morning was more than stupid, but I wanted to show them that I'm not afraid. But on the ride home, I realized I was wrong. I am afraid. I'm scared to death of losing you. That's why I've decided to make this my last case as an attorney."

"What?" Lara asked. "But you love practicing law."

"Lara, I love you more. Listen, I'm not going to turn my back on those people stuck in Alabama. There's no way I would ever do that. You can bet Tobias Incorporated won't get away with what they've done, but I'm going to sell Dick and Amy my third of the practice once this case is all finished."

"Are you sure you want to do that?"

"As sure as I have ever been," Alton said confidently. "I've made more money than I could ever spend. Life is too short, and I want to devote what's left of it to you. Your love is all that matters to me now."

Lara closed her eyes and planted a long passionate kiss onto Alton's lips. When they were finished, he pulled back and looked up at her. In his opinion, Da Vinci couldn't have imagined a more beautiful face. Lara was more woman than he could ever want, and he couldn't wait to marry her and live out the rest of his days by her side. He led her by the hand, and she followed him upstairs where they spent the rest of the night in bed making love.

CHAPTER 15

"Uncle Jerry, thanks for coming over," Jonathan said when Jerrold stepped off the elevator and into his living room. "Do you want a drink?"

Jerrold shook his head no, and Jonathan led him outside to the terrace. The midafternoon sun beamed down onto them, but they found shelter from the UV rays when they both sat down at the glass picnic table nestled underneath a gigantic blue umbrella. The air was cool and crisp despite the sun.

Jonathan looked disheveled in his silk robe and pajamas. Customarily, his skin would have been evenly toned, but this morning, it was deathly pale. His eyes were puffy and bloodshot, openly announcing that he hadn't slept in days. He sat quietly across the table from his uncle and waited patiently for Jerrold to speak.

"You look terrible, Jon. What the hell have you been doing? And don't bullshit with me."

Jonathan lowered his eyes. "I've been drinking and doing a little cocaine. Since Dad kicked me out, I haven't been able to sleep."

"You fucked up big time, you know that?" Jerrold stated. "I shouldn't even be here. Jack said you were totally off limits."

"I know I fucked up," Jonathan said as he nervously rocked back and forth. "I'm sorry, but you said I could call you if I ever needed your help."

"I did say that. That's why I'm here," Jerrold reassured him. "But that doesn't mean I'm not pissed off at you. You put our family at an extreme disadvantage by telling Felicia our secrets. What were you thinking?"

Jonathan exhaled before searching the sky for an answer. "I don't know. All my life, Fels has always been someone I could trust."

"Trust," Jerrold bellowed with a scowl that caused the right side of his face to vibrate. "You can trust her with something like your drug use or the fact that you may have stains in your underwear. But no way in hell can you trust someone outside of the fold with that kind of information. It's too big a risk. That's like giving someone a billion-dollar lottery ticket and expecting them not to cash it in."

Jonathan recoiled a bit. He had never seen his uncle so upset. "She wouldn't have said anything if Dad hadn't pushed her," he offered in Felicia's defense. "You said it yourself that he could be a bully. You know how he can get."

"I don't give a damn about what Jack is!" Jerrold snapped. "If you're looking for pity, it's not going to come from me. She should have never been able to use Azalea as ammunition. You're lucky the two of you aren't dead. There's too much at stake. And this family is bigger than family."

The harsh reminder caused Jonathan's eyes to widen. "I need a drink."

"Sit down!" Jerrold commanded, and Jonathan's ass quickly returned to his seat. "You're not going to get through this by drinking and shoveling that shit up your nose. If you want to get your job back, you need to quit feeling sorry for yourself."

"How am I supposed to do that?" Jonathan whined. "My father wants absolutely nothing to do with me. That was made very clear to me when he had me escorted out of the building by the guards."

"I believe that's why you called on me," Jerrold said confidently. "If you do what I say, you'll get back your job. I'll have that drink now. Make it a scotch and water."

Jonathan slowly rose and walked over to the outdoor bar. After a minute of bartending, he returned with two glass tumblers.

The glass disappeared into Jerrold's mitt-sized hand as he brought it to his lips. "There's still hope for you, Jon. You're not Jack's biggest problem. It's that fucking attorney, Pierce."

Jonathan nodded his head and listened intently. Hearing that Alton Pierce was higher up on his father's shit list sounded like music to his ears.

"Do you remember the timetable we set to introduce CX9 into the fuel industry?"

"Yeah," Jonathan answered quickly. "The projection called for entering after next year's third quarter when the country's oil reserves would be almost empty."

"That's good, Jon. A week ago, that would have been correct, but in these strange times, only a fool would try to predict the economy. In the last year, the planet has become a very unstable place. A gallon of gasoline is up to four dollars and climbing. You have a major catastrophe popping up in places where they shouldn't be—floods, tornadoes, droughts, and earthquakes. On top of that, this country is fighting a war with no end in sight over in the Middle East. The timetable to roll out CX9 has changed drastically. We want to introduce it to the market right now."

"Given the economic climate, I say it's a wise move," Jonathan said after contemplating his father's decision to market CX9 eighteen months early. "Especially with the fervor about global warming, CX9 will be hailed as a miracle if it can live up to its expectations. And the money will pour in nonstop."

"That's exactly what your father had in mind," Jerrold said before fidgeting with his pinky ring. "There's billions to be made, Jon. The only thing standing in our way is Pierce. If he starts crusading against us, this whole thing will turn into shit."

"Why don't we just kill that son of a bitch?" Jonathan asked after slamming back his vodka and tonic.

"It's not that simple. If Pierce dies, another attorney would surely follow his work. The only way to stop Pierce is to convince him that we're not worth pursuing," Jerrold added and then became very serious. "And that's where you come in."

Jonathan furrowed his brow and eyed his uncle suspiciously. "Me?"

"That is, if you want your job back. If so, I'm giving you the opportunity."

"How are you so certain that I can get my job back? You of all people should know that once Jack Tobias makes a decision, he never changes his mind."

"Because in few days, my brother's biggest problem is going to disappear," Jerrold said with an air of certainty. "And you are going to take all of the credit. With my support, Jack will have no choice but to let you back in."

Jonathan smirked triumphantly and pumped his fist. "Thanks, Uncle Jerry," he said graciously. "What do I have to do? Wait. It doesn't matter because I'll do anything to get my job back."

"First, you need to clean yourself up. Then I want you to take my jet down to Azalea and talk with Sean. He's waiting for you. Hopefully, by this time next week, you'll be back on board."

"Words cannot express how grateful I am," Jonathan said through an uncontrolled smile. "I owe you everything. I promise I won't let you down."

Jerrold nodded his head and smiled. "Now that is something I can guarantee."

Five hours later, after a shower and a shave, Jonathan touched down safely at the airstrip outside of Cotton City. An escort was there waiting inside of the hangar to take him to Azalea the moment he stepped off his uncle's jet. The twenty-minute ride to the plantation was made in silence.

The black SUV dropped Jonathan off in front of the mansion, and for a brief moment, he stood there in awe. Steeped in tradition, the 175-year-old structure appeared as prestigious as the day it was built. Just a few hours ago, he thought he would never see this place again. He looked up at the clouds and thanked his uncle before going inside and heading to Primary Control.

"Jonny! Come on in and close the door," Sean McMiller said without looking up from his computer. "I'll be done in a minute."

The smell of stale coffee and cigarettes welcomed him into the office, but Jonathan didn't mind. He sat down quietly and let McMiller finish his work.

As McMiller's fingertips rapidly tapped the keyboard, Jonathan took the opportunity to spy the room. Unlike his father's many offices, or even Jerrold's, McMiller's office was in complete disarray. There were overstuffed record boxes and stacks of paper everywhere. The only cleared space had been the desktop, and that had a line of Styrofoam cups half-filled with coffee, which, at the moment, were being used as makeshift ashtrays. A blanket and pillow up on one end of the couch indicated that the office doubled as a second home. Azalea was McMiller's life.

"Excuse the mess," McMiller said when he noticed Jonathan's eyes darting around the room. "They don't allow secretaries down here."

"That's okay," Jonathan said with a dismissive wave.

McMiller grabbed a thick folder before turning to Jonathan. "Let's get down to business. Do you know why you are here?"

"Hopefully to get my job back," Jonathan replied eagerly.

"Hopefully. But before we try to do that, we first have to deal with Pierce. I'm sure Jerry told you that he's standing in the way of things."

"He did. He said that we have to try and convince him to leave us alone."

"That's correct," McMiller concurred. "But he ignored the message we left for him in his office, and he's too scrupulous to accept any money. So now it's time to turn up the heat. We're going to send him a damaging message, just enough to make him feel serious pain. But more importantly, we want to be able to remind him that things could get much worse."

As McMiller casually spoke about ratcheting up the pressure on Pierce, a slight chill crept up Jonathan's spine. "What do you have in mind?"

McMiller opened a folder and handed over a stack of pictures. Jonathan thumbed through them quietly. They were surveillance photos of a woman, and it seemed as though the photographer had captured every facet of her daily life. The only thing missing were pictures of her in the bathroom.

"Who is this?" Jonathan asked. "She's fuckin' beautiful."

"Lara Gatewood. She's Pierce's fiancée."

"God, what a piece of ass," Jonathan mumbled while eyeing the photos lasciviously. "Why do you have so many pictures of this luscious thing?"

"Have you heard a word I've said?" McMiller asked flatly. "She's the message."

"Oh, I get it. Somebody's going to give her a good beating. Put her in the hospital for a few days," he said naïvely. "Just don't hurt that pretty face."

McMiller chuckled at Jonathan's ignorance. "Hospital, huh? We're going a bit further than that," he said coolly. "This job's all about shock value."

Jonathan furrowed his brow and eyed Sean McMiller skeptically. "What do you mean by that?"

"What the fuck do you think I mean?" McMiller snapped. He quickly grew tired of trying to be nice to Jonathan, especially when Jerrold specified that he didn't have to be. "Fuckin' hospital. This is a billion-dollar business we run here. When a message gets sent, believe me, it's final. If CX9 is going to make it to the market by next month, we can't afford to play any games. The gloves are coming off."

"I can see killing Alton Pierce," Jonathan said hesitantly, "but an innocent bystander? I mean, killing someone that has nothing to do with this doesn't seem right."

Without a word, McMiller went back into the folder and retrieved two more stacks of pictures. He handed them over.

"Okay, who are these people?" Jonathon asked after surveying the photos.

"They are Pierce's parents. And they'll die along with anyone else if he doesn't get out of our way," McMiller said casually. "It's going to happen no matter what you think. Just pray it doesn't have to go that far."

Jonathan swallowed hard and readjusted his tie. He finally began to see that Sean McMiller was a heartless killer with no regard for human life. He thanked God they were both on the same side.

"Sean, since you have already set the next course of action, can you tell me why I'm here?"

"Simply put, Jerry wants you to get your job back. You're supposed to take all the credit for stopping Pierce. But it sounds like you're having second thoughts."

"I'm not having second thoughts," Jonathan said. "It's never crossed my mind that innocent people would be involved."

"Well, get used to it. When it comes to this, there are no innocents," McMiller informed him. "Here's some advice. If you plan to run this corporation one day, realize that the preservation of Azalea comes before anything. That's the number-1 rule around here."

Jonathan nodded that he understood, and McMiller reached for a video camera that occupied a parcel of space on top of his desk. He aimed it at Jonathan and smiled.

"What are you planning to do with that?" Jonathan asked curiously. "I don't think this is the place to make home movies," he added with a nervous giggle.

"This is the main reason why you are here," McMiller said. "We're gonna go over in full detail our plan to deal with Pierce, and you are going to do it in front of the camera."

"Is this some kind of fuckin' joke? You want me to discuss a murder on camera? That's not something I want people to see."

"Jerry thought you would feel that way. That's why he wants to have this meeting recorded. Said it would give you something to think about the next time you decide to tell someone else about Azalea."

"What?"

"You heard me," McMiller deadpanned. "If you don't want to do this, the jet's waiting to fly you back to New York—it's your call."

The office went silent as Jonathan mulled over his options. Choose the corporation and participate in an innocent woman's murder. Or go back to New York and remain on the outside eternally. Jonathan lived his entire life hoping to succeed his father as CEO, now he could feel the opportunity slipping through his fingers.

After quickly weighing the pros and cons, Jonathan found the lure of total control of Tobias Incorporated, world dependency on

CX9, and billions of dollars impossible to resist. "I've made my decision. Let's go forward. I want in."

McMiller's lips creased into an insidious grin. "You made the right choice. Now let's get this show on the road," he said before reaching for the video camera and pressing record.

The mall at Georgetown teemed with people around noon the following Friday. A five-day heat wave encompassed the nation's capital, and its citizens flocked to the shopping center to escape the sweltering heat. The mall had central air, and its promenade looked as if it was hosting a parade.

Lara pushed through the crowd as she headed toward Destinations, where she planned to pick up some lingerie for her honeymoon. The wedding was less than two months away, and she wanted to look absolutely perfect on her first night as Mrs. Alton Pierce.

A tiny bell jingled when Lara walked through the door, and scents of love and passion from an arrangement of fresh roses and wild orchids invaded her nose. She smiled and declined service from the sales assistant before casually perusing the aisles on her own. It didn't take long for her to notice Destinations had been well equipped to satisfy anyone's libidinous needs. The boutique ran the gamut from sex toys and games to fur, feathers, rubber, leather, handcuffs, whips, and chains.

Lara wanted nothing to do with the tawdry items; she gravitated toward the section that offered the boutique's best selection of lingerie. There, she found subtle, classy pieces made from the finest combinations of lace, satin, and silk. After carefully sifting through each garment, Lara settled on a white silk and lace La Perla camisole ensemble she felt would reflect the elegance of her wedding day. She went to the dressing room to try it on.

The tiny dressing room had three full-length mirrors and a vented door; she locked herself inside and began to take off her clothes. Lara slipped into the camisole and fell in love. The creamy silk felt great against her skin, and the lace accentuated her curves in all the right places. She closed her eyes and imagined Alton's strong hands gently gliding all over the negligee before he slipped it off.

Lara was stirred from her fantasy when someone vigorously tried to turn the knob and open the door. "Someone's in here," she called out, and the turning stopped.

"Alton's going to love your outfit, you fuckin' whore," a man's voice bellowed, and the knob began to turn again.

Lara grabbed the doorknob with both hands and held on. Suddenly, the man on the other side stopped pulling the door. She dug into her bag for her phone. No signal. Lara quickly put her clothes back on.

No one was there when Lara summoned the courage to finally leave the dressing room. As she walked through the boutique, her eyes darted from side to side, half expecting someone to jump her in the aisle. All she could think about was how did someone know she was there? Lara looked around to see if someone was following her and saw a large man standing in front of a mannequin dressed in leather chaps and metal-spiked panties and bra. The thick scar on the left side of his face frightened her, and the buzz haircut told her that Destinations was not his type of place. She hurried out of the boutique.

Back in the promenade where the crowd seemed to march in every direction, Lara grabbed for her cell phone and cursed when it couldn't produce a signal after five tries. She twisted her head back toward Destinations and noticed the man with the scar trailing about forty feet behind her; it was impossible for him to blend in with the sea of twenty-something women that dominated the mall. His heather-gray eyes were locked on to her.

A sense of dread nagged at Lara once she realized she was being followed. Badly, she wanted to hear Alton's voice, but she couldn't find any reception on her phone. She turned around again, but this time the man was gone. She took a deep breath and exhaled before heading for the parking garage.

The supercharged Range Rover's tires screeched through the garage as Lara mashed the gas pedal. Her eyes stayed glued to the rearview mirror. Once she pulled out of the garage, she tried her phone again, and this time it worked. Alton answered on the first ring.

"Hey, lover. Are you calling to ask me out to lunch?" he asked buoyantly. "If so, I'm definitely free to go!"

"Alton!" Lara cried into the phone. "I think someone is following me."

"What!" Alton said after a brief silence.

"I went to the mall to purchase lingerie for our honeymoon when some man tried to come into my dressing room!" Lara said frantically. "He said you would love my outfit and called me a whore. I didn't see who it was, but he said your name. I tried to call you, but I couldn't get a signal."

"Where are you now?" Alton asked. He fumed on the other end on the phone.

"I just pulled out of the garage."

"Come here to the office. Don't stop for anyone, not even the police."

"Oh my God, Alton. This man, he had a terrible scar on his face. He looked so scary," she rambled into the phone. "He was in the boutique, and I saw him watch me as I walked through the mall. I know he was the one pulling on the dressing-room door. I know it was him."

"Shit!" Alton said after hissing loudly. "I'm sorry, Lara. Getting you involved was the last thing I wanted out of this."

Lara checked her rearview mirror. "How many times have I said that I'm in this with you? I feel safe now that I am talking with you."

"Then don't hang up. Where are you?" Alton asked impatiently. He wanted her with him.

"Not far. I'm stuck at a red light at Georgia Avenue and Q Street," Lara said as she waited for the light to turn green. "Alton, wait outside for me."

"I'll be there," he said and the phone went silent. "Hello? Lara? Hello!"

After realizing Lara was just a few blocks away, Alton leapt from his seat. He stormed out of his office and headed for the emergency stairway. There was no time to wait for an elevator. It took less than thirty seconds for him to descend four flights of stairs and even less time to get to the lobby. He was greeted outside by the heat.

Alton ignored the climate as he stood in front of the office and waited. And waited. And waited. With each passing vehicle, his excitement grew with the hope it could finally be her. But it wasn't. He tried to call her but got no answer.

Five minutes had passed and still no sign of her. Oddly, no traffic at all came from the direction of Q Street. Something was wrong. Sweat began to soak through Alton's shirt. His phone began to vibrate.

"Hello?" Alton answered.

"She's down the street," a deep voice deadpanned before hanging up.

As if on cue, two blaring patrol cars raced up the street. Alton walked out into the middle of Georgia Avenue and received what felt like a kick to the stomach. From four blocks away, he could see the rising billow of smoke.

As Alton ran toward Q Street, the anxiety swelling up inside of him made each step more difficult to take. He knew the culminations of his worst fears were waiting for him. It became impossible to fight back the tears, but somehow, he was able to push through the wave of pedestrians who found the smoke and commotion too difficult to bear.

Two fire trucks, an ambulance, and six patrol cars clogged the intersection. At least ten police officers were milling about, shooing away gawkers, and setting up barricades while firefighters battled the blaze. A news helicopter hovered overhead and filmed the havoc that interrupted an otherwise typical summer day.

Alton managed to squeeze his way up to the barricade, and when he saw the wreckage, he fell to his knees. Lara's SUV had been reduced to a pile of twisted metal and flames. The gruesome sight caused him to vomit on the sidewalk.

"LAARRAAAAAA!" Alton screamed as he leapt over the barricade.

A firefighter noticed Alton racing at full speed toward the accident. "Hey, what the fuck's the matter with you? Are you trying to get yourself killed?" he yelled while wrestling Alton to the ground.

"That's my fiancée in there! I have to save her," Alton said as he struggled to get up.

The firefighter tightened his grip and managed to keep Alton pinned. "Look at those flames," the man said. "Water's not even working, so we have to let the fire burn out on its own. Whoever she was, she's gone."

Alton's muscles slackened as he looked at the raging fire and painfully came to the realization that Lara could not be saved. "She was . . . supposed to become my wife."

"Man, I'm sorry," the firefighter said dolefully before pulling Alton up from the ground and walking him over to an EMT. "Hey, take a look at this guy. He might be in shock. That was his fiancée in that vehicle over there."

The EMT led Alton to the rear bumper of the ambulance and sat him down. After checking Alton's pulse, the EMT gave him a bottle of water and a Tylenol. "Listen, buddy, you drink this and try to relax. I'm going to check to see if anyone else needs help. I'll be right back," he said before walking off.

Alton was unresponsive; he just sat there holding the water bottle while staring at the fire in a zombie-like trance. Suddenly, his phone began to vibrate. He didn't answer until the twentieth ring.

"Alton?" It was the deep voice again. "Don't hang up or the same thing is going to happen to your parents. Their home is wired with explosives, and I have someone in Chicago waiting for my word. Do as I say, and your Mom and Dad will make it through lunch."

Alton's hands trembled as he pressed the phone up against his ear. "What do you want form me?"

"Information," the voice said. "Everything you have against Tobias Incorporated. Go back to your office and give up everything—every note, every file, and every disc. Then log onto your computer and delete anything relate to Tobias Incorporated from your hardware. We're piggybacked onto your system, so we'll be watching. Someone will drop by your office and pick up the rest. Have it ready."

"Why her?" Alton asked through quivering lips.

"You were warned, and you chose not to listen," the voice said unsympathetically. "Our hand was forced. Don't force it again. So put down the bottle of water and get moving."

The line went silent, and Alton craned his head in every direction. He was obviously being watched, but with at least two hundred people surrounding the intersection, it was impossible to figure out who it was. He peeked over at the fire and immediately thought of his parents. Alton realized he was up against an insurmountable force, and when the EMT returned to the ambulance, he was gone.

After what felt like a hundred-mile walk, Alton finally made it back to his office. He was thankful that Robin was still out to lunch; he didn't feel like wasting time explaining anything to her. At the moment, all he wanted to do was give the Tobiases anything they wanted so his parents could be left alone. He turned on the computer and began to delete his files.

While the computer deleted all things Tobias, Alton scoured his office and gathered every article of information about Tobias Incorporated he had ever compiled. Nine months of hard work, and it all fit into a small cardboard storage box. After placing the lid onto the box, Alton fell back into his chair and cried.

As the tears rolled down his cheeks, Lara's image appeared vividly in his mind. Like a slide show, the scenes played in reverse of the brief stay Lara had in his life—from the way she looked when they woke up this morning to the moment she said yes to becoming his wife, all the way back to the night when he looked into her blue eyes for the very first time.

"Why, God? Why did you have to take her?" Alton muttered into his palms between heaves and sobs.

There was a knock at the door, and Alton sat up with an alert look in his eyes. He knew someone from Tobias Incorporated was on the way over, but he relaxed when Amy Bregman walked inside.

Alton walked over to his partner and fell into her arms. He squeezed her with all his might. "Amy, Lara's dead. They killed her. Those bastards murdered my fiancée."

Amy returned Alton's embrace and used her right hand to gently stroke his back. It was a trick she used whenever she needed to console her sixteen-year-old son. "I know, Alton," she said softly. "It'll all be over once you give them what they want."

Alton stiffened, and slowly, he pulled away from her. "What did you just say?"

"Give them what they want, so this nightmare can come to an end."

"How do you know I'm supposed to give them something?" He asked, but she avoided his eyes and recoiled. "Amy, you bitch! How could you? How could you!"

"Alton, I didn't think it would come to this," she said while wisely distancing herself.

"Well, it did. So now what do you have to say for yourself?"

Amy sighed and rolled her eyes. "The money was just too much. They offered me the position of lead in-house counsel. I couldn't turn that down."

Alton shook his head. "You were the last person I thought would sell me out. I didn't even expect that from Dick."

"It's not only about the money," she said. "Lead counsel for a multibillion-dollar conglomerate. Do you know what that means for a female? Besides, I've grown tired of being third fiddle around here."

Alton winced; Amy's betrayal was causing him a great deal of emotional pain. "So Lara's dead because you're thirsty for status? I should break your fucking neck."

Amy's eyes widened as he reached out to grab her. "No, Alton! Wait! Wait!" she shrieked in terror when he managed to get a grip on her throat. "Think about your parents!"

Upon hearing that, Alton released her from his grasp and pointed to his desk. "What you came for is in that box. Get it, and get the fuck out of my life."

Amy gently massaged her neck as she walked over to Alton's desk. She reached into her pocket and retrieved a disk. "This contains a virus that will destroy your hard drive," she said before inserting the disk into the computer. She pressed the appropriate keys to activate the virus, and then she lifted the box from the desk and headed for the door. "If it's any consolation, Lara was a good woman, and I'm truly sorry about what happened to her."

The following Monday morning, Jonathan confidently walked through the lobby of the Tobias Tower. While the people around him ambled to work in a caffeine-assisted stupor, he titled his head upward and beamed a perky smile. He couldn't wait to walk into his father's office with the box he was carrying and the surprise it contained inside. Jonathan stepped into the elevator and impatiently rode up to the fortieth floor.

"What the hell are you doing here?" Jackson asked when his son entered his office. "I thought I made it clear for you not to ever show your face in this building again."

Jonathan ignored his father and continued to walk toward his desk. "Wait a minute, Dad!" he said excitedly. "Just hear me out. Listen to what I have to say."

"Have you forgotten about Felicia already? I think you've said enough."

"Dad, I know I messed up. But I swear to you that I've made everything right. I fixed everything for you," Jonathan said while tapping the cardboard box.

Jackson leaned back in his chair and sneered at Jonathan. "What the hell are you talking about?"

"Pierce," Jonathan said without blinking an eye. "He's no longer a problem."

"Come again," Jackson quickly said as he held his son's intent gaze.

"Alton Pierce is no longer pursuing Tobias Incorporated. He's taken himself off the case. His computer files have been deleted, and everything he's compiled against our family is right here in this box."

Jackson shifted forward and suspiciously eyed the box on his desktop. "Are you serious?"

"As serious as the war in Iraq," Jonathan said while confidently nodding his head. "It's over. You can introduce CX9 in to the market without a single worry."

Jackson rose from his seat and walked around to the other side of the desk. He stood five inches in front of his son and bore into him with his unblinking, cold blue eyes. Jonathan held his ground and struggled to keep from looking away, but Jackson smiled and pulled him in for a tight embrace.

"My son," he said proudly once he finally let Jonathan go. "Just a week ago, I had you thrown out of here on your ass. You could have easily hid in that penthouse and lived off your trust fund. But instead, you took it like a man and somehow found a way to solve my biggest problem. I'm very proud of you, Jon. This calls for a toast."

Jackson went over to the wet bar and returned with two tumblers and a bottle of scotch. He raised his glass and smiled. "To you, Tobias Incorporated's next CEO."

They touched glasses and tilted their heads back until the tumblers were empty. Jackson picked up the bottle and filled them again. "So tell me, Jon, how were you able to get the great Alton Pierce to back down?"

Jonathan smiled and removed the lid from the box. "Well, Dad, I've been behind the scenes with Uncle Jerry since the night we discovered Pierce was behind the man they caught at Azalea. We've been keeping tabs on him since day one, and over time, I was able to determine that more than anything, what mattered most to Pierce was his family," he said while handing his father a stack of surveillance photos. "That's his mother and father. They live in Chicago."

Jackson carefully went through the photographs of Alton's parents as Jonathan continued to talk.

"I knew we couldn't kill Pierce because of the probability of someone else coming along and following his work. I figured the only way we could get him to back off would be to threaten his parents. But in order for him to believe we really meant business, first, we would have to hit him where it hurt."

"How did you do that?"

Jonathan reached into the box and handed his father another stack of photographs. "That's Lara Gatewood, his fiancée. Unfortunately, we had to kill her," he said with an uncaring shrug.

"What do you mean you had to kill her?" Jackson inquired apprehensively.

"McMiller detonated two pounds of plastic explosives that was hidden in her car. She never knew what hit her. It's a shame because she was such a pretty girl."

Jackson didn't respond. He stood motionless with his eyes fixated on the woman in the picture. He knew her. Without warning, Jackson grabbed the bottle of scotch and broke it over Jonathan's head. Shattered glass and whiskey flew everywhere.

Jonathan fell to the floor like a ton of bricks and grabbed his head. Thick blood began to pour from the wound and saturate his blond hair. He screamed in horror as Jackson approached him and began to kick him violently in the ribs.

"Dad! What did I do?" Jonathan asked whenever he got the chance to breathe in air. "Please stop!"

"You killed her! That's what you did!" Jackson yelled as he continued to pummel his son with kick after kick until he grew tired.

When Jackson was done, Jonathan rolled into a ball and whimpered in pain. For the life of him, he didn't understand what had just happened. A few minutes ago they were toasting to his success and celebrating. And now, because of some woman, he was a bloody mess.

"Who is she?" Jonathan struggled to ask because it was extremely painful to talk.

Jackson grabbed the photographs of Lara and stood over Jonathan. He looked down on his son, who, at the moment, cowered in fear while blocking his bloody face with his arms. Jackson threw the pictures at Jonathan, and they fell all around him. He turned his back to his son and walked over to the window. Tears began to drip from Jackson's eyes as he gazed at the clouds slowly passing in the sky. He turned to Jonathan.

"I'll tell you who she was . . . she was your sister. Lara Gatewood was my daughter. The only thing in my life that was completely pure. She was all that mattered to me. And because of you, now she's gone."

CHAPTER 16

Alton gradually migrated back to Chicago in the months following Lara's death. After the funeral, he visited his parents every week, and eventually never returned back home. The memories were too hard for him to escape while staying in DC, so he moved into the guest room at his parents' suburban home and cut himself off from the outside world.

His parents were happy to have him around; it had been a while since they had the chance to see their son every day. At first, Alton relished the idea of being back home so he could keep a watchful eye on his mother and father. But being around them increasingly became difficult because witnessing their devotion to each other after fifty years of marriage was a constant reminder of what could have been. As the days went by, more and more of his time was spent holed up in his bedroom.

Autumn eventually came, and the temperature fell along with the leaves on the trees. The days shortened, and the lonely nights became unmercifully cold. For a while, Alton teetered along the borderline of depression, but his father would constantly make it a point to remind him that he came from a long line of men who were built to handle adversity. The support kept him from going insane.

Gradually, Alton began to come back around. He didn't spend as much time in his room as he used to; instead, he drove to the South Side every day to lend a hand to the revitalization project in his old neighborhood. Alton's face was even spotted around some of Chicago's charity events. He figured Lara would want that, and he pledged every donation in her name.

It was a cold, blustery mid-October Sunday afternoon when Alton decided to sit down with his father and watch a Bears game. He plopped down onto the sofa next to his father's overstuffed recliner and witnessed the Bears get slaughtered by the New England Patriots while his mother kept them fully supplied with beer and finger food. They were both asleep by the end of the third quarter.

Alton could feel his mother's soft hands rousing him from his siesta. "Yes, Mom?" he asked while peering into her doting eyes.

"There's someone here to see you," she said softly. "I invited him in, but he insisted on staying outside."

Alton slowly got up from the sofa, being careful not to wake his father. He went upstairs to the bedroom to grab his shoes and a sweatshirt. As he laced up his shoes, he wondered who was waiting for him outside and whether to carry his gun.

The wind smacked Alton hard in the face once he stepped outside. It felt like he got hit with a brick. He saw a black Town Car parked in the driveway with its engine running. Alton approached with caution.

Alton made it halfway to the car when, suddenly, the rear passenger door opened up. He stopped and waited for someone to get out. A tall man with silver hair and a matching beard climbed out of the car. It was Jack Tobias, and Alton cursed himself for leaving the gun inside the house.

"You've got some fucking nerve showing up here," Alton said as he inched closer with his fist tightly balled.

"Listen, Alton, we need to talk," Jackson said tactfully.

"There's nothing you can say to me, you son of a bitch," Alton barked before charging at him aggressively.

Jackson blocked two wild punches before grabbing Alton's hands and pinning them behind his back. Upon seeing the commotion, the driver hurried out of the car. "Get back! I'm all right,"

Jackson yelled before turning back to Alton, who was fighting like hell to break free from his vice-like grasp. "I didn't come to fight."

"You should have. What did you expect?" Alton spat back while twisting and turning desperately. "My fiancée meant absolutely everything to me!"

"Alton, listen. That was not supposed to happen. Lara was my daughter. My child. Never in a million years was she supposed to die."

Suddenly, Alton stopped fighting. "What the hell are you talking about?"

"Alton, I'm going to let you go," Jackson said calmly. "I want you to turn around and look me in my eyes."

Jackson released his grip, and Alton turned and faced him. It took a moment for Alton to weed through Jackson's facial hair, but he began to vaguely see a resemblance once he focused on those sapphire eyes. He quickly turned away.

"No. I don't want to believe it," Alton said while vigorously shaking his head.

"It's true. Why the hell would I be here? The corporation has gotten everything they wanted from you. In their eyes, they've won. What do I have to gain by putting myself out here in the open like this?" Jackson pleaded as the wind whipped around them. "I am Jonathan Bradford. Well Jonathan Bradford is me."

"You're lying. I know what your family is about—greed, murder, and deceit. Lara wasn't made up of any of that shit."

"You're absolutely right. We are all of those things. But Lara, she was completely pure," Jackson said pensively. "I want to do something about what happened to her. I want to blow it all up. I owe Lara that much. I'm sure because I need your help."

Alton couldn't believe what he was hearing. There was no way Lara could be Jack Tobias's daughter. Deep down inside, he wanted it to be a lie. But he couldn't escape the nagging voice in his head telling him that it was all true. The air instantly became hard to breathe.

"I can't do this right now," Alton said while backing away toward the house. "It's all too much."

Jackson called out to him. "I understand. Take as much time as you need. I have a penthouse at the Peninsula Hotel. I'm not going anywhere. When you're up to it, just call." He climbed into the back of the limousine and rode off.

Alton's father was still asleep in front of the television when he came back into the house. He decided to skip the rest of the game and went into the kitchen for a cup of coffee to warm up.

"Who was your visitor?" his mother asked as she sliced and diced onions and bell peppers for dinner.

Alton heaved a sigh of exhaustion. "Mom, I'm at a loss for words."

"What do you mean by that, son?"

"That was Lara's father," he reluctantly answered.

Vivian Pierce looked at Alton and smiled. "Oh, that's nice. Why didn't you invite him in and introduce him to us?"

"I wish I could have, but it's complicated. This was a surprise. I didn't know that he was her father. He's someone I don't even like. He's an evil bastard. As a matter of fact, I hate his guts," he offered with a grimace. "He had the audacity to come here and tell me he needed my help."

Alton's mother put down the knife and gently touched his arm. "Son, we don't hate in this family. It blackens your heart. And a black heart doesn't do nothin' but make you old and bitter. I've seen enough of that growing up in the South. Believe me, I know." Her words were spoken with an air of sagely wisdom. "Now I don't know what the two of you got going on, but God brought him here to you for a reason. Whether you decide to help him or not is up to you. But remember, if he is Lara's father, you know he managed to do something right at least one time in his life."

Alton leaned over and planted a soft kiss on his mother's cheek. "I see why Dad married you. You're wise as well as beautiful."

Later that evening, after wrestling with his options, Alton picked up the telephone. He called Jackson Tobias and told him he wanted to talk.

A private elevator located at the rear of the Peninsula Hotel's lobby whisked Alton up to the top floor. He patted the front of his shirt and found his pistol tightly secured to his waistline. On the drive over, he vowed to himself to kill Jack Tobias if he wasn't being straightforward. Revenge was all he had to live for.

The elevator opened up into the opulent living room of the penthouse suite. Reminiscent of a Sotheby's fine antiques exhibit, the pink marbled room was adorned with Tiffany lamps, gem-encrusted Fabergé eggs, and early Picasso sculptures and paintings. Jackson waited patiently while sitting on one of three cushy silk-upholstered sofas. Alton took the sofa directly across from him.

"We're alone," Jackson said after watching Alton's eyes dart around nervously. "You didn't walk into a trap."

"I'm not worried about that," Alton said firmly as he thought of his trusted nickel-plated .38.

"Do you want a drink?" Jackson asked while gesturing toward the heavy-looking crystal decanter resting on the table between them.

"No. What I want to know is why didn't you tell Lara the truth about yourself?"

"I couldn't."

"Why not?"

Jackson reached for the bottle and filled a glass to the rim. He sighed before bringing the glass to his lips. "You don't know, do you? You stuck your nose deep into our business, and you don't have a clue what Azalea is."

"All I needed to know was that something illegal was going on. I asked you about Lara. What does this have to do with lying to her?"

"Everything," Jackson said before picking up the glass and taking another swallow. "Azalea's the place Lara was born."

Alton rolled his eyes. "Come on. We both know she's from London. She told me how you met her mother and how she wound up at that boarding school."

"I'm the one who told her the story. It was a beautiful story, but that doesn't qualify it as true."

Alton pursed his lips. Sensing that he was in for a long story, he settled into the sofa and waited for Jackson to continue.

"This going to sound far-fetched, but what you stumbled upon is a fully operational plantation. No one has ever been able to get as close as you did. What you saw on that DVD was a portion of 976 direct descendants of the thirty slaves my grandfather's great-grandfather had with him when he founded Azalea in 1790."

"Slaves?" Alton asked after shifting uncomfortably in his seat.

"Yes," Jackson said with a nod. "Azalea has served our family for over a century and a half. The free labor has saved Tobias Incorporated billions over the years. It has survived the civil rights movement, the Great Depression, and the Civil War. It would have survived another century and a half if you hadn't come along."

"Just the sheer thought of that disgusts me. How did your family manage to go on for so long without being discovered?"

"That's another story. But I promise to get to it after this one."

Alton flashed a wry smirk. "I got nothing but time."

"With each passing generation, the plantation and the reins of the corporation were handed down to the family's most worthy son. The final decision was made by the current CEO. No women in our family were ever allowed to know about Azalea. And if you weren't chosen for whatever reason to be involved with the inner workings of the plantation, you were kept in the dark. Some family members went to their graves without knowing Azalea ever existed. In 1964, I got my turn.

"My father took me to Azalea when I was only fourteen years old. He put me and my older brother on a plane to Alabama right after school let out for summer vacation. Jerrold and I had no idea where we were going, but when we landed, I knew we were far from home. No traffic, no buildings, just blue skies and the occasional hummingbird. The air smelled so fresh, it's indescribable. Hell, the first day of spring doesn't even come close.

"My father put us in the back of a pickup truck, and he drove for a half an hour down a long twisting road. We turned our heads in every direction and saw nothing but lush rows of cotton, and it seemed to stretch on for miles. The truck finally came to a stop in front of a gigantic mansion buttressed by huge white pillars. It looked bigger than the White House. Dad told us the entire place was called Azalea, our ancestor's original home. Now it was ours. Well, at least for that summer.

"Jerrold and I raced inside to find our bedrooms. We ran those long hallways until we got tired. On the fourth floor, I found a room furnished with my clothes and a few of my favorite things from home. Jerrold found his room on the third floor. Dad always managed to split us apart. I guess he didn't want us to share the same view of the world," Jackson said while reaching for his glass. "It worked."

"Once we were settled in, Dad summoned us to the library. He sat us both down and gave a brief history of Azalea and its significance to the family's corporation. Without it, we were nothing, just another company running the rat race like everyone else. He said, like his father, he didn't want that for us. Azalea would keep Tobias Incorporated's head and shoulders above the rest of the textile industry. More than anything, he stressed the importance of keeping Azalea a secret.

"After our meeting in the library, we were sent out of house to get a firsthand look at the daily operations of the plantation. The field bosses took us over to the old mill and warehouse where the raw cotton was stockpiled, and then we spent the rest of the day under the sun overseeing the slaves tending to the cotton fields. We were exhausted by the time we counted the slaves and locked them into their huts that night. Fortunately, a hearty dinner was waiting for us when we got back to the house, and so was Sarah.

"There were only three slaves who were allowed to stay at the mansion full time—Cyril, the head servant who waited on my father personally, Mary—his wife, cooked all of the meals at the mansion. Then there was Sarah, their daughter, and she practically stayed glued to her mother's side, especially when there was an abundance of food to be prepared. The meal that night was to celebrate my father's return to Azalea, and all of his employees were there.

"Everyone convened in the formal dining room where Mary and Sarah were serving dinner. After spending the entire day overseeing the plantation, the hungry men quickly dug in. I was the only person in the dining room who wasn't scarfing down Mary's superb cooking. My eyes were glued to Sarah as she returned to the dining room bearing a tray of food. I thought she was more than beautiful. She had a smile that could make your heart skip a beat."

Alton knew that smile intimately.

"It started off as just an ordinary crush. We were both kids. Whenever she wasn't paying attention, I stole long looks at her. And when she thought I wasn't looking, I caught her stealing glances at me. That went on for a week until Sarah cornered me in the rose garden and asked me who I was. I told her. Then with those big inquisitive eyes, she asked me what it was like to live beyond Azalea's borders. And that's how our friendship began.

"Every day, after my obligations around the plantation were completed, I would meet her in the rose garden. We would spend the remainder of the day talking until the stars appeared in the sky. Well, I did most of the talking, answering her questions about living in a city like New York. She didn't even know what a city was. The only books she was allowed to read were cookbooks. I promised to change that.

"I remember the first time I gave her bubblegum. She wouldn't stop blowing bubbles. The next day, I had to cut a clump of gum out of Sarah's hair, but that didn't stop her from chewing every chance she'd get. Getting to know her made that summer one of the best times of my life."

Alton witnessed Jackson's eyes light up as he reminisced of his childhood. He wanted a drink but decided not to interrupt.

"The summer quickly came to an end, and it was time for me and Jerrold to return home. Saying good-bye was very difficult. In the seclusion of the rose garden, I must have promised Sarah a thousand times that I would return. I even left her all of my bubblegum. I thought of her religiously for the next nine months.

"The following summer, as I promised, I returned. This time I came bearing gifts. My suitcase was full of books and magazines for Sarah to broaden her horizons with, and a year's supply of bubblegum and candy. I helped Sarah hide the suitcase in her bedroom, and she thanked me with a kiss. It was the first time for both of us. That was the day we fell in love."

Jackson paused to refill his glass with more scotch. He noticed Alton making a gesture toward the other empty glass on the table. He poured until the glass was half full and they both drank in silence.

"For six years, we managed to keep our love affair a secret, but in the fall of 1971, Sarah became pregnant with Lara. I was out of school by then, and most of my time was spent at the plantation. I wanted to be close to Sarah, but more importantly, I was trying to find a way to get her out of Azalea. There was no way my child would be born there. One day in the garden, I showed Sarah a map of the world and asked her, if she could leave, where she would want to go. She chose London.

"I asked Jerrold for help, and my brother betrayed my trust. Instead of helping me, Jerrold went straight to my father and told him of my plans to smuggle Sarah out of Azalea.

"My father was furious. He said he didn't understand how I could allow a tryst to get to the point where I would compromise the plantation. I told him that it was more than a tryst. We were in love. He said he didn't care what it was, under no circumstances was Sarah ever leaving Azalea. I argued that the child she carried was a Tobias, and it wouldn't grow up to be a slave. He said I could take the baby. It was Sarah that would have to stay.

"I remained by Sarah's side until the baby was born. Lara was a week old when I removed her from the plantation. I promised Sarah that I would come back for her. But she said she didn't care what happened to her, as long as Lara didn't have to experience life behind Azalea's borders, she would be fine. She told me not to worry myself over getting her out," Jackson's eyes began to water when he paused to gather himself, but somehow, he found a way to keep from crying. "The next day, she hung herself.

"Sarah's death came as a complete surprise. I had no way of foreseeing that. I must have cried for a month straight. Her loss nearly destroyed me, almost drove me insane. Every time I closed my eyes, I saw Sarah's face.

"I was in no condition to care for Lara on my own. I needed help. So I took her to London and searched for the best nursery school money could buy. I wanted Lara to grow up in the place Sarah had chosen to live. I settled on the Gatewood Academy. They had a long-standing reputation for caring after orphaned royalty. I kept a watchful eye on her the entire time she was there. Lara stayed at Gatewood until she turned eighteen. Then she came to America to find her family, and unfortunately, we are here," Jackson's eyes were downcast as he spoke in melancholy. "Now do you see why I couldn't tell Lara the truth?"

Alton bit his bottom lip and slowly nodded his head. He wiped away a tear that was forming in his right eye.

"Though it was from afar, I loved my daughter. Even more than my other children. I was especially proud of what she made of the opportunities that were given to her. She had every right to be bitter, but she chose to dedicate her life to helping humanity," Jackson said as he reflected on the short time he spent reconnecting with his daughter. "Lara's death was not meant to be."

"Yes, it was," Alton said coolly. "What happened to Lara was a by-product of the atrocities your family has committed for the last two hundred years. You forced generations of families to work for you. They have been held captive their entire lives. Sooner or later, it was going to catch up with you. The only reason why I can sympathize with you is because I know how Lara impacted my life, and I know she impacted yours the same. Other than that, you're getting exactly what you deserve."

Jackson glowered at Alton. "I could have had you killed a long time ago. But I knew you were Lara's fiancée. I tried my best to keep this from coming to a violent conclusion."

"Look where that has gotten us," Alton quipped as he eyed Jackson cynically. "What I don't understand is that you could have put a stop to this bullshit years ago, but you of all people allowed it to continue."

"Listen, I went back to work for my family because Father disapproved of Jerrold's disloyalty to me. He said my brother should have tried to help me instead of trying to make an obvious grab for power. He shocked us both when he named me successor to the corporation.

"I always blamed Jerrold for what happened to Sarah, and I vowed to make him pay for what he had done. I must admit, in my quest to make Jerrold's life miserable, I got corrupted by the authority my father had given me. Power can be more addictive than any drug. I tried to rationalize Azalea by giving huge sums of money to Lara. I knew it was wrong."

"You were a hypocrite. What you wanted was your cake, and you wanted to eat it too. Karma doesn't allow life to work that way. But why did I have to pay for your family's mistakes?"

"Alton, you're here because I want to make this right. So you can quit fucking browbeating me."

Alton grimaced. "Don't you dare say that! Because of your family's greed, thousands of people woke up every day without their freedom. There is no way you can make that right. Not now, not ever."

"If I can't make it right, I can at least put an end to it."

"That remains to be seen," Alton said while searching Jackson's face for signs of vacillation. "If we go forward, this means the end of life as you know it. Can you live with that? Everything Tobias will be discredited and destroyed."

Jackson leered at Alton with unwavering eyes. "Jerrold knew exactly what he was doing when he had Lara killed. He was the only other person on the planet who could have known she was my daughter. He knew that her death would hurt me. And just for spite, the son of a bitch involved my own son. They can all burn in hell as far as I'm concerned."

Just before 9:00 a.m. the next morning, Jackson's jet touched down on a private airstrip in Alexandria, Virginia. After staying up half the night listening to the history of Tobias Incorporated, Alton suggested that Jackson should retell the saga to a US attorney general. Alton knew someone at the attorney general's office that he could trust. He made a call there before the jet landed, and a car was waiting on the tarmac to take them across the Potomac into Washington DC.

No one uttered a word during the ten-minute drive to the nation's capital. Alton, still reeling from everything Jackson had told him, struggled to recharge from the two hours of sleep he managed to steal during the flight from Chicago. On top of that, he grappled with returning to the place where his worst nightmare had come to life.

Meanwhile, Jackson contemplated the eventual demise of his family's legacy. He knew that once he told everything to the US attorney, there would be no way to put the genie back into the bottle; no way to stop the avalanche once it started tumbling downhill. As the car pulled into the garage of the attorney general's office, he silently cursed his brother.

The moment Alton and Jackson stepped off the elevator, they encountered a balding man on the third floor entryway with a clean-shaven face that exposed the deep cleft that parted his prominent chin. He stood erect with his hands at his sides, dressed in a neatly pressed gray suit and spit-shined wing tip shoes. His name was Daniel Breen, and he worked closely with Alton at the Society of American Humanitarians.

Daniel Breen was a hardened man, once a career military officer who had no time to start a family, especially after spending twenty years as a judge advocate general for the navy. He presided over court marshals for the four branches of America's armed forces where the charges ranged from desertion and drug smuggling to murder and high treason. When he retired from the military, Breen thought there was no crime he hadn't heard of or seen.

"Danny, thanks for seeing me on such short notice," Alton said graciously as he firmly shook Breen's hand.

"Never a problem, Alton," Breen responded humbly while shaking his head. "What can I do for you?"

"Is there someplace where we can talk privately?"

Breen led them to a small conference room with a round cedar table, four chairs, and no windows. Synthetic houseplants were placed in each corner in an attempt to make up for the lack of sunlight in the room but only added to its cheapness instead. Each man took a seat.

"Around this time last year, my team ran a civil query on twenty companies. We trolled for the usual red flags in an effort to uncover racial discrimination, sexual harassment, and other civil inequities. Our search yielded five specific companies who fit the criteria, but one of them in particular piqued my interest. Have you ever heard of Tobias Incorporated?"

"I have," Breen said with a slight nod. "They're old money. Isn't one of the sons a chair on the Energy Committee?"

"Yes, but he has nothing to do with his family's corporation," Alton quickly answered. "Simply put, Tobias Incorporated is a global textile conglomerate made up of at least thirty subdivisions with ties to everything. One of their largest divisions is an industrial complex located in Alabama called Tobias Industries. Eighty percent of Tobias Incorporated's cotton is grown there. It's a major component in the corporation, and it was one of the companies netted by my team's sweep."

"For what?" asked Breen.

Alton quickly glanced at Jackson, who sat quietly next to him with his fingers intertwined. "Local census records indicated that the rosters were littered with unaccounted for minorities. You know as well as I do that's a telltale sign for racial discrimination. I sent an operative down to Alabama to investigate, and he uncovered something more hideous than ghost employees."

"What was it?" Breen asked curiously.

"He found slaves," Alton said as he steadily eyed the US attorney, "and it cost the operative his life to get that information to us."

Breen furrowed his graying eyebrows. "What do you mean when you say he found slaves? Is that some type of metaphor?"

"Danny, I wish that were true," Alton responded flatly. "But there isn't any metaphor for what I've just said. What's going on in Alabama is the real thing. People are being held captive and forced to work against their own will."

"You're telling me that in the great state of Alabama, a corporation has slaves working for them? That's what you came here this morning to tell me?" Breen asked as he looked at Alton dubiously. His words were coated with skepticism.

"Yes, slaves!" Alton said as he tapped the table for emphasis. "The kind from our history books. You know—work or be punished."

Breen took a deep breath and used his index finger to scratch the bald spot on the top of his head. "Alton, you have to excuse me, but what you are saying sounds too incredible to believe."

After impatiently watching the back and forth between Alton and Breen, Jackson finally spoke up. "I think you should believe him. Those slaves he's speaking of, they work for me."

"And who are you?" Breen asked.

"This is Jackson Tobias," Alton offered quickly. "He's the corporation's CEO."

Breen almost flinched when he realized who was in his presence. Having lived for fifteen years in the nation's capital where lobbying for special interests thrived, Jackson Tobias was one he was familiar with. "What are you doing here?"

Alton leaned forward. "Recent events have compelled Mr. Tobias to be here, and he's decided to come forward and give up everything."

"Is this true?" Breen asked.

"Yes," Jackson replied.

"And the bit about the slaves?"

"True indeed."

"Listen, Dan, we've worked together many times before, and I know how you feel about crimes committed against humanity. That's why when this case finally opened up, I knew I had to bring it to you. I just found out the whole story last night. This might be my only chance to help stop it, but I can't do it without your help."

"Jesus, Alton, what do you want me to do?" Breen asked. "We can't bring charges without convincing a grand jury. And to get that, we need evidence."

"I know how the system works, that's the reason why I brought Mr. Tobias to you first. He is the only credible link to what's going on in Alabama. I can guarantee what he has to say will be more than enough to secure us a grand jury."

Breen massaged the cleft on his chin with his thumb as he contemplated Alton's plan of action. "If we are going to do this, we have to get a special agent in here to sit in on this interview."

"Dan, we're in DC, this city's crawling with special agents. Call one up," Alton said sarcastically.

Jackson cleared his throat. "Before you make that call, be mindful that even I don't know the extent of my family's corruption. You have to be absolutely sure the person you bring in can be trusted."

"I'll take that under advisement," Breen said before pushing his chair away from the table and leaving the room.

Alton slowly turned to Jackson. "What was that about? You don't need to question his judgment. I know he'll find the right man for the job."

"Listen, son."

"I'm not your son."

"Okay, just listen," Jackson said, unfazed by Alton's cragginess. "I'm sure you're itching to put an end to this thing, but now is not the time to become careless. My family managed to keep Azalea a secret for almost two hundred years. That didn't happen by accident. Have you forgotten about your partner? I didn't take much time to turn her against you. Until this is finished, everyone must be second-guessed."

Alton could feel the core temperature rise when Jackson mentioned Amanda Bregman's betrayal. It was a sobering reminder of Tobias Incorporated's uncanny ability to corrupt morals with vast amounts of money.

Breen returned to the conference room ten minutes later carrying a box containing a video camera, a laptop computer, and a stack of yellow legal tablets. "I made that call, and Mr. Tobias, I took your words into consideration," he said while positioning the camera toward them. "The man I called is a consummate professional who has given twenty-eight years of decorated service to this country.

"Special Agent Chuck Cole is an upstanding individual who led the charge at Waco, Texas, and was in charge of the team that captured McVeigh. He's no-nonsense and someone I completely trust. I have no doubt he will allay your concerns."

Jackson eyed Breen cynically. "We shall see."

There was a knock at the door, and in came a man wearing a sweatshirt and faded blue jeans. Standing five feet five inches tall and weighing at least 150 pounds, Special Agent Chuck Cole looked nothing like the man Breen described as the super agent who tracked down the nation's worst criminals. If not for the silver buzz cut atop his head, Special Agent Chuck Cole could have easily been mistaken for a kid fresh out of high school. Breen made the introductions, and Cole respectfully nodded toward Alton and Jackson before taking a seat across from them and grabbing a legal pad to take notes.

"Okay, let's get started," Breen said before pressing record on the video camera and glancing at his watch. "It's Monday, October seventeenth, year two zero-zero eight. This is United States Attorney Daniel Breen, and with me is Special Agent Chuck Cole of the Federal Bureau of Investigations. Seated across from me is Jackson Tobias, CEO of Tobias Incorporated, and next to him is J. Alton

Pierce, Mr. Tobias's attorney. We are here this morning to interview Mr. Tobias for the purpose of substantiating the claim of involuntary servitude taking place at Tobias Incorporated."

"Mr. Tobias, you are aware of your rights?" Cole asked, his baritone voice belied his baby face and slight stature.

"I'm waiving them," Jackson said flatly.

"You understand that by waiving your rights, you can be held accountable for anything you say that's incriminating?" Cole continued.

"Yes, I understand."

"And you're here of your own free will? No one has forced you to come to this meeting?"

"Are you serious?" Jackson scoffed. "I can't be forced to do anything."

"I didn't mean to offend you. These questions are standard fare. They're for your protection and ours in a court of law."

Alton slightly raised his right hand. "Agent Cole, Mr. Tobias knows the consequences of what he is doing. This meeting was his idea. Are you okay with that?"

"I'm fine with it," Cole said before turning to Breen.

"Formalities aside, let's move forward," Breen said. "Mr. Tobias, why don't you tell us about what's going on at Tobias Industries."

For the next nine and a half hours, Jackson spoke candidly about his family. Each revelation led to more questions, which in turn led to more revelations, and by the end of the meeting, Breen and Cole learned everything, from the plan to use CX9 to corner the fuel industry to Abraham Lincoln's role in the original conspiracy. Neither man could mask their astonishment once Jackson left them alone to use the bathroom.

"Jesus Christ, Alton," Breen said as he stood to stretch his legs. "What did you bring in here? That man is the spawn of the devil. How could something like this exist in this country?"

"I don't know. Money? Politics?" Alton responded. "All I know is that if he didn't come forward, we'd still be in the dark about this thing."

"I still can't believe it all," Cole chimed in as he massaged a cramp that developed in his hand while compiling legal notes. "The magnitude of his family's story is incredible. If it's true, this changes history."

Breen hissed. "I know. We really stepped into some deep shit here" he said before turning to Alton. "I had no idea Lara was killed because of all this. I'm sorry."

"Nobody knows the circumstances surrounding Lara's death because I was forced to keep it a secret. What's our next move regarding Azalea?"

"I can tell you what our next move should be," Cole said as Jackson reentered the room. "I'd like to take a tactical team of agents, a squad of choppers, and land right in the middle of that son of a bitch."

"You try that, and I can guarantee you that every one of those slaves will die a quick death," Jackson informed them as he retook his seat. The warning immediately captured everyone's attention.

"What would make you say something like that?" Alton asked curiously. "Why wouldn't they make it out safely?"

Jackson exhaled loudly. "Remember when I told you all about the microscopic homing devices that were injected into the slaves for tracking them if they removed their ankle monitors in an attempt to escape?"

All of the men nodded yes.

"Well, along with the homing device, we included a tiny capsule loaded with enough concentrated cyanide to kill ten men. The cyanide was implanted as a contingency method in case of a revolt, and we couldn't regain control of Azalea. Sean McMiller is the only person other than Jerrold and myself who has the authority to take such action if the situation occurred. The poison is triggered by a remote that he keeps in his belt at all times, and if you try some John Wayne style raid on Azalea, I have no doubt McMiller would not hesitate to push the button."

"I have to say this. You people are truly scum," Breen said scornfully as he retrieved a handkerchief from his shirt pocket to wipe away the beads of sweat that were forming across his brow. "Not only do you hold scores of people captive and employ them as slaves, but you feel as though you have the right to exterminate them like rabid dogs. You give new meaning to the term morally bankrupt. Don't get me wrong, I understand what you're trying to do, but I can't even stand to be in the same room as you."

"I'll second that," Agent Cole stated while glaring in Jackson's direction.

"All right, enough already," Alton exclaimed. "Let's get some control of our emotions. I know it's despicable, but what's done is done. Scolding him is not going to get us anywhere. Dan, what can you do with what we've got so far?"

"We have more than enough to convince the grand jury to return indictments," Breen answered while glossing over his notes. "I can make a few calls and have an emergency hearing scheduled for the morning. We should have arrest, search, and seizure warrants in our hands by tomorrow evening."

Alton turned to Special Agent Cole. "What can you do with that?"

Cole removed the pen he was nibbling on from his mouth. "I can string together simultaneous predawn raids on the homes of everyone who's involved with the conspiracy. I give the go word, and by sunup, Wednesday, I'll have them all in flex cuffs before anyone realizes what hit 'em. I can also send thirty agents to lock the Tobias Tower down and tape off the entire plaza to keep their employees from getting inside the building. It's this cyanide wrinkle at Azalea that bothers me. It totally takes away the element of surprise. And without that, you can surely count on those poor people being dead by the time we get in there."

"Goddammit!" Alton shouted after exhaling loudly. "Jack, is there anything you can do for us? We've come too fucking far to let this opportunity slip through our hands."

"I see the way you two look at me. Judging me. Staring down your noses from across the table," Jackson said coolly, completely ignoring Breen and Cole's disdain for him while looking directly into their eyes. "Ask me if I care, and I'll tell you without blinking I don't. I couldn't help what I was born into, no different from the Palestinian boy who was raised to run into a crowded market with a bomb. I didn't come here this morning seeking redemption or anyone's approval. I'm here solely because of Lara. I seek vengeance for what happened to my daughter. You two do what you need to do.

And when you're ready to land those choppers in Azalea, the cyanide situation will not be an issue of concern."

Early the following Friday, the wheels of Jackson's Gulfstream jet screeched against the tarmac at Cotton City's airfield, landing just as the sun peeked over the eastern horizon. Forty-eight hours had passed since the grand jury handed sealed indictments against the conspirators at Tobias Incorporated to Daniel Breen and Special Agent Chuck Cole, which they used to easily secure the necessary warrants to seize control of the corporation. Now it was Jackson's turn to uphold his end of the deal.

After waiting for the jet to come to a stop, Jackson poured himself a stiff glass of whiskey before emerging out into the mild Alabama morning where a black SUV awaited him. He climbed in, and the driver steered the vehicle toward Azalea. The sky had begun to brighten by the time the SUV rolled through the secure gates of the plantation, and Jackson ordered the driver to take him to the cotton fields.

They pulled up on top of a steep slope overlooking a vast section of Azalea's cotton fields. Today marked the final harvest of the season, and Jackson climbed out of the SUV to cast his gaze upon a mile-wide expanse of cotton stalks with large white bolls of cotton blooming among its leaves. From where he stood, Jackson could see a line of slaves methodically plucking the cotton and placing it in burlap sacks that were slung over their shoulders. As the line moved farther along, the entire field transformed from white to green. He could have stayed there and watched the slaves pick cotton all day, but he forced himself back into the SUV and headed toward the main house.

The driver dropped Jackson off in front of the mansion, and it loomed over him like a gigantic religious monument as he stood before it. With its luscious white paint glowing divinely under the sunlight, Azalea's centerpiece appeared as though it had miraculously beamed down to earth from the heavenly skies. The mansion meant a lifetime of memories for Jackson, and he eyed it pensively before going inside for the very last time.

Jackson kept his eyes forward as he walked down the mansion's main hallway. After disclosing everything about Azalea to outsiders, he dared not to look at the portraits of his forefathers on the wall. At the end of the corridor, he stepped onto the elevator and rode down to Primary Control.

Jackson noticed that there were only a few men inside of the command center once he stepped out of the elevator. It was still early, and the eight-to-four shift hadn't arrived to relieve them of their duties. Their eyes were glued to a wall of surveillance monitors, but they managed to peel them away long enough to realize their employer was in the room. Everyone dutifully nodded in Jackson's direction as he headed toward Sean McMiller's office.

"Whoa, this is a surprise. What brings you down here this morning?" Sean McMiller asked when Jackson entered his office.

"Sean, I've been watching the final harvest since I was a teenage boy. I find the mad scramble to get every fiber of cotton off of those plants very fascinating," Jackson said with a smirk as he closed the door behind him. It's been awhile since I've seen one, so I figured why not today. I'm not interrupting anything, am I?"

"Hell no, not at all," McMiller said while staring at his computer. "I'm just closing out last quarter's inventory before I hit the plantation for inspections. Why don't you ride along? Seeing the boss should be a boost for employee morale. I'll only be a few more minutes."

"Not a problem. I'm going to grab some coffee while I wait."

"You're the boss," McMiller said without taking his eyes away from the figures on the screen.

Jackson rose from his seat and walked to the coffeemaker percolating in an empty corner of the office. After learning earlier in the week of Lara's encounter with a scar-faced man only moments prior to her death, Jackson's temperature steadily climbed with every moment he spent alone with Sean McMiller.

"Sean?" Jackson said as he made his way back over to the desk.

"Yeah, Jack?" McMiller said, still staring at his computer, not realizing that Jackson was standing over him.

"Exactly how long have you been Jerrold's bitch?"

"Wʜᴀᴛ?"

Suddenly, with all of the force he could muster, Jackson smashed the glass coffeepot he was holding into Sean McMiller's face, burning him with scalding hot coffee. He fell to the floor and shrieked as shards of glass tore into his blistered skin. Jackson ignored the cuts on his own arm as he stalked McMiller like a lion bearing down on wounded prey.

"Hey! Jack!" McMiller yelped as he helplessly inched backward along the floor. "Wha-what the hell are you doing?"

"I'm evening the score," Jackson said as he wrapped his fingers around McMiller's throat.

"Even the score? Even the score?" McMiller said frantically. "What the fuck are you talking about!"

"Lara Gatewood, Alton Pierce's fiancée, she was my daughter," Jackson said as his eyes bulged with rage. "My brother knew that, and he still had her killed."

"Your daughter? Jack, I would never—I had no idea! Jerrold told me that Pierce was getting too close and that her death was the only way to protect Azalea. I was just doing my job. Believe me, I was misinformed."

"You can take that up with Jerrold when he meets you in hell," Jackson said before tightening his grip around Sean McMiller's neck.

McMiller's legs kicked wildly, and his body writhed erratically in a desperate attempt to break free. He reached for Jackson's face, scratching and clawing for something that would force Jackson to let him go. It didn't work, Jackson ignored the futile attempt at self-preservation and squeezed harder on McMiller's windpipe, cutting off the man's air supply until his eyes rolled back and his body went limp. McMiller was dead.

Jackson exhaled and wiped his forehead before reaching around McMiller's waistline and finding the cyanide trigger attached to his belt. He removed it and held it to the light. Small but extremely deadly, the trigger looked no different than a car alarm remote. He carefully put it into his pocket before unfastening McMiller's holster and retrieving his gun.

The men were still paying attention to the wall of monitors when Jackson emerged from McMiller's office with the gun held at his side. His bleeding hand trembled slightly as he raised the gun and aimed it at them.

"Everyone turn around and get up!" Jackson yelled, and the men complied. "Raise your hands!"

Jackson marched the three men into Sean McMiller's office where splashed coffee and specks of blood stained the desk. The men were stunned to find McMiller's lifeless body outstretched on the floor. They all thought there were next.

"Mr. Tobias, what's going on here?" one of the men asked.

Jackson pointed the gun directly at the man's face. "Don't ask questions. Just do as I say, and you won't end up like him. Now all of you sit on the floor, and place your hands on your heads!" he barked before reaching into his jacket and retrieving his cell phone. He pressed the talk button, and someone answered on the first ring. "It's done," Jackson said to the person on the other side of the line.

Suddenly, a fleet of Black Hawk helicopters filled the sky above Azalea. From the ground, it looked like a swarm of angry bees raring to attack the plantation. The deafening whir of spinning blades grew louder and louder as the choppers made their descent, whipping up wind and debris in their wake.

Scores of federal agents dressed in black combat fatigues carrying semiautomatic assault weapons stormed out of the helicopters once the flying machines reached the ground. Special Agent Cole led the charge of screaming agents as they spread through the plantation like wildfire. The field bosses were totally caught off guard by the incursion, and by the time anyone could react, they found themselves surrounded with guns shoved in their faces. They had no choice but to surrender.

The crack team of agents had all of the field bosses in flex cuffs in a matter of minutes, but corralling the slaves proved to be a much more daunting task. Never before in their lives had the slaves seen the men who fed, clothed, and often beat them, lying face down in the dirt with their hands behind their backs. The sight confused the frightened slaves, who began to scatter and run for their lives.

Alton watched everything from a safe distance as he sat inside one of the helicopters. He felt helpless while slave after slave darted by the chopper with terrified expressions on their faces and panic in their eyes. He wanted to help, but Special Agent Cole ordered him to stay inside until Azalea was completely secure. Alton made a valiant effort to sit still, but with so much time and heartache invested into the whole ordeal, he found it impossible to obey Cole's orders. He climbed out of the chopper and began to wander around.

At almost every turn, Alton discovered significant parts of Azalea's history scattered throughout the plantation. The old cotton mill next to the creek that flowed out of the plantation, the mosaic gardens surrounding the mansion and the mansion itself, all seemed to appear the way he imagined it would during the nineteenth century. After hearing, in full detail, the story of Tobias Incorporated's early beginnings, he was amazed at how Azalea withstood the test of time.

"Hey!" Cole blurted when he spotted Alton in front of the mansion. "I thought I told you to stay put until I came back for you."

"You were taking too long," Alton said in his defense as he approached Cole, who was standing amid a crowd of heavily armed federal agents. "I saw people running past the chopper, and I figured it was okay to come out. Was I wrong?"

Cole slung his weapon over his shoulder and pulled Alton aside. "Listen, those people you see running around here are scared shitless. They don't have a clue to what's going on. All they know is some people they've never seen before came out of the sky and attacked their leaders. They could have hurt you. Or you could've gotten lost. This place is pretty fucking big. I took a chance by bringing you along. You could at least do as I say. I've been doing this shit for a long time, you know."

"Well, from the looks of it, you weren't doing anything at the moment," Alton said while staring down at Cole.

That's because we just declared this place secure a few minutes ago. I was about to come get you. Every raid was a success. The Tobias Tower is completely locked down. Their assets are frozen, and we've taken people into custody in five different states. No one involved in this shit has gotten away. The hard part is over."

"Over?" Alton asked curiously.

"Yeah, it was easier than I thought, but we have the entire compound under our control."

"What about the people running around? They clearly need help."

"It's called shock, Alton," Cole said flatly. "It's a common occurrence when people held captive for periods of time are finally freed. They saw those SOBs tied up and probably thought they were next. We have to just let them run around until they calm down. There are a few crisis management teams on the way to help sort out this mess. They'll get these people accounted for and hopefully out of here soon after that. Jesus, can you believe this place?"

"Yeah, it's incredible," Alton said as he eyed the mansion and the surrounding area with disdain. "All of this history preserved just to perpetuate an unnecessary evil. What a waste."

"I hope once all this is over with, they burn this place to the goddamned ground."

"I hope so too," Alton concurred. "Where's Jackson?"

"He's gone."

"What?"

"We had to rush him out of here. He killed that guy McMiller to get the remote from him. Murdered him, actually, but he hurt himself pretty badly in the process," Cole said as his voice lowered almost to a whisper. "Me and my team over there were the first ones on the scene down in that control room. McMiller was on the floor with his neck broken, and Tobias was slumped in a chair holding three men at gunpoint. He had a nasty gash on his wrist, probably would have died if we hadn't gotten in there sooner. He lost a lot of blood, but I think he's gonna make it."

"You said he murdered him? Damn, that really changes things," Alton said and winced as if he were in pain. "That could destroy our case."

"From what I saw down there, that guy McMiller didn't have a chance," Cole said as he veered up into Alton's dejected eyes. "Hey, I don't like the guy, but he did what he had to do to get us in here. Damn near got himself killed doing it. That kind of effort will not go unnoticed. Don't worry, I won't let this case go to shit. Not on my watch. If it comes down to it, my team is prepared to say that Jackson killed that cocksucker in self-defense."

"I thought you Feds operate by the book?" Alton asked sarcastically as he smiled to show his gratitude.

"There is no book in a situation like this. I'll do whatever it takes," Cole said before answering his vibrating cell phone. "Fuck!" he yelled after hanging up.

"What's up?" Alton asked with raised eyebrows.

"That was the regional director back at the tactical command center calling to say congratulations for a job well done."

"What's wrong with that?"

"She also told me that somebody leaked the raids to the media. You get that with high-profile raids, especially when they occur in multiple jurisdictions. There's always some asshole looking to score points with the press," Cole said before pursing his lips and shaking his head. "Now this place is going to be crawling with those meddling sons of bitches. They'll have your whole life splattered on TV in a matter of minutes. You still have time to leave, you know, before they get here, and the circus begins."

Alton looked up at the sky as if the news helicopters would appear at any second. He had an idea of what his life would be like once the media arrived. He knew it meant the end of his privacy, and he began to imagine a brigade of news vans camped out on his parents' front lawn. Alton weighed his options; leave now and avoid the constant intrusion or stay and witness, after 150 years, the slaves finally leaving Azalea.

"I'm not going anywhere until every man, woman, and child is escorted beyond these fucking gates."

CHAPTER 17

The news of Tobias Incorporated's involvement in slavery spread quickly, sending shock waves rippling through the nation. The raid on Azalea dominated the headlines, and its footage could be seen continuously on the internet and TV. Debates sparked on almost every news outlet, and the topics ranged from whether every African American should finally be paid reparations, to questions surrounding the Thirteenth Amendment's legitimacy. Despite a few deep-rooted racist hate groups, the entire country was outraged.

Almost overnight, the corporation began to hemorrhage money. Out of fear of being branded guilty by association, companies from around the globe severed ties with Tobias Incorporated, and the well-oiled machine that once dominated the textile industry quickly ground to a halt. The corporation's stock completely nosedived and ultimately had to be removed from the market altogether. And just when it seemed like things couldn't get any worse for the corporation, the lawsuits came.

By the thousands, people lined up to sue the company. They were former employees of Tobias Incorporated who were stripped of their jobs because of a scandal they had absolutely no knowledge of, and shareholders who had lost millions in a matter of days. The corporation was forced to auction off all its assets in what seemed like a corporate yard sale to cover the cost of mounting claims. Rivals, who in the past could barely function under the corporation's ever-present shadow, swooped in like a plague of locusts and purchased everything from the Tobias Tower and the patent rights for CX9 to office supplies and company vehicles. When it was all over, Tobias Incorporated was an empty shell of itself with nothing to cling onto but its infamous name.

Meanwhile, Alton monitored Tobias Incorporated's demise from afar, wanting nothing to do with the media coverage surrounding the debacle even though he was credited as the hero who was responsible for blowing the case wide open. He managed to avoid the ravenous media's attention by hiding out at Dick Chesney's Aspen vacation home until the day came when the principals at Tobias Incorporated had to stand trial. Eighteen months had passed since the raid on Azalea, and it was now time for the people who were in involved to answer for their crimes.

It finally happened on a sunny April morning in lower Manhattan as a few hundred people crowded the steps of the majestic courthouse at One Federal Plaza. At least a thousand more spilled out onto Center Street. Among them were reporters wielding microphones like swords in a quest to capture the quote of the day, angry protesters who chanted civil rights hymns while holding up signs denouncing slavery, and curious onlookers drawn to the spectacle like moths to a flame. Somehow, a small group of police in riot gear managed to keep the anxious crowd behind a row of barricades while creating a pathway that led up the steps to a pair of revolving doors.

Alton ignored the reporters desperately calling his name as he marched through the hallowed hallways of the courthouse with Dick Chesney and Robin Alverez at his side. His mind was focused on nothing but getting to courtroom 3A before the mob of people trailing behind him and finding the best seat in the house. Suddenly, Alton stopped dead in his tracks when he reached his destination, realizing that the people responsible for Lara's death were on the other side of the door. The moment of truth was bearing down on him, and he bowed his head to pray for justice before pulling the double doors of the courtroom and going inside.

Not a single inch of seating could be spared inside of the cavernous room, and a pair of US Marshals had to be positioned outside to turn people away from the door. A stew of voices echoed off the marble walls as the impatient spectators spoke freely while the defense and prosecution teams huddled at their respective tables. The hubbub went on unchecked until the bailiff came out from the judge's chambers and raised his hands to silence the noise.

"All rise!" the bailiff's voice boomed over the courtroom. "Court is now in session. The Honorable Judge Robert J. Gawthrop is presiding."

Everyone stood silently as the elderly man draped in a flowing black robe ambled from his chambers and ascended to his lofty seat atop the bench. The judge put on a pair of silver wire-rimmed glasses before leaning toward the microphone. "You may all be seated."

Once everyone in the courtroom had retaken their seats, the judge focused his attention upon the five men and seven women who were sitting inside the jury box. "Good morning, ladies and gentlemen." His voice was low and comforting; Judge Gawthrop had done this a thousand times before. "Today, we are here in the matter of the United States of America versus the four principals of Tobias Incorporated, namely, Jerrold Tobias, Jonathan Tobias, and Amy Bregman.

"Each of the four defendants at the table to my right has been charged with two counts of murder, two counts of conspiracy to commit murder, 967 counts of kidnapping, 967 counts of involuntary servitude, one count of wire fraud, one count of blackmail, and one count of conspiracy.

"The twelve of you have been chosen to perform a most solemn obligation of citizenship. You are to sit in judgment upon criminal charges brought by the United States of America against four of your fellow citizens. The service you render as jurors is as important to the administration of justice as are the services rendered by counsel and the court. Accordingly, it is imperative that you pay very close attention to all that is said and all that occurs throughout the trial so at its conclusion, you will be in a position to fulfill your duty as a juror.

"It is my responsibility to decide all matters of the law, and you must follow my instructions on all matters of law. However, I am not the judge of the facts. It is not for me to determine which of the facts are true in this trial. That is up to you.

"Witnesses who testify in this trial are going to give you the information, and you will have to process that information. Pay particular attention to what is said. Consider the appearance and demeanor of each witness as they testify. How does the witness impress you? In what manner did the witness give their testimony? Did the witness appear to be frank, open, honest, and positive, or does the witness appear to be hesitant, evasive, or uncertain? Consider further the witness's ability to remember, and remember accurately that which the witness says they saw or heard. Ask yourself if a witness indicates any bias or prejudice. You can and should use your common sense and understanding of human nature in deciding credibility. In other words, you should consider the usual and logical tests used by yourself to determine truthfulness or lack thereof.

"Noteworthy of mentioning are the rules of evidence. Some evidence is not admissible. And when an objection is made, and I agree that the evidence is not proper, I will not permit the question to be answered or an exhibit admitted. If I disagree, the witness can answer or the exhibit will be admitted into evidence. Simply put, if I do my job properly, you will hear and see everything you should and nothing you should not.

"The defendants say they are not guilty. The United States of America says several laws have been broken by the defendants' conduct. And along this vein, we begin with the most fundamental principal of the criminal justice system, and that is that the defendants are presumed innocent. The fact that they have been charged with these crimes are no evidence whatsoever against the defendants, and may not, must not be considered evidence against them.

"In fact, the presumption of innocence alone is sufficient to warrant their acquittal unless the United States of America convinces of their guilt beyond a reasonable doubt. Not only are the defendants presumed innocent as I speak to you, they are presumed innocent throughout the entire trial. They are presumed innocent when you walk into the jury room, and during the deliberation process.

"Now, while the United States of America has the burden of proving each and every element of the charged offenses beyond a reasonable doubt, this does not mean that they have to prove the defendants guilty beyond all doubt or to a mathematical certainty. The standard is reasonable doubt.

"A reasonable doubt is such a doubt that would cause an ordinary, careful, sensible, and prudent person to pause or hesitate before acting in a matter of importance in his or her own affairs. A reasonable doubt must fairly arise out of the evidence presented or out of the lack of evidence presented. If you have such a doubt, your verdict must not be guilty. If you have no such doubt, the defendants are no longer presumed innocent, and you should find them guilty.

"Finally, I admonish you not to discuss your view of the case, the witnesses, et cetera, when we take any kind of breaks until the case is submitted to you for deliberations. Follow my instructions on the law as it applies to the charges brought against the defendants by the United States of America." Judge Gawthrop paused to lean back in his chair. "So in light of the aforesaid, I turn to the United States Attorney and ask if he would like to make an opening statement."

"Yes, Your Honor," Daniel Breen said as he calmly pushed his seat a few inches back from the prosecution table before standing and walking over to where the jury had been seated. Slowly, he walked from one end of the jury box to the other, carefully making sure he looked every last juror in their eyes. When he reached the last juror, he stopped and pointed his index finger at the defense table. "Recently, federal agents have uncovered a despicable act being committed inside one of the country's blue-chip corporations, a crime so vile it threatened the moral fiber of this great nation. Ladies and gentlemen, the four people seated right there at that table are perpetrators of that crime.

"For more than a century and a half, Tobias Incorporated has been the clear leader of the textile industry. A large portion of this country's framework has come directly from their cutting-edge innovations. If not for their contributions, the United States of America would not be the pacesetter in the global race of nations. From the very beginning, they have set a gold standard that continues on today.

"If we were here today to pay homage to Tobias Incorporated, I would be the first to say thanks. But we're not here for that because under the shimmering glow of that gold standard, the corporation has been hiding a nasty little secret."

Daniel Breen slowly backed away from the jury box and stood next to the defense table. "For decade upon decade, long after this country had done away with its most wicked institution, Tobias Incorporated indulged in slavery. Slavery. A word most of us believed had been banished to history books, but somehow, Tobias Incorporated managed to keep it alive up until this day. Driven by incessant greed, they never freed their slaves when President Lincoln issued the Emancipation Proclamation, and to further line their pockets, generations of unwilling participants were born into captivity and forced to work for free," Breen's accusatory tone grew with every word.

"I know for a fact that every citizen, upon being born in this country, has the unalienable right to the American dream—life, liberty, and the pursuit of happiness. Sadly, the unfortunate souls inside of that plantation Tobias Incorporated owned were born into a nightmare, continuous manual labor, and conditions that wouldn't even be suitable in a third-world country. Today is where it all can end.

"Ladies and gentlemen of the jury, I am going on a trip, and I want you all to go with me. We are going to a dark place where illicit deals are made with the highest ranking members of the government in the name of greed. A place where generations of innocents were bred like animals to serve a company. A place where a family of executives profited billions off the blood and backs of those poor people. A place where these four defendants bribed, blackmailed, eavesdropped, threatened, and even committed murder to keep it all a secret."

With his arms folded, Breen sauntered back over to the jury. "I hope you are all ready to go because I have the evidence and witnesses to get us there. All I need is your undivided attention. And when we get back, I can guarantee you will find all four of the defendants guilty." Breen let his last words hang in the air before walking back to the table and retaking his seat.

Judge Gawthrop cast his gaze down on the lead attorney for the defense. "Mr. Scola, would you like to make your opening statement?"

The svelte young attorney, clad in a navy-blue Brioni suit, quickly rose to his feet. "Your Honor, we respectfully decline. Our defense will speak for itself," he said confidently before sitting back down.

"Very well," the judge said along with a nod. "Mr. Breen, you may move forward."

"Thank you, Your Honor. The United States would like to call its first witness to the stand. That would be the CEO of Tobias Incorporated, Jackson Tobias the third."

With the exception of Alton, who sat directly behind the prosecution, the spectators gasped when Daniel Breen announced his first witness. For a brief second, it seemed as though the air had been sucked out of the courtroom. As promised, the trip was set to begin.

Suddenly, the double doors opened up, and two US Marshals led Jackson Tobias into the courtroom. No one made a sound as he made the long walk down the aisle to take a seat up on the witness stand. Everyone was shocked by what the once-revered man was about to do.

The bailiff approached the stand carrying a huge Bible to swear Jackson in. "Please place your left hand on the Bible and raise your right hand."

Jackson complied.

"Do you solemnly swear to tell the truth, the whole truth, and nothing but the truth? So help you, God."

"Yes, I do."

As the bailiff walked away, Jackson peered over at the defense table and saw Amy Bregman hunched over conferencing with her attorney. He moved his eyes slightly to the left and found the sight of Felicia Wennington weeping pathetically into her hands completely satisfying. Jackson buried the urge to smile and focused his on attention onto his son.

Denied bail since his arrest, Jonathan had spent the last eighteen months holed up inside of Manhattan's Metropolitan Detention Center. Fearful of retribution from the African American inmates,

Jonathan lived under twenty-four-hour protective custody. His skin was pale from the lack of sunlight, and his timid eyes darted around constantly. Jonathan had turned into a poster child for anxiety, which was exactly the way Jackson wanted his son to live out the rest of his life.

Jackson found a pair of unblinking icy-blue eyes staring back at him when he peered over at his brother. Jerrold's face began to crimson as he clenched his jaw and slowly shook his head. Until Daniel Breen approached the witness stand, Jackson steadily held his brother's venomous gaze.

"For the record, please state your full name."

"Jackson Jonathan Tobias the third."

"Please state your occupation for the jury."

"I am the chief executive officer of Tobias Incorporated."

"You're nothing, you son of a bitch!" Jerrold stood up and blurted. "You're nothing but a nigger-loving turncoat, you piece of shit!"

"Order! Order! Order in my court!" Judge Gawthrop yelled as he rapped his gavel against the bench. "Mr. Scola, I'm giving you the chance to calm your client, or he will spend the rest of this trial wearing a muzzle. Please understand that I won't allow my courtroom to be made into some kind of spectacle."

"Yes, Your Honor, I understand," Gary Scola said before sitting down and whispering softly in Jerrold's ear.

"Mr. Breen, you may continue."

"Thank you, Your Honor," Breen said graciously and turned back to the witness stand. "Are you of sound mental capacity?"

"Absolutely," Jackson answered and nodded his head.

"Are you here of your own free will?"

"Yes, I am."

"Did anyone force you to come here today?"

"No."

"Have you been offered anything, money, or some kind of reward for your testimony?"

"No, I have not."

"Are you expecting anything in return for your testimony?"

Jackson shook his head. "I expect nothing but justice."

Daniel Breen calmly walked back to the prosecution table and sat down. He placed his hands upon the tabletop and casually let his fingers intertwine. "Mr. Tobias, can you explain to the court the inner workings of the alleged conspiracy at Tobias Incorporated, and how you and the four defendants were involved."

Momentarily, as the courtroom went deathly silent, Jackson closed his eyes and reminisced of his late daughter and how she impacted his life. When he opened his eyes, he spotted Alton, who was sitting in the front row, smiling. Lara was finally going to get the justice she so rightfully deserved. Jackson cleared his throat and took a deep breath before leaning toward the microphone.

"It all began in the year 1859, in what seemed like the coldest winter in years . . ."

The End

ABOUT THE AUTHOR

Herbert Robinson is a column writer for Positive Image Newspaper. A self taught author, he developed his passion for writing after participating in a citywide poetry contest while attending high school. The Secret Kept is his first published book and he is currently writing his next novel. He grew up in Philadelphia, Pennsylvania where he still resides but also has a home in southern California. He enjoys spending his spare time with his two lovely daughters.

CPSIA information can be obtained at www.ICGtesting.com
Printed in the USA
BVOW02s0753210715

409222BV00002B/2/P